CRUCIAL STEP

Ian Laver

Crucial Step

First published in Australia by Ian Laver 2021

Copyright © Ian Laver 2021
All Rights Reserved

 A catalogue record for this book is available from the National Library of Australia

ISBN: 978-0-6451887-0-7 (pbk)
ISBN: 978-0-6451887-1-4 (ebk)

Cover design by Jan Forbes © 2021

Typesetting and design by Publicious Book Publishing
Published in collaboration with Publicious Book Publishing
www.publicious.com.au

Disclaimer
This is a work of fiction and no offence is intended. The story incorporates many true political, geographical and historical facts. All the active characters in the book are fictitious, but the names of politicians and musicians mentioned who existed at this time are true. The geographic locations are basically correct, but some map details have been altered. Key dates have been juggled in the interest of allowing the story to flow for this period in history.

To my father, Bob. I only began to know you when you passed away.

The Way Ahead

Journey travelled,
Will show the way.
Do not look back.

by Ian laver

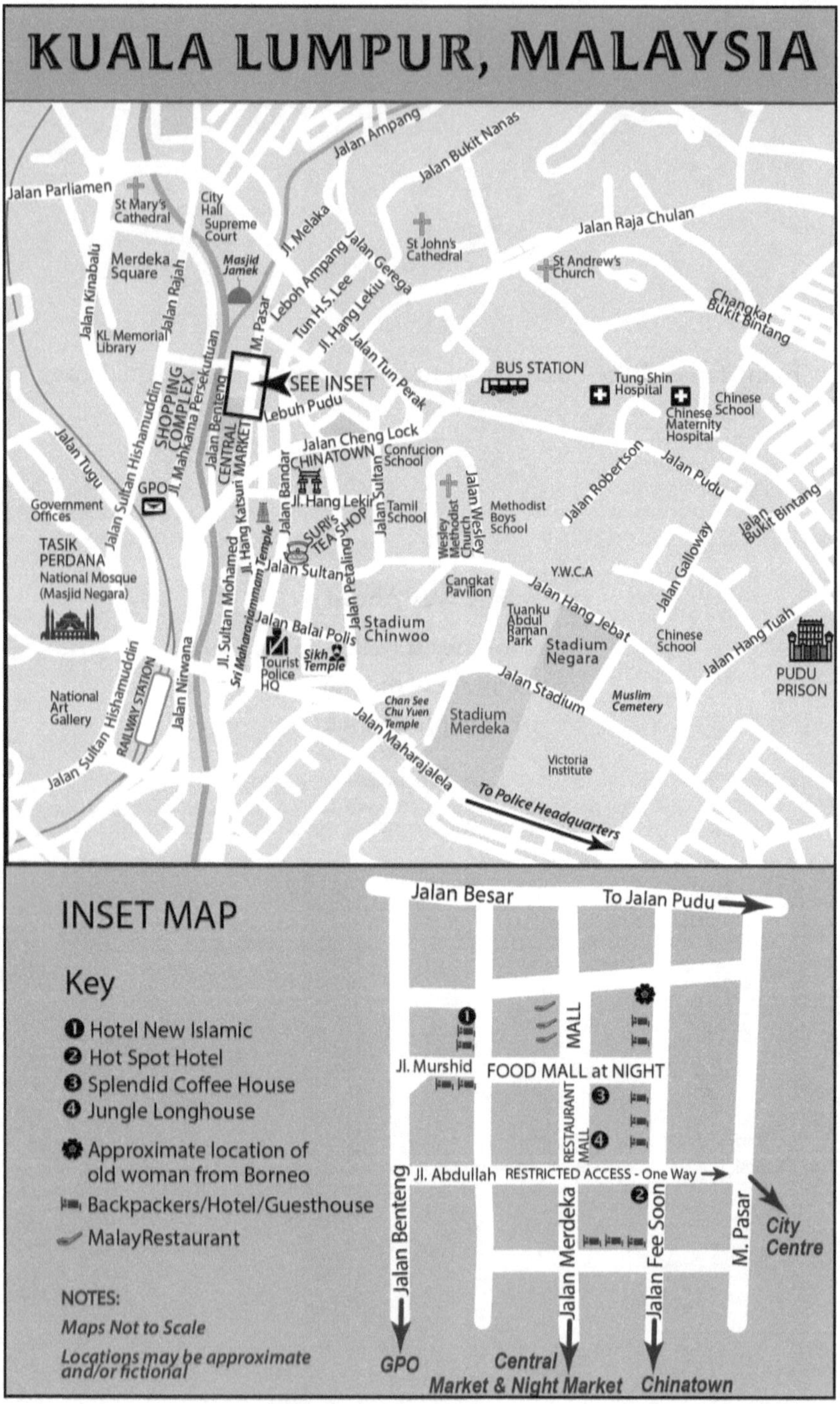

KUALA LUMPUR, MALAYSIA

Jalan Parliamen
St Mary's Cathedral
City Hall Supreme Court
Jalan Ampang
Jalan Bukit Nanas
Jalan Kinabalu
Jalan Rajah
Merdeka Square
Masjid Jamek
Jl. Melaka
St John's Cathedral
Jalan Raja Chulan
St Andrew's Church
Changkat Bukit Bintang
KL Memorial Library
Leboh Ampang
Jalan Gereja
Jalan H.S. Lee
Jl. Hang Lekiu
Jalan Tun Perak
M. Pasar
Jalan Tugu
SHOPPING COMPLEX
Jl. Mahkama Persekutuan
Jalan Sultan Hishamuddin
Jalan Benteng
CENTRAL MARKET
Lebuh Pudu
SEE INSET
BUS STATION
Tung Shin Hospital
Chinese School
Chinese Maternity Hospital
Jalan Cheng Lock
CHINATOWN
Confucion School
Jalan Pudu
Government Offices
GPO
Jalan Bandar
Jl. Hang Katsuri
Jl. Hang Lekir
SURI'S TEA SHOP
Jalan Sultan
Jalan Petaling
Tamil School
Jalan Wesley
Methodist Boys School
Jalan Robertson
Jalan Bukit Bintang
TASIK PERDANA
National Mosque (Masjid Negara)
Jl. Sultan Mohamed
Sri Mohariammamn Temple
Wesley Methodist Church
Y.W.C.A
Cangkat Pavilion
Jalan Hang Jebat
Jalan Galloway
National Art Gallery
Jalan Sultan Hishamuddin
RAILWAY STATION
Jalan Nirwana
Jalan Balai Polis
Tourist Police HQ
Sikh Temple
Stadium Chinwoo
Tuanku Abdul Raman Park
Stadium Negara
Chinese School
Jalan Hang Tuah
PUDU PRISON
Chan See Chu Yuen Temple
Jalan Maharajalela
Stadium Merdeka
Jalan Stadium
Muslim Cemetery
Victoria Institute
To Police Headquarters

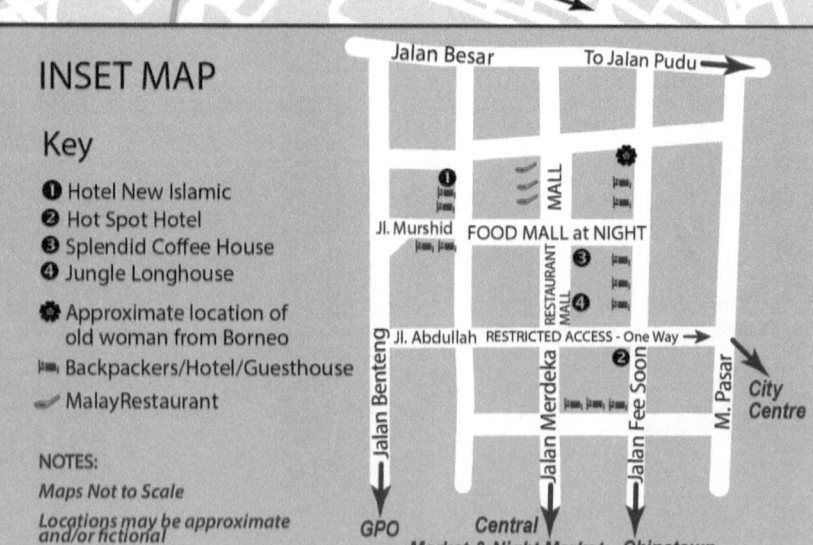

INSET MAP

Key

❶ Hotel New Islamic
❷ Hot Spot Hotel
❸ Splendid Coffee House
❹ Jungle Longhouse

✿ Approximate location of old woman from Borneo

🛏 Backpackers/Hotel/Guesthouse

🍃 MalayRestaurant

NOTES:

Maps Not to Scale

Locations may be approximate and/or fictional

Jalan Besar
To Jalan Pudu
Jl. Murshid
MALL
FOOD MALL at NIGHT
RESTAURANT MALL
Jl. Abdullah
RESTRICTED ACCESS - One Way
City Centre
Jalan Benteng
Jalan Merdeka
Jalan Fee Soon
M. Pasar
GPO
Central Market & Night Market
Chinatown

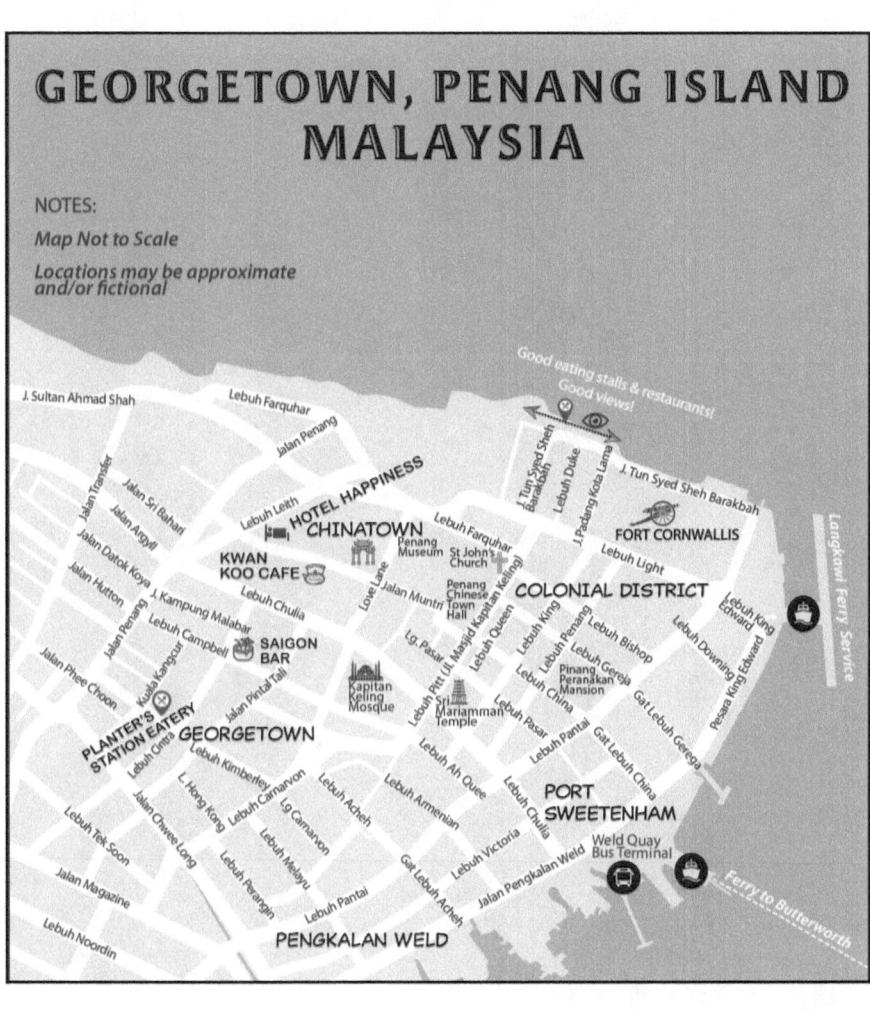

Prologue

September 1987

The last, almost empty, midnight ferry heads across the Selatan Strait towards the island of Penang, twenty minutes away.

Jack gazes at the speckled glow of lights slowly fading on mainland Malaysia as he flicks his lighter and takes a drag. Three Malay crew members come out the back and squat in the other corner. They light up fragrant cigarettes and chatter away in their native language. The ferry relaxes into a corkscrewing motion. The breeze negates the crippling humidity, out in the sea, between the land masses.

Vince chucks his cigarette into the folding wake of sprinkled fluorescent bubbles splaying out behind the stern. 'Yeah.' The ferry moves on. 'I'm going to die, I'm sick, Jack. Cancer. I don't want to go on.'

'Yeah, I know. But, mate, you can beat it. We could scheme-up some bucks from somewhere, and get some decent medical care ... just like old times, eh?' The boat sways slightly and Jack grabs the rail to steady himself.

Vince shakes his head. 'We've been mates forever; we've been through a lot. I've made up my mind. Would you ... would you give this to Gail and me boy, Theo?' He grabs Jack's hand and closes his fingers around the envelope.

Jack's brow tightens. 'You saved my life over there in Nam, mate. I'd do anything for you, you know that, but why don't you give it to them?'

The lights ahead grow in number and become brighter and Georgetown seems to get bigger.

'Why don't I do it?' Vince shakes his head. 'Why don't I do it? Because, old mate, I'm too ashamed, that's why.' Tears in his eyes pick up the glint of the weak upper deck lights. 'I can't face it anymore.'

Vince turns, walks quickly to the rail and steps over into the boiling churn of the props. A fluid movement, almost one action.

'Vince!' bellows Jack, reaching out and stumbling forward on the slippery deck.

A Malay crewman jumps up and yells, waving his hands frantically.

1

Decision Time

Chapter One

23rd December, 1987

'Official-looking one here for you, Mum.' Theo, back from his run, dropped the letter on the kitchen table on the way to his room.

Gail picked up the envelope. 'Department of Foreign Affairs,' she mumbled. Her eyebrows formed a concentrated line; somehow she knew it had something to do with Vince.

'Anything interesting?' said Theo, stepping back into the kitchen a couple of minutes later. He placed a hand on the wall and commenced his stretches.

'It's about … it's about your father.'

She placed a hand across her eyes and dragged it down over her face in a wiping action and slowly looked up at her son. There were no tears after all these years. 'He's dead,' she added in a flat voice.

Theo stopped what he was doing. Sweat prickled the back of his head. 'Oh,' he mumbled awkwardly and walked out of the room.

Hands in pockets he wandered down to the bottom of the yard and fed the chickens. 'Bloody Dad,' he almost spat, aloud.

Later he went to his room and sat on the bed, staring at a black and white photo on the dresser of his father in army uniform. No hat, dark hair, the smooth smile of a confident young man on the eve of an adventure of a lifetime. Theo thought he had the swashbuckling look of Errol Flynn without a moustache. 'Now why did you have to go and do that, eh? If you think I'm going to burst out in tears, you'd better think again.'

He picked up the picture frame, unclipped the back cover and slipped the photo out onto the bed. It landed face down. Theo read, 'Vince Perry, Puckapunyal 1968.' He lay back staring at the photo, pondering the significance of it all and glancing out the window at a struggling bottlebrush. 'I look more like the old lady than you, you bastard.'

When he arrived back in the kitchen, Gail was sitting in the same spot.

'How did it happen, Mum?'

'What? Ferry accident, well not really an accident, he committed suicide, stepped off the back of the Penang Butterworth ferry in Malaysia. I guess it had to happen, Theo, his life was a mess, I'm surprised he lasted this long.'

'Bastard,' he mumbled.

She lifted an eyebrow. 'Don't say that, Theo; despite his shortcomings he had a good side.'

She's acting like the ever tolerant and dutiful wife, Theo. 'He deserted us, Mum.' His forehead tightened, making his blue eyes more piercing than usual. 'It was a mongrel act and you know it. He never sent money ... nothing, no word for, how long, what, fifteen years? More.'

'It was the war, Vietnam changed him forever. He simply couldn't cope with life back here in Australia. You shouldn't be too hard on him.'

'Too hard! I have to say it, he just up and went.' Theo couldn't help showing his emotions. Hurt? Maybe, or was it disgust?

'Yes, I know.' Gail had been holding the sheet with the letterhead all this time. She gently put it on the table. 'Anyway, they are asking us if we want to send a representative from our family over there for the funeral.'

'I suppose you have to bloody well pay for that, too. Final insult, sink the boot in?'

She glanced at him. Gail was still an attractive woman at 40. Her vanity prevented grey from encroaching into her blonde hair and advertising her age. Theo noticed slight sun wrinkles in the corners of her blue eyes. 'No, no of course not, Jack has taken care of things it seems ...'

He remembered his father's best mate, Jack, with some affection. At least he had written to them a couple of times over the years, more than likely unbeknown to Vince, about where they were and to let them know Vince was alive ... but probably not okay. Theo still had those two letters in his desk drawer.

'I'm not going to the funeral,' she sighed. There was a certain relief in her voice, perhaps because it was all over. No real shock was evident in her demeanour. 'Anyway I couldn't get it together, or let's say I'm not prepared to get it together. Funeral is on the 4th January … mmm next year.' She gave him a hard look and began to say something but she shook her head and let the silence hang.

'Don't think I'll bother going either,' he said with a pinched mouth.

Her look seemed to soften, then she turned and toyed with the letter.

Theo sensed his mother did not want him to go. He did not want to go either. He quietly walked around the table, put his hands on her shoulders and gently squeezed. They had been a team for all these years.

Chapter Two

Three weeks later

'Hey Mum, a package from Jack,' gasped Theo, almost breathless from a fifty metre sprint.

She looked up from her magazine. 'Oh?'

He flipped it in front of her on the table, then put his hands on his knees and puffed.

She slit open the thick envelope and quickly glanced at a sheet of paper wrapped around a light gauge foil inner bundle, held with a rubber band. 'It's addressed to both of us.' She shrugged and busied herself unwrapping the foil. Her eyes opened wide. 'Well, I'll be …'

Theo stared at the big wad of dollars. 'Hell. What does the letter say?'

He stepped around behind her and they read the first part together, in silence.

'Fifteen thousand dollars each, American, not Australian,' he said, running a hand over his short cropped crown and playing with the longer hair at the base of his mullet-cut. 'Jack says Dad told him to send it to us.'

'Well I don't want it.' There was a slight edge to her voice - she was not a woman to be bought off. Her voice softened. 'You can have it all, I er … don't need it. You've finished uni, why not buy a car … pay some bills.'

'Come on, Mum, Dad wouldn't have sent it to us if he didn't want us to have something. I guess.' The last couple of words were drawn out. 'He gave you nothing but loneliness and the job of bringing up *his* son. I know it cost you a lot to educate me, remember, two jobs? I think you should have it, some sort of compensation for him being a prick to you.' *The old man is buying us off, guilt money.*

'Please don't use that language, your father was …'

'He was a mongrel to us both. I'm having a shower.' Theo walked out and closed the door with purpose. He looked down and noticed his hands shaking.

∞

After a long shower, Theo sat on the bed thinking. He remembered clearly, even though he was only six years old, the day before his father went away, sixteen years earlier. *Let down? Sure I feel let down, you bastard.* Vince told him he was only going away for a while and would come back soon. Even then, only a child, he somehow knew his father was lying.

He went back into the kitchen and raided the fridge. At twenty two he still had a teenager's appetite. The letter lay on the table; his mother had obviously put the money somewhere safe. He picked it up and read the rest of it. Jack said that his father had given him the money just before he died. Jack also wrote that he hoped to see at least him, Theo, if not Gail, at the funeral.

Theo rubbed his jaw and frowned. 'Hang on, what's this?' *Must have been a delay with postage because it was posted on the day after Dad died, Wednesday, 16th of December, 1987.* The moment was lightened when he noted the 'Priority Paid' sticker. *That'd be right.* They only received the letter after the funeral date. He glanced at the back of the envelope, *J. Deere* scribbled under the coat of arms or logo of St John's, Wayward Travellers' Project, Leboh Ampang, Georgetown, Penang, Malaysia.

He made a cup of coffee, sat at the table and read through the letter several more times. Over the last few weeks, since they received the news of Vince's death, Theo's head was crammed with conflicting thoughts. Was he being too judgemental about his father? Jack's two letters over the years tended to make excuses for Vince's behaviour. However Jack did make the points, try to understand, try to forgive, try not to judge. He reminded Gail and Theo that Vince was a decorated, brave soldier and the harshness of war had damaged his mind forever. Vince somehow lost the will to face real life. Jack had also written '*no-one is perfect.*' Theo had to concede, he also was far from perfect; sometimes treating his girlfriends or women he knew with less respect than he should have, picking fights on the football field … and those pub fights, smoking dope. *Yes Theo, you've got plenty of faults.*

In the letter, Jack suggested Theo use the money to travel to Malaysia and spend a few days with him, even if he couldn't make the funeral. He stared at the letter and the words *decorated soldier* stood out. *Theo, Theo, don't get sucked into thinking you owe him.*

Jack's comment about no-one owed anyone anything but … the thought wouldn't go away. Maybe he did owe his father the small effort it would take on his part to at least find out about his life. After all, he'd finished university, a degree in journalism, plenty of time to get serious about his first job at The Adelaide Advertiser. Maybe a short holiday, he'd be back in a month or so. While he was in Malaysia he could put together a journal of his trip; maybe even do some investigative journalism into the bargain.

The matter was firmly on his mind all day and that evening he pitched the idea to his mother.

She sighed and took a moment to respond. 'Wouldn't you be better off buying a car, you know, and getting ready for your job?' She didn't look at him.

He thought she would be pleased he was taking the initiative and going away to settle issues about his father. 'Don't you want me to go, Mum?'

She turned and fixed him with a firm look. 'Um no, it's not that, it's … well you might find out things you … er don't want to know about.'

New Adventure

Chapter Three

February 1988

He adjusted his watch, like most of the other tired, irritable passengers, at the suggestion of the captain, on his flight and as the big aluminium whale touched down it was 4.25am local time. The announcement was loud and woke him from a cramped dyslexic nether world that he knew was the only sleep he was going to get for a while. His six foot, eighty five kilo body rebelled from being crammed into a seat made for someone half his size. It was one of the few times where he wished he was smaller. Even at that hour, Theo could feel the heat and humidity of the tropics as well as the foggy haze of pollution.

He stood for a moment near the bottom of the aircraft stairs and looked out at the dazzling lights losing ground to the soft hue of the beginning day. *You're here now, Theo.* The first things he noticed, apart from the tropical surroundings, just visible, were the close air and the smell. High octane aircraft fuel mixed with many other aromas he couldn't identify permeated the atmosphere. He joined the throng and was herded across the tarmac at Kuala Lumpur International Airport. The relative comfort of the airconditioned terminal was welcome as he lined up with the other hundreds of passengers. Where did all these people come from? It seemed as if several other jumbos had landed at the same time as his flight from Sydney.

Earlier the connecting flight from Adelaide went smoothly, probably because he was ruffled by excitement on his first real adventure out of Australia. Theo had experienced only one flight in his life and that was a domestic with his mother to Perth for a family wedding. He noticed the time wasting and inefficiencies really began with the international leg at Sydney Airport. The airline employees were friendly enough but, with only two counters open at the time and hundreds of passengers convinced that they were more important than anyone else, the process was slow and gruelling. The customs and immigration people seemed reasonably organised and Theo was early enough to be whisked through quickly. This part was good because he had time to purchase a bottle of vodka, a carton of cigarettes and some film. He had been sneaking the occasional cigarette with his mates at the football club, unbeknown to his mother. Also he had grown to enjoy a sprinkle of marijuana with tobacco in a Tally-Ho cigarette paper every so often. Football season wasn't due to start until the end of March but there were a few friends he socialised with all year who smoked. This trip to Asia was a holiday and he wasn't really hooked on tobacco, as far as he was concerned. *You'll give up before you come home, won't you, Theo?* He knew cigarettes were no good for anybody and was aware it was harder to maintain his level of fitness when he smoked a lot. But most of the people he knew smoked.

The situation at Kuala Lumpur International Airport reflected much the same level of incompetence balanced with competence as at Sydney Airport. Most of the officials seemed welcoming and wished him a pleasant stay. However, it took a few minutes and a number of deep breaths to cope with the huge crowds all seeming to talk at high volume, as well as loudspeaker announcements, mostly in languages he couldn't recognise. He had flipped through his guidebook, which had a few words of basic Bahasa, in idle moments on the plane and over the last week, and he was proud he managed to reply, 'Terima kasih,' thank you in Bahasa Malaysian. He had completed a skeleton crash course two years ago in Bahasa Indonesian as well as French and Spanish, all part of the Foreign Correspondent component of the Journalism degree. Bahasa Indonesian was different to Malay but there were handy similarities, easy to remember.

Theo noticed several signs warning travellers of the penalties for possession and trafficking of all classes of drugs. He recalled the hanging of two Australians, Barlow and Chambers, a couple of years previously. He was surprised about the prominence of the sign because his mate Dempster told him that marijuana in Asia was generally no problem so long as you just smoked it and didn't take it over borders. Theo had already thought about scoring some marijuana somewhere on his trip, but had no intention of trafficking any. Maybe it was not such a good idea.

In the baggage claim area the carousel sign boasted three international flights and the moving conveyor was surrounded by eager passengers and children having rides, so he decided to change some travellers' cheques into ringgits, the local currency. It took a few minutes to work out the exchange rate and also the procedure of cashing traveller's cheques.

Back at baggage claim it was a battle for anyone and everyone to retrieve their bags because most people stood next to, with some hanging over, the conveyor belt.

A middle-aged westerner in a grey suit nodded at Theo and smiled, 'Same the world over, mate, people seem to get so excited they think they will miss getting their bags. Oh, here's mine!' He said loudly, 'Oi, lady with a baby,' and the crowd parted long enough to allow him to snatch his bag. As he passed Theo, he winked, 'That's how you do it, mate. Good hunting, enjoy your stay,' and he wandered over to a uniformed driver holding a placard.

Theo wasn't quite so bold but he had to use his Aussie Rules footballer's agility and shepherding skills to jockey a position when his rucksack came into view. 'Get out of the bloody way, you dickheads,' he mumbled. No one heard him above the din of hundreds of commuters hell-bent on making sure they were on the spot to retrieve their bags.

Then he cruised through Customs without any scrutiny other than a polite, 'Please enjoy your stay in Malay-shee-ah,' from a smiling, attractive young woman in uniform and hijab.

Theo intended to sit down somewhere in the airport, gather his thoughts and set a game plan before dealing with transport and accommodation. He also wanted to sort out and re-arrange his belongings, make sure money was in the correct pocket, and his documents were easy to get in case asked.

But once through Customs and money change it was all over. The crowd seemed to carry him with their excitement, enthusiasm and weight of numbers. Straight through the whooshing doors, Theo found himself catapulted from the comfort of airconditioning to the humid heat of Kuala Lumpur, capital city of Malaysia. His heart jumped as he spun on his heel hoping to go back inside, but the doors were final; no return. *Bloody hell, Theo what have you got yourself into?* Seats awaited no one; just steel crowd barriers with hundreds of excited locals, made up of a range of Asian faces. The sturdy barriers separated him from the mob that looked like ripping him and the other arriving passengers apart. The only thing that eased his anxiety was that everyone in the noisy crowd was smiling and laughing, as well as remonstrating. Some animated folk held up signs in chalk or rough crayon on cardboard, some uniformed drivers held up more elaborate signs. The noise level was incredible because everyone yelled and there was strong competition from diesel buses and cars as well as revving motorbikes. The intermittent roar of jet engines seemed to shake the landscape. The air was thick with the combination of Asian food aromas, diesel fumes, sewers and animal shit.

One opportunist tried to gain his attention yelling, 'Hey mister, hey you, I have taxi waiting for you, we go to hotel now, okay?'

Theo pretended he didn't hear. He whistled under his breath. 'Friggin hell!' No-one heard him.

He knew he was almost out of his depth. The guidebook warned him to be ready for a culture shock and to try and relax and fit into the hectic pace of life in Malaysia. He stood for a moment, trying to look as if he had been there before and knew the ropes but sweat dribbled down his back, fuelling his already instantly wet shirt. It felt as if water was bubbling from his hairline into his eyes.

'God,' he said. His heart rate increased but he knew he had to regain some confidence.

Obviously no-one heard him, but an official who looked like a policeman could see he was lost and pointed with his cane towards a counter he hadn't noticed inside the exit gate. He said in good English, 'Over there for taxi and bus.'

Theo nodded a thank you and dragged his rucksack and duty-free goods to the line in front of the counter. He should have noticed the sign:

Prebooking/Prepaid - Taxi and Bus.

From touchdown he had taken about two hours to negotiate the airport formalities. It was half past six and the smoky tropical sky was desperately trying to give him some eggshell blue to show he was in Malaysia and a new day and a new experience awaited him.

Chapter Four

The guidebook highlighted several clean backpacker hotels or pensions within a small radius near the Puduraya Bus Station as well as further on near Chinatown. The man in the Prepaid Office was very friendly and helpful and confirmed that the area recommended was easy to get to. Also he could easily organise the bus to Penang, where he hoped to catch up with Jack, because most long-distance buses left from there. The bus that departed from the airport was supposed to be close to where he was.

The official pointed. 'You are to go over there, see where other people are standing?'

Theo followed the direction of his arm but all he could see was people everywhere. He didn't want to appear stupid so he said, 'Thanks.' *Come on, mate who cares if you miss the bus, there's sure to be another.*

He wandered over to a group of backpackers about his age, waiting beyond the steel crowd control barriers. Trouble was, there were several groups and even though there were signs in Malaysian and English on steel poles, he was no wiser.

Touts yelled at him and waved things in his face. He did his best to relax and tried not to make eye contact with any of them. They all seemed to have either a family member with a hotel or a special price for accommodation. *Right Theo, be firm, you cannot stay at all their places.* He thanked them and continued to say he was alright because he had accommodation sorted out, even though he didn't. Suddenly he noticed with a start, movement on the retaining wall high up. A group of monkeys skittered along the top. *Concentrate Theo, find the bus or if not, at least where it stops.*

Several men in dirty clothes tried begging from some of the tourists but a police officer chased them away, waving a bamboo cane.

Theo felt confident that whatever group he stood with was within a short distance of the next group and they all seemed to be waiting for buses. Because they were like him, it was most likely they would be going in his general direction anyway. He went to the area where he thought the official had pointed to. All groups were batting away touts and opportunists and he was grateful he could hide in their midst. He steeled himself as he tried to push a path through the milling crowd.

Watch it Theo! He felt someone touching his back pocket but by the time he turned all he could see were the faces of other backpackers and locals. It could have been anyone.

This encounter gave him a degree of confidence because he was in control. No-one was going to steal anything off him as he had all his important paperwork and money in his top pockets. Dempster's advice again, wear shirts with big top pockets; never put anything in your back pockets.

Theo found a secure place close to the other travellers but not in their throng. He knew he wanted to retain individuality but he also realised he needed their numbers to keep the touts at a distance. Theo thought, with a grimace, this was worse than grand final day.

From this vantage position he had difficulty not staring at the young female, hippy backpackers in their almost see-through cheesecloth dresses, bare shoulders, and tanned legs. Tall, short, big, slim, some with more breast exposed than the guidebook suggested was appropriate for a predominantly Muslim country. He observed most of the male touts noticed them too. Theo smiled and shook his head; they were just like the blokes at home.

'Hello,' said a young woman, no older than a girl, on the edge of a group of backpackers. She had sprung him staring at her but didn't seem to mind.

'Umm … yeah, hi.' All he could think to say was, 'Where you from?'

'Belgium. You are from Australia, I can tell.'

'Spot on, right. Where are you going, er from here I mean?'

'Ah yes we fly to Kuching in Borneo today. We have been here in mainland Malaysia for two weeks.'

Theo didn't want to sound like a newcomer but he was and he was sure she could tell. 'I just arrived.'

An overcrowded bus lurched into the area, nearly knocking over the pile of backpacks as well as alerting the group she was standing with.

'Monique?' A tall young man in baggy, red, hippie drawstring pants yelled and waved at her.

Theo squinted at the sign on the bus, *Domestic Airport – Free*. He realised he was standing in the wrong spot.

'I must go, said Monique, 'Bye bye, you enjoy your stay.'

He watched her drag her pack to the bus.

He was saved the anxiety of waiting because an ancient-looking bus marked *Jalan Puduraya* arrived about thirty metres away. 'He rushed over to the mob standing near where it stopped. The bus was already about half full of mainly backpackers. Where they came from he had no idea. He thought having no idea about a number of things could easily be a regular thing. He remembered advice, again from Dempster, to not be shy, just push in.

Theo knew he sounded like a beginner but he had to ask. 'Is this the bus that goes to the Puduraya area, where the hotels are?' He waved his pre-paid ticket, hoping someone would know.

A man in a turban, and a uniform of sorts with epaulets, stood at the bottom step. Theo reasoned he had to be an official of some kind because he began yelling at someone in the distance over Theo's head. Theo thought he was a bit rude.

The man in the driver's seat, who was chewing betel-nut, took up the question when Theo asked again, and yelled above the other shouting official. 'Yes, no problem, we stop in front of hotels, no problem, okay?' He turned and spat a red geyser of juice out the opposite window.

'Sounds like there's no problem then,' mumbled Theo. 'Thanks, mate,' he said louder.

Even though the system seemed chaotic, Theo's confidence grew because so far, mainly everyone had been helpful. He didn't want to think of what it would have been like had they not been. Because he didn't have to wait to have his bags stored in the luggage compartment under the bus, he was able to jump straight on board. He noted a cardboard sign that said, *Via Domestic*. He found a seat with room to stash his rucksack in the rack above. A few local looking people jostled for seats and crammed their produce or luggage in around them, chattering the while.

Theo's breathing and heart rate returned to normal as he looked out from the marginal safety of his seat. A day in the life of Kuala Lumpur unfolded around him. He gazed around in amazement. Cars, motorbikes, rickshaws, buses and hundreds of people vied for a small share of space or the chance to conduct business. People were dressed in all types of clothing, from suits and dresses, to Muslim traditional, to Chinese workers with reed, woven conical sun hats, to beggars in rags. Dress style was typical of the information in books he had read before coming away. The sky was now pale blue with a tinge of grey smog laced through it.

'How ya doin,' buddy? It's a bit like a trip to Mecca,' said a North American backpacker across the aisle as he opened his arms to indicate the crowds and organised chaos.

At that moment the call to prayer from several mosques crossed in a confusion of noise.

Theo laughed, 'Yeah, although Mecca would probably be quieter.' In that second, Theo felt more comfortable.

The sun crept through the polluted air, indicating it was going to be a hot day. The old, rusty, dented bus edged out into the airport traffic and vibrated itself towards the domestic terminal. Even though it seemed to have a faulty muffler, Theo was glad they were away from the din and tension of the crowded airport. He had been told more than once by people who had been there that one of the key aspects of Asia, in general, was the fact that there were always crowds and always noise. Also, his friend Dempster had pointed out that there were never enough seats, no matter what mode of transport you took.

'Smoke?'

Theo looked around and thought, why not? The air was dirty enough and half the crowd on the bus were smoking anyway, backpackers and locals. 'Mad if I don't, ta.'

The young backpacker offered the packet of Marlboro and lit them up.

'Thanks mate, where you from?' He thought the friendly bloke was American.

'Manitoba, Canada.' He pointed to a maple leaf sewn to his day pack. 'I bet you're an Aussie.'

'Yep, how'd you guess?'

He laughed. 'Easy. Hey, get a load of that,' as he pointed at an obvious altercation between a group of road users. 'I'm blown out by the number of people everywhere.'

'Same here, this is nothing like Adelaide, that's South Australia, where I come from.'

The bus hissed and jerked as they followed the signs to the Domestic Airport. The people waiting appeared to be mostly local looking but included about ten backpackers. The locals had done this before and there was a rush for the remaining seats. Those who didn't manage to grab a seat sat on the floor. Theo smiled, figuring the few backpackers who didn't snare a seat learned a lesson because they were too polite, and some were left behind because there was barely standing room on the steps in the bus.

'First time here?'

Theo didn't feel the need to act big time. 'Yep, you?'

'Nah, been here several times. I like it 'cos it's so different, you know.'

'Yeah, no worries about that, mate.'

When they began to move again it was most welcome to generate some airflow through the windows that mainly didn't exist or were jammed open anyway. The fumes from the road didn't help but it was slightly cooler when they were mobile. Even though Theo was tired, his red rimmed eyes were wide open. New, interesting sights surrounded him and it was clear his new friend across the aisle, even though more experienced, was similarly amazed.

'Wow man, have a look at that!' The Canadian pointed at an old van leaning to one side, clearly overloaded with bags of cement. Four young, dirty men sat on the roof, smoking and laughing, obviously on their way to work.

The journey along Pudu Road was an education to Theo in how to negotiate a huge bus in noisy, congested traffic, with most participants appearing to ignore traffic lights or stop signs if they desired. It seemed the only authority anyone paid any attention to were the police who sported firearms on their hips. The neatly dressed officers waved white gloves and semaphored swerving, undisciplined drivers into a traffic flow that seemed to at least keep the vehicles moving. The road was shared by many forms of transport, from pushbikes, cycle rickshaws and motorised versions of the same as well as cars, overloaded buses and trucks. The noise from all this traffic was horrendous and as tired as he was, Theo marvelled at the sights before him.

His new friend kept laughing heartily at the things he was experiencing. 'Man, dig that!' he said as a truck clipped a rickshaw rider who struggled with all his skills to keep the passenger cage upright. 'I know I shouldn't laugh, but it's a riot on the roads here. If you want to see real chaos, go to India, man, it's worse there.'

Theo's eyes widened, thinking it was hard to believe. 'Yeah?'

Pedestrians also made a point of ignoring traffic lights as they ducked and weaved in and out of hurtling missiles. Theo yawned and rubbed his red eyes but with so much new scenery bursting around him it was hard for a lad from quiet old Adelaide not to be totally awestruck. He was jolted to look up ahead when the bus nearly drove up the back of a small utility, spewing grey exhaust smoke and overloaded with plastic pipes.

'How's that for a bit of economy of scale, eh?' said the Canadian pointing.

A family of six was crammed on to a small motorbike with a woman in a sari facing the rear with a small child standing on her left hip and a babe in arms. The driver nestled a boy about four and an older girl over the petrol tank in front of him.

'Not to mention safety first. At least the driver has a helmet,' added Theo, referring to the driver's turban. They both laughed.

Theo heard someone say, 'Pudu Prison,' as they passed a huge, concrete block fortress structure occupying the corner of Jalang Hang Tuah and Pudu Road. He had read some information about the place in the guidebook and was aware that the notorious jail housed many an unfortunate traveller or backpacker. Some had either done hard yards or been executed there along with hundreds if not thousands of Asians over the years. He could see two sides of the prison were painted in a rainforest mural.

'They are everywhere, buddy,' said his new tour guide, pointing to where monkeys danced and held council along the top of the walls and in the guard towers.

Even though Theo yawned almost non-stop and his eyes felt as if they had grains of sand in them he was absolutely enthralled with everything. It was so vastly different to Australia. Theo was as eager as he was determined to make a decent fist of his holiday in such a different place.

Chapter Five

The bus stopped at various locations and it was mainly locals who jumped off and more locals carrying local produce crammed on. At a location near the Puduraya Bus Station the Canadian, along with a few other backpackers, alighted.

'This is me, buddy, I'm off to Cameron Highlands. Never know, might run into each other again, small world. Take care and enjoy your stay.' He made his way down the aisle laughing and talking to others.

Theo was buoyed by the young man's outgoing friendliness.

The bus jerked on and made a few more stops and finally arrived at an area where there was a nucleus of hotels especially for backpackers. They stepped off in pairs or groups and Theo decided to join them. Even though still early morning, heat bounced off the cracked concrete pavements and the glare was intense from anything light or reflective, including prayer hats and shirts, the long white traditional dress for Muslim men.

Theo quickly put on his sunglasses and hat. He had never experienced heat and humidity like this. In Adelaide it could easily be 40 degrees but it was a dry desert heat, nothing like the tropical heat of Kuala Lumpur. Even though the city traffic was stifling it wasn't so bad when he was in the bus moving. On the street it was a different story.

He could see by the number of hotels it probably would not be a problem securing accommodation. The Hot Spot Hotel looked very much like the other hotel fronts and Theo dragged himself up the clean but well-worn concrete steps. The young Muslim man, or closer to a boy, with his attempt at a beard presenting a few tufts of bumfluff, opened his hands in apology. He had a happy round face and a chipped front tooth.

'Very sorry, sir, very sorry. Hotel full, hotel is full, sir, very full.'

Theo smiled at the unusual use of English, thanked him, trudged down the steps and tried next door at the Hotel Chung Wah. There was a young couple in front of him bargaining the room price with a plump Oriental-looking woman at the counter. As he was waiting to be served he couldn't avoid hearing power tools hammering away somewhere out the back. He was smart enough to realise it was not for him. On his way out he noticed the Indian restaurant next door. Dodging a woman selling flowers, a shoeshine boy and numerous touts giving out free tickets that were obviously a con for something, he struggled on. He gave the next hotel a big miss because it looked dirty, so he trudged up the stairs to the last one in the block. His legs seem to drag and the oppressive heat of the streets compounded the tiredness creeping into all extremities of his body. Theo knew he had to find somewhere soon or he would collapse.

The Hotel New Islamic seemed like it would do the job. He passed a young Nordic couple on the stairs who nodded and smiled. The place was airconditioned and the foyer seemed very clean with soft Malay music drifting in the background.

'G'day,' he said.

The young woman in hijab, which only gave a nun's view of her face, sat behind the reception desk. She smiled, dark eyes flashed. 'You want room?'

Theo managed a small smile, wondering what she thought he was doing there anyway if he didn't want a room. 'Yes, how much ..?'

She showed him a card with the schedule of rooms, facilities and the prices. One of the tips in the guidebook suggested that travellers always asked to look at the room before they agreed to anything.

Even though he was quite exhausted he knew he had to get this right. His friend Dempster, whose father was a manager in an international hotel chain, had lived in Jakarta in Indonesia and Kota Kinabalu in Malaysian Borneo. He had also been to Bali surfing. Over a beer or three he gave Theo some need-to-know essentials for Asia.

'May I have a look at the standard room?'

'Yes, I show.' She grabbed a set of jailer's keys from a hook. 'You follow.'

Theo noticed it was only the reception and foyer area that were airconditioned. They passed through a two-way swinging door into the accommodation section. The door creaked open and instantly Theo could see that this room would not suit him. The open window faced a noisy backstreet.

'Do you have a quieter room?'

She inclined her head. 'Window always close, use airconditioner, much better. Best price for you, 25 ringgit.' She smiled, making it seem like it was a very good deal. Her voice had a musical quality to it.

'But isn't that the price of a standard room?" Theo queried, realising he was going to have to improve his bargaining skills.

'Yes, room has airconditioner, extra cost.'

'Could I please look at the other room?' He knew she was playing with him.

They walked down the corridor. She selected another key from the jailer's ring.

'Special room for you, all the way from Ostray-lee-ah.'

'How did you know I was Australian?'

'I know these things. Special price for you, this room.' She wagged an all-knowing finger at him.

'It looks okay.' The window opened onto a side street with a glimpse of the main drag but it seemed much quieter. He nudged the bathroom door open, it looked alright. He pointed at the airconditioner. 'Does this work?'

'Of course,' she replied with a coy look. 'How long you stay?'

'Depends on how much?'

'Price depends on length of stay.'

'I don't know how long because I have to make a phone call. Okay, maybe two nights.'

'Usually 35 but 30 to you, two nights.'

'Thirty? Isn't this a standard room though?'

'No standard rooms left.'

Theo remembered the pep talk from Dempster. 'I'll take it for 25.'

'No, sorry, room 30 with airconditioner, and of course minimum stay.'

Theo sighed; he had enjoyed the banter but ... He yawned. 'Look, the list you showed me said 25 for a standard room, right?'

'Yes,' she said, eyes sparkling, 'but this room has airconditioning, okay?'

'Right, let's start again. Do you have any standard rooms *without* airconditioning?'

'No.'

'So this is a standard room, yes?' He could see she was older than first impression, probably twenty-ish.

'Yes, standard but with airconditioning, see, and bathroom attached, extra five ringgit?'

He shook his head as if to disperse the silliness of it all. 'I suppose they all have bathrooms attached? Never mind, I'll take it for 25, okay.'

'Okay,' she replied as if they hadn't had the previous conversation. Her dark eyes held an even stare.

'25, if airconditioner does in fact work. Okay?'

Her eyebrows formed a straight black line below the flowered hijab and she spoke as if struggling to not laugh. 'Here, I show you.' The battered unit burst into life. 'There, see? Working fine.'

Theo knew she was stretching it out. He had been around long enough to know that beautiful women were able to flirt like that and get away with it. She nearly got away with five ringgits, too. His tiredness lifted just being in her company.

She was all business. 'Passport, please. We have to register and check details, policy of Malaysia then we give back passport. Okay?' Dark eyes caught him off guard again.

'Right.' He pulled out his passport and handed it to her as they walked back into the small entrance foyer which doubled as an office as well.

There was a young man, probably late twenties, sitting in one of the four cane chairs. He stared at her, completely ignoring Theo. White shirt, Muslim prayer cap and dark complexion. Theo thought he looked Malay from pictures in the guidebook.

She instantly flustered. 'Er … here is your key … room nine, I will make available to you your passport when I have recorded detail, okay *sir*.'

Theo nodded. 'No worries,' shouldered his backpack, grabbed the plastic bag of duty free and headed back to his new room, thinking about the young woman. Who was the dark local man in the foyer and why did he intimidate her? He also wondered why she called him *sir*.

Chapter Six

A soft knock on the door, he didn't know how long he had been asleep. Theo rubbed his eyes. What day was it? He glanced at his watch. It was still daylight, airconditioner whirring, same day, a few hours later. He must have collapsed on the bed, fully clothed. The knock came again.

'Hang on, be right there.'

She stood there innocently holding out his passport. 'Please, sign here to say you receive it back. Thank you. Now, usually payment in advance for short stay but please pay due money on day of departure.' She didn't meet his eyes, a completely different engagement to their earlier banter.

Theo shook the sleep from his head. 'Yep, no worries. Is there a phone here I can use?'

'In foyer.' She stole a quick glance at him, dark eyes, whites flashed. She turned and took off back down the corridor in a swish of light material, nearly bumping into a young woman with a red maple leaf on her day pack.

The traveller nodded a smiled greeting to Theo as she passed.

Theo had a cold shower, being unsure of how to get the water heater operating correctly. The bathroom door had been shut whilst the airconditioner had been going so the room was warm from the day and cold water was not really a problem. The bathroom was basic with a hole-in-the-floor toilet but seemed clean enough. He brushed his teeth, organised his possessions and locked the backpack. He locked his door also, on the advice of a notice pinned to the inside, and made his way to the foyer.

The same young couple who he met on the stairs earlier were negotiating a tour of some kind. He looked at the public phone and glanced quickly through the phone book. His brow tightened in confusion. Theo decided it was far more sensible to ask the receptionist to assist him to find the number and show him how to make a call. Also he felt a need to talk with her, and help with the phone book was as good an excuse as any.

He sat in one of the bamboo easy chairs and breezed through a few tourist brochures scattered across the glass-topped coffee table. The foyer and reception area were tastefully decorated with prints of street scenes and a row of wooden masks, obviously from jungle tribes, along the long wall.

The young couple departed, nodding at him, and he stepped forward. 'Would you be able to help me with the phone ... please?'

'Of course.' Her troubled look fused away and the amused pouty expression returned. 'I make no charge for extra assistance, okay?'

He had no choice but to laugh out loud.

She responded with a quiet, musical giggle. 'This way, please.'

She zipped in front of him and he couldn't help but notice her petite, curvy body under the loose clothing. 'By the way ... er ... what is your name? My name is Th...'

'I know your name; I know many things about you. Passport okay?' She laughed. 'My name is Biru. Biru is for blue. My father's favourite colour was blue. We Muslims are bound by everything our fathers' command, just as well blue is my favourite colour also.' Some of the words joined together to form an almost unique musical flow of English.

She stood at the phone. 'Okay, what is it you ..?'

'Here.' He showed her the logo on the reverse of envelope, St John's, Wayward Travellers' Project, Leboh Ampang, Georgetown, Penang, Malaysia.

'Phone book here only Kuala Lumpur. I contact Directories.'

She picked up the handpiece and spoke in rapid Malay, or it seemed to him it was. Either way he couldn't follow except for the occasional word. He felt a strong sense of desire from her close proximity. He wanted it to last.

She scribbled down a number on the pad. 'There, see you dial that. No more need for me? We do ring back for price of call by time, okay?'

'Good, thanks, I think I can handle it from here.' She ripped off the sheet and handed it to him. He felt a pang of excitement weighed with … what? Apprehension? After all, Jack was his father's best friend, all he had from Jack was an invitation scribbled in a letter. The last time Theo recalled actually talking with him was probably twenty years earlier when Jack and Vince returned from Vietnam. Theo was only a child. There were, of course, two other letters over the period. Maybe he didn't know Jack at all. His hand shook slightly. He glanced in Biru's direction. She stared back, caught out, and smiled.

Chapter Seven

He dialled the number.

'Selamat pagi, San Johns Angli-kahn?'

'Selamat pagi, good morning,' replied Theo, not sure how to proceed. 'Um ... do you speak English?'

'Yes, of course, my name is Brian Aung; I assist with the administration around here. How may I help you?' A clipped British accent.

'My name is Theo Perry. I am looking for a ... er ... family friend of mine, Jack Deere. Is he there?'

'Aha, you mean our friend Jack, don't you?' The man chuckled. 'To answer your question, Jack is not here at the moment. You missed him by a few days. He did mention your name, though. Unfortunately Jack is not really a gifted communicator and is away much of the time. Getting a message to him is not easy but I will get the word out there and if he pops in I will contact you, if you can leave a number or an address I can ...'

'Well, I'd really like to catch up with him soon; he was a good friend of my father's.'

'Yes, I know.'

'You knew my father?'

'No, not really, but I did meet him once or twice.'

Theo could see the matter was not progressing. 'Where does Jack live, maybe I can go and visit hi..?'

'No, I'm afraid that won't be possible. He drops in here from time to time, that's how we communicate.'

'How do you know him, I mean what does he do?'

29

The other man chuckled again. 'You have many questions, young man. You need to talk to him about what he does, but I can tell you he helps out here sometimes with us.'

'But, er Brian, that's what I want to do, talk to him I mean. I came all the way from Australia to Malaysia to see him, surely he told you that?'

'No, not really, he said he wrote to you but didn't get a reply so he went away to Thailand to, well I don't think he would care if I told you, but he went to have a new prosthetic leg fitted in Bangkok.'

'Did he leave any contact details, I mean ..?'

'I'm sorry Theo; all I can do is pass on a message if and when possible.'

'Any idea when he might be back?'

'Not really but I would imagine within a couple of weeks.'

'Couple of weeks? I'll only be here for a few weeks.' Theo didn't push the white lie because he had not booked his return flight; he had an open ticket.

'Not much I can do but please keep in touch and maybe give me your contact details, okay?'

Theo rattled off the phone number on the dial and stated the name of the hotel. 'I'm not sure how long I'll be here. I'll get back to you in a day or so when I work out exactly where I'll be and when I establish a better contact.'

'Splendid. I promise to do what I can, someone here may know how to reach him, in the meantime please be in contact. Cheerio for now then.'

Theo looked at the dead receiver. 'Bugger me,' he mumbled smiling, wondering how a bloke with the name of Aung could sound like a retired British army officer. Remembering himself he glanced over at the front desk. Biru had her back to him, rifling through a steel four-drawer cabinet.

She turned, more than likely had heard much of his conversation. He hoped she didn't hear the last couple of words.

'All fixed, Mr Perry?'

'No, not really. If anyone should ring here, would you be able ...'

'Sure, sure, no extra charge,' she laughed.

'Now, I would like to ring Australia, would you please be able to ..?'

'Yes, of course, no charge again for assistance but you pay for call?' She smiled and grabbed the phone book. 'See, dial codes all here. Sometimes line is bad on international call, but we try. Ringing girlfriend in Orstray-lee-ah?' she enquired, mischievously, almost chastising, eyebrows a straight line.

His turn to laugh. 'Well as it so happens, yes. This girlfriend is by far the best girl in the world.'

She frowned slightly.

She had beautiful dark eyes. Theo liked the way she was looking at him but at the same time he wished she didn't because he was not sure what it meant. He broke the spell. 'The … the special girl is my mother.'

'You are funny, Mr. Perry,' she replied and her face lit up again.

He spoke to Gail, relating aspects of the flight and explaining generally where he was staying and what it was like. Like all mothers she was focused on making sure Theo put on fresh underwear every day, brushed his teeth and made sure he ate proper food, not potato chips. The line was crackly and faded at times but he could still hear reasonably well. He glanced at Biru. 'I'm staying in Kuala Lumpur as planned and it's a nice place, I mean where I'm staying. I like it here.'

Biru gave a smile, almost pretending not to be listening, but she appeared grateful of his comment, even though it was to someone else.

'Right, I'll be in touch.' He hung up.

There was the sound of a door closing at the base of the stairs.

'I'm going out to look around, maybe get something to eat. By the way, my name is Theo, alright? I don't know how to respond to mister.'

'Of course, as you wish. Please note there are plenty of good eating places. You go to corner and you see mall, no traffic.'

'Righto, see you,' he replied. As Theo gave her his key their hands touched. It was so slight but he was sure she deliberately did it. He tried to hold her gaze as he shouldered his day pack, and then he turned and headed for the stairs, and the street.

'Bye bye,' she added.

Chapter Eight

The intensity of the street hit him at once. The sky had lost the day but an eerie twilight hovered. A group of three young, swarthy men dressed in western style, two with American baseball caps backwards, squatted on the ground near the entrance. Theo recognised one of them as the man in the foyer with the Muslim prayer cap who had given Biru an eye-burning reprimand earlier in the day.

Being a normally friendly person and also wishing to make a good impression with the locals, he nodded and said, 'G'day, fellers.'

None of them responded; they looked straight through him. He shrugged, slightly offended and uncertain of their message but he had received that sort of response on the Aussie Rules football field when trying to be a good sport. He smiled, remembering an incident in his first A grade game. This opposition player said, *'You won't be saying nice things like that when I knock your block off, maaate!'*

He turned and strolled in the direction of the famed mall where food was available all day but more extensively from before sundown to after midnight. Sometime during his unsettled sleep earlier, he had woken with a start to the sound of the afternoon monsoonal thunder storm. The whirring airconditioner had not been able to drown out the loud, violent, house-shaking thunder and the instant flashes of intimidating lightning. In a half sleep he had opened the window and looked on in awe at the pouring rain. He had never experienced anything like it. Rain in Adelaide was still rain, and mostly in winter, but nothing like a tropical storm. It almost blanked out everything beyond a metre in a grey impenetrable sheet. The hammering noise of the falling water on the tin roofs was deafening and the fizzing sound it made when it hit the ground was almost frightening. He stood at the window for the length of time it took to smoke a cigarette and have two shots of vodka from his duty-free purchase. The rain eased and he went back to bed and fell into a jet-lagged sleep again.

There was a clean edge to the night air, even though it was still warm. Street lights honeyed everything in a dull glow and locals busied themselves setting up stalls, some with clothes and some with food. He remembered the guidebook mentioning the clothes stalls in this area were mainly for tourists. Tee-shirts, sarongs, bright beach-type shirts, straw hats, sunglasses, woven bags as well as the bottled water which he noted had become popular, even though expensive. Theo had the standard tourist pack, chlorine tablets and water purification tabs. There seemed to be more backpackers and tourists than local people milling about. He was still amazed at the number of young women around the place. Most of the backpackers were young and dressed for the climate, showing more tanned flesh than he had seen in summer at West Beach. Even the Muslim girls looked sexy in the clever way they hid their beauty. The local working people, Orientals, Indians and Malays, were obvious by their dress and banter with each other. Even though the car traffic was blocked off, Theo smiled at the fact that the locals didn't consider motorbikes as traffic and their piercingly noisy two-stroke motors spewing out oily exhaust fumes took the shine off the possibility of a quiet beer and some food. Two cycle rickshaws made an attempt to encourage westerners to go for a ride, or to have a photo taken with a tourist, but the day of the rickshaw was almost over. These young Chinese-looking men were only doing it for show, or maybe the chance to sell dope.

The call to prayer by the muezzin commenced at this hour and drifted everywhere from what seemed like several mosques. Theo was not exactly awestruck but fascinated by the compilation of noises. The aromas and smells were of so many varying origins he couldn't possibly identify most of them. The stink from the drains was one he was certain of.

Theo wandered the length of the sealed-off road which went for nearly two blocks. In that distance he was approached by a sallow youth with slit eyes. He sidled up to Theo and spoke out of the corner of his mouth like a spy. It seemed to Theo that it drew attention to the act rather than not.

'Aha, my frien' from 'stray-eeah? New Zealan'? You want drugs? Best price. Woman, clean, virgin special for you?'

Theo ignored him but wondered how the young man knew where he came from. The buildings were mainly low-rise few taller that ten floors but most four or five. They seemed to be a mixture of retail and eating places on the ground floor and residential upstairs. Touts or spruikers leapt out at each passer-by, trying to lure customers into their places. The restaurants were mainly Chinese but there appeared to be several other Asian diversities as well. There was a cluster of Indian places down one end. The Malay restaurants were along one side and seemed to cater for the young with a different violent, ear-shattering Kung Fu or action movie featuring the likes of Chuck Norris, Van Damme, George Segal or something similar playing at each venue. Theo, although being a fan of those movies when in the mood, couldn't quite come at getting his ears blown out. He was still coming to terms with jet lag and was content with a beer, something to eat and an early night.

Some of the restaurants catered for locals too, with low tables with even lower stools which enabled people to sit, kneel or squat close to the ground. Families sat around talking animatedly and eating with chopsticks.

Chinese places seemed to be quieter but not by much, and there appeared to be a competition between them also as they all had a TV in a back room hammering away. Some of the obviously more expensive ones had fish tanks in the front windows where patrons could select seafood and have it cooked especially for them. Large family groups filled the tables in all the places, sharing food, chattering away and maybe discussing the experiences of their day.

The lights were more obvious as the night had taken over from the heat of the day, and Theo could see high-rise buildings and hear the heartbeat of the city, the hum of traffic in the distance. He yawned, a sign to sit down. After some deliberation, he selected the quietest place nearby with smaller tables and less large gatherings. A TV dominated the back room with a children's show turned up to distortion in an Oriental language. He could see a group of children sitting inches away mesmerised by the flickering screen.

A middle-aged woman turned on the fan over his table and presented a menu; he ordered a beer. When she returned he asked what the best food was today. She didn't really understand so he made eating actions indicating a piled plate.

She pointed to a blackboard near the door. 'Sarawak chicken and vegetable, special today,' she beamed.

Theo wondered how he was supposed to know that but he nodded anyway. A cigarette went well with the cold beer and he pulled out the guidebook to check on a few things. He became lost in thought, unable to concentrate on the book because he kept looking out at life in the street, enthralled by the pace of the life in Kuala Lumpur. So far his friend Dempster was right, Asian cities were certainly noisy, and crowded but interesting, with things happening all the time. He sighed, thinking of Biru, and luxuriated in the feeling of being almost mesmerised when she was close. Was it her delicate fragrance? Maybe it wasn't jasmine, he didn't really know. Theo knew it was more than that. It was the wonderful feeling he had when she was near and he had only known her for, how long?

The arrival of Sarawak chicken and vegetable snapped him out of his dreams. 'Terima kasih,' he said, trying his best to sound as if he had a good grasp of the language. Dempster had told him it was always good to have a go, even if he was self-conscious about it. After a while you get good at it by trying and listening to others, he had said. Theo ordered another beer.

The chicken part of the special was nice even though it was peppered with splintered bone but the vegetables were fresh and tasty. He finished his second beer and paid the bill. Cheap, he thought.

As he stood up a strange sensation washed over him. He looked around quickly, feeling that he was being observed. Theo gathered his book, put it in his day pack and nodded a thank you to the waitress. He stepped back into the street and nosed in the direction of the Hotel New Islamic. Tired, that's all.

∞

It was about nine thirty and the street was still crowded with milling tourists, mostly about his own age but there were some older people, mostly couples who appeared to be slumming it from the big hotels. Some locals were out for a stroll or to eat and many stall or shop owners vied for trade by yelling and offering deals they hoped passers-by couldn't refuse.

The same sallow lad with half-closed eyes approached again. He tapped his nose and smiled. Theo shook his head. Maybe what he felt in the restaurant was the youth following him. That was probably it, nothing to worry about.

In the distance the noise pitch of mass vehicles could be heard periodically taking off from traffic lights on a major road, probably Jalan Tun Perak, the continuation of Jalan Pudu.

The now familiar group of three hostile-looking young men still loitered near the entrance to his hotel. This time one of them smirked at him. Theo didn't bother to respond, he just walked past them and up the stairs. He expected to see Biru; he was looking forward to it in fact and was momentarily disappointed to see a young man behind the desk.

'Hi,' he said, 'my name is Razak, night staff. You new today? You must be room ..?'

'Nine,' Theo added.

'Aaah, Mr Perry, just arrived from … er Orstray-lee-ah or been here for a while?'

Theo took it to mean in Malaysia. 'Just arrived from Australia, today.'

'Not too long flight. Europeans have much longer flight.' He smiled. 'Many things to see in Koo-ahla Lumpoor, please if we can be of any assistance do not hesitate to ask. We are proud of our country, shining light of tolerance for such a mixture of races. We can organise tours from here if you require. You may wish to visit Pudu Prison? Not have any prisoners now, closed only one month, tourist attraction now. Very notorious, also mysterious. We can arrange for pick up, guide, anything … okay?' He handed Theo his key.

'Thanks,' said Theo and went to his room.

Chapter Nine

Next morning Theo was jolted awake into the present by the noise of the street. Dogs barking, call to prayer, bells from a temple nearby, motorbikes, traffic, sweeping noises and voices in a range from talking to yelling. He had turned the airconditioning unit off in the early hours of the morning and used the fan. From previous experience he didn't like sleeping in airconditioning because he usually woke up with a sore throat. Unfortunately the fan made a clicking noise on low so he had to have it either on full or off. So, during the night he woke up intermittently to either turn the fan on or off. It wasn't so bad though because his body clock was out of kilter and several times during the night he sat at the window with a cigarette, listening to the myriad of interesting sounds and aromas wafting past. He had time to consider options in relation to Jack and figured he may as well spend some time in Kuala Lumpur, having a look at the many things mentioned in the guidebook. At some stage of his visit he was obliged to check in with the Malaysian Department of Foreign Affairs to sort out some personal paperwork related to his father and the funeral.

Not long after, Theo went out to reception hoping to see Biru. He wasn't disappointed. She was writing in a ledger.

'Good morning, Mr Perry.'

'Theo, alright? Um, I don't seem to be able to get the water heater in my room going. Is there a secret?'

'No secret. I show you.'

She swished in front of him, down the passage and through his room into the bathroom. All business.

'See here, switch?'

'Yes, I turned it on but nothing happened.'

She tried. 'Mmmm, I see.' 'Oh yes, maybe switch is not on at switchboard. Please, one moment.' As she reached up to the heater, he was magnetised by her slim, lithe body beautifully proportioned under her lightweight clothing. He felt a certain charge with her so close.

She darted past him and out the door, leaving a whiff of perfume. She returned only seconds later. Yes, sorry, main power switch off at switchboard. Okay, all fixed. Look, now heating up.'

'Thanks and er … hate to be a pain but the fan makes a loud clicking sound on low, see?' He wanted to keep her there.

'Yes, I see, but nothing to do about it now but when maintenance man come next I will have him look at it. Sorry but in tropical climate fan mechanical parts get dry and most fans are like this everywhere.'

Theo was standing partly in the doorway with his hand on the switch.

'I better go now,' she said, looking at him.

She waltzed past him, still maintaining eye contact and ever so slightly touched his hand, grasped it for a feather-second and then kept going. *What was that? So light, did it happen, Theo?*

'Sorry,' she breathed. Her smile showed she was clearly far from sorry.

Instantly she froze! Leaning against the opposite wall was the dark young man, staring. She did her best to harness dignity and lowered her head just enough. She dashed to reception. Theo held the man's stare for a moment and then closed the door in his face. 'Fuck you,' he whispered, knowing the man had seen it all – if there was anything to see.

∞

Initially Theo had wanted hot water so he could shave but at that point he had several days' growth and thought it would be a good idea to grow a beard. Even though the shower was hot he hardly needed it as the day was warming up. The encounter with the surly man gnawed away at him; it was hard to dismiss when someone gets in your space and wants to dictate terms. He knew it had something to do with Biru. Brother, chaperone? He had read a bit about Islam in Malaysia in the library at university before he came away. In the main it seemed Muslims in Malaysia were much more progressive than most other

Islamic countries because the general population was made up of a mix of Chinese, Indians and other groups. Malaysia was not an Islamic state as such. It appeared as if the country could only function best if each group was prepared to give a bit for the overall good.

Theo was on holiday and apart from checking in with Jack, he wanted to see and do as much as he could now that he had the chance. He was keen to get to know Biru better but how he was to go about that, he had no idea. Should he ask her out? Did he need to ask her family if he could take her out? Then what? Either way, he was not going to be pushed around by someone if he was not doing anything wrong. He figured he would wait until he had done something wrong, then he would be prepared to deal with it. And what would be considered to be wrong? There was nothing wrong with talking to her.

He thought it was time to get out in the street and have some coffee and breakfast. The morning was moving on and there was much to see.

He locked his backpack, stuffed the town map he had taken from the foyer yesterday into his day pack, grabbed his peaked cap, locked the door and prepared himself to talk to Biru about … about what? Maybe ask about the man who heavied her? Biru was not there. Theo was not sure if he was relieved or not.

Razak nodded, 'Selamat tenga hari, Mr Perry. Where are you off to today?'

'Um, not sure. First up I think some coffee and breakfast, then maybe wander around, have a look at a few sights.'

'Plenty of small eating places around here. You want rice, satay, chicken-rice, or western style porridge, maybe American breakfast? All within easy walk, go either way out the front.'

Theo nodded.

'Can I help you with anything else?' Razak inclined his head at an angle.

Theo wasn't sure what he meant but decided to take the question as innocently intended. 'No thank you, maybe tomorrow. Not sure exactly what I will be doing over the next few days. Thanks anyway. By the way, call me Theo, okay?'

'Yes, of course, Mr Theo. Please have a nice day.'

As he walked down the stairs he recalled his expert friend Dempster saying that the front desk jockeys always ask single blokes, *You want girl, you want boy? You want drugs?'* He wondered if Razak meant that.

At the bottom of the stairs the dark man stepped in front of him. He was wearing his Muslim prayer hat in preference to the baseball cap. The two other equally dark men appeared either side, baseball caps backwards.

'Hey, Tuan whitey boy?'

A bead of sweat trickled down Theo's back. He was still in airconditioning. 'What can I do for you?' His kept his voice level, not threatening like the dark man's intonation.

'Stay away from her, whitey boy.'

'What do you mean? From who?'

'Don't be a wise guy. You know who I mean.'

'Who do you mean?'

'Girl here in hotel. I caught her in your room, alright?' He wagged his finger.

'She was there to sort out my hot water service, mate.' Theo was gaining some confidence; also he remained on the last step to retain higher ground because he was outnumbered.

'One warning only. Stay away from her, she belongs to me. You don't understand customs of our country.'

'What, belongs to ..? Right, mate, not that it is any of your business but there is nothing going on between us, she has just been helpful, that's all, and that is, after all, her job. Okay?'

'Don't be foolish, she is not your business. Malay Muslim look after their own. Move out of this hotel, you are not welcome here … and stay away from her. One warning.' He reached up and put a flat hand firmly against Theo's chest. 'Unnerstand, big boss whitey boy?'

Theo reminded himself of football law; be ready, one step ahead, hit him before he hits you, the rules of any game. Establish control early but shake hands at the end. But this was no game. There were no rules.

Another blob of sweat stopped halfway down his back. *Now or never, Theo.*

Theo whacked the man's hand hard and fast with the flat of his hand, a fast removal rather than a straight-out punch. 'Out of my way, *mate.*' The action moved him to one side. The dark man was too busy holding his hand in shock to react. It happened too quickly for the other two. Theo was past them, out the double doors and into the humid morning. *Show them a clean pair of heels.*

Chapter Ten

Theo walked purposefully down the road and round the corner. Some of the barriers had been removed to allow restricted traffic to service some of the business premises. The traffic noise was light and nearly drowned out by music and videos playing in some of the eating places. He was sure no-one was following but even if they did, he could handle himself. However, there was some doubt deep down. He was mature enough to realise you don't go making enemies in a foreign country. By the time he stopped at The Arafat Big Restoran, sweat streaked his face. The restaurant was one of the places that did not have noise from a violent video crashing into the street. He needed a few minutes to gather his thoughts. Theo selected a table inside under a clicking fan and sat, back to the wall, to get a good view of the street. He looked up and wondered if all fans in Malaysia clicked. A shoeshine boy came over but he shook his head, pointing to his suede desert boots. The young boy was still keen to shine them so Theo had to practice ignoring him until he eventually wandered away.

'Good morning, selamat pagi,' said a small young girl in a loose hijab, similar to what appeared to be standard for women in Malaysia.

'Selamat pagi,' he replied. He glanced at the menu, realised his stomach was knotted from the recent confrontation, and added, 'White coffee for the moment, please.'

'Nescafe?' she asked.

Theo nodded, aware that the guidebook said it was hard to get real coffee unless you hunted for it. He busied himself with a copy of an

English-speaking newspaper whist glancing up without moving his head. The coffee arrived. It was hot, milky and sweet. He tried not to grimace too obviously because he didn't like sugar. He called the girl over.

'This coffee has sugar in it.'

'No sugar, just condense milk. Coffee okay?' She looked almost hurt.

He took the path of valour. 'Yes, of course, coffee okay. Could I please order … er American Breakfast?'

She smiled, obviously relieved. 'Yah, no problem.'

He lit a cigarette and contemplated his situation. Clearly he didn't want a battle with three or four thugs. He could handle one or at best two, but no more. Also, things had the potential to become ugly. Surely not, over a woman? He smiled, worldly enough to realise the situation could most certainly escalate and could compound because he was on his own in a strange city, and he didn't know anyone except Jack. Did he even know Jack? He was a day's travel away and so far Theo wasn't even aware Jack was in Malaysia. He thought about the fights some of his mates had been involved in over women but that was Australia. But in a place like this? Guns, knives? They could probably make him disappear if they wanted and no one would know. His breakfast arrived and he ordered a cup of tea, no sugar. Suddenly he looked up and out into the now busy street. The feeling of being watched hovered over him, the same sensation as yesterday.

He paid the bill and decided to go back to the Hotel New Islamic. Somehow he thought things would resolve themselves if he confronted the issue in hand. That meant speaking with Biru. He had no idea what he was going to say.

Ahead of him, about to enter his hotel, he noticed a young couple. They looked northern European. Both had rucksacks at their feet and were looking up at the sign. He hurried, thinking that if he encountered any problems with the dark trio, it was unlikely they would try anything with an audience.

'Hi,' he said catching up with them. 'Er … Just arrived?' Stupid question. 'I mean of course you have. If you are looking for a place, this hotel is okay. I'm staying here.' Clearly they *were* looking for a place to stay otherwise they wouldn't have been standing looking at the hotel entrance. He held the door open for them and followed up the stairs. There was no sign of the others.

Biru looked up.

As he was behind them he gave her the thumbs up, pointing to them. 'Key please.'

She gave it to him and turned her attention to the new arrivals. He said to them, 'Maybe catch you later,' and went to his room. The conversation with Biru would have to wait.

Theo washed some clothes in the sink and hung them up on a string he had brought with him. He had noted in the hints section of the guidebook before departing – the survivor's kit which his friend, Dempster claimed to have invented string, pegs, drawing pins, needle and thread, plumber's tape and Blu-Tack and, of course, a Swiss Army knife.

He heard a creaking noise at the door. He crept to the door and opened it quickly. No-one was there but the people talking in the foyer. He shook his head, chastising himself for being so edgy.

Theo lay on the bed, hands clasped behind his head. What to do? What about Biru? Should he show lack of courage and move out to another hotel? From what his friend Dempster had said about how seriously the Asians took the issue of losing face, he needed to be careful. Using that formula, *he* would lose face if he backed down in the eyes of the other man. If Theo didn't do as he was told, the dark man would lose face in front of his friends if he didn't take any action. Theo really needed, *and* wanted, to speak to Biru. The space around her seemed to be energy charged for him, or something near it, when she engaged and smiled. He felt an instant clouded reaction in her on both occasions when the dark Islamic man was present. What did he have over her? He said she belonged to him? Who was he and what was his relationship with her? Theo had to speak to her. And, should he go to Penang and hang around waiting for Jack who might not turn up at all? There were more questions than answers for his twenty-two year old brain.

The fan clicked and the airconditioner whirred in protest at the amount of work it had to do in the heat. The rhythmic sounds, combined with the jet lag, overcame him and the mountain of stress and fatigue crumbled around him. He fell asleep and had a dream about his father. Vince was kicking a football to him on the oval. Then it all changed. Vince and Jack were in their uniforms, laughing and smoking as psychedelic explosions echoed with Hendrix music, Vietnamese farmers with wooden guns saluted and smiled through betel-nut stained teeth, and beautiful young women danced around them. Then he saw his mother, crying, pleading ... then the dream shifted and he woke with a jolt when the dark young Muslim man looked through the bars of a prison cell and grinned at him, showing gold teeth with blood dripping down his chin. Theo sat bolt upright, sweat covering his body, almost chilled by the fan.

A glance at his watch showed it was mid-afternoon. He must have slept for hours. He showered in cold water, having no choice because the heater wasn't working again. He glanced at the words, Shower Enjoy – Model AAA, on the heater casing and tried to clear his muddled head. The bathroom was warm anyway but because the pipes were mainly encased in walls and lagging, the cold water was a relief and it brought him round. It was time to do something. He hoped it wasn't something stupid.

Chapter Eleven

Theo locked a few things of debatable value into his backpack and grabbed his day pack. He took a big breath as he locked the door, hoping Biru would be there. His heart bumped against his chest as he headed to reception.

'Good afternoon, Mr Theo,' she said smiling, eyes sparkling, almost mocking. She had changed out of the dark nun style hijab with the dark dress and was wearing lighter clothes. No more skin was exposed by the tight white scarf framing her face, and the light flowered hijab over that. Had she dressed for him?

'Selamat petang,' he replied, at least trying to seem as if he had a good grasp of the language, 'and it's Theo, right?'

Two females and a young man sat in the cane chairs, obviously discussing tourist things. A map was open on the coffee table.

Theo leant closer to Biru to hand the keys over. There was electricity again between them and the whiff of jasmine, or something soft and alluring to him. His tongue was tangled for a second and he just looked at her. She saved him.

'Theo, um … what are you going to do today?'

'Not sure, maybe check out the market area …' He needed to get to the point. He leant closer so the others wouldn't hear. 'Who is the bloke who has been hanging around here, the one who was sitting over there the day I arrived,' he pointed, '*and* who was standing outside my door when you looked at my hot water system?'

Her demeanour darkened. 'Sorry, Mahmoud is a not very pleasing man.

45

My family and his family want us to be married. I don't like the idea of arranged marriage and I make it clear I am not to be arranged. My father and mother die many years ago in road accident when I am a baby and my uncle then become stepfather. He is of the old way and doesn't understand more modern way of doing things. Many of my friends at school now not agree to arranged marriage. So my stepfather not agree with me, he still like old way for security for me but it really is benefit for him. Mahmoud's family also are of old way too and they do not understand more modern way of new Malay-she-ah, and Mahmoud himself thinks I am belonging to him. I'm sorry he is a problem for you; he is a problem for me too. I am in difficult situation.'

There was a short silence and it seemed as if she was weighing up what to say. Her gaze quickly took in the room and then zeroed in on him again. 'Maybe I go away soon to escape. Mahmoud violent man and my stepfather not say anything.' She leant closer and whispered. 'My stepfather extremely nasty bad man, I do not like him.'

Theo's eyes opened wide, shocked at the ferocity of how she said it. 'Why … why does Mahmoud hang around here?'

She sighed, seemed to relax and opened her hands in a resigned fashion. 'Sure, his family own this hotel. My stepfather get me job here three months ago but since I start they arrange all this marriage promises without consulting my feelings. Mahmoud sometimes sits here at desk on night-time shift if Razak not available. I not very sure what to do. He will not leave me alone; even though I try to say I do not want this thing, he ignores my feeling and still thinks I belong to him. I had hoped he would just accept it. He also involved in some seedy criminal thing, too, I think. He is nasty man, too.'

Theo was not sure what to say. They held each other's gaze for a fraction too long. She was the stronger of the two. 'Please try to ignore him.'

'Well, Biru, that is hard to do because he told me to move out and to stay away from you. I'm not sure what to do. Should I move out?'

'What? No, you stay; he has no right to do this thing. You and I are not to be married … are we?' She laughed, instantly embarrassed for saying something like that. 'Maybe we …'

The expression on Biru's face changed in an instant. Theo turned; there stood Mahmoud, leaning against the wall with a look of fire in his eyes.

∞

Theo left the hotel and walked almost aimlessly, but he had tried to focus on the Puduraya Bus Station to research bus times. If he got that far he thought a scout around the perimeter of the notorious Pudu Prison, to familiarise himself with the area, would kill a few hours. The encounter in the hotel foyer had unnerved him and he was no closer to any decisions. He wondered about her words, '*Maybe we …*' just before she saw Mahmoud.

Intermittently a taxi would add to the traffic noise by tooting him, looking for a fare. Vendors tried to sell him T-shirts, sarongs, beach shirts as well as street food. Sometimes a shop owner or tout would try to woo him into their shop to buy jewellery, silver or brass statues, carvings, silk cloth or other tourist mementos.

Theo looked up at the rapidly darkening sky. Woolly clouds had become lead-grey and with a tinge of anger as they tried to join up and block out the blue. Thunder rumbled in the distance. Palm trees in lonely clumps along the Jalan stirred with new energy in the oppressive heat. Items of paper and plastic flittered across the roadway accelerated by the puffs of breeze, much to the annoyance of the conical hatted street sweepers.

As he walked into the bus station, he was almost overwhelmed by the frantic hustle and bustle; it seemed as if everyone in the area was shouting at someone else. Theo remembered a visit to the Adelaide Stock Exchange as a student during lively trading and this bus station left that experience for dead. Theo nodded to himself. It was clear it would be a major task to get a ticket to Penang, let alone find where the bus left from, so he decided to wander around, checking ticket counters and bus bays. To complicate matters, taxis and minibuses operated from there as well. He thought he had it sorted out in his head as to where to obtain the ticket and what general area downstairs the buses, bound for Penang, left from. The main problem was that a number of different bus lines operated that particular route and, naturally, the prices and times varied enormously. The fumes from diesel engines and the din from loudspeakers in that area were overwhelming and it was clear to him that some of the buses should have been headed straight to the wreckers. Theo decided that when he was ready to go he would front up early, purchase the ticket, check what bay the bus left from and then spend waiting time up in the street. He knew there were agents near his hotel as well as in the hotel who could arrange tickets and travel but it was cheaper to buy the ticket at the bus station. He made a note of prices anyway.

The street was noisy too but more entertaining, with a mass of humanity surging in all directions. The sojourn at the bus station took his mind temporarily off his present decision-making predicament. As he turned to continue up the Jalan Pudu, again he had the strange feeling he was being followed. He glanced around; a Chinese man ducked into a doorway only to come out again with a box of vegetables a few moments later. He convinced himself it was only a man working. An Indian turbaned man held a newspaper up to his eyes, only to be met by a woman in a sari with two children, and they pushed off together to go shopping, out to eat or home, like any family. A beggar with no legs grinned up at him through red stained stumps of teeth and then trolleyed away on his skateboard platform. What would a beggar be doing following him on a skateboard? *Keep your nerve, Theo; the opposition is only trying to spook you into taking your eye off your game.*

The heat outside was now balanced with a level of humidity that made the air feel almost liquid. The local dogs scattered as well as the people. A particularly skinny dog with bad skin was too sick to move and it stood shuddering in the middle of the road, cars dodging around it. It appeared almost ready to die. Theo was struck by the sadness of the scene and stood staring. No one else seemed to pay the dog any attention whatsoever. Theo was jolted by another earthshaking roll of thunder as the sky released the first wall of rain, so he ducked into a kedai with tables inside. He sat, back to the wall, under the welcome moving air from a squeaky fan. He looked up, smiling for a moment, noting that the fan at least didn't click. The Sultan's High Tea Shop was a welcome break from the street.

He lit up a smoke, ordered a pot of tea, a soft drink and a plate of satay and rice, and pulled out the guidebook. Theo could see the tropical rain pounding the footpath and roadway; and the gutters overflowed almost instantly. There was a rapid change in the overall smell in atmosphere as the rain cooled the hot concrete and tarmac. He stared aimlessly into the street which almost disappeared into a grey mass of water. Slowly it eased slightly and then settled in, with a consistent hammer that drowned out most of the sounds coming from the street.

He leant forward and scanned the guidebook. Plenty of sights were listed to visit in Kuala Lumpur and a large section of the book was devoted to food. Because of the three major ethnic groups, food seemed to be one of the main attractions for foreigners. It was clear the locals took their food very seriously. The population, although geographically in Malaysia, had sizable Chinese and Indian populations as well as Westerners, a mix of aborigine and others, all vying for an equal share of self-determination in a government dominated by Malaysians. Doctor Mahathir Mohamad was the Prime Minister and had been since 1982. Theo had seen his face displayed on posters everywhere around Kuala Lumpur, including the arrival section of the airport, maybe ironically, alongside the warning for drug trafficking. His face appeared on buses, also on buildings from the airport to the city.

Theo looked up quickly. Again he had a strong sensation of being watched. There were people everywhere, it could be anyone. He tried to relax; after all, there was no reason for anyone to follow him. Mahmoud obviously didn't like him but what gain would there be to follow him? Mahmoud would more than likely think he was looking for another place to stay. The rain poured down, turning the street into a river. The air smelt almost fragrant, probably from the green vegetation and flowering trees and plants, and although still humid, there was a feeling of cleanliness. Suddenly he felt lonely. He missed his mother. He wanted to talk to Biru. More thoughts drifted through his head. Vince, Jack, Mahmoud, Brian. And, like the shroud of dark sky, he wondered what the hell he was doing in this foreign place.

'Bugger it all,' he said and then realised he had said it aloud. A man looked up from shovelling noodles into his mouth but then looked back down at his newspaper.

The food arrived and he discovered he was hungry. Why not try out some of the so-called wonderful Malaysian tucker, he thought? The rain cascaded for another hour at least and then eased. He figured he could dodge from shop to shop, awning to awning all the way back to the hotel. Just as he was about to leave a young backpacker couple slung their bags on the floor at the next table. Both were soaking wet.

'Hello, I am Franka, dis is Eric,' said the young woman in what Theo thought was a very forward, but not offensive, way.

They were both about Theo's age. 'G'day, I'm Theo,' he replied.

They shook hands.

'Dis rain, we don't get rain so much heavy in Sveden. It iss not bad, nice and warm, yah?' she said, running her hand backwards over her head. Franka had a blond female version of an almost mullet cut similar to Theo's, with a plait. She squeezed the single golden plait that hung just over her brown shoulders.

'Food time and beer time,' Eric said, folding his six and a half foot plus frame into a wooden seat. It looked to Theo as if he had size sixteen shoes and they were made to look bigger because they were a walking shoe style with thick soles. He grabbed the menu, 'The day is past the yard mast or vot it is called.'

They ordered two beers and two bowls of noodle soup.

Theo couldn't help staring at Franka's long brown legs, wondering how come all the northern Europeans he'd seen had dark tans but hardly saw the sun for most of the year.

'You obviously from Australia, yah?' laughed Eric, in a deep voice.

For a second Theo thought Eric meant perving on his girlfriend's legs. Theo recovered and pointed at his chest. 'Do I have a sign on me? Everyone seems to be able to guess I am an Aussie.' All three laughed.

Eric smiled, prominent blue eyes, 'You Ozzies have a special way about you, like you say, *gah-die*, mean good-day. Nice way of course, no offence please.'

Theo batted the comment away with a wave and a smile, definitely not offended in the slightest. After three days on his own he was warming very quickly to these two backpackers. It was made easy for him because they filled the gap with friendly banter.

Franka added, 'We met two Australians in Singapore when we arrive from Jakarta and travelled around with dem. We get on like a fire in the house, then we join together with dem and travel up here to Kuala Lumpur on de train. They kept on train bound for Bangkok. We miss dem already, like Americans say, yah?'

The beer arrived. Theo lifted his tea cup. 'Cheers!'

They responded and drank a toast.

'Where are you staying?'

'We stay at the Hot Spot Hotel, very nice place, good staff and clean, not too many bed bugs, ha. You stay where?'

'The Hotel New Islamic. A bit worn, but it's a nice clean place. Cheap enough anyway.' Theo was about to add something about a beautiful-looking sort on the desk and a nasty, unpleasant mongrel who hung around and threatened him. He realised quickly that he didn't know these people and he was glad he said no more. 'I remember going into The Hot Spot when I arrived a few days ago but they were full.'

The Swedish couple tore apart some bread and attacked their noodle soup.

'We were on our way to look at bus services but the rain made us come in here, now we meet you.' Eric laughed. 'We are not exactly sure where we go next but hope to spend some time in Kuala Lumpur, waiting for money transferred from home. Also letters at poste restante. Dis bread it tastes like cake. How long are you here for?'

Theo wasn't sure if the meaning was Kuala Lumpur or overseas but he related a general outline of killing time in the city until his friend Jack arrived back in Penang. He didn't expand on Jack, the death of his father, having to go to a government department to collect paperwork, being followed or being keen on a woman in a relationship that wasn't and promised to go nowhere.

The air seemed to be less humid. Theo felt he should give the new friends some space and head off. He didn't want to be too forward and was wondering how to suggest meeting them again to do something together. He was beaten to it.

'Maybe we meet again for food or see some sights together?' suggested Franka. 'We want to visit Pudu Prison one day while we are here.'

Theo stood. 'Yeah, that would be great. Look, we all know where we are staying so let's get together; leave a message at the front desk? I'm still finding my way round.'

Eric said, 'We could get together tonight if it is meant to happen. We could meet on the corner of Restaurant Mall when de sun goes down or de rain stops, yah? If you are there and we are there, we can eat together. If not we meet tomorrow or next day, no problem, as everyone here says when there is a problem.' He laughed uproariously.

Theo shook hands and ambled outside. The rain had stopped.

The sun came out again but the rain had cleaned up the air as well as the road, footpath and gutters. He crossed the road and could see the imposing mass of Pudu Prison in the distance but he decided to head back to the Hotel New Islamic. He had made up his mind that he would not move to another place. Why should he? He hadn't done anything wrong … yet. The rain had made the dying part of the day more pleasant as the traffic tried to do the opposite. The complacent pleasantness changed in a click as a dog came at him from a dark side street and he managed to swing his day pack at it. 'Piss off, you bastard,' he hissed. The incident reminded him to be vigilant; rabies was still rife in certain areas according to his health card.

Theo window-shopped on the way back, which necessitated a certain amount of harassment from owners plugging to make a sale. He went inside two bookshops but most of the books of any interest in the fiction section were in Malaysian, German, French or a Nordic dialect as far as he could tell. The nonfiction appeared to be either in Malaysian or English but there was nothing in the English section that took his eye. He kicked himself for not buying a paperback at the airport.

The call to prayer had begun. He smiled to himself, thinking that if you were a Muslim, you could hardly pretend to forget to attend.

Chapter Twelve

As he neared the road where the steel barriers were up for the food mall he stopped, placed a cigarette in his mouth and was about to light it.

'Hey, Mr White Boss, Tuan, books here, plenty books but I have something special for you. You look? You have cigarette for old lady almost cripple from hard work?'

The old woman sat cross-legged on a grey blanket, partly in a doorway, and her books were spread out in a neat display on the footpath in front. Her feet protruded from the red dress and the soles of her feet were dirty in contrast to the clean clothes. Theo could see she was obviously not used to wearing shoes because the soles of her feet were black and appeared hard. The second toe on each foot had a silver ring which made her feet seem delicate and almost elegant to him. He stopped and glanced down, looking for the con.

'You have cigarette for me, ha-ha,' she laughed, almost a cackle. Her beaming smile displayed a blood-red betel-nut mouth and dark, almost black, pegs for teeth. 'One only cigarette for this old jungle woman, tua wanita? Yaaaah?' She laughed again and wrapped the tail of her loose, red scarf hijab style around her neck, hiding dark wrinkled skin. Her weathered hand had a dark intricate tattoo on the back and there were two silver rings on her fingers.

Theo squatted down. It would have been against his nature to light up and walk on even though the old woman was, in fact, almost begging. He guessed she was middle-age but it was difficult to determine exactly. There was a distinctive smell, an aroma, the body odour of a working woman, but it was not offensive. To Theo she had a motherly aura with the scent of cloves and possibly jasmine flowers.

He showed her the opened pack. She took two. His eyes widened in mock surprise. He a young man, she an older woman.

'Satu for now, dua for later, yaaaah?' She dropped the other one into an old wooden box with brass inlays.

He lit her cigarette and then his own. 'Terima kasih, thank you young white Tuan from Ostray-lee-ah.'

'How did you ..? Never mind.' He remembered the Canadian on the bus and Biru said the same thing, so did Eric. His nationality seemed evident to all.

'Aha, old woman from Borneo know plenty plenty plenty.' She waved her index finger like the inverted pendulum of a clock. 'Now young Tuan, I have book for you, special price. You have been looking for this.' She slowly picked up the book, dusted the cover with a rag, and held it out.

He faltered, not sure what sort of con this was, maybe it wasn't. He glanced at the cover. *Beyond Pardon*, written by Sean Morgan. He wondered how she could possibly have known. On the cover was a picture of Pudu Prison. It was a short distance down the road from where he was. He turned it over in his hands, couldn't believe it. Sean Morgan had given a series of lectures at the university on one of the modules related to the designation of foreign correspondent. Theo remembered well and had enjoyed the lectures more than any others because Sean, nicknamed Spud by everyone in the industry, had been very witty and entertaining in his account of unusual situations whilst being at the desk in far-off places. A quick glance at the content showed the book was about the hanging in 1987 of an Australian citizen Roland Hayley, convicted drug trafficker. Theo wasn't aware that Sean had actually written this book but, being a budding journalist, he was generally up with the things that saturated the newspapers. The hanging of Roland Hayley dominated the news in Australia. He realised the hanging was only a few months ago and the book had only just been published.

He flipped through. 'How much, Old Woman ...' and added some cheeky young man drama, '... from Borneo?'

'Aha,' she cackled, 'special evening price for you, one hundred ringgit.'

He showed mock surprise, thinking this was going to be a battle. 'Mahal, too dear, I cannot afford that. Forty ringgit?' *Remember what Dempster said, halve it and less.*

She touched her breast. 'Young Tuan, very expensive book. And last page still in residence, see?' She leant across and opened the back cover. He felt that motherly aura again. 'See, last page. Many people tear out last page for rip-off, ha-ha, but here genuine article. Okay, you rob old woman. Eighty, last price, evening price? Okay, here you take?' She went to wrap it up.

'No, too dear, too dear.' He knew he had to play hard to get. 'Why evening price, is evening price dearer than during the day?' He also wondered about the story of the last page rip-off. Who would bother to do that, more so why would a vendor do it because the purchaser would return and demand money back? Squatting on his haunches, cramp and ache now threatened his calves.

'Special evening price mean really special price for you. You want this book, written for you, old woman know these things, very wise with these matters. Eighty.'

'Eighty? What about forty-five.' Theo had to stand up, squatting was killing him. He struggled to his feet, wondering how these people could squat or sit cross-legged for so long.

She must have thought he was going. 'No, no, young white Tuan, robbing tua wanita, okay, okay shrewd businessman, so young, sixty, last and final price.'

'Sixty?' he said, eyes wide. 'How about fifty, fifty is fair, alright?'

'Fifty too low, old woman probably die in street tonight.'

He turned, pretending to go.

'Fifty-five best and only last price, my family will die in street with me, losing money, not even get my buying price back.'

Theo figured that was about the right price. 'Okay Old Woman from Borneo, done, fifty-five ringgits.' He pulled the money from his pocket and handed it to her.

'You drive very hard deal Tuan. I lose money, definitely starve to death.' She laughed, that half-laugh cackle and wrapped the prized book in newspaper.

'Thank you, old woman.' He turned to go.

'You have cigarette?' She said.

He was about to say, 'Well you took one for later,' but instead he pulled one out and handed it to her.

'Aha, terima kasih, thank you, generous young Tuan, shrewd businessman. You come and see me when you want more books, best price in town from wise old woman who know all about you but I lose money, family disown me, ha! You come again and learn to me shrewd business method so I can survive, yaaaah.' He started to walk away. 'Hey, Tuan, maybe you have trouble in your life, like monkey, but long time things be okay.'

He waved, *Sure,* and walked away. Any stargazer could say that. But what about monkey? In the fading light he stopped, unfolded the wrapping and turned the book over. On the back page, in the bottom corner he noted the recommended retail price, 45 ringgit. 'Bugger,' he mumbled, ripped off. He turned, she waved and laughed. He could just hear her and make out her red teeth. He smiled and waved again. He waved his index finger, hoping to convey, I'm on to it. *Starve to death, family disown you? Sure. Lesson to be learned, Theo.*

Chapter Thirteen

Theo thought he would go back to the hotel for a while, speak to Biru, and maybe link up with the young couple he escorted up the stairs or maybe read his new purchase. He made a mental note to jot down some of the things he had experienced, and people he met, in his exercise book he had labelled *Theo's Adventures*, on the front.

He had come to the conclusion to continue to stay at the Hotel New Islamic but he was mindful of the fact that Mahmoud, whose family owned the hotel, could easily evict him. The best decision at that moment was a non-decision, sit and wait, see what transpired. He'd probably be off to Penang fairly soon. Theo wondered how he was going to set about getting Biru to go out with him; it sounded silly. He'd been in Malaysia less than a week, and was now in the middle of a controversial situation between a so-called betrothed couple. Biru wasn't promised to anyone, he told himself. Mahmoud had no claim on her, she was fair game. Anyway, all he wanted to do was see her, take her out somewhere away from prying eyes. The idea gave him a lift. There was a dark undercurrent of thought, however, that she probably would not go out with him, for a whole range of reasons. The cultural differences were many, let alone how old she was. He thought she was about twenty; she looked somewhat younger at the first meeting but on closer inspection she looked older. It was hard for him to tell with only an oval of face to decide anything on. Maybe her step-parents wouldn't allow her to see him. He was very aware that he had no idea about any of it, only that he really wanted to see her, to be near her.

The dark trio were not out the front of the Hotel New Islamic. He opened the doors gently and no one was hovering inside. He climbed the stairs. Razak was behind the desk again, sorting through a heap of what looked like receipts. He decided not to ask about Biru, no need to broadcast his intentions. Theo engaged in small talk with Razak, who still called him Mr Perry, for a few minutes, purchased an orange soft drink from the fridge and headed to his room. He turned the fan on high, unlocked his pack and took out his bottle of vodka.

He ripped the paper wrapping off the recent purchase, sat back on the bed and turned a few pages. It was an account, with extensive background, of the last days on earth for Roland Michael Hayley, an Australian hanged in Pudu Prison.

Theo poured another vodka and orange, turned the fan down and lit a cigarette. Apart from a few key photos of Roland Hayley, Pudu Prison and the author, the book was divided approximately into quarters by half a dozen picture pages of photos, some colour as well as black and white. The quarters were divided into sections or chapters and contained comprehensive information, not only about Hayley and his story or interviews conducted by the author with Hayley and others, but background about the drug scene, the role of politics by key countries and a complete section on life inside Pudu Prison. The reference section of the book contained sources of information, acknowledgements, records of interviews, police reports, references, and links with other publications, institutions and people. Theo looked at the pamphlet Razak had given him the day before. There was a range of organised tours to suit most people or groups but it was also possible to wander and have a look on your own, too. He planned to talk the matter over with Eric and Franka.

Theo was reminded of the time when the call to prayer, from the local muezzins, drifted above the clicking fan and traffic noise. He figured it was time to go for a stroll, maybe catch up with Franka and Eric. He also wanted to speak with Biru.

Chapter Fourteen

Razak was still in residence at reception. 'Aha, Mr Perry, out for eating, see action video in stereo, a walk maybe?'

'How did you guess?'

They both laughed, enjoying the light banter.

'Are you always on duty?'

'Normally night times but sometimes then Mahmoud fill in.'

'Er … where is Biru?'

'Ah, Biru day-time shift mainly.'

'I mean where is she now?'

He looked away slightly. 'Ah, Biru, not well today, maybe come in later, maybe not.'

Theo handed over his key and headed for the stairs. *Buzz off out of my head, Mahmoud.* He really wanted to speak to Biru but he had no idea what he was going to say. He bounded down the steps, through the double doors at the bottom and into the street.

There he was. Two doors down, flanked by two shadows, this time all with American baseball caps on backwards. Mahmoud did nothing other than lift his index finger like a cricket umpire and stare for about ten seconds. Theo thought it strange but he turned in the opposite direction and continued on his way. As far as he was concerned, Mahmoud could take a jump. Theo did, however, feel the dark man's gaze boring into his back, so he turned. Yes, Mahmoud and friends stood at the corner staring in his direction. Theo kept walking and turned the first corner, relieved.

'No thank you,' he said to an old Chinese woman selling flowers. She didn't seem keen to take no for an answer, probably because he looked disorientated and tired. Eventually she gave up and switched her attention to a group of Muslim girls in scarves and hijab; modern misses who giggled and gaggled like teenagers everywhere. He couldn't ignore them though because they were all very beautiful even though most of their bodies were covered up with traditional dress.

Franka and Eric stood on the corner of the Restaurant Mall. Theo had temporarily forgotten about them, his head crammed with images of Biru and Mahmoud, and Spud Morgan. They were procrastinating over the city map. Six-foot-seven Eric towered over his partner; he had an athletic body, like a soccer player who did weights. A shoeshine boy, not the same one Theo had seen before, was harassing Eric. He had sandals on and it seemed as if the boy was keen to shine them. Eric's good nature sent the boy on his way, both smiling from the encounter.

Eric held up the map. 'Aha, Theo, we are wanting to go to the night markets for food and a look around and I want to get some underwear trunks also.' He held up a pair of jocks, oblivious to passers-by.

Theo's mood changed instantly; he burst out laughing with Franka who said, 'Eric, Theo does not need to know about your underwear, yah?'

Theo felt relaxed, thinking he had known these new friends forever. 'Don't mind me; anyway I'd like to have a look at the night market too. Razak … er at my hotel said the best market is along there in Chinatown, Jalan Petalin, easy distance.' Theo pointed at the map and then in the general direction.

'Sure, we walk together, no need for taxi?' said Franka.

In a short time they arrived in the Chinatown area. The street was closed off and restaurants lined the sides of the road, just like the Restaurant Mall, but there were street-food stalls selling a variety of Asian food, but mostly Oriental. Brightly painted banners with Chinese writing were strung between buildings and even, though it was night-time, Theo was amazed at the colours highlighted from street-lights helped on by other lights from private places. All down the city block the crowds and noise contributed to an almost festival atmosphere. Most stall holders cooked food on site to eat in or takeaway. Wherever there was even the smallest of spaces, other vendors set up racks and stalls, selling clothing for locals and tourist alike. Some had kitchenware, homewares for locals, produce such as noodles, tins, dried mushrooms, garlic, salted fish, squid, prawns as well as fresh fruit and vegetables. Stalls plied their trade to the restaurants as well as tourists and locals; everything was for sale it seemed to Theo. A couple of stalls had ducks and chickens crammed into cages as well as chopping blocks and meat hanging up in the heat.

Franka shook her head. 'I do not like this thing with birds caged like dat. Dey are frightened. We move on, please? Yah?'

Theo felt uncomfortable, too.

Eric started, 'But, Franka, you eat ...' He left it at that as they moved on.

All kinds of food was prepared and cooked on site. Meat and seafood, satay, chicken pieces flattened in a simple bamboo thatch over charcoal, the smell of garlic, chilli, coriander, served on paper plates or banana leaves with a wide selection of sauces, peanut, chilli, fish and many others. Most of the stalls or carts had low tables, with jars of chopsticks and tiny wooden seats for patrons.

'Come on, Theo.' Franka waved. He had lagged back, almost totally mesmerised by the noise and range of things going on.

'Sorry, I'm amazed at all this, this ...'

They moved on as stallholders and restaurant touts competed for business, yelling in many languages, trying to attract every passer-by to eat their food. This noise was punctuated by the jangling of bells from a couple of streets away and the occasional *whoosh* of gas from a wok burner or chopped vegetables hitting boiling hot oil. Within the first five minutes of trying to wander, but more correctly dodging others, down the street, Theo and Eric were asked if they wanted drugs. Also women.

Franka said loudly, 'Why are they not asking me if I want a man, yes?' The other two laughed. Her eyes narrowed. 'Do not laugh too loud, I get the impression I am being followed.'

Theo quickly glanced around.

Eric said to Franka, 'The only people who would follow you would be drug dealers, ha.'

He nudged Theo, 'Franka, she likes the smoke, you know, and marijuana.' He made a roach smoking action, pinching his thumb and forefinger together.

Theo thought maybe he could score some puff too, but instead focused on her comment about being followed. He tried not to be obvious as he now turned and whirled a three-sixty, taking in the street scene. People everywhere, all shapes, sizes, colours, races, religions. Men and women in traditional Muslim, Oriental and Indian outfits, people in western dress, travellers, yuppies from the big hotels holding hands pretending to slum it and backpackers like him ... everywhere. Some were looking his way or past him, some may have glanced away as he looked. Some were just getting on with living. How could anyone tell in this crowd?

The enticing food aromas made it hard for anyone not to feel hungry and it was clear the three travellers were ready. They decided on an eating house rather than squatting on the road at a low table. Most of the places were not pretentious but there were a few up-market restaurants further up the road or upstairs for the more affluent. Theo managed to grab a normal-sized table with normal seats, just inside under a fan with a good view of the hustle and bustle in the street.

Theo could see that eating was a very serious business in Kuala Lumpur. The Oriental waiter recommended the Steam Boat, and whilst waiting they had a beer.

Franka said, 'We will go to the poste restante tomorrow to check on news from Stockholm, also go to bank to see if our money has arrived. We spend more than we planned but as we are here we decide to make our way to Bangkok before flying home.'

A large round container of hot soup, called Steam Boat, arrived. Theo was educated as to how to make the most of it by the two Swedes who had experienced it before. He figured the round funnel up the middle could have been imagined as the stack on an ocean liner. Underneath the stainless steel bowl a small flame ticked away, keeping it all hot. Plates of sliced mushrooms, finely chopped ginger, garlic and lemongrass, prawns, cubes of fish and pork arrived with what looked like half cooked noodles. Eric explained the general idea, and it was easy to place whatever you fancied in a small wire basket and immerse it in the soup. Everything was cut so finely and arranged to cook in seconds and Theo enjoyed the meal immensely. His mother sometimes cooked a curry when there were leftovers but the only real taste of Asia he had experienced was the same as many other Australians, Chinese or Indian takeaway.

The three drank several more beers further into the night, noting that trade increased as the night wore on and the music and chatter became louder. Eric wandered off to purchase his underwear trunks leaving Franka and Theo to solve all the world's problems.

Eric returned, seemingly deliriously happy with two pairs of underpants. They had another beer, paid the bill and ambled in the direction of their meeting place, enjoying the balmy, if not humid, evening in the city. Theo bought half a dozen postcards with the idea of at least writing to his mother. They pledged to meet again the next morning.

Theo strolled in the direction of the Hotel New Islamic. He pushed the thought of being watched or followed to the back of his mind. It occurred to him that maybe it was just in his imagination. Theo was jolted out of his comfort zone when he reached the top of the stairs.

Chapter Fifteen

Biru looked up but held her head slightly turned. He couldn't see all of her face. 'What's wrong?' he said.

She avoided his eyes. 'Nothing is wrong.'

He stepped slightly to one side of the desk. 'What's wrong with your face?' He was close to her, he could feel her breathing.

She turned and looked at him but covered her right cheek with a shaking hand. 'Accident, no problem. Your key.' She handed him the key.

'Mahmoud. He hit you, didn't he?'

She averted her eyes, embarrassed. 'Theo, you must move out tomorrow, not safe for you here anymore.'

He stepped forward, reached across and touched her face near the bruise. She lifted her gaze. Her skin was soft. She closed her eyes and put her hand over his.

'Yes, I will move out in the morning but ...' Theo tried to keep his voice even.

'No buts, Mahmoud is very angry man.'

'Can I see you ... er can we go out somewhere ... soon? I like you ...' He knew it sounded silly.

'No, please, I don't know ...' She leaned forward and brushed his lips with a honey kiss. So quick, he hardly knew it had happened. Then she stepped back, eyes wide, when she realised what she had done but she still continued to hold his hand like a feather.

There was a noise. She dropped his hand and he withdrew it at the same second when someone appeared at the top of the stairs.

Her eyes opened wide and then relaxed. It was one of the Germans he had seen earlier.

Theo looked at Biru and tried a smile but it didn't come across. He nodded a greeting to the other person and went to his room, the only thing he could do. He turned on the fan and airconditioner and sat on the bed. Theo knew Mahmoud was jealous, that was certain. How far would this jealousy push him? Next step was what to do next. Theo scrolled through a whole list of thoughts and scenarios. No doubt he would have to move out first thing in the morning, no point in putting Biru in any further danger, but he still wanted to keep up some contact with her. There were some women Theo had not treated very well in his life but it was probably through lack of worldliness or experience more than anything else. Sure he had had sex with some women and unceremoniously dumped one or two but he would never raise a hand to a woman. He sat contemplating the best course of action. Maybe he should simply drop the whole thing, forget Biru. But how could he do that? He had wanted to put his arms around her and tell her everything would be alright. He knew enough about females to know she wanted that too. It occurred to him that she took a big risk touching his hand. Then there was the kiss, he had not imagined it.

Still unsure of almost everything at that moment he instinctively stood up, took a deep breath and quietly went out the door. He figured he had to see her again, talk to her; he couldn't leave things like this, floating in space. Theo needed a direction. He could hear voices, a male and female. He slowly poked his head around the corner. It was Razak and one of the female backpackers, a New Zealander. He heard the word train. She must have been checking out to catch the late train to Singapore. They didn't see him and he returned to his room. He fiddled with the zip and padlock on his pack, thinking it was strange it was unlocked. He was sure he had locked it before going out.

He turned off the airconditioner and opened the window to let in some night-time air. Passive, almost friendly, noises drifted in from the city. There was still the faint hum of traffic he guessed to be from Jalan Pudu. Sleep came and went. Theo could not find any sensible solutions to any of the problems circulating in his head. Sometime early, just as the muezzin began calling the faithful to prayer, there was a hard knock on the door.

'Open up, this is the police!'

Deprivation Of Liberty

Chapter Sixteen

Police? Theo had fallen asleep at an awkward angle and his neck was twisted. He stumbled to the door, putting his shorts on awkwardly. He turned the key and opened the door to the length of the safety chain. 'What ..?'

'Open the door, please, poste haste, or we will be breaking it down and you will pay for it.' The voice of authority came from one of three uniformed officers Theo could make out in the grey morning light.

He was astute enough to realise there was no choice so he slipped the chain. Instantly the door exploded open and two junior officers, one Chinese looking and one Indian, burst in. He was pushed unceremoniously backwards and hit his head on the wall.

There was no time for protest but Theo spoke by instinct. 'What is going ..?'

A smartly uniformed senior officer, designated so by rank decorations on his epaulets and upper sleeves, flicked the overhead light on and pointed a cane at him. 'Silence, please, if you know what is good for you.'

The two other officers stood over Theo who rubbed the back of his head; there was no point in resisting. The click of the fan was now prominent. Through the open window the muezzin continued the campaign for all faithful Muslims.

The senior officer, Indian in looks, high forehead, neat moustache trimmed precisely in line with the edges of his mouth, slapped the cane against his khaki shorts. 'My name is Inspector Sethna. We have reason

to believe you are having drugs in your possession. Passport, please.'
Polite but firm.

Theo moved his hand towards the bedside table where his wallet and
passport were. The Chinese policeman tensed with his movement but
relaxed when Theo picked up the passport.

'Give!' He snatched it out of Theo's hand and gave it to the inspector.

The inspector opened the passport, made some up and down
eyebrow movements and then held the document against his chest.
He nodded in the direction of the two other officers. One went to the
dressing table, the other to his pack sitting on the only chair in the room.
Sweat from nowhere spiked Theo's forehead and trickled down his back.

He had not unpacked his clothing into any of the drawers and all
of his possessions were there to see. Some tourist brochures, postcards,
maps, the guidebook, and the recent purchase, *Beyond Pardon* sat on
the dressing table. The Chinese officer quickly checked the drawers
and flicked through the things lying on top. He turned and gave the
inspector the slightest headshake.

The inspector pointed his cane, 'Would you please be putting a shirt
on?' His rimless glasses caught a flash from the light above. He stood at
ease. Theo noticed he had a pen sticking out of the top of his long socks.

In the meantime the Indian officer tipped the contents of his
backpack onto the bed. He ran his hand expertly around the inside of the
empty pack. A smile creased his face as he lifted up a small plastic bag.

Theo's eyes widened, his eyebrows shot up. 'What the he..?' He was
about to say hell but was together enough to not swear, even though
hell was hardly that. Swearing would only make matters worse. 'What
is this all about ... that is not mine, I don't know how it got there, I
certainly didn't ...'

The plastic bag looked to Theo to contain about a golf-ball size
amount of green stuff, probably marijuana.

The inspector interrupted. 'You have been very foolish, Mr ... er,'
he glanced at the passport, '... Perry. You will be coming with us.'

The Indian officer placed the so-called evidence in a large envelope
and stood to attention. Theo's other relevant items, watch and wallet
were slipped into a plastic bag and press-sealed. The Chinese officer
unhooked a pair of handcuffs from his wide brown belt, which sported
a hand gun with the flap secured, and moved towards Theo. He made a

turn-around gesture. Theo rubbed the back of his head before turning around. There was no doubt in his mind that resisting would only make matters worse. A dog fight started out in the street.

'You are making a mistake, sir,' said Theo to the wall. His shirt stuck to his back and his armpits reeked. His throat was sandpaper dry. He hoped the quiver in his voice was not too obvious.

Inspector Sethna picked up *Beyond Pardon*. He looked over his glasses and said in an almost interested voice. 'You are maybe having a curiosity in the drug culture ... and prisons, Mr Perry?'

Theo shrugged as he turned around. What could he say, even if he had thought of something? When you are being framed for a drug crime, does possession of a book about the topic qualify you as being guilty?

The Chinese officer grabbed Theo by the collar of his shirt and firmly steered him into the corridor behind the other junior officer. Inspector Sethna brought up the rear, turned off the light and closed the door, a neat almost considerate gesture.

At reception Biru was nowhere to be seen. Razak stood, hands flat on the counter, eyes wide, slowly shaking his head almost involuntarily. It could have been in sympathy or total shock. Or pretending. Theo had to watch his bumbling feet as he was gently but firmly shoved every few steps. Theo glanced at Razak again and all he could register in his head was, *Surely not you?* They muscled him onwards.

Razak fired a trapped rabbit look at the police and then tried to focus on Theo. 'Mr Perry, what ..?'

No one answered him. Theo tried to shake his head and shrug as he was jerked forward towards the stairs. *Theo, think man, think.* The group went down the stairs into the street. A police Land Rover Troop-Carrier awaited them, doors open with a halo of diesel fumes filling the surrounding morning air. The driver, garbed up in the same khaki uniform, sported a khaki turban. He stood at-ease by the driver's door. Theo could hear the clatter of the injectors. Only a handful of vendors and a group of backpackers were out at that hour. Two mangy street pi-dogs looked at him in a pitiful way as if they knew his fate. It was only just light. The muezzin stopped as he was pushed into the canopied rear section and accompanied either side by the two junior officers. Theo thought he saw somebody sleeking into a shopfront, too quick to tell who it was.

Inspector Sethna rattled on to the driver alongside him, in what

Theo thought was Malay or a dialect, in a fast exchange. They weaved through the early morning traffic; the turbaned driver was expert at dodging things, twice a troop of monkeys and many times dogs. He swerved recklessly, almost as if he wanted to make the trip as uncomfortable as possible for everyone, but the other officers seemed not to notice. His jerky jabs at the brake pedal threw everyone forward and back when least expected. Theo barely noticed the traffic which was fairly heavy, even at that hour of the day.

They hurtled along Jalan Hang Tuah and swung into the driveway nearly hitting the sign, *Police Headquarters – Polizei – RMP – Royal Malaysia Police – Headquarters*. A security officer signed them in and lifted the boom gate. The Land Rover jerked to a stop under a group of tall palm trees, near the sign *Prisoner Registration Section – All incoming chargees and offenders must be processed at this point.*

The sweat covering Theo's body seemed to boil yet he felt a chill up his spine. *Prisoners? Him? Yep Theo, you.*

Chapter Seventeen

He was shepherded up the dusty stone steps, with squirts of bright red betel juice decorating the corners, and into a large room filled with police, some uniformed, some not, and prisoners. The police were identified either by uniform or weapon; a few had a side-arm on their belt, and a couple had shoulder holsters. The uniforms varied with obvious ethnic distinctions and the occasional turban. Most were male but a few female officers dotted the processing area, most in hijab or the lesser defining simple headscarf. One officer was dressed in the full, flowing, white cotton long-shirt and a Muslim prayer cap. The man had a belt with a gun, a plastic ID card pinned to his chest and black military style boots. Theo thought it might raise a few eyebrows out there in the street. Prisoners were obvious by the jangling handcuffs or their depressed or frightened demeanour. Ceiling fans in the large chamber stirred the air way up high in the already thickening morning humid heat. The domed building and anterooms were built many years ago in the glory days of colonisation and the walls appeared to not have been painted or lime-washed since then. The fans did nothing to cool Theo and the perspiration of fear soaked his clothing. He tried to remain calm and rational.

He was led, more gently now, to one of the desks marked Registration. An attractive uniformed female officer in hijab barked something in Malaysian at him. When he didn't respond she snapped, 'Name?'

He gave the details requested and the Chinese officer, who seemed to have been deputised by the inspector to take care of the processing, handed over what appeared to be Theo's passport to the woman. She recorded some details considered relevant.

Theo was inwardly shaking. Nothing like this had ever happened to him before. 'Excuse me, but ... what am I being charged for ... er ... with?' He was almost mesmerised by the dark kohl around her eyes. The lump on the back of his head throbbed and he wanted to rub it.

She smiled, an almost cynical action, in keeping with her deadpan accusing glare. She fired some rapid Malaysian as she glanced in turn at the two officers. They laughed, not heartily but almost in a mocking tone. The Indian junior officer seemed to have materialised alongside Theo.

Theo was spun and frogmarched towards another desk with a partition around it marked Fingerprinting.

He was un-cuffed.

'Hand,' snapped an almost European looking, but very dark skinned, policeman who officiously and efficiently took Theo's fingerprints. 'Wash and wipe, there.'

Hands cuffed again behind, Theo was nudged to a door marked, *No unauthorised persons beyond this point.* His sweaty feet slipped and squelched in his thongs. A tall, swarthy bouncer in uniform, pock-marked face, unfolded weightlifter's arms and opened the door to allow them through. Theo's shirt was glued to his back.

Chapter Eighteen

The long hard concrete two-metre-wide corridor unfolded in front of them for twenty metres or more and doorways fed off every three metres or so. Some of these steel doors, identified with an interview room number, were open, some closed. An open steel grill about two hundred millimetres square was positioned at eye height in every door. The walls were painted a cream colour but were in desperate need of patching and repainting. Scratches, gouges and discolouration marks peppered the length of the corridor as far as Theo could see. Signs, mostly in Malay, decorated the wall at various places. His vision was impaired slightly because sweat kept making its way into his eyes. He felt a knot of confusion in his head and wondered how in the hell anyone could work in this oppressive heat. And the smell! A stench of almost overpowering proportions, maybe human faeces, as well as urine and sweat, hung in the air like stifling, sewage humidity. As he was nudged down the corridor, Theo couldn't help wondering if accused prisoners were bashed until they threw up, or shit and pissed themselves. Maybe the smell was so unidentifiable to him because it was simply despair. He wasn't used to that! Would he be belted to confess? Confess what, he hadn't done anything! He felt, or hoped, he would be able to explain his situation. From what Dempster had said, in Asia whether you did something or not didn't matter, if the cops wanted to put you in the frame, well … This recollection made him sweat more.

As the police officers' boots clicked methodically on the concrete floor and Theo's thongs squelched, the image of Mahmoud swam before his eyes. *Bastard, it could only be him. What about Razak? No not him, surely. Where did Biru fit into this?* He didn't have time to answer these questions. He was frogmarched into Interview Room 46.

'Sit,' commanded the Chinese officer, pointing to a steel chair bolted to the floor. He unlocked Theo's handcuffs and re-attached one to a ring on the edge of the steel table in front, leaving one hand free. Was Theo supposed to feel grateful? The Indian junior officer turned on the fan and stood at ease at the door, hands behind his back, staring at Theo with no expression. Long rays of sun streaked through the shuttered window high up. The fan squeaked, Theo looked up and under different circumstances at a different time, might have laughed. The fans of Malaysia, he could write a story about that, too.

After about ten minutes, both officers left the room, door ajar. Theo was able to pull a crumpled tissue out of his pocket and wipe his eyes. At least they didn't sting now. It was difficult to focus on any particular thought about the situation he was in. It all seemed so unreal. *Surely this is a bloody dream? Wake up Theo? It didn't work – it was no dream.* His head hurt where the lump was.

Every few minutes someone or a group of persons would clip-clop or squelch down the corridor, murmuring or talking loudly. Theo could at least tell the language was mainly Malaysian.

Every now and then he heard a kind of metal tinkle noise and after some mental challenging finally realised with a start that it was the sound of handcuffs, either fitted to a prisoner or swinging on the belt of an officer.

Doors would be opened or closed … or slammed. Intermittently a thump or a sharp noise, or yell, could be heard. A scream from way down the corridor punctuated the tense environment intermittently.

Theo's head was full of questions but no answers. *You gutless bastard, Mahmoud. What about Biru?* 'No,' he said aloud. He dropped the accusation against her straight away, chastising himself for even thinking it. Her beautiful face, framed in the almost nun-style hijab. Theo shook his head; he had to focus on now, right now. He had to find out what the deal was. He was certain this would not be a problem in Australia; the police would surely let him go after checking fingerprints, or the absence of his. Also, he would have access to a lawyer.

'Yes,' Theo said to the wall, 'Yes, that's it. I'll ask them to fingerprint the plastic bag, and then they'll have to let me go.' He tried to encourage himself to feel better about his dilemma. It didn't work.

He glanced around the grubby room which needed painting like everything else he had seen so far at Police Headquarters. There were dents and gouges in the plaster and stains of all colours dark, as well as a few red blotches and streaks of red down the corners. His eyebrows shot up, wondering if the red could be blood. His heart rate levelled out again as he realised that blood turns maroon and then black so he concluded it had to be betel juice. Theo wondered about the damage to the walls, too. A scream and then a thump echoed from somewhere down the corridor, again. Theo's heart rate bounced; he looked down at his chest thinking he would see the left-hand side billowing in and out. He was temporarily relieved to see it wasn't that dramatic but he could feel the lump on the back of his head pulsating.

He was jolted from his thoughts by a dog barking somewhere outside. The persistent intermittent click of heels on the concrete down the passage continued. He wanted to use the toilet. His head and body ached. *Maybe they have forgotten about me?* He rolled his shoulders to get the blood moving again and as he was rotating his neck, Inspector Sethna strolled in. His manner was as casual as if he was coming in for dinner. The Chinese officer's entrance was a contrast as he marched in and closed the door in military fashion. The fan continued to squeak.

The inspector placed his cane methodically on the table. 'M-i-s-t-e-r Perry.' He stretched out the sound of mister. 'You have been very foolish.'

Theo steeled himself. 'Exactly what am I being charged with?'

'You have been caught with 22.4 grams of marijuana in your possession. There are serious penalties for crimes involving drugs in Malay-shee-ah.'

'The marijuana is not mine, how could it be, I've only been here a few days?' He added, 'Sir.'

The inspector smiled. 'It is totally irrelevant how long you have been here, Mr Perry. Where did you get it from?'

Theo's anger level increased and his body tensed. 'The marijuana is not mine, alright? Anyone could have placed it there. I demand, er ask you to check it for fingerprints. It – is - not – mine. Look, I need to see a lawyer!' The word lawyer was said firmly.

'Aha, a lawyer?' The inspector glanced at the other officer and a smirk crossed his lips. M-i-s-t-e-r Perry, Mr Perry, this is not a television show, we are not in America. I and only I will be deciding if you can have a lawyer. And, Mr Perry, I simply say you cannot. Is that understood?' He tilted his head. 'And fingerprints, well we are not performing that function on a crime such as this. Is that clear?'

Theo looked at him. 'What am I expected to do? What do you mean, *a crime such as this*,' he asked. Sweat prickled his forehead, threatening to drip in his eyes again.

No response. The inspector removed a packet of cigarettes from his pocket, carefully selected one and lit it with a green plastic lighter. He blew smoke up into the fan. The dog out in the compound barked again.

'Sir, the marijuana is not mine, surely anyone could have put it in my rucksack, I mean it is circumstantial evidence ...' He knew he was rambling.

Inspector Sethna rose, slipped the cane under his arm and said. 'Take him away.' He spun around and strolled out as if he didn't have a care in the world.

'I have to see a lawyer, the marijuana was planted in my bag ... please you must underst...' Theo's plea followed the disappearing inspector, out of the depressing confines of the dirty room.

The Chinese officer un-cuffed him from the table and told him to stand and turn around. Theo looked up at the barred window high up where dust played around in the rays of sun. What was he looking up there for? Maybe hoping the dog would bark, his mate, out there, free. His hands were re-cuffed behind and once again he was steered by a strong hand gripping his bunched, wet shirt at the shoulder. They left the squeaking fan to torment the dirty walls of Interview Room 46, and out the door. The Indian junior officer joined them and they marched further down the corridor.

'Excuse me, er I need a leak ... I need a toilet,' said Theo to both.

The Chinese officer stopped. 'Okay, okay.' He sighed and they stopped at a grubby door marked Tandas. 'One minute,' and he unlocked the cuffs. 'Okay?' he said.

'Yeah, no worries.' Theo was grateful for the break and of course the opportunity to void his bladder which was difficult at first because he had trouble relaxing. He glanced at the small barred window up high and thought of all those impossible escapes from custody he had seen in movies over the years. No chance here and no way he would try. Theo hoped he didn't have to try one day if he was locked up for ages. He repeated over and over to himself, he was not guilty.

He probably didn't need to, and he didn't know why he did, but he said, 'Thanks, fellers.' They looked at him deadpan.

Theo had known of a couple of players in his team who suffered from anxiety before a big game. He had played in two Australian Rules grand finals and before the first bounce had felt a jittering excitement. The big day, can we win, what about me, *am I good enough?* Their team did win one of those grand finals, year before last. He still recalled the feeling just before the bounce but it was no major hurdle for him because as soon as his opponent elbowed him hard in the shoulder, anxiety, apprehension and nervousness were forgotten because the game was underway and there was no time to dwell. This was no game at the moment and he had a bad case of anxiety. He knew he had to overcome the feeling, but how? Thinking of Biru didn't help and what would his mother think? His thoughts darkened further, realising that no-one even knew he was there. The reality of his predicament almost unhinged him at that second but he realised he had to fight against this injustice. It was all very well to tell himself to stay calm but he could not stop the sweating and shaking inside. His heart beat two to one. *Come on Theo, you can do this, you have to do this.* He kept scrolling Mahmoud's name.

They reached a door marked, *Holding Cells*, with probably the equivalent in Malaysian, guarded by another bouncer in uniform. The Malay, shorter than the other doorman, had long sleeves that seemed as if they would rip any moment. He had a crooked nose that obviously had been broken at some stage but not set properly, if at all. He nodded, what seemed to Theo, almost politely like a hotel doorman as he opened the steel door with a key from the desk. The clank behind Theo's entourage made him almost leap. The Chinese officer gripped him harder, almost ripping his shirt.

They went down some stairs and the air became cooler but more humid, if that was possible. The smell he had nearly come to terms with upstairs permeated his whole being again. The officers clip-clopped, Theo squelched, down stone flagstones worn smooth by lawbreakers and law enforcers since the colonialist masters ruled the peninsula with a grip of iron for one and a half centuries or more. They arrived at a small alcove where a huge overweight Malay, in a dirty khaki uniform, sat and grinned up at Theo through red betel-nut stumps that had once been teeth. When he stood Theo noticed he was armed and even though he was fat, not much under twenty stone, he was clearly powerful enough to deter anyone from trying anything physical. Two other similarly dressed prison guards, both sporting holstered pistols, leaned against the hewn stone corbelling, either side of a pair of open steel entrance doors.

'Aha, whitey boy, everyone love whitey-boy ass in here, yah?' he said and spat a gush of betel juice into the corner. They all laughed except Theo.

Chapter Nineteen

If Theo's fear could compound any further it seemed to and if he had been commanded to speak he would have been unable to. Fortunately the question didn't require an answer from the jailer. The two arresting officers un-cuffed him and in principle handed him over to what could have been termed the responsible care of the jailing section. They rattled off some speak in the direction of the jailer and then headed back upstairs. Another two slipshod jailers stepped forward and stood either side of Theo, close enough to intimidate with their body odour. He told himself to stand tall and tried his best to stop shaking. He forced himself to think of football games, kicking into the wind, ten goals down, raining, blowing, being injured, dead tired. *Big heart, Theo you have to have a big heart and you will get through this*. He realised, with sinking reality, there was no next week.

The jailer unhooked a bunch of keys off a board and nodded to the other two who stepped back. It was clear he was the boss and this new whitey boy was his. He picked up a truncheon from the desk and hooked it on to his belt. The truncheon was about a foot long, probably made of very hard wood with what looked like a bicycle tube stretched over its length. The man's uniformed shirt, minus several buttons down low, only just reached his belt which strained to hold his massive guts and love handles from spilling out. He came around the desk with the ease of a rover which surprised Theo; clearly a man to be taken seriously. He wasn't wearing socks and his scuffed black dress shoes appeared as if they had come from the rubbish dump. The heels were worn over on one side and there were no laces.

'Dat way, whitey boy, you no longer boss-man Tuan in colony no more. Ha-ha!'

Theo felt spit and the heat of rotten breath on the back of his head and then he was shoved towards a fork in the passages. Cells 1 – 20 with an arrow left. He was pushed in the other direction, Cells 21 – 40 – short term. Theo's heart leapt when he noted short term; it gave him a splinter of hope.

'Dat way, whitey boy!' One prison guard, strap unbuttoned on his holster, turned and disappeared, the other followed at a distance, hand on the butt of his weapon. The prison guard was far enough back for Theo to feel as if he was the sole property of the big, fat jailer.

The noise increased as they walked through an archway where cells lined each side. The jailer must have unhooked his truncheon because Theo felt it in the middle of his back. Theo was shoved, this time savagely, ahead of the smelly fat man, past crowded cells. Some prisoners yelled out, some laughed, most looked; some were too frightened or bombed to care. The plight of human wretchedness around him exuded a stench beyond pity. Poor souls unlucky enough to get caught up in the legal system. He shook his head, realising with a jolt that also referred to him. *Theo, something will turn up, you'll see.* They reached the end of the run, Cell number 30, the only cell facing back up the corridor.

The jailer pushed Theo to one side. 'Back now … sekarang!' he yelled and bashed a slow inmate's hands that gripped the bars near the entrance. The other prisoners near the front of the cell jumped back, no-one wishing to annoy the head man. The big man hooked the truncheon back on his belt and grabbed the key ring. The other prison guard stepped within Theo's vision and his hand tightened on the butt of his pistol. Big Jailer fiddled the key in the lock with one hand. He reached out and grabbed Theo by the shirt with a gorilla paw and opened the door with the other. The big steel-barred door creaked on its hinges. Theo didn't know why his focus was glued to the steel door but he thought, 'I bet that door has a memory of much misery.'

The jailer looked harshly at him. 'What you say, whitey boy. You be smart arse to me, big boss man, eh?'

Theo realised he had spoken the words out loud. 'Nothing, no nothing I didn't ...'

'Shut up your face, asshole,' and he pushed Theo into the pillar before shoving him into the cell.

Theo was shoved with incredible force but he was just able to stop his head hitting the steel post. However, he was off balance enough to slip and sprawl on the floor, landing almost at the toilet bucket. The barred door slammed shut. Only heavy duty steel could sound so final. The big jailer stood and stared, and then burst into uproarious, almost uncontrollable, laughter, his whole body shook like junket, his big fat stomach wobbled. Strangely he stopped laughing as quickly as he had started.

'You get plenty bottom play-with for your stay in dis place, whitey boy. Ha!'

Come on Theo, get on top of this. He had difficulty rising off the slippery floor. Theo landed front first and his shirt was soaked and sticky. He looked at the muck on his hands which was clearly excrement. *Don't chuck, don't chuck, breathe through your mouth.*

'Bloody hell,' he said loudly and firmly, maybe trying to sound like he was in control. He didn't know why he said it. About twenty pairs of eyes focussed in on him. He hoped they didn't see the quake in his hands. *Be strong, Theo.* He struggled to his feet, looked around the cell and his glance ended up in the original position - at the Jailer Man who continued to stare at his new piece of entertainment property for another minute or so. Whump, whump, whump! His heart rate was fast but constant at least. Theo was smart enough to not stare at the Jailer Man.

It appeared as if the Jailer Man lost interest because he turned and slowly waddled off, squirting a red betel-nut jet of goo at someone in the next cell. He ran the truncheon along the bars, creating a dull, muffled reverberation. At the other end he stopped and smashed the fingers of some poor unfortunate who must have been gripping the bars, with his lethal weapon. A man screeched in pain and someone else yelled abuse, or so it seemed to Theo.

The Jailer Man bellowed something, laughed maniacally and continued walking back to his alcove. Theo couldn't get the thought out of his mind; a gross, low-caste Neanderthal crawling back into a wretched cave.

He glanced around again, trying to get some feeling for the place, the lay of the concrete cell. Approximately twenty prisoners were jammed into about five or six metres square. Some of the prisoners went back to their muffled conversations, some averted their eyes and some continued to stare. The ones that stared seemed to be challenging him. The stink in the cell was terrible and it was stiflingly hot and humid. Flies buzzed in all directions.

He shrugged and put his hands out in a helpless gesture, thinking he may get some level of camaraderie. 'Hey, look at my shirt.' It was like talking to a vacuum.

No-one answered but a couple of men laughed nervously. Theo backed towards the tap with the intention of washing his shirt. When he turned, he was horrified by the disgusting condition of the metal tub which was supposed to be a hand basin. It appeared as if someone had vomited and not bothered to wash it away. Also he didn't need to stretch his imagination to suspect men had used it to piss in.

'Fuck,' he said loud enough, another attempt at trying to sound tough. He turned and looked around again. No one had moved towards him, no challenges so far. Sweat trickled from his scalp to the base of his mullet-cut, down his back, and down his legs. The spot where he had hit the wall earlier in the morning throbbed.

He ran the water, which disturbed the cockroaches, and used his hand to clean the basin, almost chucking at the stench that emanated from the drain. The toilet bucket, not a flush job, was alongside and stank of faeces laden with the concentrated ammonia reek of urine. Flies buzzed around his head as he washed his hands as best he could. Then he gently peeled off his stinking shirt. Theo took a deep breath, sucked his stomach in and made sure he flexed his back muscles, trying to puff himself up to maybe warn the others off. After washing his arms he used the shirt to flannel his legs, then dropped it in the basin and filled it with water. He looked out the corner of his eye and turned casually a couple of times during the process, but most of the others had returned to their original positions. The shaking had eased and his heart rate had slowed. He was more in control, convincing himself that no one had any reason to challenge him - at least at the moment. He noticed about half of the prisoners were dressed better than him. He wasn't sure what that meant but he concluded that he was safe for the moment anyway. The police had relieved him of his wallet, passport, watch and anything else he had to identify himself with. He had dirty thongs, filthy shorts and was in the act of washing a shirt that would go straight into the bin when he was released. *When? If?* Two of the inmates, Oriental-looking men, were dressed in formal business clothes, minus tie and suit coat. The others appeared to be a mix of Oriental, Indian and Malay and were dressed from poverty to casual. One man had a long white shirt and Muslim prayer cap. He sat on his own in a corner. What if someone wanted his arse? Theo was the only European. A certain amount of confidence returned when he realised he was probably the biggest person there. Well, maybe not the biggest but the tallest. He hoped he was the fittest and strongest, too. A couple of Oriental-looking men on the opposite wall looked fatter, anyway why would anyone have a go at him? The fact he was in the holding cells gave him some level of hope. A pub fight came to mind; at the Hampstead Hotel where he had no choice but to knuckle a bloke who had been niggling him all night. The bloke signalled his intention, bad mistake; Theo got the first one in, hard and fast. The bloke didn't get up until helped by his mates. *Keep that in mind, Theo.*

Theo squeezed out his shirt and, realising there was nowhere to hang it, put it on. The dampness had a kind of soothing quality about it and he knew it would be just as damp in a few hours anyway. He stood for a while, peering down the row of cells, and then sat down on a wooden bench seat as far from company as possible. What was he going to do? Surely they couldn't keep him there for ever. How could he plead his case? They must allow him to see a lawyer. What time was it? He calculated it should be early afternoon; there were no windows to define time. The caged bulbs threw a sickly yellow light over everything. Permanent purgatory. Mozzies and flies in shifts.

Someone sounded as if they were being sick in the next cell. Someone else started singing to drown it out. Theo thought the morbid song was familiar. He recognised it as record a friend of his had, an old blues singer called Son House, and the words sounded like something to do with Jesus. The blues? In a Malaysian jail? Theo listened hard; the singer was far enough away for the words to be blurred enough for misinterpretation. Some poor soul was a musician and trying to trance himself from the misery of captivity. Down in the cells there was the occasional rich throat clearing and spitting. Someone with a bad case of consumption spat. Not long after, someone in his cell used the toilet which increased the smell. He hoped he didn't have to use it. How long was he going to be in here? How long could he hold off having to sit on the toilet? His stomach gurgled but mainly from lack of food and water. Lucky for him he was badly dehydrated, he couldn't possibly have a piss in front of twenty or more hard-core prisoners. Theo kept repeating to himself, 'holding cells, holding cells.' A couple of men looked at him but quickly looked away, probably thinking he was mad like most of the others.

He sat and tried to think about Biru and his mother. The humidity was keeping his clothes damp and mosquitoes whined around his face like Japanese Zeros. He watched a cockroach negotiate the graffiti on its climb up the wall. That drew his attention to the messages and things scratched or written on the wall. Much of the writing was in other languages and he tried to decipher the differences between what could have been Chinese, Indian, Sri Lankan or other characters.

Hours seemed to drift; he had no idea of the time. Action down the corridor made him look up; Jailer Man came towards his cell, heels leaning out, casually running his truncheon along the bars. He stood for a few seconds, spat betel juice towards the corner and pointed his weapon.

'Whitey boy, you wanted by smart asshole lawyer-man. Aha, you be back, don't worry. Come now!'

Lawyer? Theo stood up straight, buoyed by the news.

Chapter Twenty

The Jailer Man jangled the keys, found the correct one and opened the door, then yelled, 'Keep back, pigs. Whitey boy, you, here!' His blubber jellied from side to side.

Theo made his exit through the steel door slow and purposeful in an effort to show some level of dignity. That was clearly a mistake because the jailer grabbed him by the shirt with incredible speed and propelled him through, clanking the door shut behind. Theo was about to protest when he was poked viciously in the kidneys.

'Ha-ha, whitey boy. You think you smart ass. In here I complete boss, you do what you told to do, quick.'

He pushed Theo again towards the alcove where the Chinese officer was standing, yarning to another prison warder.

There was a transfer process, a signature or two and Theo was once again handcuffed and they clip-clopped and squelched up the flagstone steps. The solid, dark man Theo somehow thought of as a hotel doorman bouncer, nodded to them in a polite manner as he had done when Theo arrived earlier. They walked along the dirty cream corridor to Interview Room 46. Theo almost smiled. *His room.* The door was half open and he was nudged through.

The Chinese officer un-cuffed and re-attached him to the edge of the steel table. 'Wait here,' he added unnecessarily and turned on the fan. Even with the fan going the room had the aroma of stale cigarette smoke as well as the stink of depression leaking in through the doorway.

In his damp shirt, Theo sweated as the squeaking fan whirred. He was less frightened and more in control of himself than on his previous visit. However, knowing himself very well he knew he had to make sure the fear didn't turn into anger. He knew he had a temper and it had got the better of him more than once over the years. He was astute enough to realise that a small amount of anger could be channelled, maybe used in the form of confidence, not bravado.

Theo took a couple of deep breaths and performed a small, sarcastic one-act play for his own entertainment. Aloud he said, 'Wait here? Where the hell do you think I'm going to go, eh? If I was strong enough I could rip the table from the floor and drag it down the corridor, flatten the guard on the door and walk straight out of Police Headquarters. Sure I will *mate,* but probably best I wait here, it's much more comfortable. You dickhead.'

It then occurred to him that maybe the room was wired and they would hear what he said. So he added, 'Who gives a fuck,' and gave the half open door a sneer. If it was possible to feel better, this pathetic act of defiance at least gave him a small amount of confidence. He tried to concentrate; he had to have some plan, a direction. Who arranged the lawyer? Razak? Why would he, even if he wasn't in on it? Maybe not; lawyers cost money. Maybe the good Inspector Sethna softened and decided to allow him the privilege of a lawyer? None of it made any sense at all. He must get in touch with Jack, but where the hell was he? Dope planted in his room, clearly a frame-up. *How can I get out of this? Wait and see, yes that's all I can do, wait and bloody well see.*

The dog barked. Theo thought of the dog as his. The fan squeaked. He looked up and said aloud. 'Bloody fans of Malaysia. Hey inspector, why don't you oil the bloody thing?' Theo smiled, a self-confidence booster. Not a laugh, a smile. 'Hope you heard that,' he added. 'Hey, I want a smoke.' The lump on his head throbbed in unison with a headache.

There was a damp, dark intensity weighing down the atmosphere. The fan didn't make any difference. A rumble of thunder sounded somewhere far away. He figured it was three or four, tropical time clock, the afternoon rain storm.

Sometime later, probably half an hour, a head poked around the door. 'Mr Perry?'

'Yes.' Theo could think of nothing to add to that.

'Mr Perry, my name is Josef Ibrahim; I am your lawyer, that is, if you will have me.' The man, in white shirt and bright green tie came into the room. He extended his hand. The grip was soft, typical of the Asian greeting. 'Call me Joe, English translation.' He gave a small smile.

'What … what will it cost?' Theo thought the handshake a bit limp, not like an Australian, male or female.

'Well Mr Perry, it depends but for the present, nothing as far as I can tell.' His use of English was clear with a strong American accent.

'Okay, why not, yes I agree to you being my lawyer.'

Joe sat down, opened an expensive leather briefcase and removed a folder. He pulled a pen from his top pocket and clicked it.

'Right, let's get down to business.' He rubbed the side of his nose with a forefinger, touching a neat, Clark Gable moustache.

'Right, mate, umm who … how did you … I mean who told you I was here?'

'Aha, Mr Perry …'

'Look mate, please call me Theo.'

'Yes, of course Mr P … Theo. I am here at the request of a Mr Brian Aung.'

'Brian Aung? Who's ..?' Then Theo twigged. 'Yes, I get it; he's the bloke at St John's in Penang, right?'

Joe looked puzzled for a second and then laughed. 'Bloke, oh mah Gard, you Orstray-lee-ans speak different English words. We have an Orstray-lee-an article clerk boy who is training with our firm. He says things like that, too. I was educated in America and Australian English is a different trip.'

Theo's eyes narrowed. 'So how did Brian know I had been arrested?'

He looked over Theo's head. 'I am sorry; I don't know anything other than our firm was contacted by Mr Aung to look into this matter urgently.'

'I can't work out how ..?' Theo didn't finish the sentence.

'Right Mr Per … Theo, please inform me of your situation so we can get you out of here. Cigarette?' He pulled out a pack from his briefcase and offered Theo one.

Joe lit Theo's and then his own with an old-fashioned brass lighter. He shut it with an exaggerated metallic cloonk. Both blew smoke into the fan. He saw Theo looking at it when he placed it alongside the cigarette packet. 'Made from a bullet shell, Vietnam.'

Theo nodded but was still on the previous track. 'Would you be able to find out who contacted Brian and how the hell he knew I was here? It's important.' He rubbed his eyes.

'Yes, I will do my best to find out more. Now, please a summary of your plight.'

Theo sat back and looked at the squeaking fan, almost reminiscing as he outlined the sequence of events since five o'clock that morning.

'And this Inspector Sethna calmly said that this level of crime didn't warrant fingerprints to be taken or words to that effect.'

'Mmmmm, interesting, we will come back to that in a moment,' said Joe, fiddling with his bright tie. 'Now, this is really important. At any stage did you admit ... admit any responsibility for the drugs? What I mean is, when you say, *'They weren't yours,'* you didn't indicate to the police that they belonged to someone else, someone you knew?'

'No, as I said, they were not mine and I had absolutely no idea whose they were, and I had no idea how they got into my rucksack. Except, obviously, someone put it there.' He went on to explain about Mahmoud.

'Now, this er ... Mahmoud. It seems he does have motive to plant drugs in your bag but if he really wanted to finish you off he could have placed heroin in your bag instead. We could surmise he wants to get you out of the way only for a short period. What I find puzzling is the action by the police which does seem somewhat heavy handed for a crime such as this. Don't misunderstand me; it is nasty and extreme also as to the lengths this Mahmoud is prepared to go to get you away from his woman. The penalties for anything to do with drugs in this country are severe. But I hasten to add, such a small amount ...' He flicked through some papers, '... 22.4 grams of marijuana, still serious please understand, but a vastly different story if it was heroin. Oh mah Gard, seems to me there is more to this, but ... Right, back to facts.' Joe scribbled away for a moment. 'Was your rucksack zipped up or locked?'

Theo rubbed his four-day stubble in a pincer movement, as if he did have a beard. 'Well, I was sure I did lock my bag but the lock I have would be pretty easy to pick, just a cheapie.'

'Did you mention anything about locking your bag?'

He thought for another moment. 'No, I'm certain I didn't.'

'Right, best not to mention anything to do with that and if asked, please say you can't remember, which is it seems the truth anyway. Now, fingerprints. You are absolutely sure you didn't touch the plastic b ..?'

'Joe, I told you, the bag couldn't possibly have my fingerprints on it because, it isn't mine, full stop.' Theo had leaned forward and the last part of the sentence was delivered sharply.

'Okay, okay, I have to be sure about that. The reasons they don't investigate the fingerprints is because one, it costs money, two extra paperwork which all police hate, and three, they probably thought that you would admit to the crime straight up.'

'So,' said Theo, voice rising, 'How can I prove it isn't mine? I mean, if I get done for this it reflects very poorly on the fucking legal system in this country!'

Joe's eyebrows shot up at the use of the F word.

Theo had turned pink. He wasn't finished. 'If I get done for this it means that anyone can place something, a gun, drugs, stolen property in someone's room or car or bag or whatever, ring the bloody cops and that person gets prosecuted … and no one gives a shit. Sounds fucked to me.' Anger abated, he sighed, a cross between frustration and resignation. 'Sorry Joe I didn't mean anything to do with you …' Theo realised he needed to calm down. He took a deep breath. 'Mind if I ..?' Joe nodded, Theo reached for another cigarette.

'I feel quite confident we can get the charges dropped because I'm sure they realise the case against you is very weak.' He began to rise and shuffle the papers back into the folder.

'The only person it could be is Mahmoud or one of his henchmen. No one else has any reason to do it. Mahmoud's family own the hotel and he has access to my key. Can you get the inspector in here and get the case dropped?' Somehow Theo thought that maybe it could all be sorted out straight away.

'No, I am sorry, there is a protocol but I feel sure we will have you released soon.'

Theo's hand quivered slightly as he butted out the cigarette. 'How soon?'

'I'm sorry Theo, I can't say. We have to force the police to check the fingerprints.'

'How will you do that?'

'Well as a matter of the process of law. They cannot *not* do it, it's because they can delay for the time being and it seems as if they are doing just that at the moment.'

'When can I get out of here?' Theo hoped he didn't sound too pleading.

'Theo, I will do all I can, please believe me.'

He had to push it. 'How long?'

'Tomorrow, maybe. Let's work on getting you out, okay.'

Theo slumped and almost spat, 'Fuck me dead, this fucking place, I don't know how long I'll last downstairs in that sewer. It's the worst place I have ever been in my whole life.'

Joe looked up as he placed the folder in the briefcase, eyes wide with the use of language. 'You don't mean … you have been in jail before?'

'No, what I meant was this place, Police Headquarters and the jail are the worst places I have seen and been in, if you know what I mean.'

'Yes, I understand. I will do all I can, I promise, okay?' He slid the packet of cigarettes across to Theo. 'Here you keep these.' He rifled in his briefcase and pulled out a sample matchbook. He tried a smile. 'No good without matches. They probably will confiscate them but it might help ease your stay here.'

'Ta mate, much appreciated.'

'Oh mah Gard, you say the same thing as our articles-clerk guy. He says, "Ta" meaning thanks.' He snapped the briefcase. 'Now, please have faith, I am working for you, okay?'

'Right mate, thanks, I'm not going anywhere that's for sure.'

Joe extended his hand, the gentle Asian gesture. 'Until soon my friend.' He walked to the door. 'So long for now.'

Theo recited the mantra in his head. Brian Aung, Biru, Jack, Mahmoud, Razak, Mum, Eric, Franka … Who else? He deleted the last three, although he gained some comfort from them he had to get back to … the main question. How did Brian know he was in the jail? Did Jack have contacts in the police? Then, did anyone else? It seemed unlikely. Did Razak or Biru ring Brian? How did they know the number? No, not that either. What about Eric and Franka? They hadn't made any firm arrangements to meet, so almost certainly they had no idea where he was. Razak was the most likely because he actually saw the police cart Theo away in handcuffs. Fair enough, but how did he contact Brian? He couldn't have known the number. He could have asked Biru but she didn't know the number either.

Thunder rumbled in the distance. He longed to be able to watch the storm again today but it didn't look promising. The dog, *his dog*, started barking again.

Chapter Twenty-One

The humidity level climbed a notch and added to his anxiety. Sweat poured off him, down his back, from his scalp, everywhere. As he butted out the next cigarette the Chinese officer walked in, the same fit, young man, about the same age as him, unsmiling. Was he happy in his work? How could anyone be happy if they knew someone was being framed? He was a police officer; everyone is innocent until proven guilty, surely. Theo understood what was required of him, almost familiar ground, un-cuffing, re-cuffing, marching down the depressing corridor past the private rooms. He wondered how many people in those rooms were guilty, were some of them being framed like him? Did the police have to come up with a guilty person to fit each crime? Did they care who? And, what constituted a crime? Clip-clop, squelch down the cracked dirty corridor. How come there are so many blobs of chewing gum? *Lift your head, Theo; show them you are not guilty.* He tried not to show fear; he had the shakes under control for the moment.

Thunder again rumbled like heavy guns from the front.

Familiar travel route, door opened politely by the hotel doorman bouncer … *enjoy your stay, sir?* Down the worn flagstone steps, legacy of the mighty colonial power, probably built by convicts just like him. Signed in and handed over to his keeper, Jailer Man. Theo steeled himself for the physical and verbal abuse. He did his best to internalise any sign of unhinging.

'You give me,' the big man spat, through betel-nut blood.

'What?' *Mongrel bastard.*

Any response was enough to set him off, an excuse to be brutal. He punched Theo in the stomach. Theo was quick enough to go with the punch but it still hurt. *First punch, ride with it.*

'Cigarettes, whitey boy, quick hand over or you do hard time.'

Theo wondered how he knew about the cigarettes because it was only about a third of a soft, crushproof packet and it was flat in his pocket. He made a show of getting the pack and then held out his hand. 'Sorry, I didn't know I was not allowed to have them; I mean nobody told me …'

The other two jailers mumbled to each other and laughed.

'Shut up, whitey boy. I make rules here. Next time you go up you get me full packet, okay?' He poked Theo in the chest with his truncheon and then turned him around. 'That way,' and then pushed and prodded him all the way down the cell run, past the other unfortunates, through the stench.

The nasty encounter with Jailer Man seemed to give Theo a small degree of confidence. The shakes subsided, even though he had been pushed and shoved viciously, it gave him heart because he knew if it had happened down the pub he would have been able to defend himself. Bullies like Jailer Man often backed down with a kick in the nuts, or the kneecap. He was astute enough though, to realise that the jailer was a big man and lived a life of violence.

'You bedda get used to luxury room, whitey boy,' and Theo was shoved forcefully again into the cell. He was ready this time and stayed upright.

The Jailer Man waved his weapon. 'Next time you be more polite to boss, eh?' and he burst out in the same maniacal, hysterical laughter. This time he didn't stand and stare, he was probably too eager to get back for a cigarette. He ran the truncheon all the way down to his bolthole.

The resonance of the steel door clanking shut stayed in Theo's head long after Jailer Man had disappeared. All eyes looked his way, again, like circling, growling dogs.

'G'day fellers,' he said. That was all he could think of, a try at making it appear as if he was on top of the situation, just a normal day. No response. 'I'm happy with that, too right.' Still nothing.

Thunder rumbled and the place shook. It felt to Theo like explosions but he knew it wasn't. The humidity level was unbearable, combined with the physical stench of the jail and the weight of captivity. The other prisoners reverted to what they were doing when he came in. A couple seemed to be missing and it looked like about five more bodies had been crammed in during his absence.

He found a seat on the only external corner, not the same area as before but as far away without being obvious from a sub-continental looking man dressed in dirty jeans and body shirt, with a few buttons missing, slouched against the graffiti stained wall. How long was he going to be in for? He desperately hoped Joe would work for him, it was his only hope.

Thunder rumbled and slowly subsided and Theo guessed it was raining. There was no relief in the cells. Hours dribbled by, he had no clue of the time, the caged electric light bulbs continued to smoulder a sickly yellow glow over everything, the only link keeping everyone from going crazy. Someone down the run screamed out and a commotion followed. One of the staff of jailers must have come out of the bolthole because the bars were bashed with a weapon. The voices ceased immediately. The back of Theo's head where he had hit the wall was sore and a headache throbbed. He badly wanted a drink of water but discounted the steel sink supply. At intervals others drank from there but the thought made him almost vomit. He hoped he wouldn't get desperate and have to at some stage. At least he didn't feel hungry. The presence of a couple of rats scurrying around reinforced that thought.

Some enthusiastic Muslims knelt down and commenced praying. Theo wondered if they were tuned in to a universal time machine because it was clear others in cells down the block were doing the same thing.

The Blues singer started up again, singing what sounded like the woeful shanty of a slave; he could now hear clearly enough it wasn't in English and he played a game with himself trying to pick a language. Not Chinese, that was certain and even though there were a few familiar words of Malay or Indonesian, he guessed, for the prize of nothing, it could be a hill tribe language from Borneo. He wondered about the Old Woman from Borneo who sold him the book. If she knew so much, how come she didn't warn him of this? Well maybe she did. He tried to recall what she said, something about trouble now but in the long term everything will be alright. What about monkey? Monkey behind bars? *Nice try, Old Woman from Borneo.*

Theo laughed out loud. The inmates who weren't asleep looked at him, possibly thinking he was crazy like some of the others who talked to themselves and cried out for no apparent reason.

He waved his hands, 'All okay, all okay, long time everything will be okay! Plenty plenty plenty, ha!' Immediately he realised what he had done and it occurred to him that maybe he *was* losing it. He couldn't do that. He waved his hands at those men who were looking at him, 'Can't lose it, mustn't lose it! You have cigarette, ha? Special price, special price, morning time price!' Somehow he did not care if he was talking out loud. He realised he hadn't even been in for 24 hours yet.

Sometime during the late night or early morning, Theo must have dozed for a few minutes sitting up. A big Asian man wearing a beach shirt and light-coloured shorts stained to filth stood near, blocking out the jaundiced light from the caged bulb. A sandal nudged him.

His almond eyes were hardly visible. 'Hey man, you got some cig'rettes, money?' Tattoos of dragon and snake type designs decorated his muscly forearms. He was close enough and his stance implied an element of menace.

Theo rubbed his eyes. It took a few seconds to work out where he was. 'What?'

Another Asian man almost skipped over, Harpo Marx style and stood close to Theo, looking stupidly between the two of them, but he didn't say anything. His closeness was cause for Theo to almost gag on the garlic and stale sweat radiating from their pores.

'Come on man, you got cig'rettes, money, watch in your pocket?' said the big Asian in the beach shirt. The stupid one stared. Theo couldn't work out whether the latter was indeed a simpleton or whether he was part of an act of some kind.

Theo shifted, still sitting. He realised he had to stand up, gain higher ground.

'No, mate I don't have any ...' He didn't want appear to be cheeky and he wasn't sure if these men were going to rape him or genuinely wanted to rob him. Tremors began again from the inside out. 'Listen fellers,' he said in a friendly tone hoping the fear was not obvious, 'I ... I had all that taken from me. He ...,' Theo's throat was dry so he directed his thumb towards the bolthole, 'Blubber-guts pinched my cigarettes after I got back from seeing the lawyer.'

Theo was awake enough now to realise he had to stand up. He switched to pub-fight mode.

The stupid one, Harpo, leaned in between Theo and Beach Shirt. Beach Shirt raked him the other away, with no ceremony, like a big cat disposing of a troublesome mouse. Harpo sprawled on the wet floor and sat there nodding.

Theo sized him up. Beach Shirt was shorter but several stone heavier. 'Hey bub, I'm talkin' to you, man. You hide watch in underpants, maybe money too, eh?'

'Mate, I don't have …' Theo then realised the other man was not going to believe him about not having any valuables.

Beach Shirt thrust his hand out like a moray eel and grabbed Theo by the collar as he was half up. Theo was wedged back against the wall but managed to swing a round arm which made use of the other's action. Anger gave him twice the strength because his head hit the wall on the sore spot. Beach Shirt was clearly a fighter and turned his jaw enough to negate most of the power of the hit but he relinquished his hold on Theo's shirt.

Theo's instant aggression was also triggered by fear, no time and no point being scared. *Kick the bastard anywhere as hard as you can!* But the big man came at him, trying to grab him by the throat and his shirt again, and pin him back against the wall again. By now most inmates were awake and looking, probably glad they weren't the victim. Theo had managed to move along a fraction past the end of the bench seat and he was able to use the wall to steady himself and bring a knee up into the other man's groin. Beach Shirt crumpled and let go of his shirt. Theo took another swing that missed but the next one didn't.

Suddenly another man stepped forward barking a barrage of what sounded like a Chinese dialect. Theo's barometer was up ready to hit again, this time he lined up.

'Hey, no more, man, it's okay, you win, okay?' This man, short and stocky, grabbed Beach Shirt in a firm grip and pulled him out of Theo's reach. He pointed Beach Shirt to the other side of the room, seemingly chastising him.

He came back. 'Hey man, you okay?'

Theo stood there, back against the filthy, graffiti-plastered wall, not game to say anything but ready to lash out. All he could think about was why was everyone being so brutally nasty towards him? He nodded, 'Yeah.'

'Hey man, you fight pretty good,' he said, dropping the hard endings as some Orientals sometimes do. 'You no worry about him, he opportunist, street man, like to rob people.'

Theo maintained his stance against the wall, still not convinced of his safety. 'That what he's in here for?' he queried, breathing heavily.

'Yah, yah. He bad man. I know him. You lucky I here, save your bacon. You give me, eh. You have money hidden under your balls?'

Theo almost laughed and barked. 'Listen, mate, *look!*

The other man jumped back, almost in fright as Theo turned his pockets inside out. 'Hey, *man,* you want these?' He held out the matchbook. Stick that up your arse.' The last part was said firmly and slightly raised. Theo put his other hand out like a stop sign just short of touching the other man. 'I don't want any trouble, alright?'

He side-stepped slowly so the short man was not in his space. *If he gets in your space, whack him one.* Theo was testing him. If the other man moved anywhere other than back, he had no choice.

The short man smiled, almond-shaped eyes nearly disappearing. 'Hey, mister, no problem, no problem.'

Tension slightly defused but Theo was still shaking inside. The feeling still lingered, it wasn't over yet.

The short man said. 'Man, hey man, I like you.'

Theo was on red alert again. *Did he want my arse?* 'What?' He was still against the wall.

The beach shirt man was sitting on the other side of the room glaring at him. Harpo still sat on the wet floor, quietly singing and rocking his upper body slowly from side to side. The Muslim man with the prayer cap in the far corner started droning a chant or a recital.

'Go away, mate, I've got no money or anything else.' Theo had an idea. 'But, I do have friends out there, 'he pointed, 'and if you don't leave me alone you will regret it, orright?' He didn't really feel the steeliness of his conviction, the nervous tension in his legs barely kept him upright.

'Hey man, okay okay, no problem,' he said gently waving his hands, 'But I save your ass, I thought you be grateful, you know ...'

Theo stood his full six foot, inflated his whole body and glared. 'You never know, I might put in a good word for you when I see my lawyer soon.'

'Okay, okay.' The other man was not giving up. 'Lawyer, you have lawyer? Lawyer expensive, you have money, eh? Lucky man.'

How could he explain he didn't have any money to speak of and the lawyer was being paid for by someone else, a fairy godfather?

'Australian Government is paying for me because I have been framed, okay?' The lie seemed to work for a minute.

'Aha! Funny white guy, we all framed. You want job?'

'Job?'

'Yeah, we need young person to sell, you know, important product to backpackers …'

'Mate, please leave me alone.'

Theo walked a few paces away, towards the bars at the front of the cell. Several inmates parted to give him room.

Chapter Twenty-Two

Theo stood, back to the bars and glancing around him for signs of anything. Most of the prisoners sat on the benches; some went back to lying on the floor, others back to murmured conversations in languages he couldn't decipher. Every so often someone used the toilet.

He pointed to his wrist. 'Anyone know the time?' He quickly realised how silly that sounded because it occurred to him that Jailer Man would have removed anything of value, especially watches, to sell on the black market.

Somewhere far off, Muslims were called to prayer. Someone in the jail started up, an eerie, soft but penetrating mantra. There was a shuffle and three Muslims in his cell knelt on the floor and started praying. The man with the prayer hat somehow produced a mat to kneel on. Theo knew it was daylight.

A dark youth with bruises up his arm grinned and showing black stumps for teeth turned to him. 'It morning now, I hear voices down there. You got money hidden up your ass?' He gave a cracked, dry snigger, not expecting an answer.

Ten minutes later a rubber-wheeled trolley rattled its way down the rocky flagstones, stopping at each cell. Two men with grey caps, similar to Muslim prayer hats, handed bowls of something through open hatches.

'Aha, makanan,' said the sallow youth. He chuckled, 'You best not eat this makanan, orang – man. You get plenty sicky-sick. Come on, you have money to give me? Okay, okay you be out of here soon. Good luck.'

Theo eased his way towards the rear of the cell as some moved forward. He was trying his best to distance himself from the others. Most were keen to eat. Someone handed around the bowls of what looked like gruel or porridge. Theo was not hungry in the slightest and even if he had been he would have been unable to stomach any of the makanan. Half-litre aluminium beakers of water were handed around but some were so thirsty they took two which meant the slow ones missed out. He placed the bowl of gruel on the bench alongside and moved quickly to the hatch, grabbed a tumbler and emptied it down his throat in one hit. When he returned to his spot, the gruel was gone. He almost smiled. The men seemed to be enthusiastic about the free food and the level of conversation increased. It was then he realised that he shouldn't have guzzled the water. The guidebook had said never to drink tap water without sterilising it. That meant if he had an upset stomach he would have to use the toilet in front of the growling dogs.

Mealtime came and went. Theo sat, trying to make some sense out of the events of the last twenty-four hours. Nothing made sense.

At various intervals, some prisoners were taken out of their cells by the other guards to either see their legal counsel, if they had the money, be moved to another area or maybe even released, could have been for any reason.

The night-soil trolley made its way down the run, two tidier looking Malays in uniforms of sorts, orange baseball caps on backwards, supervised the exchange of toilet buckets. They obviously had some authority, maybe trusted lifers. Theo could see them stop at the first two cells. They directed their two unfortunate assistants to replace the full buckets with empty ones under the watchful eyes of two prison guards, one opening the steel door and the other standing back, training an ancient- looking long barrelled rifle with a magazine. Theo almost laughed at the comic thought of why anyone would try to pinch a dunny bucket, full or otherwise, but he knew the prison guard was there to shoot anyone trying to escape. Manoeuvring a cumbersome-looking rifle like that in such a confined space would probably create more problems than it solved. Theo saw Jailer Man talk to them, guffawing and remonstrating, then he began the long march down to Cell 30, Theo's cell.

Theo hoped it was him being summoned to go and meet Joe, and freedom. The jitters started again, more in anticipation than anything else. He tried to suppress these thoughts as the big man continued to waddle towards his cell, only deviating every so often to hit the bars or someone's fingers whenever the opportunity presented.

Jailer Man stopped in front of the cell and stared, not appearing to see anyone in particular. He remained like that for a minute or two, seemingly deep in thought. Maybe he was. Then he burst into his laughing performance for a few minutes, and then stopped abruptly, allowing the normal sounds of restricted liberty to reign again. He spat some red betel-juice towards the bars; someone copped a hit. He lifted his truncheon like a tribal elder pointing the bone. 'You whitey boy, out here, ha-ha!' He knew exactly Theo's position in the cell the whole time.

Theo moved to the front. He noticed the Big Jailer was armed, holster flap unbuttoned; also he had stepped back quickly when the door was sprung. Theo hoped it didn't have any significance other than the jailer was on his own and ten metres away from the guard on night-soil detail.

Theo walked through, making sure he was just out of effective reach to avoid a whack from the jailer.

'Stand there, whitey boy.' The big man locked the door and pushed Theo in the direction of the alcove. 'Now move!'

Theo understood. He was being placed on toilet duties. They walked towards the night-soil trolley. Theo cringed; he hoped Jailer Man wouldn't pick up on it. They marched up to and then past the buzzing flies and the putrid stench of the trolley. Theo could not believe he wasn't earmarked for this unpleasant task. He was being teased. They reached the desk.

'Stop!' He felt a sharp jab from the weapon in the middle of his back.

Suddenly the Chinese officer appeared at the bottom of the stairs.

'You very lucky, whitey boy, you got meeting with smart-ass lawyer again, you get outing but you be back, you bet, yah! You bring me cigarettes, okay?'

They went through the transfer process and Theo was nudged up the flagstone steps by the Chinese officer. He didn't want to get his hopes up. His eyes pooled with water, a momentary involuntary thing, he was not strong enough to stop the tears. Strangely he didn't feel any shame but he hoped none of the others saw it. He had to get out.

Chapter Twenty-Three

The humidity level seemed to drop as he went upwards but the heat increased even though it was sometime in the morning, maybe nine or ten. Through the door they plodded. He managed a polite nod to the hotel doorman bouncer as they went through. The man returned the gesture, almost conveying the question as to whether Theo had enjoyed his stay. *Here mate, here's a tip.*

They continued up the dirty cream corridor and then along to Interview Room 46. *His room.* Strangely he felt more comfortable overall which showed that everything is relative. Comfortable compared to what? Well, the interview room was definitely more comfortable than the cells; he now realised it didn't smell as badly as the dungeons.

'Sit,' said the Chinese officer, un-cuffing him. Theo noticed he wasn't re-cuffed to the table, which had to be a good sign, surely. The Chinese officer marched out, leaving the door nearly closed, after turning on the fan. Theo was alone at last with his thoughts. Brian Aung, Biru, Razak, Mum, Jack, Eric, Franka, Joe … Mahmoud.

The fan squeaked, familiar territory. Where was the dog, *his* dog? Sunbeams speared into the room high up, minutes passed, maybe an hour. Sweat began to bead on his forehead; his shirt was still damp. 'Bugger,' he said to the ceiling. 'What the fuck is going on? Where is everybody? Joe? Joe? Where are you?' He wanted a drink, a cigarette, wanted to go to the toilet, too. His stomach gurgled; he wasn't sure if it was the water he had in the cells or because he was hungry.

The fan squeaked, the occasional yell or scream from outside penetrated the buzz of tense activity, footfalls up and down the corridor. An hour went by, maybe more. The door opened fully.

'Aha, Mr Perry.'

Inspector Sethna stood still, the eerie light from the corridor framing his neat profile. Theo couldn't see his face clearly. The light from the window glinted off his glasses which indicated he had moved his head a fraction. He then marched in followed by the Chinese officer. Strangely, all Theo could think about was how things seemed to be looking up. Not cuffed, door half open, only two police officers to oversight him.

The inspector sat, selected a cigarette, placed the pack on the table and made a big ritual about lighting it. He didn't offer Theo one. He blew smoke at the fan. The Chinese officer stood behind Theo, out of sight but his presence could be felt.

'Mr Perry, we have examined the fingerprints on the plastic bag containing the contraband and I suppose it would come as no surprise that your fingerprints are not on it. Someone else's appear on the bag …'

Theo whispered, 'I tried to tell you that.' The lump on his head still hurt.

'… that, however, does not prove the drugs are not belonging to you. Are you understanding me?'

Theo's forehead tightened, involuntarily indicating he was exasperated. He continued to look at the inspector's eyes. It was difficult because of the strange light in the room and his glasses.

'Did you hear what I said?'

'Yes, but … I really have no idea what the f… hell this is all about? I told you the truth, the drugs *do not*, I repeat *do not* belong to me. His face was hot and he knew it was red. 'What sort of country is this, eh? How would you feel if … if someone slipped a government pencil into the drawer of your bloody desk, rang the police chief and you were thrown in jail for theft the rest of your life, eh, what about that? That's about as bloody stupid as this whole set up is. I'm being framed and if you can't see that then you're not much of a …' He didn't finish. He was breathing heavily. Dempster's advice kicked in. *Do not lose face, man, maybe too late, who cares.*

'There is no need to be obtuse, Mr Perry. As I pointed out we are being prepared to release you.'

The relief on Theo's face must have been obvious. The inspector held up his index finger. 'There is still paperwork to be processed. You must have friends with money because Mr Josef Ibrahim is coming from an expensive law firm which, incidentally, is very choosy about who their clients are.'

Theo's whole body loosened as if someone had placed a cold flannel on his forehead. He closed his eyes and took a very deep breath. Nothing to say, no point, it could make them change their minds. The inspector butted out the cigarette. Theo looked at the packet lying near the ashtray. The inspector saw him looking and then looked away, deliberately.

Bastard, thought Theo.

The squeaking fan took control for a moment or two.

'Now, Mr Perry, we know who the fingerprints are belonging to and we still have our suspicions, we think you may be involved one way or the other. Am I making myself clear?'

Theo choked back a smart arse comment and tried to look directly into the policeman's eyes. The reflection of light made it difficult but easy at the same time. He wanted an answer, perhaps absolution.

'Yes, very clear. Do the fingerprints belong to Mahmoud, who framed m..?'

'Point one, no, they are not belonging to the person to whom you are mentioning and two, it is confidential, police business.'

'Yeah, right,' said Theo, but he added quickly, trying to sound more grateful than the *'yeah right'* that came across, 'Okay, okay. Where is Joe … Josef? When can I go?'

The inspector stood. 'All in good time, Mr Perry. Please be continuing to be sitting and we will come for you and process the release papers. I trust that will be in keeping with your expectations?'

Theo dropped both hands out and shrugged in a whatever gesture. 'Yes, I … of course.' *Whatever you say, sport.*

Inspector Sethna stood and pocketed the cigarettes and lighter, slipped the cane under his arm and smartly walked out. The Chinese officer gave Theo a stiff smile and walked out, closing the door behind him. The click of the lock was clear.

Theo looked up at the bars on the window. The fan slowly moved the spokes of dust-laden sunlight. Wrongly accused and imprisoned as well as the humiliation of it all ... 'Bastards, bastards, bastards,' he mumbled.

He wondered how long he would have to wait. Half an hour passed. The dog started barking somewhere out in a compound, maybe signalling a new era.

An hour passed. His stomach cramped. Theo knew he would have to go to the toilet very soon.

Chapter Twenty-Four

He heard a click and the door opened. The Chinese officer gave the *come-on* with his hand. Theo stood but stomach cramps made it difficult.

'Mate, I have to go to the toilet … tandas, quick!'

The policeman pointed down the corridor to the same conveniences he used yesterday. Just making it was everything as far as he was concerned. He marvelled at how anything could have such a dramatic effect on the human stomach. He was sure it was the water.

When he came out the Chinese officer was leaning against the wall. He indicated with his thumb and Theo followed. A few feet in front of the door leading into the main, domed anteroom he originally entered through, he was ushered to the right through a door marked *Debriefing Room*.

So now he was to be debriefed. Theo wondered what that would entail. Report on his clandestine undercover operation?

Inspector Sethna stood, half leaning against the table, arms folded across his immaculate uniform.

'As I was saying earlier, Mr Perry, we are not entirely certain of your innocence in this matter. Because your fingerprints are not appearing on the bag in question does not mean you are not involved in some way.'

Theo took a big breath and exhaled loudly. He was quick enough to realise that this direction, which still puzzled him, could go on indefinitely. For a fraction of a second he thought they had decided to rescind the decision to let him go. The sweats and an internal shake began again although the internal uncomfortable feeling probably was more to do with his upset stomach. 'I really don't know what you are driving at, look, sir, can I go?'

The inspector stood up straight and pointed to a pile of documents on the table. 'First you are signing your release papers and you are free to go. But we are being under instructions that you cannot sign this until your lawyer is being present.'

Theo closed his eyes, lowered and slowly shook his head, looking at the ground. *Don't react, Theo.*

Inspector Sethna nodded to the Chinese officer who had been standing, hands behind his back, near another door. He turned, opened it and walked through. Instantly the noise and bustle of a large crowded room flooded in. Theo couldn't see out because the door blocked his view but the room was large because the sound echoed off a high ceiling.

The heat, humidity and smell of freedom were so close. Theo wanted to run through the door and shout and wave his arms. He was still in low-level shock, confused as to what the police were trying to do to him. His emotions had gone from elation to confused deflation.

In walked a smiling Josef Ibrahim, Clarke Gable moustache, crisp white shirt, polished shoes, expensive leather briefcase and a bright blue tie this time. 'Aha, Theo, please, we are to sign some paperwork and you will be free to go.'

He placed his briefcase on the table and hurried over to where Theo stood. He grabbed Theo's hand in both of his and looked into his eyes. Theo was only just aware of the soft Asian gesture but the action seemed warm and genuine. 'Everything will be alright, Theo, we sign papers and we can go, okay?'

Joe sorted through the papers on the table.

Inspector Sethna handed Theo his passport and the plastic bag with his wallet and watch. 'Sign there,' he said.

Joe witnessed the action and jammed a copy of the documents in his briefcase. 'Right,' he said, snapping it shut, 'let us depart, Theo, okay?' he held out his arm, open hand. 'Please, this way.' He nodded and half smiled to the police officer.

Inspector Sethna said, 'Please be making sure you are being careful, Mr Perry.' Theo looked at him. It was still difficult to see his eyes because of the reflection of light. He had no reason to thank the policeman but he nodded dumbly, more in acknowledgement than anything else.

Theo's world began to gel as he walked towards the door. He looked deadpan at the Chinese officer and they walked into the crowded noisy, high-domed entrance hall of Police Headquarters, Kuala Lumpur, and then into the tropical heat and humidity. For Theo it represented freedom of sorts.

Catch Up

Chapter Twenty-Five

They walked down the front steps and stopped. Instantly touts and opportunists swamped them, spruiking the many services available. Taxis, accommodation, legal advice, restaurants, flowers, satay and chicken-rice and one sleazy opportunist whispered to Theo, 'You want drugs, Tuan, how about girl?'

Joe exclaimed, 'Oh mah Gard, very crowded, come, this way.' They moved down the street, away from the throng vying for a livelihood in front of Police Headquarters. 'We'll get a taxi down the road.'

Theo followed by command in a dazed state, bumping into people and struggling through the crowd. The bright sunshine, excessive tooting and exhaust noise from vehicles, diesel smoke and other fumes from charcoal fires cooking food, the constant loud yelling and the whiff of stench from drains, made his head reel.

'Here,' beckoned Joe, grabbing him by the arm and helping him into a taxi.

Theo's head ached, sweat poured into his eyes and his stomach gurgled and cramped.

Joe pre-empted his question. 'We are going to a hotel …' and he waved away the next question, 'No, not the Hotel New Islamic, another place. You have been booked in, no problem. You will be okay, Theo, all is good.'

Theo didn't feel very good at all but he did manage the smallest of smiles, an acknowledgement of gratitude. 'Thanks, mate …' He hoped they would reach there soon as his head reeled again.

'No problem, no problem, be there soon.'

They pulled up in front of the Hot Spot Hotel. Theo was glad Joe paid off the taxi driver; he couldn't have dealt with it. The blazing sun hammered the top of his head and he felt as if he was sleepwalking. It took all his effort to struggle up the stairs. They reached the top; Theo had to lean on the front counter. He knew he was swaying.

The young man, dressed in a clean white shirt, looked up from a computer screen. His chipped front tooth was prominent. 'Aha, Mr Theo, we have room for you,' he said with enthusiasm, 'my name is Yuman.'

Theo noticed the wall clock showed four thirty seven in the afternoon. Nearly thirty six hours. *Only* thirty six hours.

Joe tapped him on the shoulder. 'You should shower and get a good sleep. I will contact the office here tomorrow morning,' he nodded at Yuman 'and we will meet to go over details. Okay?'

Theo really wanted to find out many things but he was too tired, and he knew he was becoming more ill by the minute. He was not strong enough to take it further. He wanted to ask, 'How did Brian Aung find out where I was?' All he could utter was, 'Yeah, alright, tomorrow, what time ..?'

'Don't worry, I will phone ahead. Yuman has my phone number in case you need me. Please have a sleep, you look all whacked out, man.'

Joe shook hands, the soft gesture again, and walked out.

'How come I'm booked in here?' he enquired.

Yuman smiled, 'Your friends from Sweden, Mr and Mrs Franko bring your baggage from New Islamic Hotel. Also Razak worried that your baggage might not be safe there.' He looked away quickly.

Theo took a moment to realise the Swedes were Eric and Franka. Then the business about his baggage and safe? 'Why not safe?'

'Mahmoud family own hotel ...'

Theo left it at that. 'Where are Eric and Franka?' The dizziness came again and sweat played hot and cold with his forehead.

Yuman was content to change the subject. 'They go to post office, not knowing if you be released today. They be very happy to see you. They extremely worried about sequence of events. Everyone know you not guilty.'

Theo was together enough to register this comment. 'I need to clean up and lie down. Can we talk about this later?'

'Surely thing, surely thing. Please may I have your passport, by law we have to ..? Thank you, down that way, you in room sixteen.

Hot water provided free, no extra charge like other hotels. Aircon too, no extra charge, also. And western-style toilet, too. Very modern. Here.' He handed over the key. 'I bring your pack from storeroom immediately, no waiting. Your property very safe here. No one get past front counter without me knowing. Family business this hotel, very proud record.' He puffed his chest out.

Theo took the key and by the time he had opened the door, Yuman was right behind him. The room was quite warm.

'Drop it there, thanks, mate.' Theo felt vomit boiling in his stomach.

'You want anything please to let me know. I tell your friends you sleep and see them later. Okay?' Yuman turned the airconditioner on. The fan was already on fast. 'Water in jug over there. Also water filter in main reception for you to fill your own water bottle when you like, also extremely free. You drink plenty water in this climate, okay?' The chip on his front tooth gave him a mischievous look.

Theo tried to hurry him up. 'Thanks.'

Yuman closed the door and Theo rushed to the toilet and vomited. He knelt with his head over bowl for five minutes, gagging and retching. He couldn't believe how weak he felt. After a while he sat on the toilet trying to gather some strength to shower. Thunder rumbled in the distance. It sounded like his stomach. *Time for the rain, Theo. Tropical time clock.*

He had a sip of water, brought it straight up and dragged himself to the shower. The water was warm at best but it didn't matter too much as the day was still warm and humid. It felt so good standing and swaying under the tumbling water, washing the filth and memory of the last day. He wished he could erase the memory for good, forever.

His stomach lurched again but he didn't bother to go to the toilet bowl, too weak and tired. He vomited, or more dry-retched, in the shower.

Theo stood under the shower for as long as he could remain upright. There were many questions swimming around in his head. He really wanted to know about Biru. He dried himself, put on clean jocks and a tee shirt, turned the airconditioner off and switched the fan to low. Most of the contents of the jug of water disappeared down his parched throat and then he collapsed on the bed.

He looked up at the fan, his pulsating head drifting with the *click-click-click-space-click-click-click* indefinitum. *What is it Theo, Ringo*

111

Starr on drums? Ginger Baker? Drums in Africa. He had a vision of his beautiful mother stroking his hair, telling him everything was going to be alright. Biru stood waving. He couldn't hold on to that for long. The Old Woman from Borneo sat in front of a longhouse, with red gums, stumpy teeth, cackling and laughing. She held up three cigarettes. It all seemed casual and even happy but then the dreams slowly morphed into nastiness, men yelling at each other with implied violence in a jail with filth all around and then there was ... blackness.

Chapter Twenty-Six

Theo woke once to thunder, which shook the building, followed almost instantly by loud, hammering rain hitting tin roofs. Sleep overtook him again very quickly.

Later there was a gentle knock on the door. It seemed to be inside his dreams but it became louder.

He slowly shook his head, managing to shout, 'Yes?' It hurt his head.

'Mr Theo, are you okay? I hear you yell, I think.'

'What? Okay? Yeah … thanks.' He wasn't sure about anything. He staggered to the door and slipped the security chain.

Yuman said, 'You don't look so good, Mr Theo, but you should eat. You want food?'

He shook his head to register negative and almost retched.

'More water?'

Theo shook the fuzziness from his brain. 'Yes, please, more water would be good.' He shuffled over and grabbed the jug, draining what little was left into a glass and handed it over.

Yuman returned quickly, Theo was almost asleep leaning against the door. He started when Yuman said, 'Here.'

'Oh! Thanks, mate.'

Yuman's brow tightened. 'Maybe you need doctor.' A statement rather than a question.

'No … er thanks, I'll be alright, need some sleep,' he said, voice groggy.

'Your friends overjoyed you here. I tell them you sleep, see them tomorrow, okay?'

'Yeah sure. Look thanks …' Theo momentarily forgot Yuman's name, '… mate. Just need some sleep.'

'Okay, okay but I check on you early in morning time, okay?'

'Yes, I'll be alright.'

Yuman closed the door gently. Theo was at least awake enough to stagger to the door and slip the security chain. He nearly dropped the jug on his journey to the dressing table. A long guzzle soothed him only for a second or two because when the water reached his stomach it all volcanoed back up and out of his mouth. He made the vicinity of the toilet but that's all.

Theo wet a T-shirt and placed it on his head. He lay down again and the fan helped to cool him down but he pulled the sheet over himself; at least he was aware enough of the chance of catching a chill. He blacked out.

Theo woke several times, once to stabbing pain in his gut and a quick trip to the toilet. His head felt as if it would burst and his scalp was tender to touch. Another time voices in the passageway outside his room. His nerves prickled until he realised it was women's laughter. And once more much later, after midnight, the tooting of a horn followed by the wrap of a hotted-up motorbike. Each time he woke, he had no idea where he was for a few minutes. His pillow was soaked and his body ached. He put his open hands around his head which felt as if it might explode. After a few minutes he staggered over to the dressing table and gulped some more water, accompanied by a handful of paracetamol. At least he didn't bring it straight up. Somehow he must have passed out again because next awakening was the call to prayer.

Theo lay on the bed looking up at the rotating fan and trying to coordinate the click to J. J. Cale's version of Cocaine. It seemed to work, taking his mind off things. Tension and pain radiated from his brain, and his body felt so heavy he only went to the toilet when it was critically necessary. At least he felt slightly more in control of his body, and maybe his mind. The last 12 hours or so seemed like a fog and he struggled to confirm that Yuman did, in fact, visit him the previous night. Also the adventure with police officers and criminals over the last few days didn't seem real. He drifted into a half-sleep, laced with busy, harsh colours morphing into blackness, and back again.

There was a gentle rap on the door. 'Mr Theo, are you awake?'

'Yes.' He turned his head on the damp pillow. 'Be right there.' Talking hurt his whole body.

It took a full minute for him to muster the strength to reach the door.

'Ah, Mr Theo, you still don't look too good.'

Theo rubbed his eyes. 'Um, I think I'm a bit better than last night.'

'Maybe we get doctor?'

'I might wait until later, see how I feel then.'

'You have headache?'

'Yeah.' He flinched when he touched his scalp.

'Better get doctor, you could have malaria.'

'What, malaria?' The thought had not even occurred to him.

'You have body aches, very bad headache, sweats? Yes?'

'Yeah, guess so.'

'You have money to pay for doctor?'

'Yep.'

'We get doctor I think, could be showing to be very serious.'

'Might just be bad water.'

'Aha, but water can be more than bad, can be very *very* bad also.'

Theo used the door to hold himself upright. 'I have to lie down.'

'I ring doctor, you sleep. Leave door unlock, I lock from outside but still unlocked for you if you want to come out, okay?' He held up a set of keys. 'I come back with more water. You want omelette, tote?'

Even the mention of food made his stomach lurch.

Yuman helped him back to bed. Theo was embarrassed for a second by the intimacy with the young Malaysian, but he quickly realised it was caring.

'You sleep, I keep eye on door okay? I call doctor, he be here soon. I turn fan off, very bad for fever. I put water in bottle, here. Put damp flannel on your head to keep cool but must not catch fever. You sleep and I bring doctor in when he come, okay?' He placed a cool handtowel on Theo's forehead.

Theo slowly went to sleep after Yuman left the room. His head felt lighter and the lump at the back had reduced in size.

Chapter Twenty-Seven

Sometime later that morning, he woke to the sound of voices. A well-dressed man about 40, slightly taller than Yuman, placed his bag on the bedside table.

Yuman said gently, 'Doctor Munishram is here to see you, Mr Theo. I will be outside. I have rung Mr Ibrahim. Your friends Mr and Mrs Eric Franko are very concerned for you, also.'

'Aha, Mr Perry, sorry to be all business but, umm are you able to pay?'

Theo opened and closed his eyes a couple of times to try to be on top of things. 'Yes, I … I have money but I have travel insurance, also. I may not have enough money on me but …'

'Okay, no problem. Now …'

Theo handed him his yellow World Immunisation Vaccination booklet. The doctor pulled a pair of glasses out of his top pocket and flicked through the pages.

'Ah yes, good, you have vaccinations for cholera and typhoid, hepatitis A, yes good. Now please tell me what symptoms you have and then we will have a look at you, mmm?' The doctor opened his bag, rolled up the sleeves of his crystal, white shirt and sat on the edge of the bed. Theo was still slightly groggy but all he could think about was how a person could look so neat and clean in this climate.

The doctor made his examination, including temperature and taking blood, in a manner that seemed very thorough to Theo.

'I think the prognosis is better than I originally thought. Obviously I will have the blood analysed but I think we can rule malaria out.

However there are other mosquito-borne diseases which are more difficult to identify. You may have a form of influenza or some kind of viral infection, which is why I am obliged to take blood. However, I think it most likely you have a stomach infection and we will need to check the blood sample for any form of hepatitis. Do you recall any time within the last 24 hours where you have had food that has reacted with your stomach? Maybe water?'

Theo smiled. 'I haven't eaten anything in the last day and a half but I have had water and I recall my stomach felt funny not long after.'

'The lump on your head is of concern and it is possible you had a mild case of concussion as well but you say it is not so sore now? I will get young Yuman to check on you regularly over the next day or so and if you feel giddy or faint please get him to contact me. However, I think you are past that phase, alright? Maybe you take paracetamol every four hours from now.' He handed Theo two tablets from his bag and held out the bottle of water.

The doctor packed things back into his leather bag and rolled down his sleeves. 'Okay then, let us assume that it is bad water for the moment and we will review the situation when we get the results back, may take a week. Then we will have more of an idea. I will do my best to arrange for early testing. Obviously if there is something serious you will feel worse and young Yuman will contact me but I think you will be okay. It is really important you rest in the interim. Now, it is best you take paracetamol and course of Flagl for your stomach – take for one week, no need for rehydration tablets, drink plenty of water. And no need for prescription, not like Australia. I did one year of study in Sydney. Australia not so crowded as here, eh? Now, I will write the medications down, I'm sure Yuman will get it for you. In a few days I will have someone drop in an account which I hope you would honour for my services today and I will list medications that you will require, for your information. Make sure Yuman gets receipts for these medications so you can claim, okay? Also, I will get you to visit my surgery in a few days and if you are not well enough I will visit you again. Another account will be rendered, a small amount to cover my fee but the next bill will include any sundry costs like blood tests etcetera. You will able to claim on your travel insurance. There are many pharmacies; the word is almost the same in Malay, farmasi. Other medications may not be of any benefit to you at the moment. You may feel as if you can do things but it is best you rest on the bed and don't stray too far from here for a few days.'

Theo leaned back. 'Thanks doctor, I'm … I'm very grateful …' He had trouble holding back his emotions which embarrassed him.

'You are welcome, but it is my job.' He smiled and defused the awkward moment. 'Please drink as much water as you can, good water this time, okay?'

The doctor walked out, leaving Theo lying flat on the bed considering his next move.

Yuman came back. 'The doctor give me list for things from farmasi.'

Some voices were heard from the passageway and Eric and Franka looked in.

Eric said, 'Aha, you are ex-caping from jail and coming to life again, dat is goot, ah? May we..?' Eric's way of talking had a disarming, friendly quality, especially from such a strong-looking young man with a deep voice.

They came into the room. Franka held her head to one side, 'How are you feeling? We hear you get very sick.'

Theo was slightly embarrassed by the genuine concern for the second time in a few minutes. 'I'm feeling much better, thanks.' The paracetamol had kicked in and he did actually feel marginally better; even though he ached all over, the pressure inside his head had eased considerably.

Yuman said, 'Doctor says you have list of product from farmasi? I will arrange.'

'Dat is okay, we can get it for you, no problem,' said Eric.

Theo grabbed his wallet. 'I'll give you some money.' He opened his wallet. He was sure there was more money in there the other day, remembering he didn't have to go to the bank for a week because he had changed enough money at the airport. His forehead clouded. 'Bastards.'

The others looked at him.

'The bloody cops helped themselves to some of my money, didn't they?' Fortunately he didn't have any credit cards. They confiscated my possessions when they took me away. I only vaguely looked at these things when I was released, I didn't check the amount in my wallet.' Theo quickly examined his traveller's cheques. A certain relief crossed his face. 'Looks okay, I'm pretty sure, be hard to forge them and get away with it.'

He handed over what he had. 'I'll have to go to the bank soon.'

'Don't worry, won't cost much,' said Eric, 'we know where you are hiding, we can send cops around, ah?' They all laughed, including Yuman.

When the other two had gone Yuman said, 'Mr Ibrahim ring earlier, I say doctor with you. Can I ring back and say you on the mend?'

'Yes, please, I need to talk to him as soon as possible. There is much I don't know.' Theo ran his splayed fingers over his tender scalp.

'I get more water for you. I must get back to check on front reception.'

Theo had multiple questions and he needed answers from Yuman when he returned.

Chapter Twenty-Eight

Theo thought he was on the mend, even if only by degrees, and a certain confidence seemed to gel within him. The events of the last couple of days had shaken him far more than anything that had happened to him over his 22 years of life experience. He had a feeling of isolation, without much money, without friends, no family, out in the wilderness to be dealt with by others who could do whatever they liked to him and there was nothing he could do about it, absolutely nothing. What would his mother think? Where was Biru? And then the rest of the unanswered questions surfaced.

It occurred to him at that moment, yes, he really *did* have friends, people who cared about him. Fair enough, he thought, Joe may not be on the scene at all if he wasn't being paid but even so, Theo felt a genuine caring quality from the young Malaysian lawyer. Brian Aung? He must care, surely. Jack? Jack must know about this. Razak had concerns for his possessions not being safe? Eric and Franka? They care. Why would they offer to help? Yuman? He cares enough to be acting like a nurse.

His thoughts were interrupted as Yuman knocked and came back with two large bottles of water.

'Yuman, mate ... er ... look, thanks for doing all this. I really appreciate ...'

'No problem.' His chipped tooth shined, an eager look on his face.

'How come you are so concerned for me, I mean you don't know me at all?'

'Razak, fren of mine, he concerned about drugs in your room. He pretty sure you set up by Mahmoud. We ... this hotel, we are always looking for guests anyway. Malay-she-ah modern country, we want tourists to come here. We not like visitors framed.'

'Do you know Biru?' Theo had to ask.

'Yes, of course, Biru work there too.' He looked away.

'Is she still working there?'

'No she go away.'

'Away?' Theo's heart contracted.

'Yes.'

Theo asked again.

Yuman shifted his eyes. He didn't answer for a moment. 'She have problem with Mahmoud. Mahmoud think she is to marry him but she not to be interested. She modern Muslim woman, he old fashion, arranged marriage, parents agree but Biru not wanting to.'

Theo could see Yuman was uncomfortable talking about this.

'Do you know where she is?'

'No. Perhaps Razak know. His sister go to school with Biru, I think they still friends.'

'Would you be able to find out where she's gone?'

'Okay okay, I do my best. Mahmoud is low-level criminal, many local young guys sell drugs to tourists but now he have gangster men network, selling marijuana, but recently I hear he move to heroin sales to tourists. He also start to do standing over tactics to some of the businesses here in area. People wary of him. My brother share-own this hotel but he concerned because Mahmoud expanding protection racket and he could point finger at us and demand money. My brother's business partner Chinese, they go to school together,' he straightened and looked proud. 'We not very strict Muslim family. My brother worse, he privately say he not even Muslim any more. Mahmoud strict Muslim and Muslim wary of Chinese. Chinese have own way of dealing with things.' He tapped his nose like a spy. 'We should be okay but criminals always a problem for good honest businesses. Anyone complain to police, they do not do anything. Mahmoud friends with local police guys. We need to be careful because if he find out you looking for her he may do something to you again.' His eyes opened wide.

'So you are sure it was him who put dope in my room?'

'Razak think so. If him though, why he not put heroin in your room because he sell that too. Maybe too expensive? Please I not sure but I try to find out more about these things.'

'How did Josef become my lawyer ..?'

'I do not know, I only man on the desk but you okay person, Mr Theo. Don't worry, things will fall into place soon.'

'Thanks Yuman. I need to ring my mother but I don't really feel up to going out to the post office. Can I ring her from here later?'

'Yah, sure, phone in lobby. I get you some food?'

'No, thanks mate I still feel a bit tender here.' He gently touched his stomach.

'Okay, I leave you to sleep for a while but will check on you from time to time. Doctor say I have to, you may be the concussed, that okay?'

'Sure, thanks. When is Josef coming?'

'Not sure, it already afternoon. I ring him.'

The door lock clicked as Yuman walked out.

Theo was left with the noisy fan and his thoughts. At least there was some pattern forming, not too many answers but some things made some sense. Mahmoud didn't plant heavier drugs in his room – why? Maybe there would be too much explaining to do if the Australian Embassy became involved, maybe he just wanted Theo out of the way for a few days so he could cement his obsession with Biru. Mahmoud was not to know Theo would have access to a lawyer. How did Brian Aung know Theo was in jail? That was the question he wanted answered now. And where was Biru? He wanted to see her more than ever. He considered packing his rucksack and going home. Forget Jack, forget the old man, forget Malaysia, corrupt bastard of a place, and forget the last month of his life. That's when he thought of Biru. At least he was alive and on the mend. He knew he had to get to the bottom of all this. No way was he going home, losers do that. *No way.* The warm room and drowsiness nudged him into a loose sleep.

He woke to street noises and the afternoon thunderstorm, feeling weak but convinced he was on the mend. Somehow he was reassured by the daily storm because it had been a regular feature, maybe a comforting friend, throughout his short stay in Malaysia. The rain pummelled the tin roofs, and the ground; he could almost hear the gutters protest and then give in to the avalanche of water. He tried to roll off the bed and go to the window to watch and hear the rain. The effort was too much so he had to settle for lying there, watching and listening from the bed through the open window.

Theo lay on the damp pillow doing his best to focus on the most important issues needing attention. First thing was, he had to go to the bank and cash some traveller's cheques. That prompted a pang of anger because a cop, someone in the system, had been so lousy as to raid his wallet. He tried to tell himself he should feel grateful, because they did leave him some money; could have taken the lot, knowing there was nothing he could do about it anyway.

The call to prayer cranked up after the rain stopped. Theo wondered if the call to prayer was planned to begin after the rain but decided it wasn't because it was becoming dark; the time when good Muslims go to the Mosque. The call was haunting, almost trance-like. He hoped at a later time he could go and have a look inside a mosque.

Theo shuffled to the bathroom, noting that he really needed a new pair of thongs. It was too hot to wear desert boots with socks although he recalled many locals wore shoes and socks as well as long pants, and some wore suits. The cold water was a relief on his face so he decided to have a shower. He was still very weak and had to sit down on the worn tiles, letting water tumble over him.

Back in the room when he was digging for some clean underwear he noticed the books. He pulled out the guidebook with the intention of locating a bank and the post office, but he had forgotten about the book he had bought from the Old Woman from Borneo, *Beyond Pardon*. He downed some more paracetamol and lounged back on the bed, noticing extra packets of paracetamol and the Flagl tablets. Obviously Yuman had placed them there during one of his sleeps. He was surprised he didn't hear him because he thought he had slept lightly. Obviously not. He downed the required dose of pills.

Someone knocked on the door.

Chapter Twenty-Nine

'Aha, you wake. You look more better now. Sleep do you extreme good.'
'Yes,' said Theo stretching.

'I call in sometimes during your sleeps. Mr Eric bring back items from farmasi, I put them over there.'

'Thanks Yuman. Umm, did you manage to contact Josef?'

'Yes, he very busy today and also say it late and he will come tomorrow morning.'

'Okay, I understand. Have you spoken to Razak?'

'Yes, I find out some information from him.'

A current of excitement rippled through him. 'Does he know where Biru is?'

'No. She go straight after …'

'After what?' Theo's face tensed.

'She get hit in face.'

'What?'

'She get hit in face again by Mahmoud.'

'What the fuck …'

Yuman's eyes opened wide.

'Why doesn't she go to the police?'

'Police not do anything even if she do. Muslim custom, old custom, a matter of honour, not new values, man often hit woman, woman man's property.'

'What about her family? Surely Biru doesn't belong to Mahmoud, they are not married, but then it shouldn't happen anyway.'

'Parents know of this but think it okay to do so.'

'Christ almighty. What sort of law and order does this country have?'

'Yes, I unnerstan and Malay-shee-ah supposed to be more modern in line with new laws. Doctor Mahathir trying hard to implement standard practices but old-school religious leaders, sometimes, but not always, hard to change traditions. Funny thing, although not so funny for woman, Muslim man able to hit woman, Chinese or Indian man get criminal charged for doing same. Different for gambling and race track, though. Muslim man in some provinces still be flogged by cane or whip if caught at race track, Chinese and Indian man enjoy fun. Crazy, man, crazy.' Yuman threw his hands up.

Theo shook his head, unable to get the image of Biru's bruised face out of his mind. 'How badly was she hurt?'

'Don't know. Razak say she didn't want to go to work looking like potato head. He think she had enough, run away. He think that she planning to do this thing for a while.'

'Is there any way she can be contacted?'

'Not that I know but I will ask Razak. He keep low profile, he fren with her, Mahmoud know that too so I bet Biru not tell Razak anything.'

Theo placed his hands over his eyes for a few seconds. Time to move on. 'Right, do you know how Brian Aung knew where I was?'

'Brian Aung?'

'Yes, sorry, Brian Aung, who lives in Penang was the person who hired my lawyer, Josef Ibrahim. Do you know how he knew I had been arrest ..?'

'Yes I unnerstan,' after you taken by police, Razak very worried and ring Biru. Biru came to hotel and ring Australian Embassy. They not really seem worried; tell her they cannot do anything for 36 to 48 hours because most travellers turn up in that time. Then he say she get idea. She look through drawers and find notepad. She tell him she wrote number down for you but screwed up note. Razak say she like detective in movies, she rub lead from pencil over pad and number appear like magic. Some numbers not clear but she try several times and get St John's in Georgetown. Biru remember you say '*Jack*' in conversation so she ask for him. Whoever on phone not quite unnerstan' her so they ask for Mr Aung. He come to phone and evidently tell to not worry, he would deal with it. Rest being history,' he added proudly. 'She smart person.'

Theo smiled. 'I owe her, mate, I owe her. In fact, I owe many people, including you.'

Yuman dropped his head, embarrassed, keen to change the subject. 'Okay, you want food now.'

'No thanks, I'm still not too good but getting better. Look mate, I really need to contact Biru. Would you be able to find out where she is or get her to contact me?'

'Yes of course, I will do my best. I have to be careful of Mahmoud if I go around the Hotel New Islamic. I'm sure he know you are staying here, he have eyes in back of head everywhere. But do not be concerned, you are safe here because he know now you have expensive lawyer. I bet he wonder about that. Also we okay here because my brother have friends too. Mahmoud be reluctant to tangle with Chinese partner.' He tapped his nose again, secret agent style. 'Okay, I leave you. Mr and Mrs Eric Franko say to tell you they call in on you later tonight. They knock quietly, if you asleep they see you in morning, yah?'

Yuman left the room.

The Book

Chapter Thirty

Theo listened to the evening sounds coming from the street as he read up about health issues, banking, post office hours, and exchange rates. He planned to speak to Eric and Franka because they had been to the post office and he thought a bank as well. That brought on a growl of anger again because of the money stolen by the police. It was only about $35 but still ...

The light was fading so he turned the wall lamp on and flipped open the exercise book with Theo's Adventures scribbled on the front. He updated and bullet-pointed recent events since his first couple of entries but didn't feel up to concentrating on expanding the detail; he figured it would come later when his head felt better. The room only had two lights, one bulb near the fan which gave a flickering effect and one lamp on the wall along the side of the bed. It wasn't ideal but if he tilted the reading material on a slight angle he could see well enough. He flicked through the guidebook and noted some information about Pudu Prison.

Slightly bored, he picked up the book Beyond Pardon by Sean Morgan. Theo had not realised the author had written five other books as well, all of an investigative nature. He read:

Beyond Pardon

by Sean Morgan

Back cover

Beyond Pardon is a true story and contains details surrounding the case against drug trafficker Roland Michael Hayley, who was hanged in Pudu Prison, Kuala Lumpur, Malaysia on the 18th December, 1987. Renowned journalist and author Sean Morgan conducted a series of interviews with Hayley in the year leading up to the final interview conducted on the 17th December, the day before his execution.

This captivating book provides background information on Hayley; his early years and family, work history, and finally the events leading to his arrest and conviction for drug smuggling.

Sean Morgan details his journey to gain access to the prison, including interviews with officials from governments, Australian and Malaysian, as well as other parties, and provides a vivid look at life inside Pudu Prison. It is a fascinating, thoroughly researched book that provides the reader with a deeper understanding of Roland Michael Hayley.

About the author (inside jacket)

Sean 'Spud' Morgan was born in country Victoria in 1940 and this is his sixth book. He spent many years as a foreign correspondent with postings in Europe, the Middle East and Asia, but primarily South East Asia. Sean attracted the nickname 'Spud' from his early days at school because his family owned a potato farm.

His life and journalism has taken him to exotic locations, both glamorous and dangerous, including numerous daredevil operations with award-winning Australian journalist Neil Davis which took him into the conflict between Indonesia and Malaysia in 1964 and tours of duty throughout Vietnam, Laos and Cambodia, and other hot spots like New Guinea, Fiji and the Solomon Islands. In more recent times he joined up with American adventurer and journalist, Hamilton J. West and made two documentaries called 'Marching-leaf and powder' and 'Line up' about the American drug wars in South America.

Sean Morgan also teaches at Adelaide University in Adelaide, South Australia.

Theo flicked through the book reading more excerpts.

... is a true account of the last days on earth of Roland Michael Hayley, convicted of smuggling 96 grams of heroin into Malaysia. One particular train journey changed his whole life. He had made the very same trip numerous times and for the same reasons, from Bangkok to Butterworth. Malaysian Customs officers, checking for firearms due to a minor ethnic uprising on both sides of the border, stumbled upon Hayley's booty. He was arrested on the 18th of June 1983 and was charged the next day. After several appeals and numerous delays, he was hanged in Pudu Prison, Kuala Lumpur on the 18th of December, 1987.

... (Hayley's) family, lawyers, lobby groups such as Amnesty International, and even the Australian Prime Minister (along with many other Australian politicians and some Malaysian politicians also), begged the Malaysian government to lift the death penalty.

...The Malaysian government refused to grant a pardon of any kind in the case of Roland Michael Hayley. It was generally felt that the main reason

for not granting a stay of execution or pardon was because the Malaysian government was trying to show the world that they were serious about stopping drug trafficking in their country.

... traces the hippie trails starting in the late 60s, from London in double-decker buses or rusty old ambulances where travellers drew straws as to who would drive, licence or not. They headed through Yugoslavia, Turkey, Iran, Afghanistan, Pakistan to Delhi in India. And from the other direction, people with backpacks came from Darwin to New Guinea, East Timor, through the string of Indonesian islands, up the Malay Peninsula through Thailand, on to India, and some continued on to the UK, Europe or America.

... Carefree young people travelled to these places from countries where the underground had heard of Timothy Leary, Jimi Hendrix or Maharishi Mahesh Yogi. Many of these young people could boast a university qualification. The lure of magic mushroom omelettes, plunging needles into their arms, smoking bongs and hookahs packed with hash, opium or heroin, as well as other exotic substances and experiences became too much for many of these new-wave transients ...

... Attracted into this toxic mix also came physically and mentally damaged ex-forces misfits with drug addiction problems (refer Appendix – Vietnam - use of drugs by armed personnel – US and Australian forces) who had linked up with local criminals and established bars and drug distribution networks on a large scale ...

... These young travelling 'hippies' took part in a wide range of activities, irrespective of the risk, aware or unaware of the dangers. Away from home and their secure environment, the need to be careful became blurred. Most of these people made it back, content with the experience. Some became

temporarily lost but money sent to poste restante by family or friends saved them, and some pulled themselves together by sheer luck.

However, many fell through the cracks; some went as far as selling or giving away their passports, or became involved with gurus and criminals or lost their minds from excessive drug use or brainwashing by cults. Some just wandered aimlessly or sold their bodies; others bought and sold drugs to either maintain their habit or to stay alive …

… Some committed other crimes and misdemeanours from setting up other travellers for theft of passports, identity or money, and some, most certainly, committed murder (refer Appendix – Criminals on the Road - Charles Sobraj.)

… Others simply disappeared, overdosed, were murdered or crawled into the abyss. Many were not worldly enough to realise that all good things had to end sooner or later. Roland Michael Hayley was a sweeping mix of many of these things …

Theo was intrigued by what he read. It was an era he knew little about. He had heard about the Woodstock era and hippies because his mother was of that generation but did not know much about what it was like apart from some of the music. He flicked through the book some more to see what the other chapters contained. He saw that the book was very comprehensive and seemed to be thoroughly researched. The chapters he noted to be of particular interest were:

Inconsistencies with Drug laws throughout Asia and the World

Drug use and cultivation by indigenous and local people

The influence of western powers in Asia post World War 2

American drug wars

Australians and the drug scene

The influence of religion on geopolitical events

Setup and betrayal.

∞

Theo slept for the next few hours in airconditioning and without the squeaking fan, and when he woke he felt much better. He picked up Beyond Pardon. Hayley was from English migrant parents, born in 1957 in Adelaide, worked at Holden's on Port Road after leaving school and didn't return from annual holidays in January 1980.

Theo almost felt like he knew Hayley because he was familiar with areas around Adelaide. Morgan makes mention that at the first interview in January 1987, 29-year-old Hayley looked gaunt, pale and appeared to be about nine and a half stone, three stone lighter than when he went on holidays. His dark hair had thinned with a tinge of grey and it seemed prison food and lack of clean air and water had taken its toll. His six-foot frame had a slight stoop and a lean to one side as if he had a back problem.

Chapter Thirty-One

Theo woke to a rap on the door with the book spread-eagled across his chest. Weak light emanated from the globe on the wall.

'Theo, you are not yet dead?' said Eric.

Theo shook the sleep from his head, managing a smile. 'No, I am alive but only just.' He rolled off the bed, having to steady himself before opening the door.

'Aha, you look much better dan de last time we saw you,' said Franka.

'Er ... come in, please.' He flicked the airconditioner on and the fan on high again, to get rid of the stuffiness.

They gingerly shuffled in. Franka handed over a packet of biscuits. 'Maybe you eat a little now. We didn't want to disturb you but Yuman say doctor say you should be checked regularly because of concussion.'

'I think I'm over that now. I have a headache but nothing like the one I had before. I'm sure I'll be okay now. Listen, thanks for the bickies and collecting my things from the New Islamic and bringing them here, and also getting the stuff from the farmasi ... and everything.'

'Our pleasure. You owe us beer now,' laughed Eric. 'What's this?' He picked up the book.

'*Beyond Pardon*. A book about the bloke Roland Hayley who was hanged in Pudu Prison about ... umm a couple of months ago. The authorities closed the active prison immediately after but it is now a tourist attraction. I'd like to go there, you haven't gone there yet, have you?' He looked at them both.

'No, not yet but we could go together, when you are up and well again, yah? We are in no hurry. Anyway, we leave you now, do you want anything? We can get some proper food for you, because we are going out anyway for eating and walk.'

'No thanks, my stomach is still a bit unsettled but the biscuits are probably a good idea, thanks.'

After they left he risked a couple of biscuits and drank some water. Maybe a cigarette wouldn't hurt? He butted it out after the first drag made him almost pass out. Theo picked up the book again, smiling at a youngish photo of Spud Morgan trying to look serious. He recalled during the masterclasses, Spud had kept the auditorium in fits of laughter with his stories from the desk of the foreign correspondent that he labelled, '*The FUSSH desk - The fuck-up starts and stops here desk.*'

Chapter Thirty-Two

Theo woke during the night, put the book away, downed some paracetamol, turned the light off and went back to sleep. The distant sound of a dog fight moments before the call to prayer woke him to a new day. He definitely felt more degrees better but his head still ached, nothing like the fierce pounding headache he had experienced the day before. He needed to get moving on a number of things, visit the bank, pay the doctor, and of course give Yuman some money for services rendered. He wanted to contact Jack, too. *Where the hell was he? Surely Brian Aung had contacted him, must have, surely?* Also he wanted to talk to Josef Ibrahim as he still had many questions unanswered.

His stomach still wasn't right and the overall weakness of his body depressed him. The shower was welcoming and he sat on the tiles, allowing the refreshing lukewarm water to cascade over his aching head. The last lot of paracetamol didn't seem to make much difference. He washed his clothing whilst sitting on the shower base, thinking of his mother. What was it about mothers and washing? At least the lump on the back of his head had gone down considerably. After the shower he drank the rest of the filtered water and ate some of the biscuits. He was hungry which he took to be a good sign, but he was still weak and recovery would be in small doses.

Theo grabbed the two empty bottles and opened the door. No one seemed to be about. He felt like a very old man as he placed one foot in front of the other in a measured shuffle to the foyer.

Yuman heard him and looked up. 'Aha, Mr Theo you up but not away yet?' He laughed. 'You want water and you want breakfast too?'

'Well, yes that would be good but I ...'

'No problem, I arrange for you in five minute, my help arrive soon for general dog's body work. I get him to go to restoran – kedai makan – for food. Only Chinee open at the moment, Indian restoran good food but not till later in day. Do you want,' he opened his hands, 'omelette?'

'Yeah, sure that would be fine, thanks. Can I get toast as well?'

'Maybe, yes I think. We take our mug and get you coffee, too. Umm, you got ... er no money?' He took the empty bottles and filled them up from the filter systems.

'That's what I wanted to talk to you about. I had money before I was taken to jail but the bloody cops pinched most of it.'

Yuman's eyebrows went up. Theo wasn't sure if he was confused by the word pinched, the word bloody or that the police would steal money from a tourist.

He repeated the message, 'Remember, the cops stole some of my money.'

'Aaaaah, I am seeing, you show us empty wallet. Cops sometimes have bad reputation. You can get more money?'

'Yeah, no worries but I have to cash traveller's cheques. Do you cash them here?'

Yuman looked around swiftly and tapped the side of his nose. 'Ah maybe, special for you ... um Mr Theo, you not tell ...'

Theo smiled. 'Of course, I understand,' and they both winked at the same time.

Yuman added, 'You should also cash most cheques at bank for legal purposes as you may have to show evidence at airport on departure.' He winked again and they both laughed.

'Yeah. Yuman, would you be able to ring Joe, er Josef Ibrahim? I really have to talk to him today, this morning, very urgent.'

'Yes, of course, I will do so very soon. He not in office for another hour but I say to him yesterday you require him importantly. You go and rest Mr Theo and Yuman arrange everything, okay?'

'Thanks mate. And if Eric and Franka turn up, could you please tell them ..?' Yuman nodded enthusiastically. Theo turned, thinking Yuman was much like Radar O'Reilly from the TV series MASH. He did the old man shuffle back to his room and collapsed on the bed.

Half hour later Yuman arrived with breakfast. 'No tote, too early for bread but fried rice instead, okay?'

He put the tray on the dressing table. 'Coffee too. Also you have letter.' Yuman walked over to where Theo was sitting on the bed and handed him a letter.

'Letter?' Theo could see it didn't have any sender's name or address and he turned it over. The envelope was addressed to him care of the Hot Spot Hotel. 'I don't think anyone knows I'm here,' he continued.

Yuman hovered, clearly interested but polite enough to get the hint. 'Okay, I see you later, will ring Mr Ibrahim soon.'

Theo looked at the postmark. Yesterday stamped Kuala Lumpur. He opened the letter using a pen to slip in and tear the flap. His hands slightly shook in anticipation. Theo had a fair idea who it was from. He also figured Yuman did, too.

Chapter Thirty-Three

The writing was very neat, in pen and on lined paper.

Dear Theo,

I hope you are feeling better now and your stay in prison was not too much distressing. I know you have been released and I am so happy and relieved about this. I have friend to keep me informed. It is almost certain Mahmoud had the drugs planted in room. I feel responsible for what happened to you and I am ashamed that you have suffered greatly because of me.

The letter seemed quite formal and Theo thought for a moment that someone else may have written it for her. Then he remembered that she had told him she was well educated in the writing of English but daily use of the language with others created a different form. He could read her musical English between the lines.

I am in hiding and it is best I don't tell you where. Best for both of us. Do not be put off by the postmark - I posted this letter to my friend who re-posted in Kuala Lumpur. That is because it is important that no one, and that especially means Mahmoud, knows where I am. At moment I am trying to get a passport because as long as I don't have one I am unable to leave the country.

I would like to keep in touch with you so we can meet somewhere, if you would like this also. I am staying away from Kuala Lumpur but I have Mr Aung's phone number and I leave news there when I get my passport. Trying to get passport is difficult because my family don't know where I am and it is best kept like that.

I am safe at the moment staying with friends. I will leave a message with Mr Aung hopefully soon. If you don't want to meet with me, I do understand. Why would you wish to be mixed up with my problems?

I thank you for your kindness and respect.

Love,
Biru

He read the letter again. His first impression was that he was enormously happy she wanted to see him again. Did love mean love as in closeness and commitment? Or was it the polite format used in letter writing practices? His 22-year-old head had trouble deciphering all the information before him. The last few sentences gave him an out. He had thought long and hard about that. Why the hell would he want to get involved in her problems? Theo knew he already was deeply involved and connected to Biru – he wanted to see her again.

He pictured her smiling at him, with her face framed in the nun-like hijab. He could hear her telling him the words in the letter, her voice almost like tinkling, china bells. The picture came to mind of the outline of her slim, curvy body, with the light from the window behind, when she adjusted the airconditioner. He could feel the electricity again.

'Hell,' he breathed. 'What am I going to do?'

His food had gone cold but the omelette tasted good; he needed to get something into his stomach. The cold fried rice didn't look too appealing but the luke-warm sweet coffee went down well. So far he had no urge to bring it up.

He lit a cigarette, took a drag and felt dizzy so he butted it out. It didn't help his headache. Theo felt the letter clarified some of his questions but there was nothing he could do about Biru for a day or two anyway so he contemplated his next moves. He needed to speak to Joe and also try to find Jack. Sometime soon he had to fit in a visit to the bank as well. At least he had a plan.

Theo read the letter twice more, wet his finger and made Brian Aung's name unreadable and slipped it into the guidebook. The envelope flushed down the toilet in small pieces. He smiled thinking he could play at the spy game just as well as anyone else.

∞

Josef Ibrahim arrived about an hour later. Yuman had asked if Theo wanted to have some privacy so they met in a room with a desk but it was a storeroom as well. Boxes, spare furniture and bedding filled the area but Yuman made a space big enough for Joe and Theo to sit at the desk. Yuman had also arranged for his dog's body helper to collect two cups of sweet coffee from the restoran down the road. A fan was on full, wobbling as if it might fly off at any moment, but it didn't squeak or click.

'Oh mah Gard, the traffic my friend, the traffic, wow. You seem to have had a rough couple of days,' said Joe, offering the limp handshake and then opening his leather briefcase. He adjusted his red tie, striking against a crisp white shirt. His moustache was trimmed to perfection and his black hair slicked back into almost a mirror finish. Every bit the spiv, expensive lawyer. Theo smiled and thought he could easily be a film star.

'Yes, I wouldn't want to repeat my stay in jail ever again, that's for sure.' Theo was keen to get on with it, an overpowering need to know a whole range of things. 'Right, I've got some questions.'

'Shoot, buddy.'

'Best idea is for you to tell me how you came to be engaged.'

'As I explained, our firm received instructions to act for you from a Mr Brian Aung of St John's church in Georgetown, Penang.'

Theo knew the next bit but he let Joe continue. 'I found out that he received a request from a ... here it is, a Miss Biru Samaad from the Hotel New Islamic who said you had been framed. They all say that, Theo.' He smiled and then switched to serious when Theo glared. 'Okay, sorry, Theo you are the exception, of course.' He winked.

'Who's paying for all this? I hear your firm does not come cheap.'

Joe looked away for a tick. 'Mr Aung is picking up expenses.'

'Why would a Church of England representative pay for me on a drug charge?'

'No, Mr Aung himself said that he is paying, not the church.'

'Do you know a Jack Deere?'

Joe looked away again. He busied himself with a cigarette.

'Joe? I'll find out anyway.'

'Umm, yes. I know of him.'

'Is he behind Brian Aung?'

'Yes, I believe so.' He blew a funnel of smoke into the wobbling helicopter blades.

'How do you know *of* him?' Theo's throat was dry so he took a gulp of tepid coffee.

'A year or so back our firm acted for him in a case.'

Theo massaged his face. 'What sort of case?'

'Well, it is confident ...'

'Come on Joe,' Theo gave a cheeky grin. 'I'm up to my ball-bag in this and I need to know more about what is going on, alright?'

'Well,' Joe seemed to baulk ever so slightly at Theo's colourful language and took the time to weigh it all up. 'It was a drugs charge. He was acquitted, no case to answer.'

'Do, or did, the police know about that in relation to my situation?'

'Yes.'

'And?'

'When I spoke with Inspector Sethna trying to secure your release, he um ... said your name came up; a person of interest, that's all but he wouldn't elaborate on it.'

Theo shook his head almost violently. 'What?'

Joe stood and walked to a pile of boxes and turned. 'In confidence however, I have my way of being informed and money,' he rubbed his thumb and forefinger together, 'money helped me find out more. In this country, much can be accomplished with George Washingtons. Very good incentive.' He smiled at his use of the Americanism.

'My contact found out that the cops were aware, or in his words suspected, Mr Deere may have something to do with it because *his* name came up with reference to *your* surname from a simple check of records. They always do that; run the names of people through to see if anything comes up. All I know is my contact said your surname came up as flagged.'

Theo reached for a cigarette and lit up. He noticed there was a slight tremor in his hands. He took a slug of water and began talking, not from what the true beginning might be but he gave Josef Ibrahim a general breakdown about his father's death, coming to Malaysia to catch up with Jack and Jack not being in Penang where he was supposed to be. Joe peppered the conversation with questions.

'I see, I think. All I can suggest is that your father had come under the eye of some authority somewhere and the surname rang a bell ... perhaps. Also you said you have to sign some paperwork here in Kuala Lumpur with the Malaysian Department of Foreign Affairs, maybe something to do with that. Don't worry, probably of no importance, more than likely to do with immigration and as you said, the Malaysian government sent paperwork to you via Australian Foreign affairs. I think it most likely it was because your father, a foreign national, died here in Malaysia and his name cropped up as a matter of course.'

Theo's brow tightened and he chewed on his bottom lip. He butted out the cigarette and looked up at the wobbly fan.

'Now,' continued Joe, 'as far as the charges against you, the cops have nothing and your record is clear. They could, though, make a note against your name for future reference, even though legally they can't.' Joe winked. 'The police can do anything they wish. Anyway, they, the police had been watching the Hotel New Islamic for a few weeks. They know more than a little about Mahmoud Hanif.'

Theo sat forward. 'What about Mahmoud?'

'Well, please be aware this is very, you know, delicate and confidential, okay, because I am not supposed to know and my guy could be in all sorts of trouble.'

Theo nodded and circled his hand. A get-on-with-it gesture.

'The police have been watching him and his gang of penjahats

... sorry, in English, criminals. Mahmoud has a minor protection racket going, intimidating the poorer shop owners, forging student identification cards and other things like that. They sell all types of drugs to tourists, not just marijuana but hash, heroin and cocaine. That begs the question as to why only marijuana was placed in your room because he could have put a large quantity of white powder and your charges would have been very difficult to dispose of. Malaysian authorities love to show the world they are tough on hard drugs and, guilty or not, heroin for instance is a hard one to shake. I can only surmise that Mahmoud, thinking you wouldn't raise any eyebrows, probably wanted to get you out of the way for a week or two, and it would have been at least that if Mr Aung had not engaged us. Embassies don't do anything for weeks and that is only if someone pushes them because foreign travellers often disappear and turn up later. And if they don't, generally they make it someone else's problem because too much time has elapsed. I suppose the cops initially thought you may have been involved in the drugs side of it but I'm sure they could quickly see you were set up. The anonymous phone call, ha! You know, man, they get plenty of them from people who want to discredit someone. But I get the impression there was something more, I mean when I requested they check for fingerprints, they had already done that, so they were really holding you to see if they could find out anything, anything at all. I heard a whisper that the Investigation Branch had some concerns about the professional standards of the local police in this area, you know, overlooking minor criminal activities, and could I suggest Mahmoud's little crime ring might be a matter of concern.'

Theo took another sip. The coffee was almost sickeningly sweet and he felt a slightly unpleasant jolt in his stomach.

'You see, Theo, in this country certain things have been going on for ever and the relationship between powerful or persuasive guys and the cops and the military is often blurred, you know, law and money. Many people live on the poverty line and, well I guess, everyone has to make a living to feed their families. So some good citizens in authority pursue criminality with honesty and vigour, and want to rid the country of corruption. Alternatively, of course there are many who have vested interests to continue the way it has always been. In your country, or the west, corruption is of a slightly different nature but still probably just as bad. Big companies, mostly multinationals, banks, mining, media and big unions prop up and influence governments and pretend it is all above board, by the rules, you dig? Whereas here and in most of Asia, sure big conglomerates have massive power making and breaking elected governments, but the little guy gets more of the action. Yah?' He chuckled.

Theo's head was contracting and expanding, almost pulsating. He rubbed his forehead. There was silence for a moment; he tried to formulate his next question.

'What do you know about Biru? Biru Samaad.'

'Umm, only that she is the woman who Mahmoud believes to be his mengikat … er in English betrothed, promised for wife, okay? Also she contacted Mr Aung, set the ball rolling to get you out of jail. Why?'

Theo wasn't sure whether to fill him in but decided to anyway, as much for the need for Joe to be able to help as well as the need for someone to confide in. 'Well, I heard from … never mind but, I heard Mahmoud assaulted Biru around about the time I was arrested, for the second time in a few days. It seems she had enough of him knocking her about, so after she contacted Brian she ran away.'

Theo had already thought out his answer to the next question Joe was certain to ask.

'Where is she now?'

He kept his gaze level, trying not to glance towards the dresser where the letter was inside the guidebook. 'I don't know, but I understand she is safe, that's all I know.' It wasn't a lie.

Joe seemed satisfied. 'Guess that's not important, in fact if she isn't on the scene Mahmoud should leave you alone. I don't think Mahmoud is a problem for you now because of info I get from my man Friday, like Robinson Crusoe, get it? Well, he told me Mahmoud had hit the trail too because the cops want to speak to him.'

Theo's heart jumped. He hoped Mahmoud had not gone after Biru but he realised there was nothing he could do about it, anyway. He could only wait and see what transpired.

Something had been worrying Theo since the lawyer had come on the scene. 'Now Joe, you say, *"no problem"* every time I mention who's paying for all this, but surely I have to cough up something?'

Joe screwed his eyes up for a second, unsure of Theo's terminology.

'Aha, oh mah Gard, yah, I get it. I guess that is a matter for you and Mr Aung. Also you may not be able to afford my legal services. He did say all costs are covered. Might be prudent to accept that, yes?' He laughed.

As far as Theo was concerned this was another loose end to be sorted out. For a moment it dawned that he should really speak to his mother. Then he decided, 'Best she doesn't know about all this,' he mumbled.

'Pardon?'

'Oh, sorry mate, just thinking aloud.'

'Okay, Theo, I must go. Please ring me if you need anything further.' Josef Ibrahim closed his case and stood. 'Here is my card; I can be reached most days. Maybe we get to meet socially one day?' He offered the handshake again and left the room.

Chapter Thirty-Four

An hour later Yuman managed to get Brian Aung on the phone. There was an extension connection in the office cum storeroom and Theo was able to put his feet on the desk and relax. He had a headache but it seemed to be easing with each barrage of paracetamol, and the aches and pains in his limbs were progressively backing off.

'Good morning, Theo, you are out of jail?'

'Yes, thanks to you and Biru.'

'Aha, the young lady who rang me.' He laughed, 'You have friends. It always pays to have friends.'

Theo couldn't wait. 'Have you heard from her?'

'If you mean since the first time she rang, let me see, three or four days ago, no I haven't.'

Even though Theo expected it, his body slumped. 'Thanks for all you have done, Brian. Can I speak to Jack?'

'No, he is still in Bangkok; his new leg is coming along fine.' A very British accent.

'I'll have to repay you.' Theo had been mulling the money matter over in his mind. 'How ... what ..?'

'No need. Jack said he would cover the expenses, it has nothing to do with me or the church – that is important – and I'm a go-between, if you like. That is something for you to discuss with Jack.' He chuckled.

Theo rolled his eyes. 'Well, Brian, that is what I want, to talk to

147

him. Surely he has a contact number, I mean he must be staying somewhere with a phone.'

'Yes of course, I do have a number for you to ring ...'

Theo pulled out a pen and wondered why Brian didn't tell him straight away. 'Well, I'm ready.' It was difficult to keep the irritation out of his voice.

Brian recited the number and filled in details of Jack's situation, explaining it was a guest house near the hospital in downtown Bangkok where Jack stayed on trips there. Down the road was the company that made prosthetic limbs. There was a phone in the reception area and they would take a message and get Jack to ring back. That was the plan anyway but Brian made the point that sometimes there was a language difficulty or someone forgot to tell someone, and so on.

'I'll give you the number here too,' said Theo, 'The Hot Spot Hotel where I am staying in case I can't get hold of Jack, okay. I'll be here for at least a few more days.'

'Righto Theo, you also have this number and I presume you will be coming to Penang soon, too.'

'Yes, I am keen to catch up with Jack, after all he was the person I actually came here to see and, of course, he hasn't been here, has he?'

The other man chuckled again. 'All in good time. You are on Asian time now, young man.'

At that point Theo tried to picture Brian Aung. A whole range of images scrolled before him; it was hard to decide on anything. The man sounded so irritatingly wise. 'Right, I'll try to get Jack.' Theo then felt guilty sinking the boot in, perhaps sounding a little tart. He added, 'Look, sorry I er ... '

'Don't mention it, don't mention it. You have been through quite an ordeal.'

'Brian, I am keen to catch up with Biru. If she contacts you could you please ring me urgently? It is important.'

'Yes of course.'

'Okay, we'll meet soon and ... er ... thanks for everything you have done. See you.'

'My pleasure, Theo, my pleasure. Cheerio.'

∞

It took a couple of goes for Theo to get the hang of using the phone but he eventually made the connection to the Orchid Rest. Jack was not there. The female spoke very poor English. He asked if she spoke Bahasa Malaysian thinking Yuman could get a message across to her but she couldn't. The best he could do was leave a message and the Hot Spot Hotel number. He thanked her and hung up.

He heard voices in the foyer and a few seconds later Eric and Franka came in.

'Ah good morning Theo, you feeling better today, no?' said Eric smiling.

'Yes, much better thank you. I need to go to the bank today sometime to cash traveller's cheques. You went the other day, are there any nearby?'

'Sure, not far. We will take you if you like, easy walk. Not open yet. We are going out for the breakfast; do you want to join us?'

'No thanks, I already had something to eat. What time does the bank open? I have to get some money out quick because the doctor needs to be paid and I wanted to sort that out today if I could.'

'I think it is opening about ten,' offered Franka adjusting her daypack.

'Okay, we call back in about an hour and go to de bank, yah?' said Eric.

Theo went back to his room and downed some tablets, drank more water and had a shower. The day was warming up and he put the airconditioner on for a short while to cool the room down. He decided not to tell his mother anything, not at this stage, maybe never about going to jail. He knew she would only worry whatever he did so he penned a postcard with the mundane, 'Everything is fine, food great, I'm well, meeting new people, hope to catch up with Jack any day – he happened to be away – the late arrival of Jack's letter confused things etc. – Love Theo.'

Chapter Thirty-Five

Walking down the stairs and out into the mid-morning was a shock. The glare, heat and noise clubbed him. Theo realised when he stepped out into the street how unwell he still was. The last few hours, under a fan and airconditioning in his room was one thing and had given him a false security. Eric grabbed him as he took his first few steps.

'Aha, Theo, you not too steady.'

'Bit hot, mate. I'll be alright in a minute.'

Eric steered him back under the shade of the shop fronts while Theo orientated himself. At least he had remembered his hat and sunglasses. The morning was at its hottest and the humidity triggered enough sweat to soak his clothes in minutes. Growing up in Adelaide with endless days of over 35 degrees of dry heat in summer, as well as icy cold winters, had not prepared him for the tropics. He had never experienced sun and humidity as intense as in Kuala Lumpur. The cracked concrete pavement and near-molten tarmac radiated intense heat. A lone palm tree down at the corner stood at attention, fronds unable to rustle in the non-existent breeze. Cars, trucks, buses and bikes of all kinds, many hopelessly overloaded, jockeyed for position on the roadway. The overcrowded footpaths gave the impression no-one knew where they were going or what they were doing there. People shouted at others in the distance, trying to compete with the horns and loud mufflers from the cars. Bells from a Hindu temple nearby added to the din. The only levelling feature as far as Theo could determine, in his malaise, was the brilliant blue sky which, although softening the scene, also threatened with the usual tropical storm he knew was hiding on the horizon, even though many hours away.

Fortunately a bank was only two corners away and it was a relief to get away from the intensity of the street. It wasn't the bank that Franka and Eric had visited a few days ago but it was the closest, as they could see Theo was not up to a long march through the streets of Kuala Lumpur. Up the steps of the old colonial sandstone building, they moved in step with the people going in and dodged the people coming out. At the door, a uniformed guard with a blue turban stood chatting to people as he ushered them in.

The noise level increased inside, with people talking loudly and officials of some kind barking directions or instructions to others.

Eric nudged Theo and yelled, 'Dey have elephant guns, yah? Don't trumpet or we may all get shot.'

Despite his headache, Theo had to laugh. On either side of the door on the inside were two more uniformed guards, both armed with old worn heavy duty single shot rifles. Theo glanced up at the huge fans which tried unsuccessfully to shift the stifling, hot air. He was acutely aware of the damp, human intensity and wondered if others could smell him. The scent of furniture polish gave the room a small measure of reprieve. The main foyer of the bank exuded chaos in its extreme form as there did not appear to be lines to the tellers; an unruly crowd mushroomed around each grill. The crowd consisted of a wide cross-section of the peoples of Malaysia. About half were in western clothing, suits, high heels, ties, uncovered faces, but the rest was a mix of long white shirts for men, versions of the scarf from hijab to the full niqab, and saris for women, some turbaned holy men and a couple of tribesmen, straight from the jungle with their red teeth and machetes strapped to their backs. Theo had no idea what to do and was heading through the crowd to the counter marked, Maklumat – Information, where no staff seemed to be in attendance.

Franka waved, 'Here, the way is upstairs,' and pointed to a sign which said, *Cek Pengembaraan* and an arrow upstairs.

Upstairs was much cooler and quieter and the small crowd was made up of mostly westerners, backpackers. Even though they had to line up, the process was efficient. Theo was able to cash some traveller's cheques and they were back outside in no time.

'Glad to get that out of the way,' he said, rubbing his head. 'I still feel a bit weak so I think I'll head straight back to the Hot Spot and hide in my room for a while.'

'Best for you. We are going to markets and some sightseeing. We like mad English dogs in midday sun, okay?' Eric had a speaking style and his mix of metaphors lightened Theo's mood.

'Ok, no worries see you later.'

'See you,' they both waved and threaded down the crowded footpath.

Theo hurried as quickly as his weary body would allow back to the Hot Spot. He stopped out the front. He had the feeling again of being watched and spun around, trying to take it all in. There were too many faces and too many things. He had a deep-down sensation someone was watching him. He stepped inside the doorway and looked though the gap, scanning, scrolling faces. *Theo, you must be imagining it.* Theo's head was thumping again, reminding him he badly needed water. Climbing the stairs took time and effort and by the time he reached the top he had to stand and take a few breaths.

Yuman looked up. 'You okay?'

'Yeah, no worries, I need a minute to revive.' He slumped into a cane chair.

'You find bank okay?' Yuman brought over a glass of water from the filter.

'Thanks. Yes easy, right around the corner but it's a bit hot out there at the moment and I didn't realise how weak I was. Has anyone ..?'

'No.'

'Okay Yuman, first I pay you some money, sort out what I owe you, eh?'

Theo squared up the bill to date and gave Yuman a fist full of ringgits as a tip for looking after him. At first the young man wobbled his head and protested strongly and said, 'No, I can't, it all be part of our service.' Then he smiled and took the money.

Theo smiled. 'I'm off to my room; need a shower and a lie down. If anyone rings please let me know, very important.'

'I understan' no problem.'

Theo slept for the next few hours in airconditioning and when he woke he felt much better. He picked up the book *Beyond Pardon* and flicked to where he left off. He-sped read through details of Hayley's health and his feelings about being locked up. One small section stopped Theo. He looked up at the grubby ceiling and the back of his neck felt warm. He re-read the passage and it moved him, even on the second reading. It reminded him of his short stay in prison only days before and the depth of hopelessness he felt at the time.

... Hayley said at one point: Whilst I was waiting for the court case dealing with one of the minor appeals I was held in solitary confinement over the period of the court hearings. The food was better, the bed was a shade more comfortable and I had a pillow, believe it? (He coughed.) They took me to the exercise yard every day but rarely was there anyone there and if there was we were forbidden to talk. So it was a period where I was isolated except for when I had to answer questions in court. I'd been inside for about three years by then. Anyway I had a lot of time to myself and I got to know this little bird. I put pieces of biscuit on the ledge outside my barred window and slowly moved the crumbs inside over a few days, so it had to come into the cell. I talked to that bird and it fed out of my palm. It chirped to me every day until one day it didn't come. That was the day I was told my appeal was rejected. How did that little bird know, eh?

As he concluded this story Hayley's eyes moistened and a tear rolled down his cheek which was a poignant reminder of his humanity.

The interview at times was bullet form, questions and answers, and Theo skipped through. There were references to the feeling of desperation, the sounds and behaviour of other prisoners and guards which resonated strongly with Theo, given his recent experience.

Theo turned off the airconditioner and dozed for a while under the fan. He woke to his personal alarm clock late afternoon. The thunder rumbled and cracked and a thwat followed, lighting up the room. He sat for ages at the window, feeling the surrounding atmosphere turn from hot and humid to an almost unbearable degree of humidity. The air seemed to become clearer or maybe less dense for a few minutes because street noises carried clearly to his room. Then there was a rapid drop in temperature and the wind before the tropical rain exploded from the granite grey sky.

Theo's head was filled with a myriad of thoughts; his location, the things that had happened since leaving Australia, enemies, police, jail, heat, humidity, tropical rain, noise and air pollution, vastly different cultures and new friends. And beautiful Biru. All reflections spun from top to bottom and bottom to top like a gambling slot machine looking for the winning combination. He knew there was nothing forthcoming. He had to make things happen, but how? *You only win by going in hard, Theo.* The only problem was, he felt ill, hammered and humiliated. He knew he had to kick it.

Chapter Thirty-Six

Over many days, Theo nursed himself, drinking water, sleeping and reading extracts from *Beyond Pardon*.

A knock on the door roused him. Yuman told him the doctor's friend was outside requesting payment for services. Taking his empty water bottles, he walked out and shook hands with the man who identified himself with a plastic card with his photo and the name of the clinic. Theo paid what he thought was a very low consultation visit fee. He figured medical attention in Malaysia didn't attract the same level of remuneration as was the case in Australia. The messenger handed over another card with an appointment for Theo in two days' time. It was only after that, Theo thought about Mahmoud and the card being forged. However, Yuman seemed to know him.

After the man departed, Theo asked almost sheepishly. 'Has anyone rang ..?'

Yuman answered before he had finished. 'No Mr Theo, nothing. I will surely let you know if anyone does, okay?'

'Yeah, thanks mate. Have you seen Eric and ..?'

Yuman was on to it. 'Yes, they have gone to their room to rest.'

'Thanks.' Theo filled his bottles and returned to his room. He scribbled a note, asking them to let him know if they were going out to eat later, and slid it under his Swedish friends' door.

Theo slept and read *Beyond Pardon*. He smiled at some of the comments made by Morgan in relation to having to provide cigarettes and whiskey to overcome any obstacles that stood in the way of organising interviews with Roland Hayley. He also noted the interview seemed very formal and Morgan made comment that personally he wasn't sure if he could continue because he wanted to get to the heart of it all, the life of a drug trafficker, life inside, how it felt having the death penalty pending. Hayley looked ill and there was always the chance he would lose interest and discontinue the interviews. Also Morgan was mindful the Malaysian authorities could easily cancel the whole exercise. Into this mix was the chance there was still hope of a reprieve and that would have a dramatic effect on things.

Morgan made the point that the quantities Hayley had been involved with, between 50 and 100 grams, were minor compared to the big dealers who moved kilos at a time, but still, it was high-grade heroin.

Theo rubbed his eyes. He had drifted off, he thought so anyway. The book had slipped off his lower chest and had closed in the process. He put the book on the bedside table and lay back again. An interesting story; he was amazed that young people were doing all these things with their lives, living well and truly on the edge while he was booting a football around and at times feeling guilty because he had a puff of dope, smoked cigarettes, got drunk every now and then or had sex with a woman whenever he had an invitation. He still worked hard to keep his mother from finding out about his private life, whilst Hayley and his associates lived a vastly more dangerous and exciting life away from the constraints of home.

Not long after, Eric and Franka called in. Theo, although definitely on the mend, couldn't face going out. They offered to bring him something so they headed out to eat and wander the markets of the city. The call to prayer once again drifted in from surrounding mosques and it seemed to him the muezzins were signalling and encouraging each other. For some reason it made him think of home and a need to tell his mother. But tell her what?

Theo swallowed some more medications and fell into a restful sleep. Later that night the Swedish couple dropped off some samosas, fried rice and fruit. Theo was grateful because by then he was hungry.

'Eat up, we drink,' said Eric whipping the lid off a beer with Theo's Swiss Army Knife. 'We were issued dese when in army training. Bloody useless except for taking off bottle top lids, yah!'

Eric always managed to create a laugh.

The fan clicked away and they talked. The Swedes were both two years older than Theo but like him, had finished university courses, Eric engineering and Franka accountancy and financial management. The education system in Sweden allowed and encouraged students to leave school, work for a couple of years and then embark on a tertiary course. Eric had done two years the equivalent of Army Reserve which focused mostly on physical fitness and the use of small arms. Franka had worked in tourism, helping a friend whose business entailed taking people for walks in mountainous regions, summer and winter.

They discussed the education systems of their respective countries. Theo felt a kinship with them and told them more about his father and the reasons he was in Malaysia. They knew Theo suspected Mahmoud had planted drugs in his room and it was obvious to the Swedes that Theo was more than interested in Biru. They were also aware Biru had gone into hiding from Mahmoud. He almost told them that she had contacted him but thought better of it realising how much danger she was in.

'Have you heard from her?' enquired Franka.

He had to say no. He weighed it up quickly. Who would they tell? He didn't know where she was … what was the harm?

'Do I have your word ..?'

They both leant forward. 'Of course.'

'Well, yeah I have, she sent me a letter. I have no idea where she is though, all I know is she is safe, that's all the info in the letter.' He didn't want to expand. 'She's pretty cluey; she sent the letter via a friend who reposted it here in Kuala Lumpur. I guess she figured if anyone, and it seems to include her step-parents, had any idea of where she was … is, well …' Theo shrugged.

Franka mused, 'It seems strange that they would let her …'

'From what I gather though, her father, um stepfather was dead keen for her to marry into the hotel chain.' Theo referred again to the proposed marriage of Biru to Mahmoud. 'Worse still is that her stepfather was aware that Mahmoud had beaten her and it seems he didn't do anything about it, seemed to think it was okay, bastard!'

The other two looked at Theo with concern.

'Anyway,' he added, 'all I can do is wait for her to contact me again, if she ever does.'

Eric said. 'Hey man, do you really want to get mixed up with dis shit, you know, us Europeans are different to you Aussies and all dat but Islam, big difference? Man, Mahmoud sounding like a bad-ass.'

All Theo could say was, 'I hear what you are saying. Anyway, like I say, I may never hear from her again.' Saying it made his heart contract.

Eric butted out his smoke and finished off his beer.

Franka held Theo's gaze and smiled the slightest. She knew.

Theo changed the subject and talked about the book *Beyond Pardon*, telling his new friends about the lectures the journalist had conducted during his course. Then they pored over pictures and details and made plans for the next day. Pudu Prison.

Pudu

Chapter Thirty-Seven

The next morning Theo checked with Yuman to see if anyone had called. He was not surprised to find no-one had but he was still disappointed. He had been shown and he was now able to make phone calls without help. The area codes, extra numbers and other ambiguous instructions were confusing for anyone not familiar with the system. He tried Brian but the number rang out. He rang Jack and left another message with a male person this time who at least did speak good English and did confirm Jack was still there.

Theo felt much better and looked forward to the visit to Pudu Prison. He was showing Yuman the book and discussing the pamphlet when Eric and Franka entered.

Eric said, 'Selamat pagi.'

Theo nodded and Yuman smiled at the way Eric said, 'Sell-a-mat perggi.'

'Is s'lamat pahgi, roll letters together,' said Yuman.

'Right.'

'You no need to have guide at prison today, follow details in here.' He pointed to the pamphlet and the book. Theo had shown him the book the day before.

At eight thirty in the morning the tropical sun beat down on top of the traffic fumes and noise. Theo was prepared this time, with his hat, sunglasses and bottle of water. They weaved their way towards Jalan Pudu, making sure they kept with the crowd because to cross on a green light, even though legally correct, could easily have meant being hit by a vehicle. The locals knew the way to do it and that seemed to include the local dogs and the odd monkey. Dempster, who actually lived in a number of big South East Asian cities, had advised him to stick with the local people when trying to cross the road. The three joined in the foot traffic and dodged hawkers selling everything imaginable. Eric still attracted boys who showed a keenness to shine his sandals. An old Chinaman tapped Theo on the arm and pointed to his badly worn thongs. They stopped to look at his wares spread out on the pavement, shoes of all types, including the tiny slippers Chinese women used to wear. Theo thought maybe in some of the homes hidden away in this strange place they still did. He smiled at the ludicrousness of the man's vending space because the tarp was spread out in the middle of the footpath, clearly a huge inconvenience to everyone but no-one seemed to care.

Theo picked a pair of rubber thongs but was shocked to find out the Chinaman wanted more than he paid for the pair he brought from Australia. Eric roared with laughter, so did the vendor and Eric took over the bargaining. They settled on a price half what was asked and everyone, especially the Chinaman laughed like mad.

As they continued on their way the Chinaman said, 'Aha, you have tip for old Chinese man?' Theo wondered where he had heard a similar request before. The three tourists shook their heads to indicate negative. 'You have cig'rette?'

Eric bellowed with laughter again and gave him one as they moved on past the Puduraya Bus Station.

'Well I'll be stuffed.' Theo tapped Eric on the shoulder and quickly pulled out his instamatic.

An elephant decorated in colourful artwork and complete with a turbaned mahout was walking down the street. The massive animal seemed oblivious to the busy traffic, noise and fumes. The three tourists stared until the elephant was out of sight.

Theo wondered why he had not noticed the Old Woman from Borneo after they left the Hot Spot. It occurred to him, he couldn't recall seeing her yesterday either but he wasn't really on top of things then. The morning was hot and humid and they stopped near the prison, at a small hole in the shopfronts, for an ice-cold drink.

Pudu Prison loomed ahead, mysterious and foreboding, separated from them by a busy roadway. The jungle scene painted by an inmate, described by Morgan as in the Asian style, was eerily realistic to Theo on this hot humid morning. The mural seemed to him almost like a bad 8mm home movie, blurred and punctuated by the avalanche of vehicles whizzing past. When the lights changed the traffic did not seem to want to let them proceed. Eventually they chanced it with the others and threaded their way through the vehicles that refused to stop on the red light.

Theo recalled Spud Morgan's description of his first visit. Penjara Pudu 1895, written in stone, no need for more information, identified the menace of its interior. Two towers stood at attention like sentries either side of the main entrance. A band of dogs paced along the footpath and growled at each other, probably thinking they were on duty too.

Traffic noise snapped him out of his reverie. The institution was built by the British as the enforcer of colonial law and order on the locals. He could feel the almost hypnotic power of the place even though it had been closed for two months. Barbed and razor wire ran all the way around the top of the wall and was probably rusty when prisoners of war were held there during World War Two. Towers with ski-jump roofs strategically placed would have provided deadly vision for the snipers on duty.

At least a dozen guides and a swarm of touts tried their luck at selling T-shirts, maps and other souvenirs, as well as being of service to anyone who wanted it. Some tourists seemed to think it a good idea to secure a guide because they were keen to find out the history of the place but the three decided not to bother with a guide because they wanted the freedom to wander at will.

There were only a few tourists purchasing tickets as the prison had just opened. The line-up to a makeshift timber stall was short and tickets cheap. Eric and Franka went ahead and they agreed to meet at the large fountain on the west inside at a landmark on the map in twenty minutes. Theo said he wanted to look at the building from outside first.

He guessed nothing had changed since Roland Michael Hayley had been hanged. The big steel main gates were closed but the small entrance door, within the gates, was open and people handed their tickets to an official-looking man in a khaki uniform with a Gestapo-style peaked cap. The small wooden door with steel straps where Morgan had entered to conduct his interviews was situated to the right but locked with a padlock.

Theo stepped back onto the footpath; the touts thought he was leaving so they didn't follow. He wandered along the wall for a distance, taking in the mural. Although a continuous heavy green rainforest, it reminded him of scenes painted on china cups, some of the colours gently washed. He thought it was very well done, even though from a distance it looked more realistic as good scenic artwork paintings always do. He turned the corner and there was the famous sign he recalled seeing at the airport and in the book and brochure, warning anyone who passed of the dangers of drug trafficking.

Parts of the hand painted sign were faint and graffiti artists had defaced areas around it but the sign was intact. He stared at it and read aloud. The message was very clear:

DEATH – THAT'S THE MANDATORY SENTENCE FOR ANY DADA (DRUG) TRAFFICKER IN MALAYSIA. SO BE FOREWARNED.

It was quite elaborate and even though there was a Malaysian-English translation simplicity about it, the way it was presented sent a chill down his spine even though it was so hot and humid.

The traffic noise hammered his head; he had never heard or seen such congestion and noise on any road in his life. The exhaust fumes stung his eyes as he made his way back towards the entrance, past where a mangy bitch, with tits dangling like deflated balloons, looked at him sideways.

'Out the way doggie, I'm a tourist,' he said and the approaching touts took that as a signal to try to engage him again. 'No thanks, fellers, I'm right,' and he stepped forward waving his ticket and handed it to the man with the Gestapo cap.

Once inside it was free of opportunists trying their scams or selling their wares. Theo walked around to the side where Spud Morgan had entered. The concrete office complex was blocked off by ropes loosely strung across the entrance. The area was clearly unused and almost in disarray and it had become a wind trap with dust and litter gathered in the corners. The barred doors were open so he snuck in. Even though this was for admin duties only, the place made him shiver for a moment in the humid air.

He wandered out into a large stone courtyard shepherded by two stone buildings coming to a vee. According to the map, this was the northern end and only part of the jail complex. People, mainly westerners, chatted to their guides and ambled around or sat on stone steps to absorb the atmosphere. Some murmured to each other, others consulted their guidebooks or brochures. The occasional small group of tourists was herded by an enthusiastic guide through a concrete opening or past a steel entrance. Signs, some in English but most in Malay, made it clear to all as to the fact that the place had been well under the heel of authority in its heyday.

The buildings were three-storey with arches and bars everywhere and the paintwork, which was likely lime wash, had begun to peel, and some sections of wall needed replastering. Being a tourist haunt the place was generally clean and tidy, not like the reception alcove that Morgan had been introduced to on his visits to interview Hayley. The buildings had a greyness to them and it was unlikely it was much better when it was operational. Theo strolled further into the central area, up some worn flagstone steps to a long corridor with barred archways every four or five metres, and sat down on a stone window ledge. The quietness of the place was eerie, almost like the feeling he experienced on his rare visits to a church or cathedral.

He looked up at the high ceilings and listened to the strange dead echoes bouncing around. Theo noticed most people seemed to treat the place with reverence, as if it truly was a special place. There was nothing majestic about it but the people mingling or sitting tended to speak quietly and so far he had not heard anyone laugh. Intermittently a loud voice would bounce off the concrete or a tour guide would bark something but mostly the mood was sombre. Every so often, someone would open and close a steel barred door and the clank it made sounded like nothing else. He also noticed, at least so far, no one had brought children along for a visit or tour. Who would, to such a sad place, full of nothing but misery? He looked out through the bars and mesh towards the other buildings. The slight septic smell of drains intermittently wafted through the humid, fetid air to add some more authenticity. Several scratched, painted or penned messages around the alcove caught his eye and reminded him of his recent experience. Who would know how anyone in this situation felt unless they had actually experienced it themselves?

He wanted to just sit and be part of the atmosphere. Theo felt a strong need to connect with Hayley and Spud Morgan whilst he was actually in the prison, so he opened the book to the section where Spud was interviewing Hayley about his drug smuggling. Hayley explained in some detail how he had brought heroin into Malaysia and where he had sourced it from: Pakistan, India, Burma and Afghanistan. Theo smiled at the ingenuity of it all. The smuggling group used names of Indian chiefs and Greek and Roman Gods for codenames – they were well structured and seemingly those at the top were very careful.

M: So you had no idea who you were working for?
H: Not specifically, no, but I had an idea. I mean, yeah I know they were involved in the night life, you know, bars, prostitutes, that sort of shit, and of course this gave them plenty of contacts for distribution via the backpackers at all the beach and touro resorts around the place. This part of the world is thick with touros, a readymade market. Ya godda dabble a bit in drugs if you are a backpacker, don't cha? When I first started off doing it for myself I had no trouble selling Buddha sticks and blocks of hash and then of course later on, heroin. The Puduraya Bus Station was the best place here in KL. Bus comes in; touros get off, nudge and a wink, piece of cake, readymade market. It was especially easy with the young ones, away from home, crazy for some artificial stimulants, crazy for adventure. They are all at it, rooting, getting pissed, taking drugs, all their defences down, for many, common-sense out the window, perfect customers ...

Something made him look up. He looked through the bars and mesh directly at the ground floor. A dark face was there, and then it wasn't. *Not again!* There was clearly no-one there now by the pillar, only a small tour group, probably university students, ten metres over to the right. He heard a shuffle along the corridor and turned his head quickly.

Chapter Thirty-Eight

'Aha, ve thought you had been locked away or fallen in de water trough at de other fountain,' laughed Eric, his big head poked around the corner. Franka's more delicate face appeared below.

Theo glanced at his watch. 'Oh sorry, I got carried away ... er reading.' He held the book out as if it would prove it.

'Dat is okay, we figured you are lost, easy to do, such a big place,' offered Franka coming into view around the corner. Theo had a momentary glimpse of the outline of her shapely body highlighted by the light from the barred window opposite. 'Here, let me look.' She looked at him with her Nordic blue eyes, took the book from him and then absently flicked through a few pages.

Theo instantly thought of Biru, the hot water service incident, her young, lithe body, hidden in nun's garb. Eric came over and sat beside him. All three were lost in their own thoughts for a few minutes.

Eric said, 'You know, dere is a man down dere, I think maybe he iss following you? Remember when we went out for walking, before you go to prison, and you mention dat? Well, down dere but don't look now, near dat pillar. I know dese things from army training.'

'Yes, I had a suspicion a few minutes ago.' Theo glanced out of the corner of his eye but could see nothing.

Franka looked up. 'Why would anyone be following you?'

'I really don't know but I intend to talk to Joe, the lawyer.'

They nodded.

'I will investigate.' Franka flattened herself against the wall.

Eric wagged his finger, 'Spy versus spy,' and laughed, obviously thinking it was funny.

Theo's forehead tightened. 'Look, I have no idea who could be following me but either way, we should be careful. If you are with me then you are, maybe not in danger, but um … implicated?' He turned the last part into a question.

Eric said, 'Franka, she iss experienced, like Jimi Hendrix, no?'

Theo had to laugh. 'What do you mean?'

Franka said, 'He means I am good at surveillance. I worked with a company, really a friend who do adventure activities, hiking, kind of war games, you know, teams of people, storming the fort, dat type of thing.'

Theo's look asked the question.

'Well one team is to spread out and stop de other team from storming dat hill and grabbing de flag. Also we have surveillance exercises where people have to go from a place and try to outwit and also spot the person or people following. Great fun, especially in city crowds. Okay, I go and investigate but only observe. My job as instructor anyway.' She smiled. 'You wait here for five minutes and then go to the museum in Death Row, okay. I will join you dere.'

Theo was about to suggest she didn't go when she slipped back around the corner out of sight.

'Aha, she go for quick look, yah?' said Eric. 'We stay here and pretend it still us three here, talk to wall as if Franka still here so whoever is watching think we are a team still here. Yah? Franka champion at this surveillance, won prizes so don't worry.'

Eric offered Theo a cigarette. He felt well enough to have another go and the first drag was heaven. They stood there and traded small talk, blowing smoke at the peeling lime-wash walls and mouldy ceiling. The sounds of distant footsteps, clanks of steel and the strange collection of other eerie sounds added to the solid but almost supernatural feel of the place.

After the five minutes, as instructed, they made their way along the corridor to the end, down the steps and into the exercise yard. The Y-shaped steel posts holding the razor wire surrounding the yard seemed almost to be sentries on duty themselves. The presence of wire, bars and mesh, although in stages of rust or disrepair, left the visitor or the inmate in no doubt as to the restrictions in every direction. The concrete floor and, in some parts, flagstones were cracked, stained and worn.

Theo pretended not to look around but he tried to be a spy. It was apparent to him he wasn't very good at it. He couldn't see anyone in particular, but he could see everyone and any one of them had the potential to be following him. They walked past a row of cells, most with steel barred doors open, to a sign designated the *Death Row Museum*. The super security precautions were obvious.

A guard sitting at a desk smoking a cigarette looked up as they walked past, smiled and said, 'S'lamat pagi.'

It reminded Theo he needed to purchase a better dictionary or phrasebook. Franka was not there. They looked up and down the corridor before going inside where two other people, probably a couple, were examining the locked glass cases.

The room had a drainy whiff and was very hot and humid. It occurred to Theo it was that way by circumstance as much as design. A rack much like an easel stood in the corner with a photo of an inmate, buttocks exposed with a guard holding a cane, obviously ready to lash the prisoner. Along from there was a peg-board with a selection of canes used for whipping, several pieces of chain, handcuffs and various limb-restricting implements. Photos of gruesome matters adorned the walls and the glass cases contained items of interest, homemade knives and tools made from all sorts of things.

At the end of the room was a door with a grubby sign that said, '*Gallows.*' Theo surmised the sign was probably added for the benefit of tourists. A condemned man, having arrived there, would know what was through that particular door. Several glass cases had some early model prison uniforms, some with the guard's clothing and weapons necessary to retain rigid control of the inmates. Moving along, the next glass case had a dummy with a hood covering the head, a noose around the neck and the body dangling with hands behind the back.

The last glass case had another hood and above it dangled the hangman's rope. Theo almost jumped. On the back of the case, seen through the noose, was a picture of Roland Hayley with a deadpan look on his face, almost the slightest of smiles tilting his mouth upwards at the corners. It took a few seconds for Theo to compose himself; he almost felt he personally knew the man. The caption explained a few snippets of Hayley's case and the fact that the hood and rope contained therein was used to actually hang the man himself. Theo stood transfixed and couldn't break his gaze at the photo, it seemed so real.

Suddenly a sense of unease crept through him. Where was Franka? He turned. Eric was not there either. The other two backpackers had also departed. He glanced around quickly, eyes wide, took quick, measured steps to the door and looked out.

Chapter Thirty-Nine

Eric and Franka were leaning against the wall talking. Theo tried not to show the relief he felt.

'Ah there you are, thought you umm … didn't like me,' he quipped. The others laughed.

The guard looked up and smiled. That appeared to be his job as well as make sure no one walked off with any souvenirs from Death Row. Theo was keen to find out about the man who was following him.

Eric read his mind. 'Ve go to coffee shop, yah? Franka and I have seen Death Row before. You finish in dere?'

'Yeah, no worries, let's go.' There was no-one else in the corridor.

The coffee shop, along a covered walkway bordering the exercise yard, was a scattering of wooden tables and chairs. A colourful sign saying *JAIL BREAK* designated the area. Theo smiled; someone had a sense of humour. A huge fan at each corner gave welcome relief from the heat and humidity. About half the tables were occupied but they found a quiet spot in a corner, in front of one of the fans. Franka casually walked over to a table with brochures, maps, books and other tourist paraphernalia. She sidled back to their table.

A slim, young Malay in a white sarong, who could have been 16 or 25 years old, took their order.

Franka leant forward. 'Dis man is not very good at his job. He didn't even know I was keeping a watch on him. He vas watching us from de guard tower. He cannot see us now because our table is out of view but I predict he will come down from dere and appear somewhere near.

Don't look.' She hid her pointing index finger behind the map. 'Maybe at end of here. I sneak very close to him, Chinese Oriental-looking man, not very professional.'

Even in front of the fan, a bead of sweat trickled down Theo's back. 'I can't work this out.'

Eric handed around cigarettes. 'If he vas Mahmoud's man he would be Malaysian, wouldn't he not be?'

That idea had crossed Theo's mind as well. Thoughts spun in his head. Surely Mahmoud wouldn't consider him a threat anymore? Even Mahmoud couldn't give Theo so much credit that he believed Theo and Biru had cooked up her disappearance. Three mugs of coffee and three Coca Colas arrived. The young man gave a humble smile.

Eric made a fist and laid it on the table. 'Maybe ve confront Mr Chinese man and rough him up, yah?' He looked at the other two, eyebrows blond and in a hard line. Then he lifted them and laughed. 'Just kidding.' Several other patrons looked up at the big Swede.

Theo exhaled. There was no way he was going to confront anyone but the whole thing of being followed disturbed him.

Franka slowly stood. 'I go and check out our guy.' Before anyone could say anything she went to the bookstore again.

Theo turned to Eric. 'Mate, I don't get this, just don't get it.'

They sat in silence. Theo yawned and it reminded him to drink more water. He took some tablets and guzzled. He looked over to where Franka was supposed to be but she wasn't there. He felt the presence of someone and a blob of sweat started the journey down his back again. She appeared from behind.

'I have been around de perimeter and I find him walking towards the entrance. He walked through and I go up to guard tower and I observe him crossing road at the lights and keep going. I'm sure he didn't see me but …' she shrugged.

Theo exhaled. 'Are you sure ..?'

She said quickly, 'Oh yes definitely, he was following you because when we were up on ramparts we saw you go upstairs to where we found you. We wander to fountain and then back and he still there looking up at you.'

They finished off their drinks, paid and left. The only things they all wanted to look at were the cells and the hospital.

The areas where the cells were located seemed to Theo to exude an even more depressing feeling. The three of them wandered, all lost in their own imaginations. The top floor where the cells opened off had been painted recently with a shiny paving paint and the walls were in good order and painted a creamy white. Up and down the row it looked almost neat and tidy but Theo guessed that was because the guards had full control of this terrain, different to the exercise yard and the open sections of buildings where graffiti, scratches and grubbiness reigned. A strip of solid mesh down the centre between the ceilings made it perfectly clear to anyone there was no way out through there.

The other floors had caged fluorescent lights in the corridors which gave the place a dull respectability. The cells in some parts had arched doorways and others a normal rectangular doorframe. They all had barred doors and a number. Signs directed inmates in English and Malaysian as to what they could and couldn't do. The natural light through the bars was reasonably good and Theo could imagine prisoners being able to read and play cards. The order and relative neatness and cleanliness changed inside the cells. Every room had dozens of sayings, anecdotes, messages or brandings on the walls. The writings were in English, French or a European language but the rest appeared to be Indonesian, Malaysian and possibly several Oriental dialects. This indicated that prisoners of probably every country on earth had spent some time in there. Often crude drawings or scratched outlines of male and female genitals and sexual acts decorated the walls. Grubby, chipped and peeling graffiti scarred the surfaces and Theo wondered what stories they told. He remembered Roland Hayley talking about the violence and bullying in such a place, and the feeling hung in the air. In some cells were intricate beautifully painted murals of countryside and beaches, and some were finely detailed artwork like eastern religious paintings, obviously done by really talented people. Surprisingly, or maybe not, most of these wonderful pieces of artwork were not defaced like most official signs, with lewd sexual drawings and common graffiti. Theo thought maybe there was honour or recognition of greater art among thieves?

The cells were harsh; everything, including the bunk, was made of concrete and a notice on the wall indicated that up to a dozen prisoners had to live in a space not much bigger than a small caravan. A glance at the toilet bucket made Theo sweat and a bad memory came back of his stay in prison only a week ago. Although these toilet buckets were clean and set up as a reconstruction Theo could imagine how bad it would have been. His body began to quiver and a claustrophobic feeling came on and made him sweat even more. His head had been tight from the recent illness and this confinement brought on a real headache again. An image of his mother and father came into his mind. And then Biru. His eyes pooled with water. He needed company, had to get out of there.

Theo caught up with the others when he had composed himself. 'I reckon I've had enough. I might wander to the front gate via the hospital.' Eric and Franka were almost through as well, and agreed.

'Have you seen old mate, you know, our ..?' Theo asked.

Old mate threw them but Eric understood quickly. 'No, ve have been searching for him but I think he hass gone.'

Theo drained his bottle and, although it tasted like warm swimming pool water, he was grateful for it. The day was very hot now and he quickly examined the hospital area and sat down for a minute. The whole complex silently required the visitor to take a moment and contemplate, take it all in. The medications he had been taking made him tired and his thoughts shifted to the situation he was in. He could see his football coach clearly at three-quarter time. *'Come on fellers, you're five points down and kicking into the wind, you've been training all year for this, one quarter of football in your whole life. Come on you bastards, let's get out there and win!'* He shook his head; maybe there was plenty at stake right here in Malaysia, right now. Sure, he could bail out and go home. Or he could sort things out as best he could. *And Theo, you kicked that goal, put your team in front. Remember? How could you forget, eh? You were absolutely flattened, received a free kick, could hardly walk but you kicked that ball straight between the big white sticks, ump didn't have to move except signal a six pointer. You were so sore, weren't you? But mate after that goal, you were so high you hardly felt a thing. You played harder after that, right?*

He stood up with purpose and walked towards the front gate. Three dogs started a fight nearby. It didn't last long because a guard threw a lump of concrete in their direction and they scattered yelping. Theo stopped several times and looked up at the imposing buildings, his mind crammed, but somehow he felt stronger about things and he was determined to actually do something rather than wait and have things done to him. Near the entrance he managed to find a section of concrete wall in the shade unoccupied so he sat down. He glanced around but he had shaken off that sinking feeling of being observed.

Shortly after, Eric and Franka appeared and they all walked out into the bustling city, in the direction of the Hot Spot Hotel. Franka suggested she drop back and see if the tail was still at it.

Theo didn't want her to do it, thinking maybe she was putting herself in danger. When he insisted so strongly she could see he was serious, so she agreed. Eric made the joke that he could do the following because no-one would notice a giant flatfooting in amongst the crowd, which lightened the moment.

All Theo could think about was having a long drink of cold Coke and lying down in the airconditioning of his room. But he had some very important things do before becoming horizontal.

Chapter Forty

'Mr Theo, Mr Theo, telephone call for you,' the young man said, eyes sparkling.

'Who?' he panted. His heart raced, and not from the climb. Theo had struggled up the steps, leaving the others on a mission to the poste restante.

'Mr Aung, half hour ago. No, he didn't say message only other than you ring back soon. You can use office. I organise ring back timing for cost?'

Theo was thankful that Yuman understood he didn't want to talk in front of anyone in the main reception area. Also the return walk from Pudu Prison had tired him. His hands shook slightly as he fingered the dial on the desk phone. He sincerely hoped Brian was there. What was the message?

Theo waited, glancing up at the wobbly fan. The strange ringtone burred in his ear. As the seconds passed, his disappointment grew and he dreaded the connection running out. Brian picked up. Theo wondered if the other man heard his sigh of relief. Brian, in his infuriating way, took some time to relay the news. Biru had rung and there was a number for Theo to ring.

Theo's heart leapt as he fossicked around in his day pack, like a man wearing welder's gloves, for a pen that wouldn't work until he had scribbled an Olympic Games collection of circles. He had to ask Brian to repeat the number to make sure it was correct.

'Make sure you say your name is Walter Graves from the Australian Embassy and ask for Farah Mahomed, alright?' Brian pre-empted the question. 'She is being very cautious; she says there could be people listening in.'

'Yep got it, Walter Graves and Farah Mahomed.' He scribbled the names down. In his haste to hang up and ring Biru he nearly forgot to ask about Jack.

'Oh, Jack is still being Jack, the mystery man.'

Theo closed his eyes and pressed them shut. 'Yes and..?'

'He rang me from hospital in Bangkok and he said he would ring you soon.'

'Why doesn't he ring me? I have left two messages for him; I get a different person each time.'

'Yes, he is hard to catch.'

Theo rolled his eyes and asked again. 'When is he going to ring me?'

'Very soon, be patient. Communication by phone in Asia is not as easy as it is in your country.'

Theo was going around in circles. He wanted to talk to Biru. He took a deep breath. 'I'd better go, thanks Brian. Um … I'll be coming to Penang soon and I look forward to meeting you.'

'Of course, and I look forward to meeting you. Jack has told me so much about you.'

'Okay, mate, if Jack happens to …'

'Yes, it goes without saying, I will let you know but he will be ringing you soon. Mind how you go.'

Theo decided to interpret *'mind how you go,'* as a figure of speech like *'see you'* or something similar. A trickle of sweat rolled down each side of his face and made his new beard itch.

His index finger traced the numbers, trying to go slowly so he didn't make a mistake. A woman picked up and rattled off in what Theo thought to be Malaysian.

'Excuse me … er maaf, permsisi … mm do you speak ..?'

The woman on the other end sounded like she smiled, and switched to English. 'Yes of course, this is administration, what can I do for you today?'

'My name is Walter Graves from the Australian Embassy. Could I speak to er … Farah Mahomed please?' He hoped the woman wouldn't ask anything more.

'Please wait a minute; I will see if she is in.'

From that click to the next click was the longest minute he had ever experienced.

Click. 'Yes, she is coming to the phone and is now entering from another room. Please don't hang up as we transfer you.' *Click*.

Another click, this one sharper. Theo was becoming good with clicks by now but then ... dial tone. He frowned at the handpiece, swearing under his breath, and put it against his ear again, more in hope than anything else.

Click. Relief, at least the connection was still there like the sound down a long pipe. A few seconds ticked by. 'Hello, um Mr Graves?'

It was her, Biru, her beautiful voice. Theo couldn't speak for what seemed like minutes. A feeling of panic-stricken warmth spread over him.

'Mr Graves?'

'Er ... yes, Miss ... um Farah Mahomed?'

She laughed. 'Yes.' She whispered, 'for the moment I am being that person. You are Australian Embassy and I applying for visa endorsement in case anyone is asking here, okay? I really thought you would not ring me, I say to myself why you would be getting mixed up with problems for me.'

Theo's tongue was tangled but he managed to say, 'When ... when can I see you?' It sounded stupid to him and he thought it must have to her.

It sounded as if she smiled. 'We don't have much time, the longer we talk the more chance there is being for someone to listen in and get ideas. I still have not my passport but I have friends here and they try to help me. Can I meet you? I have been thinking of nothing else but you since ...'

He didn't know what to say. 'Yeah, sure, where ... when?' He could picture her, smartly dressed, eyes flashing, hijab framing her face.

'I cannot tell you where I am right now but I will go to where your contact is, I have friends there. I also know your other friend is to be there soon, too. I hope to arrange the transport within three or four days. I say no more, okay?'

He was mesmerised by the way she spoke.

She said, 'Mr Graves, are you still there?'

'Um ... yes.' He came to, and smiled at the absurdity of it all. 'I'm going to ...'

'Yes, I know you are to be doing that and we will use our contact number and I will advise further. Important, do not ring here again, okay? Ears maybe in walls,' she said in a breathy whisper, 'I cannot wait to see you.'

'Yes ...' He was not sure what he was answering. 'I really want to see you too.' He thought it sounded a bit limp.

There was a noise at the other end, maybe a door slamming? She whispered, 'Yes, me too, quick I must go,' and then much louder, 'Thank you for contacting me, Mr Graves, I must go, please.' The line went dead.

177

Chapter Forty-One

Theo sat under the wobbling fan smiling for a few minutes. All he thought about was her saying she had been thinking of nothing else but him. A noise outside, in the street, in the reception area, he didn't know from where but it jolted him into reality. His scalp tightened. Theo knew he couldn't have asked where she was, but that was a positive. He forgot to ask *how* she was, did she know where Mahmoud was, what was the situation with her family, and did she have enough money? He had made the phone call reasonably sure of what he was going to say. Sitting there in the storeroom he reckoned he'd made a botch of the whole thing. He needed to tell her how much he wanted to see her; he was *longing* to see her. Then he began to feel like an idiot, doubt crept in. He tried to think back to what she said. Did she mean she was thinking of nothing else but him, literally, or was it only polite conversation? Then, the abrupt ending – had she been discovered?

Theo put his head in his hands and rubbed his face. The headache was back with a vengeance. He needed more water and paracetamol. He told himself to snap out of it and look at the positives. She made it clear she wanted to see him, what more did he want. 'Right, Theo, it's all okay at the moment,' he said aloud.

He walked out to the reception area.

Yuman looked up. 'Yes sir?' said the young man, full of enthusiasm.

Theo stood up straight, making an effort to at least appear to be on top of things. 'Yep, no worries, I need some water but I still have to make a couple more calls, okay.'

He filled his bottle and returned to the wobbly fan.

Theo dialled Jack's number and grumbled, 'Come on, come on,' the whole time and then added, 'that'd be right,' when it rang out.

Next call was to Josef Ibrahim. He explained the situation about the person following him, pointing out that the man looked Oriental rather than Malay. Joe was surprised because he said he thought Mahmoud was elsewhere and he didn't know who could be doing it. Theo asked him to dig up information, anything he could on Mahmoud. Joe promised to speak to his people and get back to him.

Theo hung up and sat rubbing his temples in contemplation for a few minutes, trying to get his thoughts in some sort of order. He was not over the illness and was aware he should not overdo it. He went to his room and lay down.

'Biru Biru,' he murmured to the clicking fan but he was asleep in seconds.

Chapter Forty-Two

Theo sat up with a start. Thunder reverberated. It took a few nervous seconds to orientate himself. The events prior to collapsing appeared before him one by one. Pudu Prison, Roland Hayley, his Swedish friends, being followed by an Oriental type, Brian Aung, no Jack. Biru. Biru? It took a few seconds to remember that he had spoken to her on the phone.

Then a dark thought pressed on him. The fact that he hadn't asked whether she was okay or not plagued him. Was her face still bruised? He reassured himself that she was okay and they were soon to meet again in Penang. Theo drank some water and it occurred to him that he felt better as well as hungry. A shower later and feeling positive, Theo knocked.

Eric opened up. 'Ah, you look more well than before.'

'Yeah, much better. Look, I might go and get something to eat; do you and Franka want to join me?'

'No thanks, we arrive back only a short time ago, maybe after rain completes, yah?'

'Sure, we can meet at the Splendid Coffee House on the corner, perhaps on dark?'

'Okay, er ... Theo?'

'Yes?'

'Keep to main area and watch for that man who is following you.'

'Yes, right. I had forgotten about it. I will be very careful. I won't be going far anyway, just want to get out of here for a while.'

He stuffed *Beyond Pardon* into his day pack and went to reception.

Small talk with Yuman was always pleasant. He didn't need to ask questions, Yuman read him.

'No, Mr Theo, no phone calls. You feeling better?'

'Much, thanks, mate. Look, it's Theo, not Mr, okay? I'm heading out for a while.'

Theo headed down the stairs and into the late afternoon street life. Bikes, motorised and pedal, battled the bigger vehicles for their right of place on the road and the noise from horns, exhausts and people completed the picture. He was glad of his hat as he became aware of the slightest change in temperature and atmosphere. After a moment he realised how silly he might appear to others standing there looking at the sky for guidance, so he hurried in the general direction of the Splendid Coffee House.

He threaded his way, dodging vendors selling souvenirs, T-shirts, sunglasses and other items of interest to backpackers and tourists. It was hard not to notice the young females. Almost see-through hippy cheesecloth dresses and tops, distinct absence of bras and the outline of panties and his imagination made him shake his head. Some of the northern European women wore short dresses and had beautifully tanned legs going all the way up. It made him wonder what the locals thought of them. He observed several groups of young, local men hanging around and staring at the girls. He shook his head again when thoughts of Biru came into focus.

Suddenly he realised he hadn't checked for anyone following him. Casually he glanced around. At least there was no distinct feeling of being observed.

'Hey, Tuan, Mr White Boss, selamat tengah hari, apa khabar. I have something for you! Very special and only for your eyes.'

He stopped and turned in the direction of the cackle. 'Aha, apa khabar, how goes it, Old Woman from Borneo,' he laughed, a genuine response.

'You have cigarette for poor old woman, tua wanita yah?' She smiled, red teeth and all. Only a small number of books decorated her blanket and this time she had a few tiny statues and strings of beads.

'I bet you say that to all the tourists, Old Woman from Borneo?'

Theo squatted alongside her and pulled out his cigarettes. There was that aroma again, almost familiar and unique. A motherly aura mixed with cloves, jasmine or something he still couldn't identify. She unwound her scarf slightly which revealed her very dark wrinkled neck.

Theo could see clearly the tattoo on the back of her sun-hardened hand. Two silver rings glinted.

'Alright, why not,' he said and made a big deal about offering her one; she took two, dropped one into the tiny wooden box and stuck the other in between her red stumpy gums. Theo laughed out loud as he lit her up. 'You took two.'

'Aha, White Tuan Boss very observant. Now, special evening price.'

'You don't have many books today.'

She took a drag and smoke leaked out her nose and mouth, creating a fog. 'Oh I have plenty, plenty, plenty, but put away ready for afternoon storm coming soon.' Thunder rumbled like a jet taking off in the distance.

'Okay, Old Woman from Borneo, what do you have for me?'

'A book, special phrase and dictionary book of official language of Bahasa Malaysian … very important for you to have for negotiating treacherous foreign country.' She laughed slightly more softly this time, not as sharp, more an old woman's chuckle.

Theo wondered for a moment how she could know he wanted that particular book as he took it from her and looked at the cover. It seemed new, in good condition.

'You need for communication with official government people as well as ordinary people in street. Special price for you …'

'How much?'

'Thirty ringgit.'

'Thirty ringgits? Nah, too much.' Theo remembered the advice; stall for time, don't get pressured, halve it. 'Fifteen.'

'No no no, because this book just for you almost fire sale price. Twenty five!' she snapped, grabbed the book from him and went to wrap it in newspaper.

'Hang on, hang on.' He took it back from her and flipped it over. The recommended retail price was scribbled over. He glanced at her, wondering if he caught a slight smile. 'Fifteen.'

Her look hardened. 'Twenty.'

Come on Theo, stick up for yourself. 'Fifteen.'

He detected an almost offended demeanour cloud her face. It took a cool moment before she spoke. 'Book still have last page, very valuable to have last page in residence, special evening price. Twenty.'

He waited her out, looked around and stalled for another second or two. 'Eighteen.' His calves ached so much he had to stand. She must have thought the deal might be off.

'Okay, okay, old woman most suredly die of neglect and starvation in dirty streets.' She let a moment hang and then added, 'Twenty.'

'What? You said okay to eighteen.'

Thunder shook the buildings and a slight puff of breeze stirred the canvas awnings.

'Twenty last price. Cannot sell less than buying price.' She still held a look halfway between seriousness and being offended.

Come on Theo, don't fall for it. 'Eighteen.'

'You shrewd businessman so young.' Her demeanour changed instantly and she smiled broadly. 'Okay, you win, eighteen. I good mind not to give you complimentary fortune prediction but to seal deal and for good will you give me cigarette and I throw in special fortune extra for free.'

Theo knelt down, smiling.

Thunder boomed and lightning flashed like a wonky fluro.

She wrapped up the book and as he handed her the correct money she grabbed his hand. 'Rain coming now Tuan, Old Woman must go back to jungle.' She laughed again. Her hand was warm and soft. 'Free prediction Tuan as promised for you. Woman in your life in bad situations, be careful you not get used, maybe not your business. Cigarette to clinch deal, yaah?'

'Old Woman from Borneo, you drive a very hard bargain.' He opened the packet, she took two. He raised his eyebrows in mock horror. The air thinned further and smelled sweet. Odd blobs of rain, almost as big as golf balls, hit the pavement five metres apart. He was well aware of the need to find shelter. She gathered her remaining books in the blanket. When she stood he was amazed at how small she was, barely up to his armpit.

The old woman wagged an index finger at him. 'You find out many secrets soon young Tuan, you need to be careful.' She was gone before he could respond. He stood staring, also amazed at how lithe and agile she was.

He wondered again how she knew he wanted a phrasebook. Theo didn't have time to wonder because the blobs of water joined quickly to become tropical rain and he knew he had to move fast. He dashed the twenty or so metres to the awning of the Splendid Coffee House. Wet but not soaked he turned to look at the rain, even though he had seen it almost every day since arriving.

Someone caught his eye for a second and he squinted thought the grey sheets but could no longer see anyone in the doorway. The road in front boiled with water and flooded around the parked bikes and battened-down stall carts. The moving bikes and vendors' barrows quickly found safe destinations or threw sheets of plastic over their wares. Others sheltered from the downpour in shopfronts and doorways.

Followed Again

Chapter Forty-Three

'Over here?' A young waiter beckoned, pointing to a table with a fan overhead. 'You see better and hear good too.' He spoke loudly but the hammering of the rain made it difficult to hear. A Van Damme movie played on a screen nearby.

Theo signed rather than yelled, 'No, here is fine thanks, mate.'

He selected a table away from the street, in the corner where it was shielded from the noise, but not the video screen. Damp clothes made him conscious of catching a chill. He dumped his day pack on the table and sat with a good vista which made him smile, thinking of the cowboy movies where the hero always had his back to the wall. He looked out through the teeming rain and almost convinced himself there was no-one out there trying to get into his head.

Then he saw the man, further along at the next doorway. There was no doubt, it was the same man he'd seen a moment ago but he looked Malay, not Oriental. Theo busied himself opening his backpack for a moment, then pretended to look towards the video screen. Out of the corner of his eye he zeroed in on the man. No doubt about it. Who was he, was it Mahmoud's man? The memory of jail, of being humiliated, of being framed made the hot feeling of anger boil up from deep down. He willed himself to calm down and think of himself as the predator from now on.

Theo sat for a casual while and flicked through the phrasebook.

The friendly young waiter ambled over to his table. 'Hey man, menu?'

Theo reminded himself to remain casual. 'Terima kasih. Is that right?'

The young man smiled, 'No, not spot on, but pretty good. Try to say tree-mah-karssee, like tree. Say T and almost roll reemah, okay?'

'T'rima kasih, how's that?'

'Bang on, mister,' he said.

Theo smiled, very much aware the young in Malaysia might be watching far too many American movies. The aroma of garlic, chilli and other spices tickled his nostrils. He ordered chicken satay and rice with a pot of Chinese tea.

Theo leaned back and massaged his face. His hands slid to the back of his head. The lump from a week ago had gone down but was still tender to touch. A sour memory flashed of the incident when he was shoved, with absolutely no chance of defending himself, backwards into the wall.

Every few minutes he snuck observations out the corner of his vision, easy to do without being spotted because the rain provided a screen. The man was still there.

'Tea, man?'

'T'rima kasih.'

'You goddit.' The young waiter placed the pot on the table and grooved off, eyeing some girls who walked in.

He lit a cigarette and poured a cup. A few leaves floated around the rim and it made him wonder if the Old Woman from Borneo really could read his future. How did she know he wanted a phrasebook? How did she know he was involved with a woman? How did she know this woman was in a jam? It was dead easy to come up with those predictions. Every tourist wants a phrasebook; most young men would be trying to form a relationship with a woman, the place was crowded with them, travellers and locals. Woman in a bad situation? Well, it could mean anything from missing a flight or a bus to losing a passport, or at a stretch, could mean a drug deal gone wrong. And none of his business? If it was a local woman, the family could be after him, if a prostitute the pimp could be after him. If a backpacker? Maybe the boyfriend could be jealous. As far as finding out many secrets? Well, that could apply to almost everyone on earth.

Theo picked up the phrasebook again and smiled, content with the thought he got the old lady back from ripping him off last time. He turned the book over and glanced at the recommended retail price, too hard to read as it had been scribbled out. His eyes opened wide when he noticed another sticker underneath. It took a couple of careful minutes to peel it off without damaging the writing. The recommended retail price was 16 ringgits. He burst out laughing; she had done it to him again. A couple of backpackers looked up from another table; obviously his laugh had been louder than Van Damme machine gunning bad guys down. The whole mini adventure with the old woman gave him a warm feeling and he didn't care if she had the upper hand, it was not being cheated, it was the way business was conducted.

Theo was concerned, however, about the man across the street. He feigned a glance in that direction, with a pretend look at the menu, and turned his head at the same time. The man was still there. *Well I'm watching you now, mate.* His outward bravado did not match his internal reservations.

Food arrived. The heavy effect of chilli and delicacy of the other hidden spices made it very tasty. Since arriving in this strange land he had been intrigued by the food stalls and the huge variety of things available. Now he was feeling better in the stomach he pledged to try something new each time, if possible. The restaurants ranged from low cost – what he called 'chew and spew' – right through to high-end expensive dining and they tended to sell their own version of general fare with a few different things available. Some restaurants were very western with Mexican tacos and American hamburgers, set up mainly for tourists. The street food was a whole different thing and stalls sold just about every type of Asian food, meal or snack ever invented plus more creative things for the adventurous. Theo could imagine this type of food being sold to locals for hundreds of years.

The rain still fell but appeared to be easing and pedestrians began to dart from shelter to shelter. He picked up *Beyond pardon* and continued reading. The detail seemed to drone on, as often is the case with non-fictional accounts of events, but occasionally something would stand out. His mind wandered, thinking of ideas for his life as a journalist.

∞

Theo jolted into reality at a bark from a motorbike in the street. He wondered if he would ever get used to the noise. Familiar music cranked up from the other room. Jimmy Barnes. He smiled; Jimmy was loud even when the video clip was turned down. Over the road, the Malay man was still in the same spot.

He put the book down and rubbed his eyes. The rain stopped and the cloud cover dissipated, bathing everything in late afternoon light. The air had a clean quality to it but he knew it wouldn't last with all the traffic.

Theo opened *Theo's Adventures*. He had not expanded on very much so far, however. His overall intention was to document everything, important or not, and then expand, delete and rehash later on. All this he had learnt in his university studies and the presence of the book *Beyond Pardon* had given him incentive. Maybe the Old Woman from Borneo was correct; possibly he had been subconsciously looking for it when she appeared out of nowhere and presented it. Theo thought it was a very unlikely scenario.

He decided to write in diary format with the idea to use sections of it if when he was trusted to write an article or a column. Also the possibility of using the information in a longer piece appealed to him. He thought about the job at The Adelaide Advertiser, due to start in a month's time. Theo had been overwhelmed with joy, when he received the acceptance letter in December, not so much that the job was the best in the world, but it was a job and several of his university friends had not as yet managed to secure employment. The position entailed research on various projects for news and current affairs as well as assistance to the reigning journalists with regular columns. He was told the sports editors jealously guarded their areas but he was encouraged to not let that deter him from whatever he wanted to pursue. His new boss had suggested Theo jot down anything he saw or experienced on his trip so that it could be used at a later date. He was promised that within a few months he would be able to write an article, short though it may be, as it was the tradition for the chief editor to allow all the newcomers the chance to establish themselves with something of their own. Theo already knew many of the staff because he had done his traineeship at the newspaper on a casual basis in the printing room and warehouse as well as assisting editors, marketers, financial advisers and political commentators. His supervisor had been very enthusiastic about Theo's Malaysia trip. Theo's application for a small fee was made as a joke and taken as such but he was told if he came back with anything interesting it could be the launch of his career. That was meant in jest too, but Theo could see his trip had been interesting so far, and as long as he managed to document everything, story ideas would become apparent.

Theo did not realise how much he would miss his mother. He didn't realise how much he relied on her and it had become increasingly apparent since leaving how much they actually relied on *each other*. She had impressed upon him the importance of being independent and capable of taking care of his life from an early age. '*Make your bed, tidy your room, wash the dishes or you don't get any pocket money,*' and as he became older, '*mow the lawn, wash the car, do the gardening, do your washing, iron your shirts.*' He smiled, remembering her saying, '*Don't need to iron your underpants, no-one can see them but they have to be clean in case you have a road accident!*' Theo could never work out why someone would look at your undies after an accident, particularly if it was *that* sort of accident. He vowed to ring her soon.

He wrote down points of interest in the book, looking intermittently out at the street scene as if that would trigger inspiration. The pedestrian traffic had increased and any road traffic servicing the restaurants or stalls had ceased, probably because more barriers had been erected restricting some roads to one way. Soon other barriers would go up further down the city blocks and some areas would become malls or restricted traffic for evening and night-time trade.

The humidity level had slowly risen but Theo's clothes were still damp from the shower. The Splendid Coffee House had slowly filled and only a few tables remained vacant. The waiter came over, probably to encourage Theo to buy something more as he was occupying a table for three or four.

'Howya doin,' man. More food, beer perhaps?'

Theo rubbed his jaw, Eric and Franka should arrive soon. His stomach felt ready for a beer. 'Beer thanks, bud.' He added the last bit for a stir.

'You goddit,' replied the young man spinning on a heel, trying to impress two young women who had clearly noticed him.

Theo nodded in their direction; the one in red smiled, which gave him an excuse to look across the road. The man was still there.

He continued to write and look up and around but the feeling of being watched was strongly with him again. It could have been as simple as feeling the gaze of the two female tourists who he did catch glancing at him from time to time. But it was not. He looked up quickly, using the menu again as a shield. The man was still there. Theo was sure he was being watched now, dead certain. He leaned his head against one hand, pretending to write and was able to glance up intermittently and observe the other man from between his fingers. He was Malay in appearance, probably not much older than Theo, short to medium height, casually dressed, greyish shirt, no glasses. Theo smiled dryly at the cliché because the man stood out, reading a newspaper and wearing jeans in the hot weather. He was jolted to attention.

'Beer, dude?' The waiter placed the ice-cold bottle and glass on coasters.

'You bet dude, Tiger okay?' bantered Theo.

'Sure buddy.'

They both laughed. The two girls looked up at them as the waiter flicked his towel from behind his back to flop over his shoulder. A deft move he clearly had practised and thought the girls would be impressed by. He cruised like a film star in the direction of their table.

Day was in the losing battle with darkness and was signalled by the call to prayer from several different directions, like 3D. Bells from the nearby Hindu temple heralded a similar function.

U2's, 'With or without you' came on as the next video clip. The screen was in the other room but it didn't matter to Theo as someone turned up the volume and drowned out the muezzin's call. He poured the beer, lit a cigarette and contemplated his next move. A tap on the shoulder made him start.

Chapter Forty-Four

'Aha Theo, you hide in back.' Eric pulled up a chair alongside. 'Where's Franka?'

'She is meeting a friend from Hollant who is attending conference and is staying in ritzy hotel far from here. She is staying tonight with her and will be getting a taxi back here tomorrow.' He leaned closer to Theo. 'A man, not same man but a man, do not look now but he is standing ...'

'Yes, I've seen him,' said Theo, almost proudly to show he was more observant than before.

'Whoever he is, he is not excellent at his job,' mused Eric.

'I'd like to know what he is doing, I think I will go and confront ...'

Eric waved a forefinger. 'You have bad idea and good idea. I will go and grab him and then *you* confront him while I am holding him clenched.'

A bead of fear journeyed down Theo's back. He wanted to be proactive but was this the way to go? It was clear that Eric could talk this way because he was so big and looked intimidating. However, Theo knew he needed to show some courage in front of his friend. He remembered when he was in jail, the feeling of being on his own, how he puffed himself up, trying to look tough, and those times at the pub when he had to show some bravado. In a pub fight it was important to get the first strike but there was always a good chance you would shake hands afterwards. Confronting a criminal, who could be armed, in a foreign country was an entirely different matter. He tried to block his last thought.

Theo sat up straight. 'Right, mate what do you reckon?'

'Okay, dis is fun but for the moment we have beer and wait for darkness.' He signalled the waiter, pointed to the beer on the table and gave two fingers. 'Drink up Theo; you need the courage of de Dutch.'

The beer arrived. Theo said, 'T'rima kasih.'

The young waiter gave him the thumbs up. 'Hey man, you speak like local dudes,' and wandered off, smiling in the direction of a table full of girls.

Eric ignored the glass, took a long guzzle from the bottle and tabled his guidebook, opening to a flagged page with the map of the city. 'What we do is dis, we wait for about five minutes, be dark then and I pretend to say goodbye to you, I go out front door, make big show of walking to corner, up dat way. We here at present.' He pointed with a big finger. 'I slip into shop doorway and peek out. You walk out of here, do not look in his direction and you go dat way, slow and casual. We haff to make sure he really is following you, can't beat up wrong guy.'

Theo jumped. 'Beat up?'

Eric burst out laughing, 'Kidding, kidding. Okay, back to story. You walk to corner, turn right into Jalan Fee Soon and go to all the way past markets to next corner, and den right into Cheng Lock, over river bridge, right again into Mahkamah and you see railway line on left. You go up past GPO and there is shopping complex.' He traced the route with his finger. 'By den we know for sure if he is following you. Take that road left before building and then go right which is lane behind shopping complex is for goods and storage, you turn down dere. I know it's dere because Franka and me we stop for joint.'

'What?' Theo was feeling hotter than the night was. 'You smoke dope, here in Kuala Lumpur?' His eyes felt as if they would burst.

'Sure, Franka love puff, I only help out not let her do on her own.'

'Christ almighty, mate I spent the worst 36 hours of my life in jail for bloody dope that wasn't mine. I've had the odd smoke at home and I admit I was considering scoring here 'cos I heard things were pretty easy-going in Malaysia but mate, for Christ's sake, be careful. Maybe you should read this book; this'll frighten the shit out of you.' He reached into his day pack and pulled out *Beyond Pardon*. 'Here, take it for a couple of days. There's plenty of research material in there so flick to the bits that are interesting, mainly the interviews with Roland Hayley. I've nearly finished it anyway.'

'Thanks.' He slipped it into his cloth shoulder bag. 'Okay, back to story of surveillance. I will follow you both and when you turn into lane behind shopping complex you walk about twenty metre down, you turn around and walk back. He will be then between you and me. Presto, we catch dis guy in trap.' He leant back looking pleased with himself and took another mouthful of beer.

'Right.' Theo drew the word out, doubt hovered. 'What ... what if he is armed?'

'No problem, dere are workers along further and others walk in and out of roller doors. I know, we nearly get busted by a guy who came out for smoke, proper smoke like cigarette.' He laughed loudly. The two girls a couple of tables away looked up. 'Franka and me we make out we are smooching and playing sex so the guy get embarrassed quick and went the other way. Anyway, so if we confront our guy he won't risk any physical play. We, or you, ask him what he is doing following you and I be right behind him. I know some Asian smart defence moves, we learn in army. If he hit the road well so it is, nothing lost, we play safe, okay all settled.' The last few words were more an order rather than a question.

Theo's mouth had the chalky feeling again. The mouthful of beer didn't make any difference. He knew a cigarette wouldn't help but he flicked out a duty-free and lit up anyway. He pushed the pack towards Eric to give him a minute to think.

Theo was treading water. Eric could see that and opened his palms like an offering. 'What could possibly go wrong, yah? We have it all covered. This is modern city, no one pulls weapons in public and not at tourist anyway as tourist has special police to report any subversive activity.'

Theo felt sure the person following him was one of Mahmoud's thugs. Dangerous as it was, he had a right to find out what was going on; it was time for answers.

Theo sat up straight again, realising he had slumped. 'Okay mate, yep let's do it.'

Eric held up his bottle and they clicked. 'Yah.'

They went over the plan again and to Theo it all seemed so simple but he knew, from playing football, even kicking with the wind, you could still lose.

'He is still dere so I make big issue of going. Hey Theo, those two girls keep looking at us; maybe we come back later and talk to dem for fun. I can tell the one in red is in love for you.' He laughed loudly and went to put money on the table.

Theo waved him away. 'I'll get it, mate.'

Eric stood, winked and laughed as he walked out.

Theo signalled the waiter with the international sign of writing the tab. Sweat dribbled down his back and he wished he was under the fan again. He wasn't sure if it was tension or because it was hot and humid. The humidity had eased up after the rain but he knew it would come back with a vengeance.

The young waiter arrived with the bill a few moments later. He dropped it on the table and was about to skip off when Theo indicated he wanted to pay straight away. He rounded the bill, taking the suggestion from the guidebook about giving a small tip for good service. Also Theo figured he would come back to this place because he liked the waiter and the food was good.

Theo noticed his hand slightly shaking. He stole a sneaky glance at the mystery man who was still there trying to look inconspicuous and he wondered what he was letting himself in for.

Chapter Forty-Five

Theo stood, picked up his day pack and walked past the two girls, smiling as he went. It was slightly cooler outside, a balmy tropical night. Traffic barriers were obviously up and the evening crowds had started to mingle and seek out places to eat. The smell of food drifted tantalisingly, but it was punctuated by a whiff from drains or from the small piles of garbage piled intermittently as if in secret code for the workers. The hum of distant traffic on the motorways rose and fell like the surge of surf in the night air.

He wandered along, pretending interest in street stalls, politely rejecting hawkers, and then turned into Jalan Fee Soon. He glanced in all directions except behind, not wanting to give the stalker any hint. Theo was experiencing high anxiety and it was difficult to give the outward appearance of calmness. He had to keep reminding himself to be steady and hold his nerve.

Even though at times the street was noisy, he found it comfortable not having to dodge motorbikes and cars. As he approached the markets, vehicles were not permitted but motorbikes and rickshaws were. The market area was very crowded and he sped up, hoping his tail could keep up. Sweat soaked his shirt and adrenalin pumped through every part of his body. He swung right into Jalan Cheng Lock, a major road, and the noise and pollution of the night-time traffic hit him hard. In addition to the road congestion, pedestrians of all types jostled for position, some going home, some going out, some trying to sell things, some hanging around looking for opportunities, and some begging.

A man on a skateboard with no legs and one arm scooted with great skill between the waves of people, managing to put up his good hand hoping for alms. Theo stopped to look at the man and almost forgot where he was and what he was trying to achieve. He swallowed a couple of times in mild shock and gave the man some small coins.

A young Indian girl dressed in worse than filthy rags, with a very young baby on her hip, tried to engage him with sad pleading eyes. 'Please mister, pleeeeeez, you give?' He had no more small change and kept walking.

Sweat dripped in his eyes and he pushed and was pushed by the avalanche of people. Then he felt a feather-like touch. Someone slid a hand in his back pocket going for his wallet.

'Hey!' he said, loudly and jabbed his elbow back at that direction.

A slick Asian boy grabbed his ribs and skittled off so quickly that Theo could not have described him if asked. He was thankful he had put his wallet in the front pocket of his shorts anyway. Good old Dempster. A couple of people stopped and stared but basically no-one showed any concern, as if this was normal behaviour.

Some people were in traditional dress of some kind. Men wore various outfits; some in long white shirts and skull caps and braided kurta collars, and others with various headwear, from turbans to coloured cloth, but many were in western dress – trousers, shirts and some even with a tie. Women's attire varied, some in almost jungle garb through to modern clothing, even in high heels. The racial mix amazed Theo and he wondered how they all progressed together with such a variety of religions and ideals. Many, even some in western clothes, chewed betel nut and every so often a corner of a wall was splattered with red juice in a designated spot. Theo thought spitting on the football field was bad enough.

He crossed at the lights with the crowd, making sure to have a group of people on the side where the cars were coming from because some vehicles ignored the red light and manoeuvred their way through the pedestrians. He turned into Jalan Mahkamah Persekutuan and continued past the GPO. The area housed larger buildings, more like the big business hub, and there were no food stalls or small shops. Marked off areas were allocated for the parking of motorbikes and pushbikes. Pedestrian numbers thinned out but being a major thoroughfare the vehicular traffic was heavier than Theo thought possible. Larger vehicles, buses, trucks and commercials whizzed past, some spewing choking, diesel smoke.

He lifted his forearm in an attempt to cover his nose and mouth. The piles of garbage on the footpath seemed to increase in size and he noticed a garbage truck up ahead and dirty-looking men with equally dirty turbans shovelling from a pile into the truck. None of the piles looked old but the soaking rain had helped to disperse some of the rubbish into the drains.

The onslaught of the noise, traffic and crowds had temporarily put his mind off the job in hand. He resisted the urge to look around but somehow felt there was someone there. Well there was, Eric. He hoped anyway. *Be there Eric old mate, be there.* The street lights threw a misty kind of fluorescence that buzzed with attracted flying insects in the humid air.

Theo arrived at the shopping complex and then swung a left and walked for the width of the building which housed a few fashion boutiques or commercial offices. Most were closed or closing up, clearly open only for business hours. Theo's mouth felt like sand, his clothing was soaked with sweat and his hands trembled. At the laneway, he hesitated for a second taking in the layout of the area. The area was illuminated with the occasional street light. It took all his strength of character to not to look behind.

He turned and walked slowly into the lane, past a well-lit loading dock and piles of pallets. About three quarters the way along, a forklift was stacking large boxes and near it two men in overalls sat on pallets smoking cigarettes. Fifty metres seemed to Theo to be a long way away in case something happened. The churning in his stomach felt like a jumble of clock springs. He knew he had to get on top of it all. A flashback reminded him of the vacuum when the siren sounded a fraction before the first bounce on the football field.

The reek of garbage hung in the humid air. Two dogs looked up from foraging in a pile of rubbish and went back to their work, obviously more intent on their prize than him. He walked to within 20 metres of the men. They either didn't see him or didn't care about his presence. They continued to chatter and puff away. One of them laughed. The sound was louder than the forklift.

He turned quickly, detecting a flash of movement behind a rubbish skip. It had to be the stalker. Sweat poured down his back and his scalp prickled. Eric's words swam in his head, '*What could possibly go wrong?*' A big image zipped around the corner, silhouetted by the entrance light for a nanosecond and melted into the shadows. Eric, surely? So the stalker was now between Eric and him. Supposedly.

Theo walked back in the direction of the entrance. The rubbish skip where the scuffling noise had come from was five metres away. Theo still hoped the image in the shadows, now ten metres away, was Eric. Theo clenched his fists; the springs stopped winding and tensed solid in his stomach. The skip was two metres away. The big image crept to within three metres.

Theo stopped, balanced himself, one foot in front of the other a short space apart. He knew this was the moment. He had to do it.

'Hey mate, come out from there!' It was then it occurred to him that the man might have a weapon. 'I ..,' his mouth felt full of sawdust. 'I know you are in there.'

A rustle sounded like rats behind the skip. There was no escape, only two ways out. Towards Theo or in the other direction into the arms of … 'Come out, *now*!' Theo made the last word loud. He thought his finger nails would burst the skin of his palms.

A shape appeared and dashed in the other direction as quick as a cockroach.

'Stop, buddy,' boomed a Viking command, enveloping the man in a bear hug. 'Calm down, I vill crush life out of you if you resist, yah, okay?'

Theo started breathing again, fear and anxiety was more his friend than enemy at that second. Eric wrestled the man forward with ease, almost lifting him off the ground. There was just enough light.

'Okay, mate why are you following me?' Theo felt better now, in charge. He stood, feet apart, ready as he would ever be.

The man was dressed in jeans and casual short sleeve shirt. Theo could make out a tattoo on one forearm, but not clearly. Theo guessed him to be about the same age as him, five foot nine or ten, slight build but maybe wiry. A prominent nose between dark eyes in a swarthy complexion made him look very much a Mahmoud man.

No answer. Theo thought the man might not understand English. He tried to focus on the Malaysian phrasebook and scrolled a few

Malaysian words in his head, attempting to construct a sentence to communicate. 'Bolehkah anda capak English … er … Englasi … er … Inggeris … um do you speak English?'

Still no answer.

Eric increased the tension of the bear hug and lifted the man off the ground. Whilst it was clearly unpleasant for him it was not enough to cause any damage until Eric increased the pressure another notch. The man tried to kick backwards but Eric lifted him higher off the ground and outwards.

'Come on mate, who are you and why are you following me. If you don't cough up we'll hand you over to the police.'

The man could hardly breathe but he grimaced which looked almost like a sarcastic smile.

Eric's eyes widened suddenly. 'Theo quick! Behind!'

A barrage of sharp Malaysian language hit Theo as he half turned. He could see it was the same two men, who had been smoking down the other end by the forklift. One of the men tried to grab Theo around the neck but panic and natural instinct made Theo bring up his elbow hard and fast into the other's stomach. The intruder staggered back, winded and temporarily dazed, but the other man came forward in a Kung Fu stance and swung his foot within inches of Theo's face.

'Fuck!' yelled Theo and moved in the only way he knew to get the first punch in; he had to get in close. He took two quick steps, too close for the other man to manoeuvre an effective karate kick. Confidence came with fear and adrenalin and Theo pushed the other man's flying foot upwards which sent him cartwheeling backwards into a pile of boxes. The man rebounded almost instantly and rushed at Theo with surprising speed. In that second Theo could see the man had lost his head by rushing rather than calculating.

Theo took a quick step to the side like a matador. He knew how to play dirty by raising the elbow. The effectiveness of the forearm jolt was helped by the speed of the other man and he hit the ground shaking his head and wondering.

'Watch out, Theo!' yelled Eric, still unable to do anything because he was still holding on to Mahmoud's man who struggled wildly.

Theo turned. The first intruder was on his feet and coming again at him.

Theo yelled again, 'Fuck!' as he managed to fend off several karate kicks.

The other man was on all fours and about to stand. Eric could see what was happening and pushed Mahmoud's man hard into the rubbish skip, probably hoping to negate him for a few precious seconds whilst he went to help Theo. Theo was okay with one but two obviously reasonably skilled fighters was another thing.

Eric almost danced in and swung a haymaker that fortunately for the first man only just clipped his shoulder and although obviously hurting, didn't stop him coming again. Strangely Eric's question, *'What could possibly go wrong?'* pounded away in Theo's head.

Suddenly someone yelled, *'Police.'* Everyone stopped circling in mid-fighting pose.

Chapter Forty-Six

Mahmoud's man staggered out from beside the rubbish skip, holding a card that glinted in the light. 'Stop! Berhenti! Police!'

Theo and Eric stared at each other. The two workers looked at each other and all four looked at the policeman. Then all five looked from person to person. All of them breathing heavily.

Theo said, 'Police? What the ..?'

'This is all a big mistake, I am a police officer,' said Mahmoud's man, rubbing the side of his head where he had come in contact with the steel skip. He staggered over. 'See, my ID?'

Theo examined it. 'Abdullah Bangga, PC, Polis Diraja Malaysia.' He was about to ask what Diraja stood for when he flipped the card over and saw the words Royal Malaysian Police (RMP). He handed the card to Eric.

'Malaysian Police Fingerprints and Records, okay?'

The first intruder put his hand out, massaging his bruised shoulder with the other. 'Apaka?' he panted and shrugged his shoulders. Both of them examined the laminated card.

The tension in the air eased to confusion. Everyone looked at each other again.

Theo faced the policeman, brow tightening. 'What the hell is this all about?'

The policeman took a moment and it appeared as if he wasn't sure how to begin.

'Well?' persisted Theo, slowly bringing his heart rate and breathing back to the present. He kept firing glances at the other two as he said it.

'Okay, I am under orders to follow you, that is all I can say.'

'Well, you better say more, mate or …' Theo had an idea. 'Or I'm going to the Australian Embassy and …'

The policeman held his hands out in an offering gesture. 'Sir, I am under orders …'

'Under orders? Look, mate you are going to have to tell me what is going on, who gave you the authority to tail me, and why?'

The two workers stood looking on, moving nervously from one foot to the other. The one who had spoken a moment ago obviously realised the conversation was being conducted in English and he had no idea what was going on.

He said, 'Saya tidak faham?' The two of them slowly walked over to the policeman handing over the warrant card. He rattled off some Bahasa Malaysian to the policeman and a rapid exchange of dialogue followed.

After a few minutes the two intruders laughed and both put their hands out wide and shrugged.

The first man said, 'Maaf,' followed by a few words, then they both bowed almost apologetically towards the two westerners and walked back along the lane in the direction of the loading dock.

Eric and Theo shrugged as well and looked at each other again. Police Officer Abdullah Bangga shuffled a bit closer and pulled out a packet of cigarettes, offering the two tourists one. Both were still confused but Theo figured a smoke might be of some benefit. The peace pipe. Eric lit them up.

Abdullah pointed in the direction the intruders went. 'They were only trying to help, thinking you guys were assaulting and robbing me, a Malaysian national, okay?'

Theo sighed, impatient to find out more. 'Fair enough I suppose but why were you following me? Sorry to be a pain in the arse but mate, I need to know, alright?'

Abdullah took a drag. 'Okay, this not going to go down well for me, I'm in the fingerprint section and apart from a bit of overall police training, I've never done this surveillance stuff, that for professional guys, okay?'

'But why follow me?' Theo snapped but then remembered losing his temper could make things worse. At least it seemed they weren't under arrest, or were they?

'Okay, it because you are low-level priority. Investigative section short of staff and I get dummy, see?'

Theo took a quick drag and blew the smoke out quickly. 'No I don't bloody well see. Why low level but who gives a fuck, I want to know who authorised all this?'

The policeman's eyes widened at the use of the four-letter word. Theo caught it but his tension had risen and he didn't care about offending people. Also he wanted answers, he was owed answers.

'I can't tell you that.'

Eric took a big breath and stood up to his full height in an attempt to intimidate the policeman and it seemed to work because the man was even younger than he first appeared, a real rookie.

Eric spoke in his deepest Nordic voice. 'Ve vill have to be going to our respective embassies then. Come on Theo, let us go now.'

'Okay, okay, hang on.'

Theo wondered if he knew any words other than okay. 'Please tell us who you are working for. Last chance.' Theo figured the poor bloke was going to be in trouble because he didn't do a very good job with surveillance.

'Inspector Sethna.' He glanced around nervously, thinking the boxes and skips had ears.

'Why?'

'Because he still thinks you may have something to do with Mahmoud Hanif.'

'Well I bloody well don't, right? And what else?'

He looked away. 'Nothing else.'

'Come on, mate, what else?'

'Look, I get into trouble for all this.'

'What else?'

'Maybe have something to do with lawyer and Mr Deere. Okay, that's all I know, please I seconded to loosely keep an eye on you after other officer got made.'

'Other officer?' Theo rubbed his jaw in a pincer movement.

Eric was quicker. 'Other officer being Oriental-type man who follow him,' pointing at Theo, 'earlier on at Pudu Prison, yah?'

The policeman ran a hand over his eyes and it seemed he was contemplating what to say, or how much. 'Okay, okay. You guys are pretty good at this, picking up surveillance.'

Theo was about to say that the police were pretty bad at it. 'Right, what do we do now?'

All three looked at each other.

'Okay? I have to report this to the inspector. He will be raving mad.' His outward demeanour portrayed the fear a schoolboy might show before telling the teacher he cheated.

'I want to meet with the inspector,' said Theo on a whim. Then it occurred to him that the inspector could easily throw him back in jail. 'Er ... um I'll bring my lawyer.'

'No, no, you can't do that.'

'Why? I have every right to clear my name. Look, mate ... er ... officer or whatever you are, I have done nothing wrong, I was wrongly arrested, I was framed, I was bullied, followed, intimidated and all the rest.' That's all Theo could think of at that moment.

'Best I can do is report it as it is,' the young policeman said resignedly. He looked at the two tourists. Er ... um could we ... um omit this little scuffle we had earlier? I mean those two guys, they'll say nothing, one thing for sure here in Malay-she-ah, local people want nothing to do with police. If the inspector knows you jumped me, maybe I get sent to archives and sort paperwork in crypt.' His attempt at humour brought a smile to the others' lips.

'Yeah, I guess we can keep it quiet, but I will be setting up a meeting with Inspector Sethna one way or the other, or my lawyer will represent me.'

'I understand, okay. Should we be saying you walked up to me in the street, say on Jalan Fee Soon near the night market and asked me what I was doing, okay?'

Theo received a nod from Eric. 'Yep, that's alright with me but please tell him we wish to see him, my lawyer will approach him. Also tell him I am pissed off at all of this underhanded stuff.'

'I tell him you are not happy rather than, you know ..?'

Theo rolled his eyes. 'Righto.' He had another idea. 'Do you have a business card in case I need to contact you?'

'Umm ... no I ... er ...'

'Come on, mate.'

'I could get into trouble about this.'

Theo held out his hand, palm up.

'Okay, okay,' and he fished out a card from his top pocket. 'You know I won't be able to give you any information, I mean I am a police officer and you are a … a ..?'

'A what?'

'What I meant was, a … er … a person of interest.'

Theo wasn't about to argue because he could see he was at least of interest whether he liked it or not. 'Yeah, fair enough I s'pose.'

The three walked back to the entrance to the lane and Police Officer Abdullah Bangga said, 'Okay.'

The situation was not exactly awkward but unusual and the three men shook hands. They parted ways, police officer to the right and the two friends to the left, back to backpacker haven.

Theo and Eric didn't talk much for the first leg of the trip back but as they were crossing the main thoroughfare to the night market, Theo felt obliged to say, 'So much for your comment, *What could possibly go wrong, eh?'*

They both laughed; people looked at them and thought perhaps they were on drugs. The banter kept up all the way back, making light of the adventure they had experienced. Several drug dealers approached them thinking a sale was a possibility because of their buoyant behaviour.

Chapter Forty-Seven

The crowds in the streets thinned out by the time they arrived at the Restaurant Mall.

Eric said, 'Hey, why we not go and see if those girls are still at the Splendid Coffee House?'

Theo didn't care one way or the other because as soon as the word girls was mentioned, an image of Biru came to mind. But still, he thought, some female company would be good for a change. However, he had to ask, 'I thought you and Franka were, like, a couple?'

Eric laughed. 'Yah we are, but you know, we haff separate lives, you know. We have our own friends at times.' He winked. 'Us Svedish are very liberal minded, especially before we get married, try before buy.' He laughed uproariously again. 'Franka she probably haff fun with her friend also, away from prying eyes. She probably smoke dope, too.'

'Keep your voice down, mate,' whispered Theo, not keen to broadcast any subversive behaviour, with the memory of jail foremost in his mind.

The Splendid Coffee House was loud and rocking, with the film clip of Talking Heads '*Stop making sense.*'

'Hey, I'd like to see this, mate,' said Theo.

The place was packed; barely standing room and the same girls weren't there either, so they kept going. A couple of other places featured Jacky Chan and Bruce Lee videos respectively, loud and violent, so they decided on the quietest place they could find, the Jungle Longhouse, to have a beer. A Chuck Norris video had started in the main area and Chuck was karate-chopping his way through half a dozen bad guys with the aid of quadraphonic stereo surround sound. The place was about half full of young people keen to kill a few hours watching popular time-wasting entertainment. They selected a table in the corner, furthest from the speakers, and ordered beer.

Theo had to talk loudly, 'Well, that was a surprise to me, I mean that bloke being a cop.'

'Yah, at least dat should put your mind at rest to show Mahmoud is not around dese parts.'

'Yeah, but why are the cops following me? They wouldn't have let me go if they thought I had any link whatsoever with that arsehole Mahmoud. Remember he said it's got something to do with the lawyer and Jack. I really have to catch up with Jack but the bastard almost doesn't seem to exist. It's bloody strange; I mean Jack knows I'm trying to contact him. I really do have to find him and I'm not sure how safe I am in this country.' He lit up a cigarette and blew smoke at the wobbling fan. 'I'm heading to Penang soon to catch up with Biru – don't know what's going to happen with that – and hopefully Jack will front up there soon, too.'

'Yah, we go to Penang soon too, but first to Cameron Highlands on de way. You come with us there too?'

'No, I think I might go straight to Penang, probably the day after tomorrow, but I should wait and see if I get word from Biru ... or Jack for that matter. Yuman said there is a night bus leaves here about nine or so every day. Eric, I really don't know what the hell is going on but if I don't get a call from Joe tomorrow I'll go and see him. Seems as if he has the answers to a few of my questions and he ain't telling me.'

'At least you might now have a contact in the cops,' suggested Eric. 'Abdullah seemed as if he might believe you, otherwise he would not have stayed around and explain to us, things, yah?'

They had another beer and glanced at the screen intermittently. The volume on the sound track had been increased and they had plenty to talk about so they had to shout.

'Thanks for backing me up, Eric; mind you, mate, I wouldn't have done that epic surveillance thing on my own. I was going to walk down and confront him as he was standing in that doorway over the road. Plenty of witnesses, in the well-lit street ...'

The movie finished, they paid up and wandered out into the mall.

The air was cooler but still humid and the noise of the traffic many miles away sounded almost like the sea. Theo looked for the Old Woman from Borneo but she was not there. Apart from a number of dogs growling and barking at each other, the street was almost empty.

Theo said, 'I wonder where the monkeys are?'

'They must go to bed early,' replied Eric.

Despite being tired, Eric's comment caused them to laugh hilariously. They traded jokes all the way back to the hotel and parted company in the reception area, after agreeing to go sightseeing the next day. Yuman, Radar O'Reilly, informed Theo, before he could ask, there were no messages.

What an eventful night it had been. Theo poured himself a duty free and lay on the bed thinking about the last few hours. He felt good about himself for a change; even though he had to admit he had been fragile at times. What if one of Mahmoud's mates had a gun? What if it was a mongrel of a cop who had decided to arrest them? Questions still remained but at least he felt safer not having Mahmoud hovering in the background. He was puzzled about the police; why were they interested in him, or Jack, or Josef? He knew they were the questions he was going to ask Joe first thing in the morning.

He couldn't sleep; thoughts, scenarios, ideas and facts spun around in his head. He went over to the window and sat on the sill, lighting a cigarette. The fan continued to click and it seemed to coordinate with the barking pi-dogs in the street. Where was Jack?

Theo had a drink of water and lay down again. He tried to focus and list the things to be done the next day. It almost did the trick. Biru wandered in and out of his consciousness. All he could hope for was that she was alright and he would see her soon. Before his crammed brain surrendered to sleep he was still wondering why they shook hands with the policeman. Finally he satisfied himself; maybe it was simply the right thing to do. As simple as that.

Chapter Forty-Eight

The call to prayer woke him from the best sleep he had managed since arriving in Malaysia. Chanting drifted from a Chinese or Hindu temple nearby, punctuated by local dogs barking. He went to the window and looked out. Only a small piece of sky was visible but the early morning tropical blue was uplifting. He knew it was too early to go for breakfast or make any phone calls but he decided to jot down all the questions he could think of.

The first call for the day was to his mother. He had posted off two postcards so far but he knew the mail took at least a couple of weeks if not more. Australia was a couple of hours later in time zone and he hoped she would be around the house somewhere at about nine in the morning. He had given up trying to remember what day it was.

Second up was a call to his lawyer Josef Ibrahim, his supposed friend, Joe. Theo figured he would be able to inform Joe about who had been following him rather than the other way round. Also Joe was to find out anything he could dig up about Mahmoud. But the important thing was for Joe to set up a meeting with Inspector Sethna. Despite his reservations about returning to police headquarters, he had to find out why they were intent on following him, so he wrote down some questions. The information from Abdullah that he was of interest because of Joe and Jack troubled him. Theo needed to find out why Joe and Jack were *persons of interest* to the Malaysian police. He recalled Joe saying, '*You probably couldn't afford me.*'

The next call was to Jack's accommodation in Bangkok but he was not available.

Hopefully his final call would be to Brian Aung. He had plenty of questions to ask because Brian was now, whether he liked it or not, the liaison person in this whole affair.

Feeling confident and as prepared as he could be for the day, Theo ducked out to the small Malay-Chinese breakfast bar called Kesudian, which served banana porridge and snacks. The porridge reminded Theo of his dad, who used to get up early and make porridge for the three of them. That was one of his first memories, before the war, before his father went away. He had to get out of that frame of mind so he grabbed a copy of the New Straits Times, written in English, and leafed through the pages, noting world news and events and the cricket scores. He read the sporting section and headed back to the Hot Spot via where the Old Woman from Borneo would have been if she was there. He was slightly disappointed but he quickly realised it was only early and she seemed to be a later person. Others out and about included some shop owners and a street sweeper with a conical hat followed by a small utility with a water tank and a man on the back hosing the pavement. Some cars and bikes weaved their way through and the occasional backpacker wandered, either looking for early food or accommodation. As usual the dogs of the city strutted around growling at each other, using up their energy so they could sleep all day and bark and bite people at night.

Yuman was on duty when he arrived back and Theo was able to ring his mother in the privacy of the cluttered office. She was on the verge of going shopping so he was lucky. He found he could only talk about superficial matters like weather, people, fun, new friends, great food and interesting sights. 'Just posted a couple of postcards and I'll try to get one away every week. Money holding out very well, plenty left … yes I'm doing my own washing.' When it came to Biru he couldn't even mention her name, fearing it would all come out wrong and unnecessarily complicate things. He did, however, tell her he was still in Kuala Lumpur because Jack was away but he hoped to see him very soon. There was no way he was going to tell her about jail or being followed, or having a fight. She spoke of status quo things to update him about news from home. Nothing had changed in his absence.

The three and a half minutes spent talking to his mother gave him a lift, even though he shook his head a few times at her unnecessary concerns. Didn't she think he was smart enough to change his underwear every day? He concluded it was the role of mothers to police matters such as those.

Next call was to Josef Ibrahim. It took several clicks to get through to him. Luckily for Theo the lawyer was in early due to a court appearance.

'Hi, Theo, you beat me to it. I was going to ring you today. By the way, howya doin'?'

Sure you were going to ring me, thought Theo. 'Pretty good, Joe.' He was eager to hear what Joe had to say. 'What news do you have for me, mate?'

'Plenty. My contact tells me that Mahmoud is in Denpasar, or somewhere in Bali. The reason we know, or think we know, is because he is being watched by their customs people, but for what, I'm not sure. But, buddy, the important thing is, certainly for the present, this guy is not and has not been following you, and it is most unlikely he has had a man watching you, okay? He is a small-time drug guy, that's probably why the Indonesians are keeping an eye on him.'

'Well that is good to know. *And?*'

'Also man, I find out something else.' It sounded like he lit up a cigarette. 'The police have been tailing you. Very funny stuff, man. They are embarrassed a bit because your Swedish giant sidekick made the cop guy at Pudu, better than Dragnet.' He laughed. 'Wow! I also hear on the grapevine that you made the new guy they put on you as well. You're pretty smart, Theo, but it doesn't pay to embarrass the cops, man.'

'Embarrass the cops?' Theo snapped. 'They are following me and I have no idea why, for fuck's sake.' There was a silence. 'Sorry, mate … Well what should I do, I mean surely I am within my rights …'

'Sure, sure. Theo, you must understand in this country you only have rights if the authorities agree to let you have rights, get it? Savvy?'

Theo held the phone away from his face and sighed. 'Yes, okay, I get it but what should I do or what should be my course of action? I mean, I want to set up a meeting with Inspector Sethna to try and work out what the … the heck is going on.'

'Bad strategic move, guy, meeting the good inspector, bad move. However, you have a perfectly good lawyer here. No reason why I can't make the approach because they cannot detain me but they sure can you if you come in. Not saying they would, but police here in Malaysia are pretty powerful guys, okay?'

Theo's breathing returned to normal but the room was stuffy which didn't help. 'Right, Joe then can you do that, set up a meeting?'

'I'll do my best but I must check with Mr Aung to confirm he, or they, are still paying for my services. It may sound somewhat callous and money focused but the firm I work for does the billing and I only get a small fee. These things cost money, amigo.'

Small fee? Theo smiled and looked up at the ceiling. *Sure, I bet.* 'I understand, Joe, I get it. So what should I do now?'

'Simply carry on as you are; if you think you are being followed ignore it for the present anyway, okay?'

'Ignore it.' Theo said, deadpan.

'Yeah, man, don't worry, I'll sort it out.' A hearty laugh followed. 'We still haven't had that social get together either, Theo.'

'We will, maybe when you have news we can meet, right?' Theo wondered who was going to pay for the drinks.

'Okay, bud, we'll be in touch.'

Theo could see the snappily dressed lawyer with his $200 shoes, polished like mirrors, resting on the elk skin blotter atop the teak desk. 'Righto, Joe, I look forward to hearing from you and … er thanks for all you are doing.'

There was another laugh. 'Sure man, sure. Adios amigo!'

Theo hung up. He felt better about Josef Ibrahim and was confident the lawyer was being straight with him, even though in a salesman's fashion. Theo wondered again, who was paying?

Chapter Forty-Nine

Theo heard Eric talking so he wandered out to the reception area, rubbing his eyes. 'Morning people,' he said as he pulled out a coke from the fridge and handed over the money to Yuman.

'Thank you, Mr Theo.'

'Yuman, it's Theo, okay?'

'Yes, Mr Theo.' They all laughed.

Theo told Eric he'd had breakfast earlier and still needed to make another call so they agreed to meet at the Splendid Coffee House in an hour and work out a plan for the day.

Theo made phone call number three – Jack. He rang the number; a different person answered again so he left a message. He was disappointed but he reminded himself Brian did say Jack was going to ring *him* – soon.

He decided not to ring Brian, figuring it would be better to wait until the end of the day in case Jack did actually ring either of them. He looked at his list; doctor and a visit to Foreign Affairs to sign some paperwork, all in the same direction; Foreign Affairs could wait if they did not have time. He wanted to have a look at the main mosque in Kuala Lumpur, Masjid Negara, but that was a kilometre or two away and could wait until tomorrow. The Hindu temple where chanting and periodic bell ringing emanated every day was not far away, past the markets. There was no point in arranging a bus ticket to Penang yet. Theo checked out the bill with Yuman and went back to his room for a shower.

Twenty minutes later he was seated alongside Eric who was finishing off with coffee.

Eric smiled. 'Mista Theo, you will never get Yuman to call you by your first name. Dey always call me Mr Eric or Mr Jansen or even Mr Franko, or something like dat. Sometime dey call Franka Missus Frank, not her last name. We find it is normal polite form of address a lot in South East Asia.'

'Yeah, Biru and Razak were the same. I guess I'll have to get used to it, eh?'

Theo ordered a coffee and explained what he had learned from Joe and what was to happen from here on, if anything, regarding a meeting or information from Inspector Sethna. Theo's doctor's appointment was in half an hour's time so Eric decided to go back to the Hot Spot and ring Franka to see what she was doing for the day. They agreed to meet up later that morning at a place they picked from the guidebook, Ibu Suri's Tea Shop on Jalan Sultan not far from the doctor's surgery.

The sun was hot and he was glad he brought his hat again. Theo dodged and weaved his way through the morning traffic, pedestrians, stallholders, beggars and spruikers, towards the doctor's. He stepped back several times to take a few photos. Jalan Sultan was a major thoroughfare and it was a battle to cross the road but he stuck with Dempster's advice and crossed with a depth of personnel between him and the oncoming traffic – in case.

The doctor's surgery was on the sixth floor. The lift didn't work so he had to use the stairs and he noted every floor had a small restaurant of some kind, and one floor had a food hall. The wonderful aromas coming from the food being cooked on site was enough to make him hungry even though his stomach was still bloated with porridge.

'Another good place to come and eat if we run out of choices but we won't be able to talk,' he mumbled.

No-one could hear him above the clatter of plates and generally loud conversations mixed with orders and instructions being yelled across the rooms. The sounds bounced off the shiny surfaces and he stood for a moment taking in the scene, in a food court which occupied the whole floor, and he was almost mesmerised by the din. Around the perimeter were stalls selling almost every type of food he had seen since arriving.

He found the surgery with some difficulty after becoming lost in a catacomb of passages, most of which were crowded with people and merchandise, and the thought of what could happen if there was a fire passed through his mind. What made him slightly jittery was the fact that he couldn't see any fire extinguishers or sprinklers.

A list of four doctors' names appeared on a frosted glass door. He entered the waiting room, instantly shocked by the number of people crammed in there. Two ceiling fans wobbled and spun with the pretence of cooling the close, hot, humid air. The patients ranged from reasonably healthy-looking to obviously in need of medical attention. People squatted or sat on the floor because all seats were taken, some seats with two people sharing the space. Some children cried, some yelled, some played whilst other patients chattered away to each other. Despite the chaos, the place appeared to be very clean. Theo thought the better of turning around and going because he needed to find out the results of his blood tests.

He went to the crowded reception where two obviously overworked women tried to keep the room in order.

'Yes, how may I help you?' said a plump woman with a red dot on her forehead, dressed in a multi-coloured sari. He gave her his details and the doctor's name.

The woman smiled, 'Ah yes,' as she ticked his name on a register. 'Please one moment, you may be standing over here.' She pointed to a space almost behind the counter where she was seated. She picked up the phone and fired a few quick words Theo couldn't catch.

The woman could see his agitation. She waved, 'Momen, momen, not long.'

About five minutes later Dr Munishram stepped out from a passage. 'Aha, Mr Perry, nice to see you again, please come this way.' They shook hands.

Theo felt special but did wonder how the other poor patients felt with him being put at the head of the queue. It dawned on him that it was probably because he had money, not because he was a white Tuan. Also he had travel insurance. Money paves the way.

They passed several other rooms, one sounding like a torture chamber, and the doctor held open another door as if Theo was royalty. In contrast to the front waiting room the doctor's office was neat and well equipped with a wide array of instruments laid out on benches.

The doctor rested one buttock on the edge of the desk covered, but seemingly in order, with charts, reports and other paperwork.

'Now, Mr Perry, how are you feeling?' he said, reaching across and opening a file, clearly Theo's.

'Pretty good, thanks, my stomach has settled down and the headaches have subsided.' The doctor checked Theo's head where the lump was. 'Any pain from this?'

'No.'

'The blood tests all came up negative; you may realise we could only test for known mosquito-borne diseases but you seem to be okay there. Also, no reading for hepatitis types but sometimes it takes a while to show up.'

Theo exhaled and smiled. 'That's great news.'

He wrapped Theo's upper arm and carefully watched the gauge drop. 'Yes, blood pressure normal. I think you most likely had stomach poisoning from water with a slight touch of concussion. When you get back to Australia you should have another blood test for infectious diseases, in particular Hepatitis B, most unlikely you have Hepatitis C but get tested in case. I see you have been vaccinated for Hepatitis A so you should be okay there.'

The doctor stood. 'Right Mr Perry, you are free to go and enjoy the rest of your holiday. I have prepared a report to add to your health card and for your insurance as well, okay?' He picked up a sheet of paper from the desk.

'Thanks, Doctor.' Theo couldn't believe how efficient this process was. He tried not to think of the masses in the waiting room.

'You will of course be presented with an account at the front desk. Here is my card.' He stuck out his hand and they shook.

Theo went to reception and the woman with the red dot typed out a bill. Theo surmised that even though the amount was less than half what he would have had to pay in Australia, he was paying probably three or four times what everyone else was paying. He was handed a receipt and walked out into the passageway, thankful he didn't have any tropical diseases.

The smell of food was too overpowering so he braved the noise and purchased some samosas, with red hot chilli sauce, served on a paper towel and a square of newspaper. He walked down the stairs and into the humidity, wondering what Eric, Franka and he were going to do next. Hindu temple or city centre? The idea of a location with airconditioning seemed appealing to him at that moment.

Theo wandered towards Ibu Suri's and had the feeling of being observed, again. He spun around.

Flagged Name

Chapter Fifty

'Hi Theo.' Eric could see the look of alarm on Theo's face. 'Okay, okay, I am good guy. At least you are getting good at surveillancing.' They both laughed at the absurdity of it all. 'I walked around corner just as you walk out of building. Perfect timing, no?'

'Where's Franka?' Theo offered Eric a samosa.

'She is having a great time and will be going city centre Golden Triangle for shopping soon. I will go dere as I will be needing canvas shoes for walking in tea plantations.'

A few minutes later, over condensed milk coffee and the clatter of cups of a nearby kedai, they decided to split up again and meet in the Golden Triangle shopping precinct in an hour or two which would allow Theo to go to the Department of Foreign Affairs in the meantime. Theo explained that he was required, as a formality, to sign some papers to do with his father's death.

Theo said, 'It shouldn't take long.'

Eric laughed.

'What?'

'Shouldn't take long like, *what could possibly go wrong*, yah?'

They laughed again and picked a location to meet later. Eric paid the bill.

∞

The Malaysian Department of Foreign Affairs was housed in a building that appeared to only have government offices. The building itself was one left over from colonial days and had a very British feel to it. Big stone pillars identified the entrance along with a uniformed, armed guard each side behind ornate lecterns. The guard closest to Theo asked, in English, his business and inspected his passport. The guard made a record of the details and politely handed it back, and he was directed towards a reception booth identifying departments, including Foreign Affairs. Theo felt somewhat out of place as he squelched in his thongs across the vast marble floor covering the foyer. He was acutely aware he should have worn his airport clothes. More reception booths identifying other government agencies and departments radiated out to the lifts almost like a ritzy hotel.

'There we are sir, you go to lift number four and up to third floor, okay?' The dark, well-dressed young man looked down his nose as he noticed Theo's thongs and casual dress sense. He handed Theo a plastic ID card with a number, marked 'Visitor.'

After a short interlude of Kenny G equivalent in the lift he found the office and was asked to take a seat in a small waiting room. Two other people sat reading magazines. The airconditioning was welcome at first but he felt cold after a few minutes. Progressively over the next twenty minutes the other two were ushered away by different office officials.

'Come on, come on,' he mumbled, hoping the woman behind the desk didn't hear him but hoping she could see he didn't have all day.

Another fifteen minutes passed and Theo was about to ask if there was a problem when a slender forty-ish woman with dark, almost burgundy hair, dark features and friendly eyes called his name.

She smiled. 'Sorry to keep you waiting, Mr Perry, we had an urgent matter to deal with and then I had trouble locating your file. My name is Mrs Ismail. This way please.'

Any anxiety Theo had was negated by the friendly way she introduced herself, also the flippant way made the excuses about urgent matters and locating files. She was dressed in western style, sensible medium high heels and a snug-fitting business suit that highlighted a well-maintained figure.

They entered a comfortable carpeted office. She rolled her hand indicating a seat. 'Right, Mr Perry.' She quietly went to the business side of the desk and sat down.

'Please, call me Theo.'

'Okay, we have some paperwork for you to sign, mostly routine but complicated slightly by the fact that your father was an Australian citizen, but also because he held a permit to work here in Malaysia because he was in partnership with a Malaysian national in a business venture.'

The words, partner and business venture caused Theo to sit up straight. His demeanour must have been obvious.

'You surely were aware he lived here on and off for many years?'

'I sort of knew he lived in this part of the world, on and off, but wasn't aware he had a business partner who was Malaysian, I mean.'

'Okay, I'll give you these papers to sign, they are straightforward, in relation to some minor personal possessions and his ashes being held by a Mr John Francis Deere, who lives in ... Penang I believe. Your mother returned a letter to me stating you were going to see Mr Deere.' Theo nodded. 'She also supplied us with the details we needed to confirm in relation to his date of birth and informing us you would be coming here to sign things which is of course cheaper than getting international solicitors to do it, right?' She laughed in an understanding fashion.

She walked around the desk and placed a document in front of him, pointing to the flagged sections to sign. It was mainly confirming family details. For a few seconds the fragrance of her perfume reminded him of his mother. She took his passport to the photocopier and then went to a bank of filing cabinets and pulled out a file.

Because she had mentioned Jack's name he was compelled to ask. 'Is there any information on Jack ... er John Deere?'

'No, just that he is holding the ashes and a few other items listed as minor personal items not itemised. I had some difficulty locating some of your father's details. Initially when your mother contacted us I thought it would be just a formality. I do several hundred or more of these every year, tying up paperwork dealing with the death of foreigners.' She went back to the desk, sat down and handed him back his passport.

Theo finished signing and looked up, interest piqued, hearing the word difficulty.

Mrs Ismail continued, looking at him with brown eyes and smiling slightly. 'I discovered that the file was flagged by our international police which meant there may have been an ongoing investigation of some kind, or perhaps an unresolved matter.'

Theo's brow tightened, he had thought all this would be just formal paperwork. He ran an almost shaky hand over his short hair. 'Do you know anything about um … this investigation?'

'No, like I say, the file was flagged but in view of the circumstances, I mean his death, look Mr … Theo, sorry to be so blunt as this; what I mean is, it seems that any investigation was dumped as a result of his, if you like, your father's untimely death.'

The airconditioning seemed to warm up. Theo felt damp under his arms. He shook his head and pulled out the small notebook containing some questions written down earlier. Suddenly he felt like a child in front of this woman and he knew he needed to snap out of it. It took a couple of moments to remind himself he had a degree in journalism and there were questions that needed to be asked. He stared at the page for a few more seconds, unsure because the questions on the pad were now mostly irrelevant in light of the new information to hand.

'Umm … Mrs Ismail, as you can probably imagine, no what I mean is, most of what you have said is news to me.' He shook his head again and took a deep breath. 'Do you mind if I er … ask you a few questions, I need to try to understand some things?'

She continued to look at him amiably. Her mouth had a slight curve, the beginning of a smile. 'Of course,' she replied, opening both hands, palms outwards. 'I don't have much detail but I am happy to help.'

The voice in his head told him she was okay, willing to at least hear him, to a degree anyway. So he decided to start from the beginning, or near it. 'My father, Vince Perry, left my mother and I back in … about 15 years ago. All we knew was that he was going to work in … er in Thailand.' Theo relaxed, forgot about being a journalist for a while and opened up, telling her things he could remember about his father. 'We heard nothing from him over those years except for two letters from er … a friend informing us Dad was alright. We had no idea he was in Malaysia. You said he had a Malaysian business partner?'

'Yes, it is a common occurrence for overseas business people to team up with a local business person, helps to allow that person to stay here to work. Otherwise a foreigner can only be issued with a short visa and they have to leave the country periodically and re-enter to continue working here.'

'Do you know who the partner was?' Theo made to jot down details like a real journalist.

'Yes and no.' She smiled. 'What I mean is, the name stated here is Ameer Faziq but that would probably be only a name to secure the visa. Mr Ameer Faziq would probably hold an executive position in a corporation. We have complex visa restrictions but there are agents who handle these immigration issues, big business people seem to be able to pull strings, if you know what I mean. The present government is keen for overseas trade and business so ...' She shrugged and held out her hands like an offering again.

'Who was this person associated with, I mean what business was he in?'

'Not much detail, just says financing but there is a pencilled note, "Malacca International Corporation". I take that to mean an international banking and/or finance company based in Malacca, more than likely luxury hotels or entertainment investments.'

Theo closed his eyes for a second, wondering what he had launched into. 'So would it be reasonable to assume that Vince was involved in the ... er *entertainment* industry?' He knew he was beginning to sound like a real journalist.

'That would be a strong possibility. Theo,' she stood and reached over to a pile of files, 'we need to move on now; I don't think I can really help you anymore.'

Theo knew he couldn't dally around all day. 'Oh, yes of course, no worries.' He did not have any more questions in mind.

She handed over three more documents for signatures. He read them as best he could; it was all about verifying he was himself and was Vince's son and he did indeed represent the Perry family. She photocopied them, placed all his copied documents in an envelope with her card stapled on the front, and handed it to him. The meeting was over and she walked him to the door and shook his hand in the soft Asian style.

'I hope you enjoy your holiday, Theo, you have my card if you need anything further in relation to your father.' She said smiling, and added almost as an afterthought. 'Be careful, I hope you find what you are looking for.'

'Er right, thanks er ... Mrs Ismail.'

Theo walked out of the building into the blazing sun and it was only after a few minutes he realised he was walking the wrong way. He pulled out the map and headed off in the right direction, still scrolling her words, '*Be careful, hope you find what you are looking for.*' He wondered again what he hoped to discover on this journey.

A dog looked up from a pile of garbage and barked aggressively as if Theo was about to steal his booty. It brought him back to the present, reminding him to concentrate on '*being careful.*' He skirted around the dog, aware of the fact that most of the dogs in Kuala Lumpur did not like westerners.

Chapter Fifty-One

The Golden Triangle was the showpiece of modern Malaysia's might in South East Asia and it took Theo much longer to get there than he had anticipated. After walking for ten minutes, the heat, humidity and traffic noise wearied him. On the occasional street corner a cycle rickshaw driver pestered him, offering a lift. Yuman had told him that rickshaws were being phased out due to the amount of traffic on the roads but he said if you can get one, the drivers are desperate because taxis are cheap so don't pay any more than two ringgits: the usual price for a short trip was about one. He stopped at a drink cart, downed a cold soft drink, and at that point decided to grab the next rickshaw he came across.

'Hey, boss Tuan, you want?' He pointed to the seat with a hood over it.

'Maybe.' He kept walking. 'How much?'

'Where to, boss?'

'Golden Triangle.'

'Four ringgit.'

'Too dear. One.'

The man laughed and rode on, then stopped.

'Two, boss, last price.'

Theo had to hold out, if only for personal pride. 'I know it's one because that's all I paid yesterday for the same trip.'

'Hot day boss, one and a half.'

'Sorry mate, nice day for a walk.'

'Boss Tuan, you win, okay one.'

Theo smiled, so did the man and they pedalled on through

the horrendous traffic to the shopping complex. Theo had the opportunity to practise every swear word he knew. Almost every minute provided a life-endangering manoeuvre. He had his backpack over his face because the exhaust of big trucks and buses blurted smoke straight at him. However, he managed get a photo or two when something exciting happened. When they arrived at the intersection of Jalan Sultan Ismail and Bukit Bintang, Theo was shaking and soaked in sweat from heat and fear.

The laughing man with the Viet Cong helmet said, 'Good trip, boss Tuan.' and he laughed outrageously. 'Best shopping for tourists down there, also good eating mall and market along there and left, okay?'

Theo gave him two ringgits. He didn't have any change but also felt sorry for him, knowing how much work the man put in and how little he made. Theo handed over a couple of cigarettes as well and stood at the kerb and waved him on his way. For a few moments sadness hung over him when he thought of how privileged he was being an Australian, how well off he was and how little most of the people around him had. The sun beat down and he had to find some shade.

They had agreed to meet on the corner where he had been dropped off. It took five minutes of pushing and shoving through the street crowds to establish that his two friends were not there, but it was understandable because Eric had suggested they check the corner every half hour on the hour. A group of Hindus moved through the crowd chanting, selling marigolds and ringing bells, and Theo was glad to sneak inside the shopping mall to escape the noise.

The airconditioning was welcome relief from the heat of the pavement and he ambled around for a while, eyes wide open at the variety of goods on sale. Most of it in this mall seemed geared for tourists: clothing, souvenirs, travel apparel, books and a bank of travel agents. At the far end electrical and whitegoods were more for locals.

The crowd was mostly tourists of all ages but some teenage locals made up the remainder. Theo could see they were from the middle or wealthier class with plenty of disposable money. They were a stark contrast to the people who scratched a living in the streets. He shook the melancholy feeling and set a course to check the corner again, as it was on the half hour.

Eric and Franka almost bumped into him, they were looking one way and him the other.

'Hey, watch it, man,' said Eric in a gruff voice.

Theo joined in and replied loudly, 'Hey mate, stop shoving will ya or I'll report you to the police.'

They jostled and laughed their way into another food hall where Franka suggested they go because it was quieter and there was a string of milk bars and café s where you could sit and talk. Real coffee was available, too.

Eric had briefed Franka about their surveillance operation the night before but he must have made it sound less complicated and less dangerous than it was. Just talking about it made Theo glance around a few times to be sure no-one was watching them. Theo prided himself on how clandestine he could be, faking rubbing his nose to see in one direction, running his hand through his hair for another and reaching to the floor to pick up a tissue for another. Eric noticed and burst out laughing.

'What?' protested Theo.

'Nothing, nothing.'

Franka thought they were keenly observing two scantily dressed young women making their way through the tables. 'You guys, you cannot help yourselves, hah.'

Both men chuckled.

Over the next hour they visited several handicraft places and a museum full of old weapons and colonial paraphernalia. Theo purchased a small set of wooden block print stamps but nothing else caught his eye.

When they walked out into the street the afternoon storm had started. Franka suggested they go to the big international hotel over the road and grab a taxi from there. They dashed across the road with the lights, still risking their lives, and made it to the comfort of the hotel, slightly damp. The doorman beckoned a taxi for them and they piled in. Eric gave the doorman a handful of ringgits. The man frowned and glared at them, obviously the amount was not what he was used to but Eric showed the doorman his empty hands and hooted with good natured laughter as they pulled out into the increasing rain.

They arrived at the corner near the Hot Spot and an argument erupted with the taxi driver who, unnoticed by the tourists, had not used his meter. The amount he wanted was ridiculous as far as they were concerned and Franka saved the situation by threatening to go to the tourist police and report the driver. They agreed on a quarter of his asking price which was probably too high but they parted company, the taxi driver smiling and the tourists forcing smiles. They dashed to the Hot Spot and scrambled up the stairs, soaked with tropical rain.

'Mr Theo, Mr Theo, Mr Deere he ring for you,' exclaimed Yuman, waving his arms.

'What, on the phone now?'

'No, no, he ring two hour ago, maybe more. I try to tell him …' Yuman still continued to wave his hands trying to explain he did his best.

Chapter Fifty-Two

'That's okay, Yuman, no worries, not your fault.' Theo squirmed in his wet clothes.

'He say he ring back, I not know what time you be back so I say ...'

'Don't worry mate, it'll work out.' Theo wondered about his luck.

Eric said, 'We see you later, yah?'

Theo nodded and turned. 'Yuman, was there any message?'

'No.'

'Should I ring him?'

'No, no good, Mr Deere say he not at that number. He say best he ring you later. Mr Theo, maybe he ring soon, I tell him you be back in later afternoon.'

'Right Yuman, I might go and shower and have a rest, would you please ..?'

'... surely thing, I will come and get you if there is any phone call, okay?'

'Thanks.'

The shower was welcome and Theo did some washing in the hand basin. There was a knock.

'Mr Theo, Mr Theo, come quick Mr Deere on phone.'

Theo dashed to reception and grabbed the phone. 'Yes, yes, Theo here.'

'Theo? Theo me boy, how ya goin?' The line had a pipeline echo.

Even though the line was bad he recognised the voice, after eighteen years. His tongue locked and no sound came out of his mouth for a moment.

'Christ, don't tell me the line is ... Theo, is that you old mate?'

'Yes.' Theo found his voice, 'Yes it's me, Jack, where … I mean how … umm how are you going?' He finally strung some words together that made sense.

The phone connection was shaky for a start, which did not help. 'How's things, long time no see, eh?' The old familiar voice.

'Pretty good, Jack.' Theo's eyes pooled slightly. He looked around in panic for a second thinking Yuman might see his display of genuine emotion.

'Lookie here, mate, I'm sorry I've been so hard to catch, had to have a minor operation on my leg, nothing to worry about but put me out of action just the same. Anyway, tell you all about it when we get together. And Theo, I'm real sorry about Vince … er … ya dad, ya know?' The voice reminded Theo so much of his father. After all, Vince and Jack were good mates before going to Vietnam and after as well.

'So umm … when are you coming back to Malaysia?' Theo was still slightly choked up. He hoped Jack didn't notice. It wasn't a very clear line, the sound echoed down the pipe.

'Pretty soon, mate. Got my new leg all but fitted. Have to go in again for some final adjustments tomorrow, also have some business things to deal with, so I should be heading back within, say, three days?'

Theo's heart jumped a beat. 'Great.'

'Listen, mate, it was a bit of a pity my letter didn't reach you in Australia until, I think Brian said …'

'Yeah, about two weeks after the funeral, I …' Theo was almost going to lie to say he wanted to go but he managed to hold it back. There was time to talk about that at a later time.

'Yeah, anyrate I thought you weren't coming so I pissed off to Thailand – needed a new leg.' He chuckled. 'Also, I heard you recently had a bit of a scrape with the … er authorities … best not talk about it over the phone.' He continued, 'Where are you at the moment?'

'I'm in Kuala Lumpur still …' Theo suddenly realised Jack knew where he was because he had rung. '… er I mean, Hot Spot Hotel … not far from the night markets, up from Chinatown.'

'Yeah, I have a fair idea. How's your mum?'

'Pretty good, keeps telling me to shower every day and change my underwear.'

Jack chuckled.

Theo continued, 'Anyway, I was planning to head up to Penang in a day or so anyway.' He decided not to say anything about Biru.

'Aha, off to Batu Ferringhi to ogle the nude sheilas on the beach, eh?'

Theo laughed. 'Well, I have to take in the sights while I'm here.'

'Righto me old mate, I'm really looking forward to seeing you. A lot has happened in the world since we last met. You were only about five or six mate. Have you grown any bigger?' He chuckled.

Theo had to have a go. 'To laugh at that I'd have to be no older than five or six.' He laughed anyway.

'See, you did laugh. Anyrate, mate, I'm going to have to hang up soon, someone else wants the phone. I'm in touch with Brian in Georgetown on and off and you have his number so we'll talk through him. I'll let him know soon's I know what I'm doing.'

'Yep, sure thing.'

'And mate, I'm really looking forward to catching up with you, right? Oo-roo for now.'

Theo couldn't remember much, it had been such a long time since he had spoken to him, but the way Jack spoke brought back memories as if it was yesterday. The last few minutes had brought the letters alive. He felt as if he knew Jack better than his father. Jack had written twice during that time, in addition to the funeral advice, but Theo realised it was the lifeline Jack had slung out, perhaps hoping Theo or his mother would not forget Vince, for all his faults. Theo saw an image of his father and Jack in uniform, cracking jokes over a beer, both laughing. And there was Jack rolling a cigarette, leaning on his crutches, looking as if he had two legs and not a worry in the world. It was only a year or two later that Theo heard someone mention in one of the adult conversations he wasn't supposed to hear that Jack's leg was blown off by a land mine. For a young child it was a terrible shock. He also heard that his father had saved Jack's life.

Theo put the phone down and, under the wobbling fan and the noise of the thundering rain, sobbed uncontrollably. He had to wait a while and then put his sunglasses on as he went to his room. He didn't want Yuman to see him like that.

Chapter Fifty-Three

Later Eric knocked on the door. Theo had steadied but still felt sad, but he tried to focus on happy thoughts as he jotted some information in his *Theo's Adventures* exercise book.

Eric handed back *Beyond Pardon*. 'Interesting reading. You know dis guy?' He pointed to the author's name.

'Well, not really well but I met him when he ran masterclasses … er lectures sort of thing, on being a foreign correspondent, very witty bloke, had the class laughing most of the time.' Theo wagged his finger, trying to play the voice of reason. 'I hope you and Franka pay attention to the penalties handed out in this country for drugs of any kind. Mate, I tell you, that short amount of time in jail changed my whole perspective on drugs – at least in this bloody country anyway.'

Eric smiled. 'I pay attention but Franka she is liberated woman, thinks she hass rights, yah! See you later.'

∞

Theo joined the Swedes on the corner for a visit to the Sri Mahamariamman Temple, the oldest place of worship for Hindus in Malaysia.

They hired sarongs to comply with modesty requirements and shuffled around the crowded enclosure with the hundreds of other devotees. Prayers were being conducted at the time and trance-like chanting competed with bells. The place was full of colour, flowers, incense, statues of gods and a feeling of holiness.

'Someone could sell the earplugs, they'd make a big living,' said Eric, with his hands over his ears.

They followed the custom and made a small donation to a devotee who wouldn't let them leave until they did. Outside they stood looking up at the five-tiered stone structure, fascinated by the colours and details of the carvings in the tower, highlighted by floodlights. The crowds of mainly devotees poured in and out and a few beggars tried their luck.

Afterwards they ambled back to the Restaurant Mall and selected the quietest place to have a few drinks. Theo told Eric and Franka about his phone conversation with Jack and how good it was to speak to someone from home.

'I will be going to Penang in a day or so,' he said, 'depends on getting a ticket. Yuman says buses go there regularly so I shouldn't have any trouble. He can organise tickets from here.'

'We are going to Cameron Highlands for a week, meeting friends for walking trek,' said Eric, lighting up a cigarette. 'Then we go to Penang. You will be there for a while?'

'Yes, not sure how long but I'd say at least a week, most of the time in Georgetown I think but also Batu Ferringhi too. Not sure what other touro things there are but I hope to have a good look around the island.'

'We must catch up together again, okay?'

The day had been eventful and tiring for Theo and he excused himself and headed back to the Hot Spot. The others were going to one of the restorans in search of a movie they might fancy. He wanted to make a call.

∞

Theo walked past where the Old Woman from Borneo had been on the other two occasions. For some reason he wanted her to be there but really did not know why. Maybe to talk to her but, he really couldn't answer why. Was it because his mother was so far away? Maybe it was because the phone conversation with Jack had made him homesick. He realised he needed to snap out of thinking about scenarios.

'Mr Theo, I have news, well not much but some.' Yuman waved his hands. He looked past Theo as if the walls really could hear. 'Razak find out that Biru okay, he think she in Miri, stay with old school frien, working in tourist hotel,' he added again excitedly, 'but she okay.'

'How does he know?'

Yuman tapped his nose and leant forward, broken tooth glistening. 'Ah, he frien of brother of her frien, who have brother as well who play tennis together.'

Theo was surprised she was in Borneo but whether true or not, didn't matter so long as she was out of reach of Mahmoud, and maybe her family. He had to test the information even though he was confident Yuman was on his side. The only drawback was if Razak and Yuman, and who knows who else, knew where Biru was, what about Mahmoud and his followers?

'What about Mahmoud?'

Yuman's eyebrows pinched. 'I think he gone somewhere, Razak think Indonesia. Word on street he is looking after interests in Bali, maybe a bit hot for him here because big police looking at local inspector for this district.'

'Um, how do you know this?' Theo felt a shiver.

'My brother say everyone lie low at the moment because police activity cracking down on drugs.' He tapped his nose and glanced around. 'Student cards, money change, cash no receipt, network here very nervous because government agenda want to show West that Malaysia tough on drugs and crime but for local guys, small business owners, other things tied up with that.'

Theo asked again. 'How do you know all this?'

'My brother get word from partner, Chinese shop and business owners feeling the pinch.' Yuman looked around nervously. 'Common knowledge on street.'

Theo could see Yuman didn't want to say any more; even in Australia he suspected that the local crooks always had word on what the cops were up to most of the time. And he guessed that Yuman's brother probably had at least a money-changing scheme going if not being involved in some other slightly colourful illegal activities.

'Right, look thanks for the information.'

Theo had to play dumb and pretend he did not already know about Biru and Mahmoud. He informed Yuman that he would be leaving the day after tomorrow to travel to Penang to meet up with Jack.

Yuman said, 'Ah, yes of course,' and then he smiled, 'I happy for you. Long time you wait to see your frien and I hope everything is okay. How long will you be there?'

'Not sure, depends on Jack but I also want to have a look around Penang Island and maybe other places too. Not sure when I will come back to Malaysia, I mean in years to come that is, in the future, I have to start my new job in a couple of weeks.' Theo noticed that when he said he was coming back, it seemed to make Yuman light up. Theo wasn't going to mention Biru.

'What if Biru want to see you?'

Theo found it hard to hold the young man's sparkling look. He added, 'But I will be in touch with you and I hope I see her. I … er, am not sure what, you know, not sure about any of that only other than I would like to see her again … er, and you of course … and anyway I'll come back here and see you before I fly out back to Australia.'

Yuman nodded. 'Yes, of course. You want me to organise ticket for Penang?'

'Yes, maybe, but I want to check out where other buses go as well, for future interest, you know?' He wanted to go back to Puduraya Bus Station. 'Eric and Franka are going to the Cameron Highlands; don't think I'll go there, might do on the way back. Anyway, we'll talk tomorrow morning after I've thought about it.'

'Okay, Mr Theo, no problem.'

Theo had made the decision to ring Brian in the morning. He was well aware Brian said he would let him know if Biru rang, or if there was any further information from Jack. He wanted to talk to Brian, maybe to get suggestions for a place to stay, maybe just to talk.

He grabbed a Coke from the fridge, handed over some money, bid goodnight and went back to his room. The night was still warm and muggy so he turned on the airconditioner and the clicking fan for company. He poured a vodka and Coke, lit a cigarette and opened *Beyond Pardon*. Why did he want to go back to Puduraya Bus Station? It provided a wealth of vital information for the things he was writing about. Also he somehow felt a link with Roland Hayley.

On The Move

Chapter Fifty-Four

Oil palms drifted by, acres and acres of them. The bus had been delayed at some points since departing from Kuala Lumpur due to roadworks, but that didn't matter to Theo. Slowing down enough to take in the scenery had its benefits, least of all reducing the frightening speed at which the bus hurtled along. Theo thought a video monitor, above the driver and slightly to the left, turned up to full volume, was installed to keep everyone's attention focused on it rather than the road. It was so loud that even with tissues in his ears he could hear it clearly. The movie playing was a Bruce Lee classic with ridiculous violence scenes that had Theo chuckling with the man alongside him, whenever his vision was drawn to the screen. The bus was about half full of backpackers and the rest local people, including many children. The locals who watched the movie chattered much of the time and the ones who didn't, slept.

Theo wondered how anyone could possibly sleep through that level of noise. A few of the backpackers put tissues in their ears and slept, probably because they were exhausted. Theo had the fleeting thought he was becoming a local; two weeks ago he would have been nursing a migraine headache.

Despite the noise it was difficult to stay interested in the movie for long periods because of the Chinese dialogue soundtrack and the English subtitles underneath were small and difficult to read. His mind wandered, mesmerised by the fields of oil palms sliding by. Periodically Theo was jerked into wakefulness when the bus swerved as the driver either fiddled with the TV controls or appeared to watch the movie. When roadworks were in progress the driver overtook anyone in front whenever possible and at times Theo thought they would have a head on. Because they were not travelling fast it was almost amusing but when the bus found new sections of the highway he had to close his eyes.

The bus was airconditioned and had 'No Smoking' signs everywhere but most of the passengers ignored the signs and lit up. Some people had opened the windows near them and the airconditioning didn't work very efficiently anyway. Theo figured that if the driver was set on frightening everyone and was smoking as well just under a sign that said the opposite, then Theo was well within his rights to light up. The Malaysian man alongside him had obviously decided to ignore the smoking rules too and he beat Theo to it by lighting up himself and offering Theo one.

Theo thought the nicotine would help but he couldn't stop himself doing the driving with the driver. He was sure he had put a dent in the floor where the brake would have been, much to the amusement of the man alongside him, who couldn't speak English very well.

Theo hammed it up. 'He's not going to pass ... bloody hell! He is ... shooooooot, we just made it ... No way! Frigging hell, we're rooted this time ...' and things similar. They both laughed.

Despite what Theo considered to be very close, if not a miracle, they didn't smash into anything. He begrudgingly had to give credit and be impressed with the skill of most road users, pedestrians as well. It was clear to him that the level of tolerance everyone appeared to have for each other was far greater than people back in Australia. He had concluded days before when near roads and on the footpaths of Kuala Lumpur, because there were so many people and so many vehicles, everyone mucked in and gave a bit. At home cutting in on someone usually meant a punch-up at the next set of lights, or worse, a cricket bat through the front windscreen. He noticed they never seemed to completely give way but always gave enough for someone else to sneak in. It led him to believe that because of the huge numbers of people, they had to get on and consider others, to a degree anyway. Maybe it *was* the Asian way Dempster had talked about.

Theo must have drifted off with the rocking of the bus. He had been thinking of the second visit to Puduraya Bus Station. The main reason for going there was to absorb the feel of the place because he wanted to expand on what he was going to write in his articles about travel in Malaysia. Before leaving that morning he asked Yuman to arrange his ticket but Theo wanted to experience the intensity of the crowds. He remembered Spud Morgan said the best and only way to write a really good article was to have a sense of place and actually be there, right in the guts of it. He wandered around glancing at chalkboards and notices about bus travel to Penang as well as information on other trips to consider for later in his stay. He laughed; no one paid him any attention. He was aware people didn't wander around inside the bus station; it was more like nudged and hustled. For some deep-down reason he couldn't explain, he wanted to understand how Roland Hayley, and others like him, actually felt.

He watched the buses coming in, the thick diesel fumes and engine noise, as well as people yelling at each other, some trying to snare tourists into purchasing tickets from them, others trying to communicate with a lackey on the roof of a bus loading or unloading baggage. On at least three occasions he felt someone try to invade his pockets and when he looked around he could detect no-one in particular, just mobs of people.

Theo managed to find a spot by a pillar where he could observe the comings and goings, and at times he jotted down points of interest. He also took a few photos as candidly as possible. As well as the travellers, sellers of tickets, freight agents, porters and workers loading and unloading, there were countless vendors selling souvenirs, cigarettes and clothing. The food sellers had hot and cold food, satay, samosas, and thali-type meals with rice on banana leaves, sweet treats of all descriptions, icecream, and fruit of many varieties Theo had never seen.

He watched backpackers everywhere and his mind went back to Roland Hayley's descriptions of the way it was. Theo could see it was still the same because as Hayley described, young travellers disembarked, some alert, many bleary-eyed, and because Theo was looking at the overall scene in a different way, he could see these people were vulnerable. Far from home, very short of money, many naïve and most wide open to scams of all kinds. From his vantage point he could actually detect one rough-looking character sidle up to young hopefuls, whisper something, and exchanges of money and some transaction take place. The young man was dressed in reasonably clean clothes with a shoulder bag but he was unshaven and his hair, although not long, was unkempt. At another place where Theo purchased a coke from a young Indian boy, he watched a bus unload and observed someone who could easily have been a Hayley character. This young man definitely looked down and out; skinny, dirty, with long, knotty hair and seemingly oblivious to anyone watching. This person was selling some sort of drugs, probably marijuana, almost openly and both seller and purchaser seemed unworried by any consequences. In view of the drug policy of the present-day government, Theo was amazed there didn't appear to be any police around. Then it hit him! Maybe there were! His hands started to shake involuntarily and fresh sweat prickled his scalp. He left the area soon after and as he walked out he saw a sign that he had not noticed before telling travellers to watch out for pickpockets and … people selling drugs.

When Theo was a block away he calmed down, realising that even if there were police around, he didn't have anything on him that could be deemed to be suspicious. Then he realised with a start, it did not seem to make any difference before.

∞

The Penang bus had '*Luxury Clipper*' painted brightly along the side with palm trees and a beach scene. The driver, a compact, dark jovial type, baseball cap on sideways, cigarette dangling from his lips, sat, eyes closed with hands clasped behind his head, legs sticking out the window whilst listening to the radio turned up full bore. His assistant, with a pirate's style bandana wrapped around his head, checked people's names and ushered them onto the bus. Theo waited until almost last to make sure his bag went in the luggage compartment rather than out the other side of the bus and away in the hands of an opportunist. This advice had come from Dempster and also a backpacker he met at the hotel. The assistant poked the VHS video into the player, thus disturbing the driver, and then promptly went to sleep curled up on the top step. He didn't wake up until they had a toilet and food stop at The Coffee Kedai - Tea and Cakes.

The first movie featured Claude Van Damme in '*No retreat, no surrender*' and everyone in the bus appeared interested for a short time.

The sound track was in English but the lips of the actors didn't match the dialogue. The Asians on board seemed to be more interested than the backpackers although Theo knew some of the tourists were stoned because he could smell marijuana smoke. Not long after they pulled out of Puduraya Bus Station a young female backpacker, no older than eighteen or nineteen, leaned across the aisle and offered Theo a smouldering marijuana roach. He declined, saying that he had a bit of a hangover from the night before. He could not help looking down the front of her loose cotton top as he talked to her. Theo wished he could tell them about his stint in jail so they would know the dangers of what they were doing but he realised he would look like a puritan, or a liar. The number of young women backpacking around, some on their own, amazed Theo. The incident with the joint, looking at her firm breasts and slender legs made him slightly unsettled. The young man alongside her identified himself as her boyfriend because he had a hand on her tanned knee.

Some sections of the highway, Theo thought, might have been built by convict labour because there didn't appear to be any heavy machinery around. What could have been corrective service officers, not armed with firepower but looking severe with lengths of cane in hand, stood around and directed the workers. The labourers were all very unkempt; some with shirts, some not, some had Oriental, woven, conical hats, others had almost Italian-style handkerchiefs, or squares of rags with the corners tied. The unlucky ones wore nothing in the blazing sun as they dug, shovelled, and carried earth and rocks in woks. Theo felt sorry for them and wondered why they did not use wheelbarrows. The background of rice paddies and palm trees, punctuated by the odd buffalo and what was termed coolie labourers with poles over their shoulders balancing buckets or woks of dirt, completed a rural scene Theo imagined South East Asia had looked like for hundreds of years.

Periodically Theo was brought back to the present when Van Damme machine-gunned down an army of bad guys and then proceeded to punch and kick the rest of them on his way across a compound.

∞

As they trundled on, Theo had more time to think because the bus swerved around potholes and reading was difficult. Sometimes the driver either couldn't be bothered slowing down or didn't see the big holes because the overladen bus bottomed out several times. The stoned backpackers looked at each other and laughed when the bus hit the big ones as bags dislodged and people were thrown about like flotsam. The sleeping Asians continued to sleep.

The new addition, a travel book by Eric Newby sat on his lap. On his last night in Kuala Lumpur, returning to the Hot Spot, she was there.

Chapter Fifty-Five

'Aha, Young White Boss Tuan, here! I have book for you. Special. I know you look for book, right now.'

Theo jerked with surprise. Not only had he forgotten to look for her on the way home but in conversation he had told Franka earlier in the evening he needed to buy a book to read on the bus, some escapism type reading, but even then had not really thought of the Old Woman from Borneo.

Theo straightened up. 'Maybe I don't need a book.'

She had more books than usual spread out on her blanket and some other jewellery items as well. 'Yah, yah, you do, I wise old woman, I know these things. You want to expand mind, read plenty. This book collector's item, very valuable but I save for you.'

He squatted and opened his packet of cigarettes. She took three. 'Three?' he scolded.

She put two in a little box and laughed loudly, showing red teeth and gums. He lit both their cigarettes.

He knew he had to play along, he wanted to. 'Maybe I already have too many books.'

She wrapped her scarf loosely around her turkey neck. 'This book very special, written by early model traveller who set standard for world travel writing. Special evening price.'

Theo had not heard of Eric Newby but he flicked through a couple of times, trying not to seem too interested. 'Look, Old

Woman from Borneo, I have too many books already, I have to carry them. How much?'

She laughed her half cackle, 'Ten ringgit, just for you.'

'Ten? Naaah! You've got to be joking, too dear, mahalnya.'

'No, no, not too dear, special collector's book, you keep and make fortune.'

'Five.'

'Five? No five too small, I lose money, I starve to death on street, be laughing stock. Eight.'

'Eight? But this book is second hand, printed in ...' Theo squinted, '... 1958. No, no. How about,' he rubbed his jaw, 'Six.'

'I tell truth, book worth plenty, plenty now, wait till years' time, worth fortune. See print date, first issue. Six no good, see back page also is still in residence, most important for collector's antique book. Seven.'

Theo burst out laughing, remembering the previous two encounters where he had been done. 'Okay, Old Woman from Borneo, I will have to sell my body on the street now to pay for this, okay? Seven.'

'You so wise young Tuan, you shrewd businessman.' She wrapped the book up in newspaper. 'You now qualify for free fortune pronouncement. Wait, I contact spirits from jungle.'

She looked up into the polluted evening air. 'I think you go to meet woman far from here, she create danger for you, maybe.'

You covered your bases there, Old Woman from Borneo. How could she know I am leaving tomorrow? Come on Theo, lucky guess, all tourists move on and woman? Easy, plenty of them around. Danger? Choose from getting one pregnant to a jealous boyfriend. 'Where am I meeting this woman?'

'Aaaaah! Ooooooh, vision not clear but you leave here soon and wait, but you come back here.'

That's a safe bet, KL is the only international airport in Malaysia. 'What about danger?'

'Can't tell for sure. You give me cig'rette for going away present?'

Theo smiled again. 'Yep.' He opened the pack and gave her one. She looked at it as if it was an insult. 'Alright, alright,' and gave her another two. He walked away from the encounter wondering how she could know those things but it did not take long to convince himself it was all circumstantial and anyone could make similar predictions.

∞

The bus braked hard and the book fell on the floor as they pulled in for another toilet stop. Perfect timing – almost in unison with the credits on the video screen monitor.

Chapter Fifty-Six

This bus stop was more primitive than the previous one with squat toilets and brown-coloured water, obviously from a bore, coming out of the taps.

There were a dozen food and drink stalls with low tables and squat stools. He purchased some lychees and a mango. The driver hit the air horns and they were soon on the road again. The highway was in slightly better condition and not long after, they pulled into Butterworth, the mainland port and city linking Penang Island.

The bus station was near the ferry terminal. Theo had considered taking the ferry but Brian suggested he go back that way because often the bus times did not coordinate with the ferry times and there would probably be a wait. Brian told him the causeway bridge was an interesting sight as well. Theo also had another motive. He wanted to find out which ferry his father had stepped off the back of when he died. If Brian did not know then Jack would. Theo was content with the decision because the dock was crowded and noisy, also he wanted to do the ferry trip, back and forward.

He took a few shots with his instamatic and hung around lost in thought, looking into the harbour for a while. He straightened up with a jolt and glanced back towards his pack, still visible in the luggage rack under the bus.

Port-related activity continued in the late afternoon sun. A mosaic of fishing and recreational boats, peppered with ancient-looking Chinese junks, sampans and clinkers, floated at anchor or chugged out to sea. Other craft bumped and rocked against the wharf and two ferries were tied up, loading and unloading. One ferry sat stationary, engines bubbling and boiling water at the stern, adding more diesel fumes to the scene. Palm trees stood in groups and other tropical trees lined the road. A slight sea breeze began and slowly ruffled the glassy sea surface into mini ripples, and the palm trees began to stir.

Theo looked back at the bus. Most of the locals stepped off, including the smiling man who had been alongside him, and the luggage holds were open for people to retrieve their baggage or produce. The pirate coach assistant yelled out names and distributed items. Theo jumped down and found some shade, lit a cigarette and kept an eye on his bag. Several touts were doing the rounds trying to sell accommodation or restaurant recommendations to the backpackers who had decided to stretch their legs and probably make sure their packs stayed on the bus, too. The bus driver, cigarette hanging from lips, stood at the doorway and wouldn't let any of the touts on to the bus.

Theo glanced over at the young backpacker who had offered him the joint. She stood talking with her partner and the couple she had shared the smoke with. The female of the other couple was of similar age and in Theo's eyes just as beautiful. It made him think of Biru again.

Boarding another bus parked alongside was a group of uniformed Australian personnel from the Butterworth Air Force Base, smoking and chattering. Accompanying them were similarly uniformed Malaysian officers and some local women, wives and girlfriends, Theo thought. Two other buses pulled in, dropped off passengers, gained more and then pulled out.

Theo casually glanced around, sure no-one was following him. There were no suspicious-looking characters on the bus as far as he could tell. After about half an hour, Theo jumped back on board and the bus filled up with local people going to Georgetown. There were not enough seats and several sat in the aisle, on the floor or on top of their bags.

The bridge, stretching 13½ kilometres, joins Penang Island to mainland Malaysia. In the late afternoon a heat haze, mixed with industrial smoke or smog, hung over the island like the ring around Saturn. Large sea craft, tankers and container ships dotted the bay on either side. The bridge had four lanes and prompted the driver to push the bus as fast as it would go. It seemed as if something was due to explode. Differential and gearbox whine made it difficult to hear the violent video but it was in Chinese anyway without subtitles. As they neared the Georgetown side roadworks came into view and the driver was forced to slow down, which was a relief to some of the passengers. People began to talk excitedly as they went past the other end toll office and along the expressway towards Georgetown.

Theo was instantly interested as they moved almost at once into the suburbs, mesmerised by the quaint buildings, most of Oriental design with ornate carved stonework and brightly painted exteriors. He made note on his map of a colourful temple he saw when the bus stopped for a moment before starting again and swerving down an impossibly narrow street, vying for space with cycle rickshaws, handcarts and pedestrians. Theo realised with a pleasant shock that there seemed to be fewer motorbikes and other vehicles than in Kuala Lumpur. The people seemed to be mostly Chinese-looking and many wore the traditional conical sun hat.

The bus eventually stopped at the Weld Quay terminus, which appeared to be as much a market place. Vendors of all things added to the noise and confusion as passengers tried to claim their luggage. Theo was quick to grab his backpack and took off in the direction of Lebuh Chulia where the bulk of the cheaper hotels were. Several touts harassed him with all sorts of deals but he fended them off, saying he knew where he was going because he had been there before.

He had spoken to Brian yesterday and quizzed him about places to stay and eat. It seemed there were plenty of suitable hotels to choose from and luckily he was able to speak with a young man who had come from Georgetown. The backpacker had booked into the Hot Spot and was sitting in the foyer reading some brochures when he overheard Theo talking to Yuman.

Theo was headed for the Hotel Happiness, and if not that, the Hotel New in Lebuh Ho Fat, a supposed short walk from the bus station. The quaint names of hotels and eating places caused him laugh out loud which made several people look at him. Rickshaw riders constantly stopped to offer a lift but he wanted to walk after sitting for most of the day in the cramped uncomfortable bus. However, thunder rumbled in the distance, sweat soaked his clothes and he didn't want to be caught in the rain. Street names were mostly in what looked like Chinese and many didn't seem to have any name at all. Within a short time he could swear he was going around in circles.

'You best get transport,' said a young Chinese man of indiscriminate age.

Theo mentioned the name of the hotels and the boy said, 'Four ringgit.'

'Nup, too dear.' Brian had said don't pay any more than two.

'No, no, long way, long way, have to go there.' He pointed wildly.

Theo had studied the map earlier and was sure it wasn't that far.

'No thanks, mate, I'll walk.' The sun beat down. Theo asked directions from a friendly-looking man selling jackfruit.

'Ho Fa Row deferen. Hotel Happiness in Ho Fa Lay, Jawtown big place, lon way, okay?'

Dropping the hard consonants in the typical Chinese way made it difficult for Theo to decipher but he understood the drift. Ho Fat Road was different to Ho Fat Lane. He hoped he was not going to regret the decision to walk. Theo continued in the direction the man had indicated.

The rickshaw driver appeared again. 'Long way, long way, take much time.'

Theo kept walking.

'Okay, okay, three best price.' The adolescent put his hands out as if he was making a huge sacrifice taking on a fare so cheap.

'Sorry, mate, too dear,' and Theo kept walking, straps of his backpack digging into his shoulders.

Okay, okay, you win, two.'

Theo hoped it did not look as if he had lost face but at that moment he was past caring so he jumped in and they pedalled off, nearly collecting a food trolley in their haste. Theo tried to relax but they hurtled along. 'What's the bloody hurry?' he said to the driver but he didn't hear. At least it was a way to see the place as they scattered a pack of dogs lying in the middle of the road.

The streets were narrow, some one way, and the buildings were very Chinese. Temple dogs and various colourful statues sat at some doorways, and banners of dragons and huge letters fluttered from the maze of electrical wiring stretched across the streets. Produce was laid out on mats for sale in awkward places and mobile food carts and barrows dotted the roadway, sometimes making it difficult for traffic to negotiate. There were many opportunities for photos and although he had plenty of duty-free film Theo figured it would be good to get the films he'd already taken developed. With the promise of the afternoon storm, however, people darted all over the place packing up or preparing in readiness. They pedalled down lanes and narrow roadways, some fighting for space with motorbikes, other carts and pushbikes. The accesses looked much the same, crowded, noisy, and some more than others topped off with the aroma of spices, cooking food, garbage, dog shit and two-stroke fumes. Most roadways had open drains, more so than Kuala Lumpur, where rotting vegetable matter, mixed with paper and plastic, baked in the stifling heat. A dead dog added to the stench in one lane and Theo hoped the rain would wash it all away.

After a longer time than Theo imagined, they pulled up amongst a bustling crowd of mainly vegetable vendors at the end of Ho Fat Lane. Theo could not see any hotel and he had the feeling he was in for an interesting experience at the least. He was about to ask about that when the boy pointed to a sign almost overshadowed by numerous smaller Chinese signs high up.

'Righto, mate, understood,' he said, climbing out, noting that the drains were covered up.

Food aromas drifted in the air. He felt slightly guilty about the rickshaw boy because it was in fact considerably further than he estimated but Brian's words echoed softly. *Don't pay any more than two.*

Theo dug out two ringgits.

'Two okay for passenger but two for baggage.' The boy held out his hand. The original happy face Theo remembered was replaced by an oily smile.

'What?' said Theo loudly, 'You can't just jack up the …' as he handed over two ringgits.

Chapter Fifty-Seven

'We agree on two from passenger but baggage always same price as person, okay?' The okay was added as if it was all settled and the fare was four.

Theo took a deep breath and released it with a sigh. 'Sorry, mate, we did not agree to that at all.' He put his palms outward.

Theo knew he had to remain calm and not threaten because someone was bound to lose face and he was determined it not be him. Suddenly a loud female voice stopped everyone within the radius. A plump Chinese woman burst out of the laneway and yelled at the rickshaw driver. Theo stood watching her wag her finger and talk sharply. It sounded like a Chinese dialect and she was reprimanding the boy but Chinese at high volume sounded confrontational normally to Theo anyway.

She said to Theo, 'He give other rickshaw boys bad name. You no pay for baggage, fare of passenger include baggage, always, okay?' She turned to the rickshaw driver, 'He no need to pay for bag, it included.' She shrieked at him, 'You go, go, go!'

'Right.' Theo shrugged at the rickshaw boy but could think of nothing else to say so he picked up his bag.

'This way to Hotel Happiness, my name Mama, some call me Big Buddha Mama but that take too long to say.' She laughed, breasts wobbling, 'I proprietor of hotel.'

Theo realised he would have taken some time to find the place because the hotel sign was difficult to see among other signs and the entrance was down the lane about twenty metres. Signs mainly in Chinese decorated many of the walls in all directions, with English translations in smaller writing on many of them, advertising travel agents, small restaurants, produce and souvenir shops for tourists. There were only signs intermittently in Malaysian.

They walked to the front counter through a group of tables, some occupied by backpackers drinking beer or coffee.

'We only have budget room, okay?' He nodded. 'How long you stay?' She opened up a register and took a pen out of a jar.

Theo had been thinking about this question and was no closer to a resolution. 'Well, I'm not sure, but initially say two days. I ... um ... have to meet a friend of mine, I'm not sure when he ... er ... sh ... not sure, and I ... er want to go to Batu Ferringhi for a couple of days and come back, you know ...'

Mama looked at him, eyes wide, all business. 'Okay, okay, you stay two days and we know more later?'

'Yeah, I should know more soon ...' He was glad he hadn't mentioned Biru's name.

She waved her hands, 'Okay, okay, no problem. If you decide to go to beach for day or two we hold room for you, many guest do same, small deposit require though, okay?'

Theo was thankful she could read him thinking; she must have gone to the same training school as Yuman. She took his passport, photocopied it and handed it back with a key. 'You go that way.'

Theo was thankful he could get in because he had given Eric and Franka the list of hotels he was going to try. The Hotel Happiness seemed nearly full as backpackers wandered in and out and some sat out the front. Either way, as a last resort he told them to leave a message with Brian Aung at St John's Church if other things failed. He gave them Brian's phone number as well as the address of the church.

Theo walked past the entrance and into the foyer. He stopped, overwhelmed, and looked around the room. Although the building was very old, everything was clean, bright and functional. Shutters, doors and walls were painted all colours and old, well-used furniture sat in practical positions. A row of brightly painted dragons formed an ornate cornice and at each opening off the main room sat a pair of temple animals breathing fire. A family of Chinese chattered away in a room adjacent. The fragrance of incense burned as offerings at various places where small Chinese Buddhas sat smiling welcome. The incense hid any smell of drains.

Theo wandered over scrubbed paving stones and past a bigger version of the smiling Buddha. He stopped, stepped back and rubbed the Buddha's stomach which was the extent of his knowledge of Buddhism. He wound his way through a courtyard surrounded by miniature cane palms, tropical flowers and plants. A ferocious dog-dragon sprouted water from its mouth into a small pond full of goldfish and colourful carp, most at least a hand long. After the heat from the street it was a most welcoming place to be. Theo stopped again and stood for a moment to take it all in. Several backpackers walked past acknowledging him.

The spotlessly clean floors were painted brightly in cream gloss paving paint and the walls in a variety of clean colours. The rooms were in rows in a dormitory style but partitioned off into separate rooms. Each door was painted bright gloss red with a gold number in English and a Chinese character underneath.

He placed his pack on an old lowboy that could have been five hundred years old, turned on the fan and glanced around his room. The partitioned walls stopped about a foot from the roof with insect wire filling the gap. The budget rooms had no bathrooms. Theo didn't mind because it was very cheap and the young man he met in Kuala Lumpur convinced him it was the best place to stay if he could get in, and he could upgrade to a better room if he wished.

He went down the corridor to the ablutions area. Fortunately the toilets and showers were segregated because partitions started two feet off the ground and finished at about six and a half foot, not much privacy. The toilets were Asian style, holes in the very clean floor, and the showers had open drains that flowed into bigger drains outside in the corridor. Each shower cubicle had a tiled trough for those who wanted to wash, splashing water over themselves with a mandi. The shower was no more than a spout sticking out of the tiles about five foot up but there was pressure enough to get wet. The tropical storm arrived as he stepped under the gusher and because the weather was so hot there was no need for hot water. He stood for ages, scrolling events in his mind and looking over the partitions as rain poured down outside, filling gutters and flooding drains. Feeling clean but exhausted he went back to his room and lay down.

∞

He awoke sometime later to the sound of the local mosque calling and was momentarily confused as to where he was. It came back quickly. The fan whirred, didn't click or squeak or wobble. Theo smiled, the private joke all his. He turned it to low and lit a cigarette. He wondered for a moment why there was a mosque nearby because everything he'd seen so far was so Chinese he had forgotten about any other group living here in Penang. Familiarity returned when dogs began barking.

He made some entries in *Theo's Adventures* book. Later he went to reception to check on phone availability and rang Brian to make contact. Biru had not contacted him. Brian agreed to meet him the next morning. Theo had a beer at one of the tables out the front, chatted with a couple of backpackers, went for an orienteering stroll, then ate at a dim sum restaurant down the lane.

Back in his room again, he poured a generous slug of vodka into the mouth-rinsing plastic cup and topped it up with orange. He opened *Beyond Pardon* and flicked through. The interviews became somewhat repetitive; Hayley talked about his lawyer and legal team and the arguments raised. Then he talked of life inside and stories of other inmates. Theo put the book down, closed his eyes and wondered about the whole sad story. He could relate to Hayley's plight, someone caught up in the twists and turns of life. Not everyone would end up like Hayley. Theo thought the poor bloke simply made bad decisions, one after the other. Theo's short stint in jail was not a patch on Hayley's incarceration but he knew one wrong move, not even necessarily away from home either, and anyone could get into something they couldn't get out of. He also wondered if he ever would have read Hayley's story if he had not come to Malaysia and had he not known Spud Morgan. And then he started wondering about the Old Woman from Borneo.

Chapter Fifty-Eight

The morning sounds of Asia woke him early. Barking dogs, people talking loudly, beep beep of vehicles, the ding of bicycle bells and someone sweeping outside his door. Gongs sounded accompanied by hypnotic chanting in the distance and he thought he heard a call to prayer somewhere in the mix of sounds.

Even at seven in the morning, the day was warm and humidity hung in the air like treacle. Theo decided to go round the corner and try a place mentioned in the guidebook where banana porridge was a specialty. He wandered into the courtyard and stood for a minute looking into the cool water at the fish cruising beneath the strands of seagrass water lilies. Even though noises drifted in from the street, he was calmed by the beauty and serenity of space. The thought of food moved him on and he waved good morning to Buddha Mama and a young male assistant at the front desk. He was only a few feet outside the entrance when a rickshaw driver, parked under a frangipani tree, yelled out.

'Hey boss, you want lift?'

'No thanks, mate, not going far.'

'No problem, no problem, my name Tung, quick hop in.'

'Sorry, mate, I'm only going around the corner.'

'I be your special guide for stay, okay?'

'No thanks.' Theo kept walking to the corner and turned.

'Special price, guide for day?'

'No thanks I'm not going far.' Theo went to walk into the Kwan Koo café.

'I wait for you here, okay?'

Theo stepped over to him. 'Thanks mate, I don't need a rickshaw at the moment, I'm about to have breakfast, right?'

'Okay, no problem. I wait for you outside, here, okay?'

Theo threw his hands out and shook his head and said in a friendly, but firm way, 'I – don't – need – a – rickshaw but thanks anyway, okay?'

Theo sat under a fan at a table near the back with his back to the wall. A dreamy teenager, who shuffled over dragging her sandals, dropped a menu on his table. He looked out into the street. No-one out there looked suspicious and he was feeling content within himself. All he could see were industrious people hosing or sweeping the pavement in front of their shops as they yelled to each other and laughed. He felt good because he was certain no-one was following him and it occurred to him they may have given up.

He ordered banana porridge and the girl delivered a copy of the local paper as well, written in English. Most of the content was local politics of which he had no specific interest, but the sporting section had cricket scores. After breakfast he wandered out the front.

'Still here, I wait for you.'

Theo kept going in the direction of St. John's. The morning was hot and humid and apart from the occasional tree, the buildings provided intermittent shade.

'Where you go? I take you.'

St John's wasn't far, even taking into account one-way streets. Theo finally gave in. 'Okay, okay, how much to St John's Church?'

'Four.'

'No thanks, tidak.'

'Jawtown big place, okay three.'

'Listen … er … Tang, one.'

'Me Tung … two.'

'One, I was told I should pay no more than one.' He knew that was a lie but it seemed necessary.

'Oh no, one too small. Two best morning-time price.'

Theo kept walking.

'Okay okay, you win. One.'

Theo smiled, feeling as if he really was getting the hang of it without losing face. Tung looked solemn for a second or two, maybe trying to look cheated and then he grinned. They pedalled off towards St John's. In the heat people were out selling or eating at mobile food carts, cafés and restaurants. A group of middle-aged tourists with cameras around their necks huddled with a guide. Theo had not seen any tourists since leaving the Hotel Happiness.

Building types varied but were mostly one and two storey, separated by an arch into a courtyard or a stone temple entrance. Signs, mainly in Chinese, decorated the buildings, and flags as well as banners hung on electrical power wires across roadways. Theo could not help looking up, mesmerised by the creative, electrical wiring wrapped around transformers and poles, seemingly tangled like discarded fishing nets. He wondered if anyone actually managed to electrocute themselves or whether fires ever started due to a short out.

Tung took them through lanes and narrow roads, more than once only just avoiding a collision. Eventually an old man with baskets full of ducks piled high in his front rack and with almost non-existent vision, did actually collide with them but it was just a friendly nudge. It was all the more graphic because Theo was in the seat in front of the rider. Tung and the old man argued almost heatedly and the old man remonstrated and pointed to Theo several times. Theo figured the old man wanted some money because of the belief tourists have plenty even though it was clearly the old man's fault. Theo winked at Tung and pulled out a cigarette and pretended to light. Tung understood and a couple of cigarettes later, both parties walked away smiling.

Theo was thankful they were taking the back lanes because the wider roads were more impersonal with cars, motorbikes, buses and trucks all vying for limited space. They weaved through local traffic which consisted of handcarts, barrows, pushbikes with trailers or big cages in front of the rider. The occasional motorbike or car seemed to spoil the scene which, although far from tranquil, was quaint, and if he blocked out the motor transport, he figured it was as it had been a hundred or more years ago. Several times Theo looked for the imaginary brake with his foot, but eventually he gave in and tried to relax because the speed everyone was moving at was very slow and the danger of anything serious was small. The humid air was punctuated by bicycle bells, people yelling and Oriental and occasionally Indian music coming from shopfronts. Theo had not noticed very much Islamic or Indian influence so far but he did notice a mosque on the skyline as they turned a corner. He knew from the guidebook that there were some Chinese temples near the Masjid Kapitan Keling. After about ten minutes they arrived at a big stone church on a half-acre of lush, freshly mown lawn, shade trees and a smattering of outbuildings.

Theo put his hand in his pocket to pay.

'No pay, no need, I wait for you.'

'Mate … Tung, I could be here for hours, best I pay now.'

'No problem, I wait.' He smiled and his eyes almost disappeared in his Chinese face.

'Tung, I could be ages in here.'

'No problem, I wait. I be your official driver.'

'I can't afford to pay for you to wait here all day for me.'

'Boss, no cost, I wait, it is my job.'

Theo persisted. 'How much?'

'No fee, only cost of one ringgit for trip here and fee for next leg of journey.'

Theo handed him a couple of cigarettes. 'Righto mate, suit yourself but I'll be a while.'

Theo left Tung lounging as his own passenger, smoking under the shade of a tree.

∞

The church, typical of old British colonial sandstone construction, stood behind an iron spiked fence. A small sign saying *Wayward Travellers' Haven Project* with an arrow pointing next door caused Theo to look in that direction. He remembered Brian saying something about Jack helping out there.

Theo walked through the open double gates and looked up at the big sign identifying St John's Anglican Church, Penang. Information as to days and times of services and functions and a phone number for general enquiries filled the rest of the space with smaller font.

A nun walked out the front door of the church and nodded to him as she passed. He glanced towards the administration offices on the right and slightly to the rear. One building to the left and near the back of the property appeared to be the rector's private residence and two other smaller outbuildings completed the scene. Theo looked at the church doors was reminded of how long it had been since he went to church. He turned and wandered towards the administration building.

Some children were playing down near one of the smaller buildings at the back. An old Chinese man sat reading a newspaper at a wooden table under a giant fig tree. Theo continued on towards the admin building.

Someone called, 'Theo?'

Chapter Fifty-Nine

He turned.

'Theo! I'd recognise you anywhere.' The grey-haired Chinese man wearing a white shirt and dark trousers stood up and waved. 'Over here.'

Theo walked over, slightly unsure of the situation.

'Brian, Brian Aung. What a pleasure it is to meet you my son.' The man gently grasped Theo by the shoulders and embraced him, like family. 'Splendid.' He swung his arm in the direction of a teak chair.

Theo shook his head. 'It's ... well, I didn't expect ..?' The man was not as old as he looked from a distance.

'What? A dumpy little Chinese fellow with a British accent?'

When he laughed his eyes reduced to slits in his chubby face. Theo thought he looked like the smiling Buddha at the Hotel Happiness. A good match for Buddha Mama.

All Theo could say was, 'What can I say?' and he laughed too.

'My father was with the British diplomatic service and my mother was, of course, Chinese. Half and half. I suppose God gave me the education and British accent, and the Buddha gave me the Chinese look.' He stroked his all but non-existent beard which consisted of half a dozen long hairs. 'Tea?'

Theo nodded. Silence followed for a comfortable minute while the tea was poured and Brian slid the packet of biscuits towards Theo.

Brian reached for a packet of Lucky Strikes on the table. 'Hope you don't have this filthy habit. Cigarette?' He offered Theo one and chuckled.

CRUCIAL STEP

Theo smiled; it was comforting to be with such a happy person. 'Thanks,' he said and lit up.

Brian exhaled. He held the cigarette between thumb and forefinger. 'Now, Theo, please tell me about yourself.'

'Before I do, have you heard from Biru ... or Jack for that matter?'

'I haven't heard from your lady friend Biru but I had a brief chat with Jack yesterday. He said he spoke to you and by all accounts he should be here tomorrow or the day after. Now about you, Theo. You obviously survived jail?' He smiled but he wasn't making fun.

'Yeah, just.' A shiver ran through him at the thought. 'It was the worst experience of my life without a doubt. I was framed by Biru's boyfriend, Mahmoud, or at least I'm 99% sure it was him – he was the only one who had any motive because there was no reason for anyone else to put dope in my room when I was out. Also ... well he's not, and he never was, her boyfriend either but her family and his family had arranged for them to marry. She had resisted from the start and when I came along – we didn't do anything, I mean kind of, you know ... er ... touched ...' Theo felt a flush, 'and he happened to see us ... you know.'

'Aha, affairs of the heart. This may not be my business, but ...' He waved an outward palm and smiled at the contradiction as he continued, 'I probably don't need to tell you to be careful with your situation; Muslims, Chinese and Indians too, take these things seriously, in point of fact, some more seriously than others. In all but the very liberated Muslim families, women are considered to be property and arranged marriages are commonplace. In years gone by, her family may very well have had you beaten and her killed, terrible. Fortunately these days, women are grouping together and trying to change all that, I mean now we have, in the modern Malaysia, women lawyers and laws are being changed to give women equal rights. Sounds good in principle, of course, but there is still a long way to go. You may have difficulty understanding this but for Mahmoud, it is a question of honour and you are threatening an Islamic tradition that has been around for a very long time. So, in effect, he is just defending honour; his, Biru's and both their families.'

Theo's confusion showed on his face. 'Honour?'

'Yes, he would be thinking only of protecting the woman who has been promised to him.'

261

'Protecting? But he has slapped her on two occasions I am aware of …'

'Yes, that may be so but a woman is seen as high value and he sees it as his duty to be responsible for her. And you are a threat.'

Theo shook his head, 'You are right, I do have difficulty accepting this.'

Brian smiled and wagged a finger. 'I didn't say accepting it, I said understanding it. I agree with you, I have difficulty accepting it too but I have as much of a problem accepting any culture that allows women to be treated in this way. Unfortunately, also, in our so-called civilised western culture, many women are bullied and treated appallingly. It is most unfortunate that some men feel the need to be like this. In fact, to bully anyone is unnecessary.' He flicked his hand, dismissing the topic. 'Anyway, Theo, may I ask what you intend to do when she does show up?' He took another drag.

Theo shook his head slowly.

'Aha, seems as if you haven't thought very clearly about that. Please, if you need to talk about this I may be able to help.'

Theo realised he badly wanted to unload his thoughts. 'Help? Yeah, look I … we haven't even talked about anything, I hardly know her. Nothing really has happened between us, she may not even turn up, I mean, when I went to jail, she disappeared. At first I thought Mahmoud had taken her but then I figured she had been planning on running away before I came on the scene. Some of the things she hinted at earlier indicated she wasn't very happy with being sold off to become Mahmoud's property.'

'I too was of the opinion she had been thinking of running away prior. She said her family had her life planned out for them more than her. Theo, if she does turn up, you should be very careful about being seen with her in public. A young Muslim woman walking hand in hand with a western, white man would indicate to the Islamic police that she is a prostitute and she would definitely be punished, if not murdered.'

'Islamic police?'

'Yes, Islamic police, Muslim police same thing. Probably as far as the government is concerned they don't exist, but I can assure you they do. They represent the more strict code of practice for Islam called Sharia. These men, and it is always men, wander around and spy on other Muslims and if they catch anyone betting or drinking or co-habiting with another race of person, well they dish out punishment.'

'Oh.' Theo pulled out his cigarettes, offering Brian one, who shook his head. As he lit up he again wondered what he was getting himself into. He hardly knew anything about her background, in fact he hardly knew her at all.

'Yes, I would point out, you have much to think about. I must say, Biru seemed like a very nice, polite young lady and she gave the impression she had her head screwed on. It must be very difficult for progressive young women who wish to throw off the shackles of male domination and family traditions. In many Muslim families, the women are forbidden to work and can only have friends approved of by their fathers or brothers. As far as having a relationship with a man, well firstly the man has to be highly recommended and there has to be a chaperone present until marriage. This is not the case for all by any stretch and it does surprise me sometimes when I visit Kuala Lumpur and I see many obviously Muslim women in western attire. I mean we have women in government, as lawyers and in the corporate world, so maybe things are changing, at least in the big cities.'

Theo took a sip of tea and then picked up a biscuit to fill the silence. He knew there was a lot to learn.

Brian switched topics. 'I only met your father a couple of times; he seemed a decent sort of fellow.'

Theo nodded. 'I see, right. I didn't really know my father very well, he left Australia when I was six and didn't come back as far as I know in all that time. Before he went to Vietnam, we used to go to the footy and the beach and things but I don't remember much.' Theo almost said, '*He was a bastard to my mother and me, never wrote, never let us know he was okay, nothing, bugger all.*' Then he returned to the conversation. 'But, Jack took the trouble to let us know dad was alive, alive but not well in his mind. The war messed his head around. Mum said it was shell shock. I guess that's why I'm here to see Jack. Believe it or not, I seem to remember Jack better than the old man, you know? I get the impression my father and Jack were up to something over the years.' Theo looked directly at Brian.

His eyes almost disappeared when the face took on a smile. 'Maybe, I suppose they were involved in some business enterprises, they had to survive here but ...' he shrugged, 'I'm sure you will be asking Jack about all these things.'

'Do you know anything about how he died? I mean what part of the boat was he on, how could he just step off the back and, you know, and no-one sort of stopped him?'

The answer surprised him. 'Well, Theo, it is no secret he stepped off the back of the ferry through the gap where the tow line is. It's very easy to do. It was late at night and I believe there were only a handful of crew members playing cards or something. Anyway, my son, you should not dwell on this. It was indeed no accident, or should I say your father chose to step off. There were witnesses and it was fully investigated … um … probably more rigorously than if it was a local who did the same thing. I hate to say it and it needs to be said, from what I knew of your father, he had many problems, mental illness they say and it seems he'd had enough of living. Sometimes in this life things just happen, it is as simple as that. No need to make it complicated. If you wish to pursue this you should speak to Jack, he was there at the time.' His eyebrows levelled. 'Naturally you want to know many things but could I say, maybe finding out finer details uncovers things you don't wish to address. What do you expect to find, anyway?'

Theo thought for a moment. 'I don't really expect to find anything, it's more … I want to see, look at the ferry, that's all. I don't know, curious I guess …'

'Now, something important. Another pot of tea and a Chinese version of Digestive biscuit?' He laughed, eyes disappearing. The wise, Chinese side of Brian Aung dominated. Clearly he was not going to talk about things that were not his business.

Theo respected that and liked the man very much. 'Yeah, why not.'

Brian grabbed the newspaper and they walked into the administrative building where he introduced a middle-aged woman who sat at a reception desk.

'Theo, this is Lisa Lu who is here most of the time. I help out sometimes when they are short. If you need to get in touch with me she can get in touch with me.' He turned, 'Through here.'

He led Theo out the back to a kitchen where an urn bubbled and he directed Theo to a covered patio outside. 'I'll make a pot of tea.'

Theo was left to his thoughts for a few minutes and even though it was hot, the fragrant garden gave a feeling of coolness with shades of green and flowering plants. He hadn't even considered any of the implications of being involved with Biru. He had no idea what he was going to say to her. She was trying to obtain a passport but what did that mean? Were they going to go ... away? Where? Theo thought his only sin was to like her but where to from there?

Maybe it would be best if she didn't show up at all and possibly that could happen anyway. Brian hadn't heard from her so maybe she had no intention of fronting up. That would solve ... what? It would solve her family or Mahmoud wanting to kill him, anyway. But Theo knew it wouldn't solve him wanting to see her.

A small bird flittering in the frangipani tree caught his attention and he recalled a short passage in *Beyond Pardon* where Hayley befriended a bird. He was jolted out of the silence.

'Here we are. They say tea doesn't solve all the world's problems but it jolly well helps.' Brian put the tea tray down on the table. 'Help yourself to the biscuits; they are much nicer than the real Digestives. Chinese make them, they are very good, you know. These are better than the ones we had out there.'

Chapter Sixty

Theo broke the comfortable silence. 'When Biru spoke to you last, what did she say?'

'Not much. She said she had to be quick using the phone at the place where she was staying because, obviously, no one was supposed to know where she was. She said she was trying to organise a passport and visa for Australia. I formed the impression she had been trying to sort this out for some months, maybe longer, because she complained about delays with bureaucrats, something like that.'

Theo nodded, 'Yeah I got that, too.'

'She rang me. I suspect she was in Borneo but that is a guess because our connection dropped out for a second and I was on a sort of party line – lines must have crossed – then someone mentioned Nia Caves in this other conversation – I was about to hang up when I was reconnected again. Damned phones, happens all the time. Anyway she didn't say much more, only asked if she could leave a message here in a day or two. Then she gave me the details I was to pass on to you and then she said she had to go, it all happened quickly. Before she hung up she gave me the number to give to you. I knew roughly where Nia Caves are and I looked it up to be sure. They are in Sarawak, near Miri,' said Brian smiling, obviously proud of his detective skills. 'Of course she could be anywhere and someone happened to mention the caves in a broader context.'

Theo nodded. 'I spoke to her straight after your call, she quickly said she should be here in a few days, about now in fact, and would get a message to you. I am a bit surprised she hasn't contacted you in the last few days.'

'Oh well, remember you are on Asian time now, Theo.'

They both sipped their tea with the distant hum of traffic wafting in the midday heat as the tinnitus of cicadas gently rose and fell.

'What is the Wayward Travellers' Place next door all about? Sounds like a rock band.' Theo indicated with his thumb.

'Wayward Travellers' Haven or Project,' corrected Brian. 'I suppose it does. It was started and named by a gentleman who took far too many drugs and lost his passport … as well as almost his life. He wasn't a member of a rock band but he played beautiful classical guitar.'

Theo leaned forward, interest piqued.

'Yes, a hippy fellow by the name of Hartford Whittaker, an American who spent many years in Iran, Pakistan and India. Interestingly he had studied to be a priest with the Catholic Church but must have become disillusioned so he decided to travel, maybe looking for truth or the meaning of life. Many chaps do, it seems, particularly fellows with high IQs you know.

'He drifted and fell into making a living taking advantage of travellers, well maybe not exactly stealing from travellers but let's just say selling hash and marijuana. This is back in the early or mid-sixties. Somehow or other he became tangled up with a guru, a cult, in India, along with many other flower people, and he gave his soul, or being, to this Indian guru named Maha Vaastu who had founded an ashram. They called themselves Mujtahid Mandir, loosely translated means Divine Temple, something of that nature. I suppose it was a racket because people surrendered their souls which meant their identity which I surmise meant their passports and earthly possessions. The ashram was a big farm where everyone worked, grew fruit and vegetables as well as marijuana to make hash, and worshipped. After a time he managed to come around and realised it was all a big brainwash so he somehow or other moved on to Malaysia.

'In the late sixties crossing borders was quite easy without a passport if you bypassed the official crossing point but when he arrived here he had to re-apply for a new American passport. That was not an easy task and is a far more difficult task today, but anyway he reverted back to his Christian roots. That brought him here to St

John's and he kicked his Catholic roots and became an Anglican and took on the role of lay preacher.'

Theo nodded.

'At about that time many young tourists, mostly the ones travelling on a shoestring, seemed to get caught up with flower power and all that. The eastern religions, yoga, meditation and so on were appealing to these young people, and let's face it, most were fresh out of school or college or university, just children. Naïve, many were, at best. Some sold their passports to criminals for money, some gave them to gurus or charlatans, believing god would provide. I suppose these young people were so stoned and starry eyed, they thought the world would be like this forever. Sitting around, taking drugs and I believe, having wild sex.' He smiled. 'I was a younger man then and my family was stationed in many of these places, particularly India.' He started laughing and Theo realised with a jolt that maybe Brian had been doing the same.

'When I was old enough I worked at various jobs around Asia. You realise, when you look Chinese but you speak like a Brit, it's hard to say what race I am. I spent some time in the UK but I didn't really fit, plus I didn't like the cold, so I came back to Asia.'

'So what happened to this ... er Hartford bloke?' Theo wanted to bring him back on track.

'Oh, yes of course, Hartford Whittaker,' he said, 'Yes, well he realised there were many lost souls out there ... umm, wayward travellers like he had been. So he set up the 'Haven' for people to drop in. His idea was to help pick up the pieces, get them off drugs, get them home, find some work for them to help with costs and to deal with the various embassies and consulates to sort out passports and travel matters, and I suppose to encourage the odd person to become a Christian on the way. However, the idea of the place was that it had to be non-discriminatory, non-religious, you know, non-judgemental in any way. That was because he had been there and knew what it was like to be, if you will, sucked in and spat out with nowhere to go.'

Theo was about to ask; Brian picked up on it.

'Oh yes, Hartford. Sadly he died a few years ago, I think he had malaria combined with hepatitis and in general I think his years of bodily abuse caught up with him. He was only fifty something, about my age.'

'Umm, some time ago, on the phone you did mention Jack had something to do with the place?'

'Yes, but only recently, in the last few months. I have known Jack for many years, on and off.'

Theo thought he detected the smallest of smiles. Brian's eyes closed in what Theo had noticed to be a sort of mischievous mannerism. 'What did Jack have to do with the place?'

'Jack, yes, well he came out of the blue, as it were, and offered to help out with general things, like counselling those with serious drug problems, helping with clerical work, drafting letters to embassies and governments and believe it or not, carpentry work. You wouldn't think he has only one leg, you hardly notice. The place has attracted a number of local youth in recent years. Sadly drug usage has spread here in Malaysia; you don't have to be a backpacker to have a problem. Unfortunately, many of the rickshaw fellows and taxi drivers sell the stuff, marijuana or heroin, to tourists and I surmise the temptation is too great and they get tangled up in the whole sorry saga.'

Theo wondered whether he had it wrong about Jack and his father. 'You said Jack came on board recently? What did he do, I mean where was he before that?'

Brian Aung smiled again, that mischievous look crossed his features. 'Aha, my fine young friend, you will have to talk to Jack about that. I will say, however, Jack Deere is the most Christian non-Christian I know. But I should further point out that he does tend to swear a lot.' He winked.

'Are you a Christian, Brian?'

'Interesting question. I suppose I am but it's more that I have a spiritual side; I believe that a God of some kind created everything and because I was brought up in the Christian way, I have rekindled that. Although I did spend many years off the rails but I have done a complete circle and come back, if you will. My Chinese side is too complicated.' He smiled. 'I am what could be classed as a fine weather Christian in as much as I go to church on Sundays but don't worry if I miss a week or two. Having a God to take responsibility for my faults, and the faults of others, is very much a benefit, don't you think? Also I rather like the idea of community, worshipping together on a Sunday, makes me humble for the naughty things I've done and makes me feel good for the coming week.' He smiled again in a reminiscing way.

Theo nodded and was about to ask about the '*naughty things*' but decided against it. It was time to change tack. 'How well did you know my father?'

'Not very well, I met him some years ago when I met Jack. They were members of the Planter's Club. They let anyone in there these days.' He laughed. 'What I meant was when the British handed over to the new Malaysian government in 1957, the management was forced to allow Indians, Chinese and ethnic Malays to join. These days the club is very cosmopolitan and no-one seems to be too touchy anymore along racial lines. However, ethnic Malays are not supposed to drink or gamble but they make use of the dining facilities. There are plenty of card games and other forms of gambling and of course the club gathers its funding almost solely from the sale of alcohol. Anyway, I didn't know your father well at all. He seemed like a decent sort of chap.' Brian shrugged and poured another cup of tea.

'Right, Brian, I might head off so I hope to catch up with you again soon. I'll give you the number of where I'm staying but I'll ring you whenever I get the opportunity.' He handed Brian a business card with the name of Hotel Happiness printed on it.

'Yes, of course I will advise you if Biru rings. It has been lovely to meet you and please do call again, I'm almost always here. I'm sure when Jack turns up I will get to see you again.'

They shook hands.

'It was also great to meet you, Brian.'

'Remember, if you need to talk about umm … anything please come and see me.'

'Okay, thanks Brian, see ya.'

'Cheerio.'

Theo walked out the side of the building and towards the front gates. He heard someone whistle.

'Hey boss, ready for trip?'

Theo had forgotten about Tung.

Chapter Sixty-One

Tung suggested a sightseeing trip down along the esplanade and the waterfront. The young rickshaw driver knew the area well and recommended a small eating house where a slight sea breeze tickled the lazy palm trees lining the road. Theo had time to reflect on the morning's conversation. He was surprised Jack had offered his help to the Wayward Travellers' Haven. It was possible Jack and his father were not really involved in anything seedy. Theo, however, had now formed an opinion deep down that that his father and Jack had been connected with something sinister, but if so, what?

As he looked out at the fishing boats, old junks and tankers in the distance, he couldn't help analysing things that had come to his attention since he arrived. Joe, the lawyer, had acted for Jack on some court case. He wondered if his father was involved in some way. What was the police interest that linked his surname to his father's? Why had there been a flag against his father's name? And the Malaysian business partner – Ameer Sayerfiq, who is or was he, some casino criminal and what was *he* mixed up in? Where did Jack fit into all this, if he did?

He knew there was a lot to think about in relation to his father. Why had he jumped from the boat, why suicide? Why had he run away from his life in Australia? What were his feelings towards Theo and his mother? Could it have been as simple as Vince having shell shock and not being of sound mind? Theo tried to shake the feeling of sadness that overcame him. He realised they were big issues and he began to understand they had been with him nearly all his life. He jotted down a few questions needing answers and then ordered a beer.

Theo opened *Beyond Pardon* in an attempt to take his mind off the direction of his thoughts but after a while he realised he hadn't even turned any pages. Thoughts of all those other things he had not even considered in relation to Biru and the barrage of matters he had mental blocked scrolled through his head like a gambling machine. Maybe she would not turn up which would solve everything. But he longed to see her and it was clear to him that he didn't care about any of the consequences. The idea that she could be using him to get out of the country surfaced again and although he did not want to believe this, his rational side accepted that it was a possibility. They had known each other for such a short time and in very constrained circumstances – he needed to see her, talk to her, touch her.

His gaze settled on a massive tanker at anchor way out and he allowed his thoughts to drift. He thought of the young Belgian woman, Monique at the Kuala Lumpur airport, and the young backpacker who leaned over to offer him a joint in the bus.

He spent the next couple of hours smoking cigarettes and making notes in his *Theo's Adventures* book. He divorced his mind from the jumble of things crowding his head by concentrating on the details for the article he was determined to write. Mid afternoon he wandered out the front to find Tung asleep in the rickshaw. He didn't want to wake the faithful servant but he had a cold Coke for him.

They made their way through the afternoon heat, the long way Theo was certain, back to the hotel. He wondered if there was a scam involved but surprisingly, the fee for Tung's services was multiples of one for each leg of the trip. Theo thought about it, played hard to get for a moment, and then laughed and gave him a bit more as well as some cigarettes. It was the equivalent of a couple of dollars to drive him around all day. He liked the young man who was probably only a couple of years younger than him and figured it would be handy to have someone to ferry him around in the long term.

'You want me wait for you to go out again?'

'I'm not going out now for a while but I might go out later. I really don't know, not sure what I'm doing.'

'I wait for you?'

Theo was touched, thinking what a tough way to earn a few dollars but he also realised the rider was scheming for business. 'No, no need, mate I really don't know what I'm doing. If a fare comes up you take it, okay?'

'Sure thing, boss, I keep eye out for you; this my area of Jawtown,' he said and pedalled off yelling at another rickshaw rider across the road.

'Mr Perry, Mr Perry, phone message for you.' Mama looked up from talking to someone and waved her hands animatedly. 'Phone not long time ago.' She handed Theo a note.

The writing was neat but slightly ambiguous.

'Mr Deere he rang. To ring back in short time later.'

'Thanks. Mama, did he say ..? No, don't worry. Do I ring him or will he ring ..?' He quickly realised that Jack would ring back because there was no phone number on the note for Theo to ring.

'Oh yes, Mr Deere he ring you here at hotel later in afternoon time, okay?'

'Yeah, right. Will it be okay if I go to my room?'

'Oh sure, it okay, we go and come and get you when he ring. Small charge for service but not much, okay?'

Theo smiled, thinking of his mother. 'Sure, no worries.'

Theo's head spun like the vacuum before the bounce of the ball. Finally he was getting close to meeting Jack and resolving some of his questions.

Jack Deere

Chapter Sixty-Two

Theo didn't bother showering in case Mama came for him. The window was high up but he had an interesting view of a brightly coloured tile roof awning, with the branch of a flowering frangipani cutting across the patch of sky in the rest of the frame. The sky showed downy, cottony strands dragged across brilliant blue. He knew the storm was on the way.

Theo sat in a cane chair and tried to make notes but the thought of meeting his father's old friend made the task difficult to concentrate on. His whole being was full of emotion, anticipation and a certain amount of dread he had to admit. Jack used to spoil him when he was a child. Uncle Jack.

'Call me Jack, Theo. Uncle makes me sound old,' he used to say with his infectious laugh.

Also Theo couldn't forget Jack made the effort to send him those two letters letting him know his father was alright. He didn't have to do that. Jack did not have any responsibility for Theo.

Theo's eyes dampened. He almost chastised himself, telling himself he was an adult and should not worry about the meeting. His father was dead, nothing would change. There was a need to relax and be who he was. He shook his head finally and smiled, bringing himself out of his malaise with the thought that Jack would certainly just be himself.

He heard the sound of shuffling, dragging thongs or sandals, coming towards his room. He was at the door before the knock.

Big Buddha Mama was startled because she nearly knocked on his face. 'Oh! You very quick to answer door, must have mystical powers. Mr Deere is on phone now, okay?'

He followed her waddle through the inside garden to the front desk and she pointed to the phone. Thunder burbled in the distance.

'Extension lead let you sit in chair over there.'

Theo picked up the phone. It was warm and his hand was slippery and hot from the humidity. The handpiece slipped out of his hand like a cake of soap. 'Ooops, bug … er sorry, Yeah … Theo here … um Jack?'

'None other old cock, how the fuck are ya?'

Theo smiled, reminded of what Brian had said, '*He swears a lot.*' 'Not bad.'

'I only arrived back a couple of hours ago, came by train, easier than flying from Banggers.' He answered the question Theo was about to ask. 'I've got a bit to do this arvo,' Theo's heart dropped for a second, 'But I'd like to catch up with you for at least a few minutes today to, you know, say g'day sort of thing. Then we can spend some time together tomorrow when I get all this shit I need to deal with out of the way.'

'Yeah that'd be great, Jack, where do ..?'

'I'll come to you; I know where the Hotel Happiness is. You going out at all?'

Theo's turn to smile and relax a notch. 'I'm pretty busy, Jack, but I guess I can abstain from having fun by waiting here for you. Course I'll be here, can't wait to see you. Remember, Jack, I came here to see you, right?'

'Yeah, guess you bloody well did. Okay, matey boy, see you in about an hour.'

Theo decided he had time for a shower. Questions scrolled through his head. What would Jack look like? Would he recognise him? The cold shower didn't get rid of the jitters and apprehension.

Chapter Sixty-Three

Theo was on his second beer, at one of the tables scattered out the front, when Jack arrived.

First up Theo didn't recognise him. There was always plenty of action out the front in the street; rickshaws, hand carts, pushbikes and people milling – tourists and locals. Jack looked like a tourist being dropped off at the hotel. Wearing a bright beach-style shirt tight across the chest and upper arms he looked a cool, casual bloke. The long pants and shoes didn't seem to fit into the surrounds. He handed the rickshaw driver some money and looked around. It was the slightest of limps, or more an awkward movement, that gave him away. Theo had been looking for an older man with greying sideburns and maybe a walking stick. When he saw Jack, he realised he was only in his forties, certainly not an old man.

Theo stood up and eased his way through the tables. They stood looking at each other for a few seconds.

'Well I'll be rooted; you still look like a kid.' Jack laughed and threw his arms around Theo.

They stayed embraced like that for a long moment. Theo couldn't speak, tears almost filled his eyes. Jack was slightly shorter than him but more solid.

Jack smiled, obviously better at this sort of thing than Theo. 'Right mate, let's have a fucking beer, eh?' His demeanour was all larrikin.

'Yeah, let's,' he managed to say, turning his head and signalling Mama for two Tigers to hide the embarrassment of his emotions.

'Been a long time,' said Jack. The wrinkles were there and a slight greying at the temples. His brown hair was medium length which contrasted with Theo's image of a close-cropped army style cut.

'Yeah.' Theo had been waiting all this time with much to say, questions to ask, but he couldn't formulate anything.

Jack filled the void. 'Been a hectic week up in Bangkok.'

'Umm … what did you do there?'

'Well, I had a new leg made and fitted, that was the main thing but also had to have a minor op on my leg, stump, the old leg used to rub the shit out of it but it's goodoh now. I have business interests there as well.' He moved his head from side to side, easing the tension from travelling.

'Yeah, what sort of business?'

'Well a number of things, shares in a backpackers' hotel, adventure hikes. We can talk about that later but, what about you, eh? You've grown up.'

The beer arrived. They clinked bottles.

'Here's to it, the future,' said Jack, 'it's all we have, eh. How's your Mum?'

'She seems to be moving along with her life now I'm almost off her hands.'

Jack smiled in a reminiscing way. 'Now, about you? You just finished uni, right?'

'Yeah, but first up, thanks for, you know, organising the lawyer and stuff …'

Jack gave a no worries shrug, sticking out his bottom lip. 'Well, Brian did all the work and he kept me posted, bloody good bloke, Brian, eh.'

'Good, seems to be enjoying life bit more now that I'm almost off her hands.' Theo was happy to change the subject, move to familiar ground. He went on to tell about his university studies, the job waiting for him. Jack punctuated Theo's story with questions showing real interest.

'It's really important to get a decent education, mate,' said Jack, 'I mean me and your dad had plenty of opportunities when we came back from, you know, Vietnam. I look back at those times and we could have got work, the seventies was a time when there were plenty of jobs to be had. It's because Vietnam fucked us up, or that's the excuse. Oh sure, the war turned out to be an unpopular one, I guess all wars are but not like this one. Many, if not most of the people back home could see that we shouldn't have been there in the first place. I guess I was bitterer than most because I lost a pin, but coming to this part of Asia after the war was the best thing I could have done because it was like a new start. My life was a mess, in a different way to your Dad's, that is. Unfortunately, your dad was right next to a really huge explosion not long before he returned to Oz and he never really got over it.'

Theo nodded and offered Jack a cigarette.

'Ta, yeah I guess it was a bit like running away but we sort of had to, you know. My marriage was well and truly up the shit, Charlene and I should never have been married, we were way too young. She had moved on and was seeing another bloke so I had no reason to hang around. Anyway, mate. I wanted to say or needed to say to you, don't judge your father too harshly, alright? I mean …'

Even though Theo needed to talk about all that he wanted to change the subject, for the moment at least. 'Right yeah.' No chance.

'You do know that your old man saved my life?'

'Yeah, Mum told me about it.'

'Horrible shit but as you know, I managed to tread on a mine that blew off my fucking leg from the knee down, neat as, and apart from millions of cuts and bruises, not much other damage. Still got my balls.' He cupped his hand. The attempt at humour didn't lighten the reality of the incident. 'I was lying there; blood every-fucking-where and a couple of our blokes who had advanced ahead of me had been shot; I found out later they were dead. Anyway I'm lying there dazed, didn't sort of comprehend my situation, too shocked to yell or scream I think at the time. Vince who was to the left and behind us runs full pelt over to me, bullets going everywhere, mostly machine gun bullets, and he grabs me and slings me over his shoulder, firing as well until his gun was empty and he runs back with me over his shoulder to the safety of our position. Had all this told to me a few days later. He risked his life for me.' Jack's eyes took on a glint. He sniffed lightly. 'You alright with this shit?'

Theo's eyes had widened to almost shock. He hadn't expected such a graphic account. He nodded.

'Straight after that, he stormed a Vietcong position that had our blokes pinned down. He won a bravery award for all of that, completely committed, almost foolhardy but when things are going haywire it sort of pushes blokes into split-second decisions. Not long after that act of incredibly unselfish behaviour, he happened to be near a big explosion and that is what fucked his head. He was my best mate and I tell you the world is a worse place without him. I want you to know that. He was a really good bloke but he couldn't handle the day-to-day things, like living. The war knocked the shit out of him.' Jack's forehead glistened with perspiration and his eyes had a haunted look, wide and attentive. This was clearly a personal and very emotional few minutes for him.

Theo felt it was his duty to say something. 'I understand ... you were mates for a long time.' He knew he needed to change the subject. Fortunately he was beaten to it.

Jack appeared to relax a bit, took a big drag and blew the smoke out in a long funnel. 'But enough of that, plenty of time to talk about that later, only if you want, of course. How long you staying for?' He butted out his cigarette.

'Oh, about another couple of weeks, could stay longer but my job can't wait forever. I have to confirm my flight soon.'

'What about this Muslim sheila?'

Theo started. Then he realised Jack had organised the lawyer from Biru's phone call.

Jack leaned forward. 'I meant Biro,' he said with a mischievous smile, 'She's the sheila at the hotel, right?'

'Yeah ... er her name's Biru, anyway I guess I need to tell you a bit of a story. I was going to fill you in later on, all about this sheila, being followed, getting framed, the jail nightmare and all that stuff.' Theo outlined some basic facts to give Jack an idea of his situation, making sure to not give away too much info about Biru's plight but stating she would be in Penang any day. Theo wasn't even sure what he was going to do himself, let alone tell Jack what was going to happen, so he left the story there.

Buddha Mama came over with two more beers and they drifted off into polite conversation for a while, not touching on anything really important. Jack did most of the talking.

Then Jack said, 'You must come around and meet my ... er wife Van, Vanessa. We have a son, Harvey – I call him Harve – 11 years old. You would be welcome to stay but our place is very small, you'd have to sleep on the floor, or standing up.' He laughed. 'Right, matey boy, I better piss off, got a fair bit to do. Maybe we could meet tomorrow, arvo would be best. Which reminds me, there is some stuff I have to do for Brian, too – I guess he told you a bit about the Wayward Travellers' Haven? Yeah, well I can get that out of the way in the morning and maybe we can meet mid arvo at the Saigon, it's a small bar-type thing. It's in a lane, Min Lu – off Leboh Chulia, turn right at the night market sign, can't miss it. That sound alright?'

'Right.'

'Oh, by the way.' Jack reached into his top pocket. 'Here's a photo of your old man, I guess you have ... er haven't seen him for many years, maybe you wouldn't recognise him.' He looked away, embarrassed.

'Thanks, I only have a photo of him when he was in Puckapunyal.' The colour photo was easily recognisable even though Vince was older and sported a straggly black moustache. The face was slightly puffy, as if he had just woken up, unshaven with a couple of days of stubble, the dark hair was longer but the familiar traits were there.

'It was taken er ... maybe a year ago.'

The photo reminded Theo of something he wanted to ask. 'What was the name of the ferry that, you know ... er Dad ..?' He slipped it in his pocket.

Jack's forehead tightened. 'Aaah, yes. You really want to know?'

Theo looked down and then around, 'Well, you know I was ...'

'Of course, I guess why wouldn't you?' Jack stood up. 'It was the Palau Barung, rusty old baby. Brings back bad memories, mate.' He leaned closer, 'Listen Theo?' He cleared his throat. 'You don't want to dwell on this shit too much, you know? Your old man was a good bloke and my best mate but unfortunately he couldn't cope. The important thing to bear in mind, Theo, he thought the world of you, you have to believe that, alright?'

Theo thought, *sure, Jack, that's why he went off to Thailand, eh?*

'Look, mate we will talk about all this stuff over the next couple of days. Consider this, something I sort of learnt over the last ten or more years; Asia helps to put death in the right perspective, somehow ...'

Theo nodded in a non-committal fashion. 'Yeah, sure.'

Thunder sounded in the distance and a breeze ruffled the greenery of the pot plants. Theo stood.

Jack looked up at the darkening sky. 'Right, mate must go, let's say about three-ish tomorrow arvo at the Saigon?' He patted Theo on the shoulder. That wasn't enough and they man-hugged.

'I'm sure I can find it.'

Theo managed to introduce Jack to Tung who was only too pleased for the fare. Theo ordered another beer, deep in thought, and looked out at the hustle of the street.

Mama placed a beer in front of him. 'He your brother?' she said smiling.

'What? Nah, just a friend.'

'It funny, western people say we Chinee look very same but boy, same thing for you whitey men, you look same to us.' She laughed and added, 'If you need ticket for ferry or for minibus trip to Batu Ferringhi special discount best price for guests, we can fix from here, okay?'

'Yeah, thanks, I will.'

Theo sat for a moment fondling the photo, finished his beer and then made a call. After initial pleasantries he couldn't wait to tell her.

'Hey Mum, I finally met up with Jack.'

'Umm ... oh, that's great, dear, how ... how is he?'

Theo went on to explain the meeting, clearly relieved to have made the connection after so long.

His mother finally managed to get a word in. 'Is he ... is he happy, well?'

'Yeah, he is obviously older than when I last saw him, but, you know, not much older.'

'Does he still crack jokes?'

'How did you guess? Yeah, look Mum, I really got on well with him, it was as if we had known each other for ever, if you know what I mean.'

'Yes, I sort of do. He ... he always liked you as a kid ... anyway, do you have enough money?'

The conversation moved to other things until the line went fuzzy and he had to hang up.

Later that night, Theo wriggled in a half sleep. The significance of seeing Jack again after so many years had a profound effect on him. On the one hand, it was wonderful to see him because Jack represented many lost years and there was a genuine bond between them. On the other, seeing Jack stirred up emotions from those lost years. Despite the disappointment with the absence of his real father

Theo realised Jack filled that role even though he had been absent too. Theo did not have the opportunity to ask Jack any of the questions he had written down and it was possible he may not have received any satisfactory answers to some of those questions, either. Then thoughts of Biru peppered the rest of the night and words of wisdom from Brian Aung kept surfacing. He tossed and rolled in the tangled sheets wondering again what he had got himself into.

Chapter Sixty-Four

Next morning they drifted through the streets towards the ferry terminals, Tung pedalling, smoking and singing, Theo smoking and lost in thought. The morning was cooler than usual because it had rained for most of the night. The sun had only just come up in a cloudless blue sky. Theo decided to go down to the wharf early and inspect the ferries and maybe take a boat ride.

He had been prepared to walk to the ferry terminal but Tung was there in front of the hotel. Tung had slept the night in his rickshaw, under a sheet of plastic to keep the rain out.

'Hey, boss. You want ride?'

'Yeah, why not, thanks.'

They arrived at Raja Tun Uda, the Georgetown Ferry Terminal, and even though it was still early the place was bustling with activity. The building, which served as a waiting room, part storage and ticket sales was noisy and crowded.

'I wait for you,' Tung said firmly.

'I could be a while; you should grab any fares you can.'

'That okay, I wait.'

Theo felt some level of responsibility for Tung but at the same time felt a pang of annoyance at the assumed regimentation of his movements. 'Mate, how about we say ten o'clock back here, eh? Then you can plan your day.' Theo stuck his hand in his pocket preparing to pay.

'No, that okay, you pay later.'

Theo didn't want to argue because he was mindful that being a rickshaw operator was a tough way to make a living. 'Here.' He handed Tung a couple of cigarettes. He had run out of duty frees, except for a couple of packets he was saving for later, and was now smoking what the locals were, tobacco with cloves. He looked at the packet and knew he would have to give them up before he arrived home.

Tung pedalled off to the shade of a tree where the tea and coffee stalls were.

Theo lit a cigarette and walked through the wire gate into the enclosure. Two monkeys were standing guard on the stone pillars on either side of the gates. They stopped preening each other for a moment and looked at him suspiciously. He stopped and saluted them for a laugh. Two shy women in long colourful sarongs and hijab, carrying baskets, giggled at him. This sequence of actions lightened his mood, at least for the moment.

A scattering of green shade trees and the occasional palm dotted the perimeter outside the fence. Theo walked towards the dock. Two ferries were tied up and he could see one in the distance trailing white water, indicating it was heading to Butterworth. Along the dock, fishing boats, junks and other craft loaded and unloaded quickly, clearly not being permitted to tie up for long and occupy a key berth. Men chattered and yelled as they threw gear and ropes to each other. He walked past the first one, Palau Rawa.

'One down,' he said aloud hoping that the Palau Barung was in service today.

He walked up to the other ferry which was being loaded and appeared to be the next to depart. Palau Undan. 'Nope, you ain't it either.'

Theo stood for a moment and looked at the ferries gently nudging the wharf and swaying in the crystal clear water. Cranes lifted and swung equipment and freight in all directions. The scene would have been a picture postcard had it not been for the rubbish gathered around the pylons. The rumble of the diesel engines at idle and the ever present whiff of exhaust fumes also detracted. He wandered over to some meagre shade, fascinated by the noisy loading of a Chinese junk. The men were singing some sort of sailors' shanty to break the monotony of the obvious hard and heavy work. The timber vessel looked very old, even though he could hear a diesel motor rumbling away down below. The sails were clearly still used and Theo thought it was a plus for the world that such an old vessel would still be in service with so many more modern forms of sea craft available.

Theo looked over at the ferry being loaded and wondered how many times his father and Jack had done the trip, back or forward. How many times had his father stood at the stern? Theo wandered, head down, hands in pockets towards the terminal, which was a huge corrugated iron shed. The inside was lined with plasterboard, and steel mesh seats, in rows, filled up the area. The noise and bustling crowds, some tourists but mostly locals, reminded him of the Puduraya Bus Station in Kuala Lumpur. Several of the ticket windows with bars were open and lines, or more groups of people, nudged each other and chattered excitedly in front.

The ferry schedule details were painted on the wall at one end but chalkboards confused things and displayed the current amended daily details. Brian had told him the ferries ran more by need than schedule. Even though one may be listed, if there were not any or enough passengers or not enough freight or vehicles, they sometimes cancelled that service. Also, often a ferry was replaced because it needed mechanical service from time to time. Times were chalked on boards at the side of each window and appeared to be for some other service, maybe water taxi?

Theo walked up to the information counter. 'Selamat pagi, er do you speak English?' His question was too complicated to try in Bahasa Malaysian.

'Yes of course.' Theo thought he looked like a policeman with epaulettes, badges and a cap. 'What may I do for you, sir?'

'Is the Palau Barung in service today?'

'Let me see this thing. Yes, it is running now but will be loading vehicles at Sultan Abdul Halim terminal in Butterworth in now time. It is due here within one hour.' He smiled and almost bowed.

Theo said, 'Terima kasih,' to the man's sweat stained back as he was called to the other end of the counter.

The ticket counter lines were much shorter than before so Theo bought a ticket. The cost was 40 sen, a fraction of one ringgit. Nothing. He purchased a packet of Marlboro cigarettes in case wheels needed to be oiled. The cigarettes were imported from somewhere and were not really the original thing but that didn't matter – he had developed a taste for the clove cigarettes over the last week or so.

Theo had time to spare so he wandered along the wharf again and around the warehouses. Men drove forklifts as frantically as they drove on the road. Sack trucks whizzed everywhere and Theo was amazed no-one collided with anyone else. He sat on a pallet under a listless palm tree out of the sun and looked out at the glassy sea. The smell of spices, coconut and diesel mingled in the humid air. Two pi-dogs stood at about ten paces and studied him. Theo picked up a rock and held it up to show them. They padded away. A biting, cutting announcement, like sideshow alley, from the loudspeakers wired to a pole above, made him jump. The next ferry was preparing for departure.

The Palau Undan had loaded the final vehicle and the engines gained in pitch. Water churned and bubbled white and fluorescent at the stern of the large, steel ferry and it nudged the dock a couple of times whilst the men untied the ropes. A loud horn blasted a much more important path, above the other noises, through the still morning. He could see another ferry not far out but couldn't decipher the name. He knew it had to be the Palau Barung.

He was pleased enough, perhaps satisfied, to finally be able to go on board and relive where his father and Jack had been. His father had stepped off the lower deck outside at the stern, behind the vehicles; he had been able to glean this information from Brian a few days earlier. Somehow he had to go to the exact spot; to him it was a pilgrimage. Theo realised it might not do him any good and could cause dark thoughts but he was compelled to do it. He asked himself what he expected to find and concluded he did not expect to find anything; he had to see, that was all. His father was dead and he could do nothing to change it.

The departing ferry rumbled and shuddered into a half circle and slowly powered clear of the small craft nearby. The two ferries passed along smooth parallels about fifty metres out. Theo could just make out the name on the rusty hull. Palau Barung. It was time for a boat ride.

Chapter Sixty-Five

Half an hour later, Theo was standing at the stern of the ferry. He looked up at a cracked Perspex sign that identified the craft as a mixed passenger, freight and vehicle ferry.

Earlier, at the point of boarding, the vehicle area on the lower deck did not allow passengers to enter through that entrance and he was forced to join the crowd walking onto the general passenger deck one up. He hoped he could go below and actually stand near where his father had stepped off the back.

Theo moved with the crowd which consisted of mostly local people, carrying bags, cases, bales and baskets of chillies, dried fish and vegetables. A large contingent of children ran around yelling, seemingly unsupervised. Theo was shoved and hustled as he glanced up at the sign:

Due to dangerousness of sea craft adults are warned to supervise those children at all times.

He figured the original version in Malaysian appearing below was more accurate. Rows of steel mesh seats, facing forwards and backwards lined the central part with similarly constructed benches around the perimeter. Even as he stepped off the gangplank onto the boat, most of the seats were taken and the ones that weren't were used by children jumping and playing.

Theo tried to walk down the stairwell to the vehicle deck but was told firmly in sign language, by a man in greasy overalls, the access was one way only for owners of vehicles. Theo was disappointed in this but was going to give it another try later.

No seats were available and some passengers sat on the floor. It was humid and hot in the main cabin and Theo leaned against the side bulkhead and lit a cigarette. The ferry shuddered and jerked and slowly negotiated away from the wharf. Once the ferry had cleared the inner harbour, the engines reached full pitch and he made his way out the back of the passenger section which overlooked the lower vehicle deck. Even though the sea was calm, the boat settled into a waltzing, corkscrewing motion and he had to grab the rail every few steps to steady himself.

He leaned against the rail and looked down. There was a pushbike tied to the side rail with a huge basket lashed to the bar in front of the seat and the handlebars. In the basket, with heads sticking out of holes obviously made for that purpose, were probably a hundred ducks. Three people down there, probably crew, squatted and played cards nearby.

He went to the stairs and no-one was on guard. At the bottom, a man in a sarong, chewing betel nut, no top and a dirty, uniform cap, came over and put his hand up.

Theo explained in English but he didn't have the vocabulary to explain quickly in Malay that all he wanted to do was go and stand at the back and look. The man shook his head, obviously no, pointing to a sign which said:

Passengers are prohibited from this area while the ferry is in motion.

Theo thought fast. 'Cigarette?'

The man looked concerned for a moment. Theo thought he was about to become angry. Then he said, 'Aaaaah, dua.'

Theo gave him two to show he understood dua and then gave him another two, saying, 'Empat,' to clinch it. He followed that by saying, 'Terima kasih.' The man stepped aside smiling, obviously happy he had clinched a deal out of nothing.

Theo went to the back rail. He looked from the similar Perspex sign as he passed, down to the bollard in front of the open area where rope was coiled. The sea boiled, churned by the huge diesel motors, into a neat V-shaped wake that slowly disappeared into the deep blue millpond sea. The crew looked up and Theo offered them a cigarette each, pointing at himself, waving his hands in an expansive way to show he wanted to stand near the rail but he would not be a problem. None of them seemed to care, especially with a free cigarette. He pulled out his instamatic and took a couple of shots of the ducks and then stepped towards them. He squatted and stroked one on the head with his index finger, thinking their lives were surely coming to a sad end and probably sooner rather than later. Another head with a longer reach pecked him. He wasn't ready and jumped.

'You little mongrel,' he yelped.

Obviously the men had looked up as he stepped towards the ducks. They laughed. Theo smiled, feeling like an idiot and opened his arms in a *'what the heck'* gesture.

He stood at the stern, mesmerised by the churning water and the perfectly formed wake. The men returned to their card game and as far as he was concerned, he was the only person in the world right there right then. Theo looked at the spot, most certainly where his father had stepped off. He tried to feel something but his head was in neutral. If someone wanted to walk off the back of this ferry, no-one could stop them. It was obvious but it made him wonder why he still hung onto the thought his father may have *accidentally* stepped off. The discomfort created by the rumble of the engines and the shuddering deck was pleasantly negated by the slight breeze that sucked the diesel fumes away. Theo stared back towards Georgetown. A large container ship in the distance shook him out of the trance-like state as the reality settled upon him. It was clear his father was at the point in his life when he'd simply had enough. As simple as that, Theo told himself, he did not want to go on living. He recalled Jack and Brian saying the same thing. Sadness visited him for a moment but Theo slowly felt the weight lift off his shoulders. He knew he would never understand but he felt nearer to accepting it.

Theo was shifted out of his preoccupation as the pitch of the engines changed and the wake slowly caught up with the boat. The lower deck quickly became an ant's nest as vehicle owners started up their engines and the sound of the ship's horn was nearly drowned out. The area rapidly filled with exhaust fumes as they glided into port. Theo felt he had done it and fought his way up the stairs to the passenger deck where people were so excited about disembarking, they all tried to get off at once. The gangplank was ridiculously crowded and he was concerned it might collapse. The whole exercise was complicated further because the people with bicycles, rickshaws and freight couldn't wait either.

Theo walked to the back. The Butterworth wharf was much the same as the Penang side; cranes and derricks dotted the dock but the amount of activity was much the same. People milled, going places, pointing, buying and selling, but all the while most were yelling above the noise of diesels or motorbikes or the clanking of machinery. He looked up and over at the spot where he stood a week earlier. A long-haul bus was negotiating the traffic and pulling out.

He glanced down and the ducks were gone. He looked out into the crowd of vehicles, people and bikes and he could see the man pedalling and wobbling into the mass. Theo took a photo, knowing it would not be much good because of the distance but he knew it would jog his memory in the future. He looked at his pecked finger and laughed. Laughing seemed to click him out of the dark mood that had hovered over him since the previous night.

The trip back was more of the same but for some reason there were fewer passengers. He returned below to the rear of the vehicle deck. No-one paid him any attention but he had clearly been accepted as friendly because crew members smiled and nodded to him. He smiled as much to himself as them. It made him feel good that people who didn't know him could be so accommodating and friendly for no reason. Thinking it could have been because of the cigarettes, it still made him happy.

During the last part of the 20-minute journey his thoughts returned to Biru. He really wanted to see her but still couldn't get his head around what he was going to do if and when she turned up. Brian's warning continued to play inside his head; both of them could get beaten or worse for liking each other.

An incident came to mind as he looked out beyond the wake at the white bubbles folding back into sea. A gentle breeze had tickled the shiny water giving it an almost frosted glass look. He recalled a time when, a few years ago, he had applied for scholarships and cadetships with various publishing companies and newspapers. He was sitting on the bed, head in his hands worrying if he would ever be accepted and then, at the same time, worried if he was accepted by several of them and *then* having to make a choice. What to do? His mother had been walking down the passage and saw him sitting there. He told her and she burst out laughing and grabbed his head and kissed him like he was a baby. It embarrassed him and she knew it and they almost wrestled in a playful manner for a few minutes. He remembered her exact words. '*Theo, if that is all you have to worry about then don't. Things always sort themselves out, no matter what. When it happens, you will know what to do.*' And when it did happen, he did know what to do. Well, almost. His mother and a teacher guided him but he made the decision.

That was years ago. Biru was a whole different situation. He shuddered thinking how difficult it would be for her to obtain a Malaysian passport. He forced himself to think clearly, confident Jack and probably Brian would know what to do.

When he walked off the ferry, saying, 'Selamat pagi,' to some of the crew members, his new mates, it was still morning and he had a plan.

Chapter Sixty-Six

Theo bought two Cokes and handed one to Tung. They drank and chatted for a few minutes. Tung said, 'Back to hotel or sightsee, Mr Theo?'

'My name is Theo, not mister, alright? Back to hotel via the post office.'

Theo waved at the monkeys who had grown in number to about ten. Some were teasing a couple of dogs by darting in close and showing their teeth. When the dogs lurched at them they jumped up on to one of ridges on the tiered pillars.

The activities so far, topped off by the walk from the ferry through the crowd, made Theo weary. He wanted to check poste restante and see if there was a letter from his mother. Then he figured on a shower and something to eat. Fortunately the breeze had increased, unlike most other days at this hour so far in his visit to Malaysia, and trees lining the roads stirred. The incense smoke wafted out the front of the Chinese temples and mingled with vehicle fumes and drain smell. The trip back was uneventful except for a close encounter with an overloaded truck that swerved towards them as it was endeavouring to miss an oncoming bus. The bus was trying to overtake two rickshaws that had pulled straight out without looking. He managed to pull the camera out and take a few shots.

The Georgetown General Post Office was an old stone colonial building with pillars and a high ceiling. Big fans whirred up high but didn't seem to make much difference to the heat. He found the 'Held Mail' section and to his delight there was a letter from his mother.

He ripped it open and eagerly read the contents. His mother's neat backward-sloping writing made him realise how much she meant to him. It was only two pages and although the news was mundane, it linked him to her and things at home. He stuffed the letter in his top pocket and battled his way through the touts to Tung and his rickshaw.

As he entered the Hotel Happiness Buddha Mama yelled, 'Phone call message for you.' She handed him a piece of paper. 'Brian he say you have phone number.'

'How long ago?'

'Half hour.'

'Thanks.' His hands trembled slightly as he read the note. He turned to Mama. 'Can I please ring from ..?'

'Sure thing, please take phone, cord go to seat there.' She pointed.

He dialled. A woman answered in Malay. What's her name? Lisa. She speaks English. 'Is Brian there?'

'No, Mr Aung out.'

'Er ... Lisa it's Theo here, we met the other day, I'm a friend of Jack's.'

It took the next few minutes to establish Brian had gone shopping. Theo's head spun. Shopping? He further established Brian had not left a message, or could have, but she did not seem to know. It was not the problem of her not understanding English, it was because she was one of those people who did not embrace her job. Theo then thought the job could be voluntary and they had to take whoever they could. He left a message for Brian but had no expectations he would receive it.

Theo finished his beer but he really wanted a shower. Shopping? There was no point in being angry; he figured if Brian did not ring back in the meantime he would go to the church because he was not doing anything else anyway. The same arrangement was made with Mama who promised to call him when the phone call came in. She also reminded him of the small extra service fee.

After the shower Theo returned to the front counter. There was no message so he decided to head in the direction of the church and wait for Brian. He was going to have to kill time because he was not meeting Jack for at least two hours. Fifteen minutes later Tung dropped him off in front of St John's Church. Theo went to the administration area and who should be sitting at the desk but Brian.

'Aha, you decided to come here in person.' He stood and smiled. 'You could have rung me, save a trip.'

Theo almost rose to the bait. 'I did ... I did, ring I mean, didn't what's her name, Lisa, give you the message to ring me back? I was out this morning ...'

'She was here when I returned from shopping but she gave me no message.' Brian could see Theo was annoyed. 'She's new here, only been in the job for a couple of weeks and she does not get paid much. I apologise on her behalf.'

'Anyway, Brian, you rang me?' Theo rolled his hand in a circular fashion.

'Yes of course. Biru rang and informed me she is arriving tomorrow sometime.'

Theo's mood brightened and his heart cranked up. 'What time ... where is she staying ... where do I meet ..?'

Brian laughed, losing his eyes for a second or two. 'Many questions, I don't know what time but she is staying with a friend, a school friend I believe, all very secret. She will ring here when she has settled in. She said she still has to be careful, even though the Mahmoud character seems to be out of the picture, for the moment at least. She is very concerned for not only her safety but yours as well.'

'Mine? I thought Mahmoud ...'

'Not Mahmoud, her family. She informed me they are very angry with her for not agreeing to marry Mahmoud and also for defying her stepfather in this matter. And, they have reported her to the police as well as the Islamic police. She only knows this from a friend of hers at the hotel she worked at ... called ... Razak.'

Theo shook his head slowly, not sure what to do. The thought of whether it was all worth it crossed his mind again.

'Remember, I made mention you should be very careful in this matter.'

'Yes, you did, but you did say you may be able to help.'

'Well, not exactly, I believe I said if you wanted to talk about it, I would be happy to talk and advise. Oh well, maybe I did say I may be able to help.' Brian chuckled, sat down again and pointed to a cane chair.

'What should I do?'

'Theo, you should really have thought this through.' He leaned back and laced his fingers behind his head.

'I ... um, yes, I have tried to reason it through many times but I can't come up with a direction until she shows up. I hate to say it but I almost secretly hoped she wouldn't turn up so then there would be no issue at all, you know?' This was untrue because he would be devastated if she did not turn up but he also knew he would be more able to make decisions once he saw her again.

'Mmmmmm. Could I ask ..?' He didn't wait for a reply. 'You say you like her and that is obvious, but do you intend to travel with her, and bear in mind that would be very dangerous in Malaysia or, for that matter, Indonesia? Or are you planning to head back to Australia and, if the latter, would you want her to come with you?'

Theo lit a cigarette to gain precious seconds. His heart went at it again. He took a drag which made his anxiety state worse. 'As you know she wishes to apply for a visa to Australia, I mean she already had that in mind before I came into the picture. I would be able to help get her some sort of residency, happens all the time, mobs of Vietnamese and some Chinese asylum seekers, boat people. I happen to know this because we did a thesis on the defragmentation of Vietnam after the war, after Saigon fell. So to answer your question, yes, I would like her to come with me.'

Brian nodded only, allowing a quiet forum for Theo to continue with the talking.

'I mean, really, I hardly know her. I have considered any number of things, for example, it's clear she had the wheels in motion for some sort of escape well before I came on the scene.'

Brian replied, 'Yes, that appears to be so.'

'I suppose it is always possible she is using me to get to Australia but I sort of figure, if that's the case, so what? We land and she says, 'See ya later,' so what again? I would like to think we could be a couple ... or something.' Theo was embarrassed saying the last sentence. 'We haven't had much time to get to know each other very well yet and I know it is weird, but I feel strongly connected to her. I have never felt this way before.'

Brian tilted his head and closed one eye. 'She told me she had applied for an Australian visa about six months ago and was having all sorts of problems because as a Muslim woman, she has to have a passport firstly, obviously, and before that, parental approval or family approval anyway, and probably more.'

'When she rang did she say anything about the visa?'

'No. I guess you'll have to wait and see. Theo, from what you have told me it seems as if your heart is in the right place. Throughout our lives situations bob up from time to time. We are, in the main, forced to take one path or another. I can't tell you what to do, of course, but I think your intentions are honourable, so follow your heart. The decision will be easier once you have spoken to her; you will have a better idea then.'

'Yes.'

Brian leaned forward. 'Have you told Jack about it?'

'Well he knows about her in general terms; there was no need to say too much 'cos there was always the chance she wouldn't show.' He knew there was still that chance.

'See how things go. May I suggest you think very seriously about not getting too intimate with her, you …' He cleared his throat, 'At least here … you get my meaning? Her family may have a good idea where she is; also we can be certain some people know more than we do about the whole business. So need I say again, be careful?'

'I intend to. Right, I'd better be off, I'm meeting Jack. Thanks for taking the time to talk with me.'

'Anytime. I suggest you be at the hotel tomorrow morning in case I ring.' He stood and they shook. 'Mind how you go then.'

'Righto, see you.'

Chapter Sixty-Seven

The Saigon appeared to be a small bar/café-style eating house because of the narrow frontage on the crowded lane. However, all the action was inside. The stone archway, guarded by two huge porcelain temple dogs, opened up into a large courtyard, shaded by awnings and huge planter boxes with trees and flowers. Bars with stools ran down one side and a dining room and a room with a dance floor disco edged off to the other. Theo stood for a moment and with no sign of Jack, selected a table shaded by a bamboo awning. It was pleasant enough inside the closure as big pedestal fans raked the area from the corners. Clapton was playing Born under a bad sign, not too loudly, from speakers in the dance room. The place was not crowded with about an even mix of older tourists, backpackers and a few obvious upwardly mobile locals.

Theo was a few minutes early so he decided to use the time to read through his mother's letter and maybe more of the book the Old Woman from Borneo had sold him. He smiled as he read his mother's letter. After the third time he stuffed it back in his pocket and pulled out Eric Newby's book Slowly Down The Ganges. A quick flick through gave him an idea for his Theo's Adventures. His exercise book was still mostly in note form and he was still chewing over ideas as to how to pull it all together. Eric Newby's book, although dated, gave him the idea that he could document his story as an ongoing column that could run over a number of weeks, or months.

A beautiful young Oriental girl, almost a woman, took his order and he was momentarily distracted checking out her legs. Someone put on The Rolling Stones Start me up and a crew of tourists whooped.

'That won't do you any good,' said Jack from behind him. 'The sheilas waiting on the tables here are not for sale.'

Theo stood and they shook hands, both smiling. Theo was reminded of that mischievous look.

'However, mate,' continued Jack, 'if you want a bit of that sort of thing, all you have to do is go and sit at the bar.'

Jack signalled the young waitress, indicating two beers. She smiled in a way that made Theo think they knew each other. Jack also waved at a man with a blue turban behind the bar.

'Now, Theo, first up, how has your day been so far?'

He briefly explained the ferry ride, not delving into too much detail. 'I know you think I shouldn't have revisited the ferry, but I needed to, you know. But I think I've got it out of my system now.'

'I didn't mean you shouldn't have, it was really for me I was meaning. I have pretty bad memories of that night as you can probably imagine. Anyway old matey boy, we have a heap of things to chat about but first up I have to tell you something.'

Theo's eyes widened, thinking for a second there might be some heavy confession coming up.

Jack noticed and put his hand up. 'No, no, it's alright, relax. Maybe some of the things we talk about later might make you jump but all I wanted to say was that I own this place. So we can do what we like, okay?'

The beer arrived. Theo was introduced as a friend to the young waitress whose name Theo didn't really catch, Ming, something like that.

'To us, to your father, your mother, my present wife, my poor departed wife and of course, my son Harvey. I'll explain all that family stuff to you later and if we don't get too pissed we can go back to my place later. Right?'

'Fine by me.' They clinked bottles.

'Now, if you excuse me for a sec, I have a bit of business to attend to, need to speak to my staff.' Jack stood up and walked to the bar, grabbed a clipboard and stood talking to the turbaned Indian. His limp was not noticeable and he walked with a straight back, almost military.

Theo needed a few minutes to pull out his notebook and think about the questions he was going to ask Jack, either tonight or over the next few days. Also, how much was he going to say about Biru?

'Right mate, let's catch up. Another beer?' He ordered beer, peanuts and satay. 'As you can see, this is how I make a living. I have to confess when I first bought the place, about 11 years ago, it was pretty seedy. The way things work, to own anything, a westerner has to be in partnership with a Malaysian national and can only own a maximum of 49%. My wife Van owns the other 51%. I hope you will come around to my place and meet her later. I told you I have a son, Harvey, he's 11 years old. Van is not his mother. His mother Xin died not long after he was born. She was my first partner in this business. Harvey was born and she … unfortunately died.'

Jack looked away for a second as the beer and food arrived. Theo thought there was something more but Jack welcomed the intrusion.

Jack leaned forward and pointed. 'What's that for?'

Theo opened his book lying on the table. 'Remember? I'm a journalist. I'm writing an account of my travels, part of my first assignment for The Adelaide Advertiser. My editor told me not to waste a good trip.' He shrugged. 'So I'm not. I have jotted down some things I wanted to ask you, though. It's easy to forget things. You said things were a bit seedy when you took the place over?'

'Yeah, a real dump. Look Theo, I'm not proud of this, you've probably guessed or you'll find out anyway but we used to sell drugs from here. We had a neat set-up with the local police and, well it helped pay the bills. It was mostly soft stuff, hash and marijuana, in the beginning anyway.'

Theo's ears braced. 'Was my father involved? Relax, Jack,' he quickly added, 'I'm not putting this in my book. This is not an interview. I'm not a real journalist. Yet.'

Jack nodded. 'Yes, we both were, it was the only way to make a living. When we went to Thailand, after leaving Australia, we worked for a mate of ours who was married to a Thai. You could only get three month visas, so to stay in the place you had to leave the country for 24 hours and then return and get a new visa. Bit like here. It was all sheilas, drink, drugs, you know, we were young but it was more me than your old man. He went along with it. He never really had a thing with any of the sheilas, and some of them were drop-dead honeys. He really wasn't very well, morose, depressed; nothing could pull him out of it. Anyway, Theo, none of that had anything to do with you or your mum, he was almost not of this world anymore.' Jack's eyebrows formed a straight line. 'I wanted to tell you, I know I've said it, but your father really did care very much about you and your mother.'

Theo wanted to respond with a barb but decided to let it go. More beer arrived.

'This is how it happened in Vietnam. It's hard to explain but basically he was caught in crossfire, this was a few days after he rescued me. I didn't see the thing, obviously I was in hospital in Saigon but he and a few of our blokes were trapped in a drain, like an open drainage trench between rice fields, by the Vietcong and they also had some heavy-duty artillery. So they bombarded our blokes for a time and one explosion was that bit too close. Our choppers came in after and hammered the jungle, got rid of the enemy. Your old man walked out of there, sopping wet, covered in mud; he looked normal but he didn't react when people spoke to him. They discovered he was stone deaf and sort of non-responsive. His hearing started to come back a week or two later when he was in hospital but he never recovered from that incident. Well, he appeared to on the surface but it sure wasn't the same old Vince. It moved his head into another area.' Jack downed his beer and nodded at the blue turbaned man.

They sat in silence and Theo felt obliged to finish his beer to cover the vacuum.

'Sorry, I didn't mean to … but it's important you realise, he thought the world of you.'

Theo felt his forehead and eyes warm up and he was grateful to be able to look away. Thunder rumbled in the distance, followed by a whip-crack fluorescent flash nearby which made the fairy lights along the bar flicker out and the fans stop.

'Aha, set your watch, Theo, time for some rain.'

The lights flickered and came on and the fans cranked up again. A slight gust of cooler air tickled the canvas awnings. More beer arrived. Theo could feel the effects of the alcohol. Somehow he didn't mind because he felt safe, with a friend. 'When was your son was born, I mean, what made you start a family here, so far from home?'

'You know what?' said Jack, almost musing, 'I think my home is here, Theo, in Asia. This is where I belong. I'm married to a Malaysian; Harve ... er Harvey, my boy, is half and half. I was, well let's say Vince and I felt like Martians when we returned to Australia after the Vietnam War. We were fucked in the head and we thought, because of the moratorium marches and stuff, people were down on us. Looking back, a lot of the resentment was possibly more in our heads than was actually true. I suppose I felt we would be welcomed as heroes and all that shit but maybe our egos were the only thing bruised. We were still kids then, Theo.' He laughed, almost forced, but it broke the serious strain of the conversation for a second. He pointed, 'About your age now, Theo, younger. Sorry mate, didn't want to insinuate you are a kid. War of any kind is a cunt of a thing. It's because we had been in a controversial war, we had killed human beings and been maimed by the enemy – people exactly the same as us, fighting for their own country. And, mate, most of us were just out of school. Only the hardy don't get damaged by that – physically – or mentally. Also the handling of Agent Orange, a raft of other chemicals and asbestos as well had an effect. All added up. Other people got damaged, I mean wives, family, kids – like you – friends and the like back home cop it, some tenfold.' He took a deep breath and his smile was forced at first and then became genuine. 'Anyway, how's your mother?'

'She seems to be happy enough. She spent several years in a quandary after Dad left. I was only little but I knew she suffered quite a bit. When I look back, it must have been hard on her, even though you sent those two letters telling us he was okay, I think she often felt that maybe, you know, maybe he would come back one day.' Theo felt a pang of deep sorrow. 'As I got older there were times I thought that if I wasn't around she could have moved on, you know maybe married again, something like that.'

'Did she um ... did she have any relationships with any other blokes?' Jack looked away.

Theo was drunk enough to not consider the question too intimate. 'Yeah, a few but really I guess she always had me to take care of. As I grew older I could see she was missing out a bit, you know, most of her friends had blokes ... she had me.'

'Your mother was, is, a good person, I always liked her. More beer? Shit, we'll get wet here.'

The rain started and spray fizzed into the area where they sat so they moved into one of the alcoves off the side. Someone turned the music up to drown out the noise of the rain on the roofs and awnings. Theo thought it sounded like Grateful Dead.

'Now Theo, time for you to tell me a bit about yourself. What about this journalist's job? When do you start?' Jack's voice did not betray the six Tiger beers he had consumed.

Theo noticed and hoped Jack did not notice his own voice slurred at times. He expanded on some of the things not mentioned earlier, in relation to the job, although he was drunk enough to not remember if he had covered them. It did not seem to matter; their conversation drifted into how the footy was going back home, who he played for, what he thought of the Hawke government and other comfortable matters.

The rain poured and before long ended as abruptly as it had started. They hardly noticed they were on to the next beer.

Theo felt bolder. 'When I went to Foreign Affairs in Kuala Lumpur, I found out that my old man had a business partner named, let me see …' Theo turned a couple of pages. 'Here, Ameer Sayafiq, who was supposed to be a businessman associated with the gambling casinos in Malacca. What was that about?'

'Yeah, that's easy. I said before, for any foreigner to work and stay here for any longer than three months, you have to be in business as a minor partner or married to a local. It can be complicated but if you know how to arrange it, it's a piece of cake. Early on we went out of the country for 48 hours and then came back but the government tightened up on that for a pile of reasons. In my case, I married Xin and she worked here. Then, long story but basically she died and I was legally able to stay because we had a son etcetera. At that time we were working in bars and clubs in Kuala Lumpur and here on and off, and it was easy to arrange through an immigration agent – with the help of a fistful of ringgits – to get residency for your father and other blokes we knew. There are agents with an ear in government like lobbyists who handle these matters.'

Jack glanced up to see if Theo understood the drift and took a slug on his beer.

Theo said, 'What part did Dad play, I mean what sort of business?'

Jack looked away quickly and then back again. 'No part really, his involvement was just on paper.' Jack knew the answer wasn't good enough from the look Theo gave him. 'Well, it was purely an arrangement on paper just to get residency. He, Vince, never even went to Malacca as far as I know, it was a scam. To say it was common practice would be an understatement. Plenty of foreign nationals are involved in all sorts of businesses because the government wants the lion's share of control over any business here, and may I say Asia in general. I can tell you; most successful tourist operations or business ventures were either set up by foreigners or with foreign dough. The government is pretty smart because they allow lobbyists to arrange residency so foreigners can pump money into or set up businesses but they still like to make sure this country has the controlling share. It's the opposite in Australia; any foreigner can come in and buy and own whatever they like, well not exactly but a bit like that. That will bite Australia well and truly on the arse one day when Aussies find they don't own anything.' He looked up at the ceiling several times and seemed to reminisce. 'Whitlam tried to buy back the farm after many years of governments of all colours giving away Australia's assets to the highest overseas bidder. The Asians in this part of the world are smart alright, they like to keep tabs on their wealth; maybe that is what I like about the place.'

Theo was on the way to being really hammered by the drink but he was still on top of things. 'You say you were working in bars and clubs. What sort of work?' He hoped it didn't sound too probing.

'Oh, organising food and booze, supplies, furniture, electrical stuff, arranging musicians and bands, sometimes filling in for bar staff when someone couldn't make it in. And of course drug supply, small scale, you know. And occasionally organising sheilas, you know ...'

'Dad had a flag against his name. Do you know what that was about?'

Jack rolled his cigarette packet slowly, a pensive gesture. 'I guess you have a right to know. It started off as a minor issue but I guess drugs are never a minor issue. We knew most of the bar and club owners around the place and we used to get the benefits of cheap grog at times, you know, from over the border, no tax sort of thing, and to be able to tap into the availability of sheilas, you know, prostitutes. Also money changing and of course, marijuana and hash. To run a business and this is the backpacker and tourist industry, the local cop had to have a share as well as many other people up and down the line – I mean some politicians who,' Jack wiggled fingers indicating quotation signs, 'gave the approval for us to operate. This included hotels, adventure stuff for backpackers. In Australia you just pay licence fees to public servants.' He laughed and lit up another cigarette. 'It's a different sort of corruption to how the west does things.'

Theo wondered where he had heard a similar statement before.

'Where was I?' said Jack, taking a slug.

Theo's head went into a slight spin.

'Yeah right. Anyway, bear in mind everyone in the game was doing it, somehow our names were bandied around, this is a while back, maybe eight years? There was a bloke called Bacchus who worked for us indirectly and he became greedy and got caught.' Jack looked over at the bar and waved. 'But, could have been a competitor too or someone in the chain of dope supply, or someone with a grudge, who knows, and it's not really important, someone dobbed us in. However, we, that's your old man and I, were charged with, 'Aiding and abetting in the supply and distribution of illicit substances,' something like that. We were shitting ourselves because it was only soft drugs and everyone else was doing it. Anyrate, we easily beat the charge and these days, yes, I still pay protection money because someone I know or know of, whispered in the right ear and helped get us off, so it worked both ways. On the one hand someone wanted us out of the way and on the other, someone wanted us in.'

Theo was together enough to say, 'Joe, Josef ...' Theo had trouble saying it. 'Er ... Joe the lawyer that's where he ..?'

'Yep, Joe's firm of upstanding lawyers acted for us and the charge simply went away. He had just finished his articles then and was only a junior assistant. He pretends to be a good Muslim but really he's just like us, when he gets the chance he sneaks in a drink, likes the horses ... you know. But he keeps it pretty quiet though. By the way, how in the hell is that bastard?'

It was Theo's turn to laugh. 'He's okay I suppose, I can tell you I was bloody pleased to see him. Mate, Jack, thanks for sorting all that shit out, I'd still be there if it wasn't for ...'

'That's alright, no worries, but it was lucky that sheila, er what's her name, Biro ...'

Theo laughed again. 'Biru, like Bee-roo ...'

'Yeah right, sorry, anyway what was I say … oh yeah, lucky she had Brian's number.'

There was a comfortable silence.

'Why was Dad's name flagged?'

'Mmmm … maybe because of Joe's firm of lawyers and, I wouldn't mind betting my name has a flag, too.'

Theo was sober enough. 'And do you reckon that was why the police gave me such a hard time?'

Jack ran his hands over his face. 'Yep, could be. I must have a word to Joe and see if I can make that shit go away because I'm legit these days, that is, except for the protection money I pay. We take a hard line on drugs here, ha-ha, I mean in this place, plenty of shit out there in the street but we keep it clean in here. And we don't do the sheilas thing anymore but we do allow some selected ones to mosey in and hang around the bar if they keep it low key.'

The call to prayer echoed around like simulated surround sound. It seemed they were both ready for a break in that line of talk.

'Do you ever get used to that?' said Theo.

'Used to what?' They both laughed together and clinked bottles as some samosas and satay arrived.

Theo was thankful for the food which helped to soak up the alcohol a bit. The bar became more rowdy and someone turned on the video screen to get the best of Billy Idol. Theo could see a group of backpackers laughing and whooping it up and he thought he recognised one of the blokes on the bus from Kuala Lumpur. They had another couple of beers.

Jack said. 'Getting a bit loud here now, want to go for a drive?'

Theo said yes but as they staggered through the crowded bar and out the front, he wondered if Jack was going to drive because he certainly couldn't.

Chapter Sixty-Eight

It was as if they stumbled out of a predominantly western stage set into China. The laneway was crowded with food stalls and people talking and socialising. Colourful banners and lanterns decorated the buildings and along the main road at the far end a man-powered red dragon snaked across the entrance, accompanied by bells and drums and firecrackers.

'This way,' said Jack, laughing. 'Time for a bit of night-life, eh?'

They moved through the crowd to the corner of Chulia Street where Jack spoke to an Oriental-looking man who waved at someone else and in a few seconds a car pulled up. They slid in, Jack slightly more awkwardly than Theo, and the car pulled away. Jack rattled off some instructions to the driver and the vehicle slowly weaved its way along the road.

Theo asked, 'What lingo was that?'

'Mandarin. It probably sounds like I speak it fluently but I don't, however, I get by. That's Van's language and we try to encourage Harvey to speak it as well as English and of course Malaysian. I speak basic Malaysian, Vietnamese and a little Thai as well. Now, let's go for a bit of a tour of the city and then back to my place, right?'

Theo nodded but it made his head spin. He was happy and content to be on a tour and be looked after for a change. They drove around the streets for a while then down to the port and the ferry terminals.

Theo pointed, 'Well I'll be, look at that!' Three monkeys squatted on top of the stone pillar at the entrance. 'I wonder if they are the same monkeys that were there this morning?' Theo stuck his head out the window and saluted them.

Jack laughed, 'I wonder if they are the three wise monkeys?'

They were both drunk and Jack attempted to add to it by bringing out a bottle of whisky. He measured capfuls, with great difficulty in the swerving vehicle, which they knocked back. Jack pointed out landmarks and explained matters of history about Penang and Georgetown.

'You might be wondering why your old man wasn't a partner in my business?' Jack didn't wait for an answer. 'Well he didn't want anything to do with owning anything. Many times I offered to bring him in or help him get something set up but he always smiled and shook his head. He was happy enough pulling wages and getting a few bucks from ... around the place. I tried to encourage him to do it so he could put some money away for you and your mother. You had to know him ...' Jack realised his mistake. 'Sorry mate, bad choice of words, you always wanted to fucking well know him, what I meant was, knowing him like I knew him, the man before the explosion and the man afterwards. If it was the man before the blast he wouldn't have left you and we wouldn't be having this conversation because he would have been a better dad to you. Oh fuck, you know what I mean.'

Theo's eyes and forehead became warm again.

'Theo, the man afterwards couldn't deal with business things or much else for that matter. I handled almost everything for him.' Jack rolled his palms outwards and looked out the window.

The last few words were slightly choked and Theo realised Jack was almost crying, too. They travelled on, each looking out their own window, allowing time to gain composure.

A short time later as they drove along the esplanade Jack put his hand on Theo's shoulder. 'We've discussed quite a few things tonight, you know, about drugs and things. I don't want my boy to know about any of that shit. He knows nothing of my past and Van, well, she is no innocent either, her past is colourful too and she knows about me, of course. One day, I'm sure my son and I will talk about these matters but at the moment he is still just a boy. You understand?'

'Yeah, no worries.'

Half an hour later they arrived in quieter streets at semi-detached stone dwellings built in the colonial style typical of Georgetown. They stopped in front of an old but brightly painted stone and timber house that had hardly any garden and opened almost on to the street. Half open, old but painted, timber shutters lined the front and two bicycles leant against the wall. Jack paid the driver and ushered Theo in through the open front door. Some Oriental music Theo couldn't pick played softly in the background.

'And who have we here? You must be Theo,' said a female voice with the soft Chinese "t" in "must".

Jack said, 'This is my wife, Vanessa, Van if you like.'

A petite, very attractive woman with a black pageboy haircut, dressed in a cheongsam, a flowered silk dress, stepped forward, extended her hand and smiled. 'Jack say so much about you I feel as if I know you already.'

Jack took her in his arms and kissed her, almost Hollywood style. She was a small, slim woman and was dwarfed by Jack's bulk. She giggled at Jack and pushed him away good-naturedly. 'Harvey will be home soon. Doesn't look like you need anything to drink but I bet you will. Please, Theo, this way.'

The house was, as Jack had said, very small and they went down the passage, past two rooms, probably bedrooms, through a lounge furnished with Asian artefacts, cane chairs and a glass-topped coffee table with ornately carved dragon legs. The rear of the house opened up to a garden similar to the one at the Hotel Happiness, minus the fountain.

'Now sit.' The way she said it was welcoming, not an order.

Meanwhile Jack had turned up with three beers and they clinked bottles.

Theo didn't have the chance to say no to another beer. He said, 'Looks like I'm drinking myself sober.'

Van did not understand but Jack rattled off some Mandarin and she laughed. It was cool and comfortable sitting in cane chairs looking out into a Chinese garden under the soft lighting.

Van stood. 'Now, something for us to eat?' It was a question not requiring an answer.

When she went out towards the kitchen, Theo noticed she was petite and curvy, highlighted by her tight dress with splits up the sides. She seemed to glide on soft, silent slippers and it made him think of the tiny slippers the Chinaman shoe seller had on display.

Jack and Theo smoked cigarettes and chatted. About ten minutes later Van returned with trays – noodle soup, cold sliced duck, chicken with peanuts, rice and half a dozen small bowls of assorted vegetables cooked in many ways. Even though they had eaten throughout the afternoon, Theo found he was hungry again.

Not long after, Harvey arrived home. Theo had been wondering what the 11-year-old looked like, having a Chinese mother and Jack as a father. Theo may not have been a judge in such matters but he could at least see that the boy was good-looking. He looked Eurasian and was blessed with smooth, slightly olive skin. The boy had very polished manners and also seemed older, or worldlier, than his age.

Harvey said, 'You can call me Harve if you want, only my mother calls me Harvey.'

Theo and Harvey warmed to each other and chatted whilst the other two busied themselves clearing the table and washing the dishes in the small kitchen to the side.

Harvey told Theo about his schooling in Georgetown and added, 'I am going to school in Singapore for the first term next week.'

That prompted questions about how he felt about boarding school and sport and subjects. The boy was obviously enthusiastic about it all and if what he said was true, he received good marks for the subjects he liked. The others returned and the group chatted about everyday things, drinking pot after pot of fragrant Chinese tea, until late in the night.

'I'd better go,' said Theo.

Harvey's eyes shone. 'Hey, Theo, can we go out together soon, you know to the beach or something, before I go to Singapore?'

'Yeah, sure.'

'Theo, there is no need to go back to your hotel now, you can stay if you want,' offered Van. 'We can find a corner for you.'

Harvey looked at him, eyes wide.

Theo thought, and hoped, Biru was coming tomorrow. 'Thanks, I'd really like to but I'd better head back to the hotel, a few things to do tomorrow. But Harvey … er Harve, maybe over the next few days, it's just that I have to meet someone tomorrow sometime, it's very important, not sure what time though.' Theo was touched the boy wanted to be with him. 'I promise, before you go away next week, okay?'

'Thanks,' said Harvey and, very much the grownup, shook hands with Theo.

Theo was about to ask about taxis but Jack said, 'Plenty of taxis around, we'll get one out the front.'

Theo thanked Van and said goodbye to them, promising he would see them again soon.

Out the front they sat on a stone ledge alongside the bikes. Jack said, 'Oh shit, I forgot. I have a box of your father's things locked in the safe at work. The landlady gave it to me; she said they could be personal so she stuck some things in a shoebox and hid it from the cops. I told her take whatever else she wanted of his, a few clothes, shoes, things like that people could use and we chucked out meaningless stuff like, you know, toothbrush, old newspapers. The cops may have glanced through it but I doubt it somehow. They were satisfied it was ... er suicide. There wasn't much left of his gear. He rented a small room a short walk from here and even if he did have things, they were snatched by people down the line.'

Theo's heart beat harder. 'Snatched?'

'Yeah, I don't think anyone pinched anything really personal, the local people aren't like that, but I'm sure the landlady and others grabbed practical stuff like soap, tissues, pens and notepaper. She took the pillows, cane chairs, coffee table, you know, no use to you or me. The stuff was worn and old. Mate, he lived a really frugal, lonely life but that is what he wanted, simply because he was so ill in the head.' Jack squeezed Theo's shoulder in a comradely way and looked directly at him for a moment. 'I have his ashes also, for you to take.'

Theo realised there was deep love for a lost comrade in Jack's look. The silence took care of the need to answer.

Jack looked away for a moment and then said, 'It's that Biru sheila arriving tomorrow, eh?'

Theo was now the boy again, feeling sheepish and uncomfortable about the new subject. 'Um ... yeah.'

'Mate, I'd hate to see you get yourself in the shit but you be bloody careful how you deal with all that, right?'

Theo felt himself nod in the artificial lighting of the street. Firecrackers went off somewhere in the distance.

'I can see she means something to you and you think you may owe her but ...'

Theo bristled slightly. 'No, I mean, yeah. No, I don't know what to do really. She is supposed to arrive and I was going to see how it went. I really need to talk to her. She's supposed to be organising a passport, as well as a visa for Australia.'

Jack looked at him. 'I know it ain't my business but have you considered the fact she may be using you, if you know what I mean, for her ticket out of here?'

Theo somehow thought he had to justify it. 'She was trying to organise these things well before I came on the scene so it is not all down to me being here. And I haven't coughed up any money.' But he knew he would, if she asked.

'Anyway, be careful where you meet her because, forgetting her family and this boyfriend who ain't too keen on you, there are Islamic-type police who wander around trying to spot any Muslim not toeing the line. If she hasn't got a safe place, the church is quiet most of the time, and even if there is a service there are sections off the main area. Also the *Wayward Travellers' Haven* next door, there are several doors in and out of there, too. Anyway, if you need any help with her passport or visa let me know, I may be able to help.'

They stood as Jack hailed a taxi. He stuck his head in the driver's window and rattled off some Malaysian and handed him some money.

'Okay, mate, good to see you and I can get one of my blokes to drive you and Harve around the place in a few days when you get organised. You may have noticed I have a phone at home but I never use it for anything other than family. Ring Brian and here is the number of the *Wayward Travellers' Haven* and the Saigon, someone will know where I am.' He handed over a business card.

'Thanks, Jack, for everything.' He had been refused several times during the night but he tried again. 'Can I give you some money for ..?'

'Sorry, mate, your money is no good when you are with me.' Jack grabbed Theo and gave him a hug.

Theo climbed into the front seat with the driver. As they moved off Jack winked and mouthed the words, 'Be careful of that sheila.'

It was almost quiet in the street and the laneway in front of the hotel. Theo was ready for bed. They had consumed a lot of beer and the first part of the afternoon was somewhat of a blur. He had drunk himself sober, almost anyway, but he was astute enough to know he would have a headache in the morning. He wondered if he had asked all the questions he had listed. No way. Jack's words rolled around in his head. '*Be careful of that sheila.*'

Biru

Chapter Sixty-Nine

The call to prayer, tangled up with Hindu bells, dogs barking and horns tooting, brought Theo into the next day. His body and head were more dull than hungover but it amounted to the same thing. The copious amount of jasmine tea they drank must have helped because he had certainly consumed more beers than he could count, plus a few hits of whisky. He downed a handful of paracetamol with the rest of the water and lay back looking up. The fan made his head ache more and his stomach churned. Jack's words would not go away and he wondered what would happen on this day. Her beautiful, musical voice had disturbed his dreams all night and he couldn't delete her luscious figure from his thoughts.

The morning was already warm and he had a long cold shower. He wanted to be near the hotel for when Brian rang so he grabbed a small table on the edge of the garden, more in than out. He couldn't face breakfast so he ordered a pot of coffee and briefed Mama for phone calls and messages. To his amusement she reminded him again of the small charge for the personal telephone answering service.

The sound of water gently gushing from the dog-dragon fountain, the muted sounds from the lane, the murmuring of staff, clattering of dishes in the kitchen and the waft of incense gave him a lift, despite his hangover.

This was an opportunity to flick through Eric Newby's book again and make some notes in his exercise book. Several ideas had surfaced as to how he was going to put all these travel things together for the editor. Even though his head was still pressed with a frontal headache he managed to eliminate Biru from his thoughts some of the time.

Whenever he heard the phone out the front he started and with Mama babbling away he was rapidly brought back to reality.

After a couple of hours he amused himself taking photos of the garden, fish, plants, statues and ornaments. He went to the toilet and when he returned Buddha Mama was standing at his table.

'Where you been, important call for you? Please, may have to pay small fee extra for waiting time. Jus joking.' She laughed and her jolliness made Theo laugh, too. 'Please, a Mr Brian on line, now. You take your personal seat there, no extra charge ... for today. Ha!'

He grabbed the phone. 'Have you ... is she here?'

'Yes, she is staying with a friend not far from here. She says it is not a good place to meet. Unfortunately she is still having trouble obtaining a passport.'

Theo could feel his heart pulsating against his ribs. 'Jack suggested I meet her at the church, or next door.'

'Yes, I see. I think the church might be best because there is not much in the way of functions today. Anyway, I have her number and she is by that phone now. Please let me know, firstly, if you wish to er ... continue the relationship and secondly about the passport, alright?'

Continue the relationship? Theo had not even really started. 'Okay, yes ... thanks ... her number?'

'Theo, best she goes into the church from Leboh Song, from the back there is a small door there, you go in the front doors, alright?'

Theo hung up quickly and dialled the number.

'Hello, Farah speaking.'

Farah? Oh, yes of course and the voice was familiar. 'Theo here,' he said with a tongue that seemed bigger than his mouth.

They were both waiting for the other to speak and then they both spoke at once. They laughed at the same time, too.

'Theo, I have been waiting for very long time to see you. I have trouble with paperwork but I tell you later. You want to see me? You have not rethought things?' Her soft voice mesmerised him for a second. 'Theo?'

'Um ... sorry. Yes please I want to see to see you, today, soon?'

'It not good place to meet at friend's house ...'

'Can you get to the church, St John's?'

'Yes. Okay I have things not to be avoided here right now but we can meet at noon. Oh Theo, I want to see you.'

Theo looked at his watch. Two and a half hours away. 'Yeah, for sure …' He pulled himself together and explained the plan and hung up.

His hand slipped as he replaced the phone piece.

'You look like you very happy,' said Mama. 'Look like you have girl fren? Ha!'

'Yes … I'm about to meet a friend, haven't seen for a while.' He terminated the conversation, not wanting to elaborate. The less she knew about things the better.

She waddled off laughing and yelling at someone through the kitchen door.

Chapter Seventy

Theo showered, shaved and preened. He cleaned his teeth three times and selected his cleanest clothes which were only blokey clean and wouldn't remain clean for long in the climate. He quickly realised her clothes would be the same. He had to force himself to calm down and take it easy, to not be too eager and remember to be careful.

At eleven o'clock he could not stand it anymore so he decided to walk to the church rather than go with Tung. Also, he didn't want to go out via the front of the hotel because Mama was sure to ask him where he was going or something; she was a very perceptive woman.

He found a way out through the back of the hotel, past a small vegetable garden and a shed where an old man was repairing a bicycle. Theo nodded politely and kept going, thinking there was a good chance the old man would report his departure to Mama. The church was about twenty minutes' walk and after about five minutes he realised his clothes were already damp with sweat. He was a few minutes early as he turned into the street where the church was, when a woman called him.

'Theo, Theo it iss you!'

He turned as she was heading towards him. 'Oh, Franka, I didn't expect to see you for a few more days at least.'

She walked up to him and hugged and kissed him. Old friends reunited. 'Good to see you, ve just get in from the Cameron Highlands, ve cut our time short because weather rainy. Ve book in to Hotel Happiness, big jolly woman in charge dere say you go out back way of hotel for walk.'

Theo was right; Buddha Mama knew exactly where he was. 'Yeah, um, I have to meet someone soon.'

'Eric hass the headache and wants to lie down, I go for a walk and tour around town for a while. Hey, ve catch up for drinks tonight?'

'Yeah, maybe ... it depends on things but we'll get together soon anyway.' Theo thought she noticed the hesitation in his answer and he felt guilty not confiding in her. 'Anyway, have to go but I'll tell you all about it later, okay?'

She gave him a soft smile and touched his shoulder. 'Yah, I understand.'

She leaned closer, 'Be careful Theo,' pecked him on the cheek and wandered off.

He arrived at St John's Church, looked up and down the road then walked up the steps and realised he was shaking.

It was cool inside but Theo's anxiety negated the relief. Sharp sounds of footsteps bounced and echoed off the stone walls and shiny surfaces under the high ceilings. He noticed a man in a cassock down near the altar busying himself with something. Theo slowly moved in a 360, trying to orientate himself inside the huge cavern, as his eyes slowly adjusted to the dark. An old couple sat staring towards the altar and two women kneeled at separate places in the pews. The man in the cassock was too far away to pay Theo any attention even if he knew he was there. In one of the side chapels Theo could see an old woman with a basket of flowers, replenishing the vases. A quick look around didn't reveal Biru so Theo slowly walked the perimeter, checking every possible place where anyone could hide. He noticed four entrance doors and another door marked 'VESTRY.' He looked at his watch. The big hand showed a fraction past 12. He willed himself to relax.

He sat down in the middle of one side which gave him good vision of the four doors that opened directly from outside. Brilliant colours emanated from the incredibly intricate leadlight windows high up. A prayer book lay on the bench and he picked it up, feigning interest. He didn't notice her approach.

'Good morning,' said the old Asian woman in perfect English. She had an armful of what appeared to be hymn books. 'Oh! Now is that the time? Doesn't time fly? It is good afternoon then, I mean. May I help you in any way?'

'No thanks, I'm … contemplating.' He felt clammy, even though it was pleasantly cool.

'Yes of course,' she nodded in an understanding way, smiled and shuffled away.

The man in the cassock clicked and clocked around the altar. It made Theo wonder why men in churches didn't wear rubber soled shoes. Another quick glance at the watch. Ten past. A bead of sweat trickled down his back. It wasn't that hot, or humid for that matter.

The man with the noisy shoes clipped out. A door closed. A door opened, Theo looked up, the old woman again carrying a box, probably candles.

Twenty past. *Where was Biru?* He licked his dry lips. He stood up and walked the circuit again, checking all alcoves and potential hiding places. Theo decided to sit on the opposite side. No Biru. Half past.

A young couple came in the far door, genuflected in front of the altar and then knelt down in the front row of pews. After fifteen minutes they left. Theo wanted a cigarette. He drummed his fingers on the wooden pew. *Biru, where are you?* He walked to each entrance door in turn, opened the doors gently, looked out, saw no Biru and he went back and sat down again, in a different spot.

Ten to one. Theo's clothes were soaked. He picked up the prayer book again and feigned interest, with difficulty. One o'clock. He decided to go and see Brian if she did not show in the next few minutes. Maybe she had rung him? Something must have happened. He would wait until one twenty.

Theo glanced at his watch. It was time to make a move.

He walked the circuit again and snuck out the side door closest to the administration building. Fortunately Brian was at the desk.

'Aha, Mr Theo Perry.' After the jovial greeting Brian switched. 'What? Are you alright?'

Theo realised he must have looked worried. 'Well, yeah, er no … Biru has not turned up. I was to meet her at noon, has she rung ..?'

'No. Ummmm …' Brian leaned back. Always calm. '… maybe she couldn't get away. Relax, my boy; I'm sure things will be okay. Have you looked in all the nooks and crannies inside the church?'

Theo lit up a smoke and almost burned the red hot end down to the filter in one drag. 'Yes, at least half a dozen times,' he said as smoke leaked out his mouth and nostrils.

Brian tried to lighten things. 'Golly, that's the way to get lung cancer.'

Theo wiped his face with his other hand, in no mood for humour. 'I'm sure, no, certain, she said noon today. May I use your phone and ring that number?'

'Yes, of course.'

Theo rang and a woman answered in what Theo thought was Malaysian. He hung up. 'Bugger, I don't want to get her into trouble at that end.'

'Right, Theo, I'm sure everything is fine but we will investigate this matter. You go back inside and I will scout around the outside.'

They went out. Brian said, 'I'll do a couple of loops and then meet you inside.'

He took off towards the back and Theo went inside. He looked at his watch, not quite twenty five past one. Theo tried to balance the thought of missing her with the fact he had only been gone a few minutes. He walked the inside perimeter and then sat down in a different place. Brian arrived ten minutes later.

'I checked the other buildings; no-one else has seen anyone wandering around lost. I think she has been delayed. Maybe you should go down there and pray.' He pointed towards the altar.

'What?' Theo looked at Brian who smiled so much he burst into a chuckle and his eyes almost disappeared. 'Very funny.'

'Righto, Theo, you may as well stay here and continue to wait. I will go back to my job that I am not paid very much to do and maybe she will ring. I will try that number again but if Biru does not answer I will hang up. Rest assured I will be discreet. Anyway, it is best to relax, everything will be alright.'

The afternoon slowly disappeared and Theo didn't have to look at his watch when the thunder started. Sad and frustrated, Theo was increasingly feeling he had been set up. But why? It did not make sense.

He went back to the administration building, tried the phone again but it rang out. He decided to return to the hotel and have a few beers with Eric and Franka. He walked out the front with a mixture of heavy heart, deep concern, a little fear and a very large amount of irritation.

'You want lift, boss?'

'Yeah, why not, Tung.' He shook his head, wondering how Tung knew where he was.

Chapter Seventy-One

The trip back to the Hotel Happiness was a blur. Theo tried to reason things out; nothing but questions surfaced. At least he was together enough to not do anything rash. He told Brian he would contact him later in the evening when he'd thought the whole thing out. At first he thought there were only two scenarios. One, she was waylaid and for some reason couldn't contact him, or two, she had decided she didn't want to go through with seeing him or involving him in her quest to get out of Malaysia. Then, a third idea came to mind. Maybe she was in danger. And then it expanded into danger from whom – Mahmoud, her family, the police? Had she been kidnapped? Beaten? Murdered? Theo told himself to ease up.

An hour and several beers later he was sitting with Eric and Franka at the front of the hotel. He had been apprehensive at first about telling them about the situation but Franka had said, 'You look troubled, maybe we help.' Theo was sure Franka knew. Eric added that the best cure for it all was a few beers, universal for all problems.

They ordered some food but Theo was not hungry.

'Maybe we comb the streets?' said Eric with a shrug.

'No, Georgetown iss too big, it would be a waste of time. Ve have no idea where she is staying and she may have even flown the cage, yah?' Franka, the voice of reason.

'Maybe ve go back to church and wait dere?' said Eric.

Silence dominated the sombre mood and the rain added nothing but gloom.

Franka explained their situation. Eric's father had been involved in a car accident and they had to return to Sweden the following day, flying from Penang Airport to pick up the international flight in Kuala Lumpur. The extent of the injuries was not too severe but Eric was needed to take over his father's business. Theo had trouble taking all this in but he politely nodded, thankful that Eric's father would be okay. He did however, realise he would miss them both and at a time like this, with the whereabouts of Biru unknown, even more.

The rain continued to pour down and flood the laneway out the front. Theo didn't hear the phone due to the noise of the rain. He felt a tap on the shoulder.

'Someone for you on phone,' said Mama and with a mischievous look whispered, 'Girl fren? Farah Mahomed, you be careful with Muslim woman, they very big trouble for white boy tourist, okay?'

'Umm, no it's not ... doesn't matter.' His nervous system went into overdrive. He felt like he was going to throw up.

'You know where phone is, special line juss for you, ha!'

Theo looked at his friends, they had heard Mama.

Franka winked. 'You best get it.'

His heart raced. At least she is alright. She must have been held up.

He took a big breath. 'Theo here.'

The other end was silent. He was about to ask if anyone was there when she said, 'Theo, I ... I do not know what to think ...'

'Why, what's wrong?' His hand shook.

'I see you with your girlfriend, I not sure if you want to see me, if you have girlfriend we maybe not ...'

'What ... what girlfriend?'

'Out front of church you hug and kiss western girl, maybe no place for me ...'

'Western girl? No, no Biru, that's Franka, she's a friend, she is ...' Theo figured a small lie would not hurt, '... she's married to Eric, she's a married woman, they are friends of mine, she just arrived from the Cameron Highlands, a friend only, she's married ...'

Silence dominated for a painful moment, he was about to speak again.

She said, 'Oh I ... I am thinking you already with woman ...'

'No, Biru. No. There is no-one else; I really want to see you. Can we meet tonight?'

Silence. He was about to speak again.

'Okay, I try to get away. We can meet at church?' Silence again, it seemed as if she was thinking. 'In one hour, okay?'

'Yes, yes for sure, see you soon.'

Theo couldn't keep the smile off his face, rain or not, he would see her in an hour. He asked Mama if he could make a call, so he rang Brian.

Eric and Franka were clearly happy for him, knowing now she was not in danger, and they celebrated with another beer. Theo's nerve endings felt delicate and he had difficulty concentrating. He knew it would be worse waiting at the church.

Franka said, 'I didn't think I give you big passionate kiss but this shows Biru must be serious about you, more than just using you to get out of Malaysia, I think, yah?'

Arrangements were made for them to get together either later that night or the next morning before their flight.

As Theo wandered towards the front, Buddha Mama wagged her finger at him. The message was clear, be careful. He inwardly bristled, wishing he could be careful on his own without advice from others. The rain had ceased, leaving the street, drains and air almost sparkling clean as the evidence of wetness glinted in the dying sun.

'Boss, ride to church?'

'How did you guess, I need to pray again.'

Tung looked at him, not knowing whether to smile or mind his own business. He chose the latter and they pedalled towards St John's.

Theo was nervous but he kept telling himself everything would be alright. He tried not to think about what he would do when they met; he knew there was nothing he could plan anyway. A couple of streets away they could hear the church bells ringing.

They pulled up in front. Tung stood, balancing on the pedals and yelled, 'I wait for you?' And at that second the bells stopped.

'No, mate, not this time, I'll make my own way back later.'

He paid Tung and gave him a handful of cigarettes. Darkness had almost descended as he waited a moment for the bellringer to go. Theo opened the side door.

Chapter Seventy-Two

Dim lighting in the alcoves and sets of lit candles provided enough illumination for Theo to see Biru was not there, not obviously anyway. His nerves jittered as he slowly walked the perimeter. An old man and woman sat in the front pew and departed out a side door two minutes later.

He sat and picked up the same prayer book as before, willing himself to calm down and be patient.

'Theo?'

He turned and stood. She was about five metres away. The voice was familiar but it did not look like her. 'Biru?'

She took several silent, almost ballerina steps towards him and stopped. The shapely young woman dressed in western-style clothing looked nothing like the girl he remembered. She peeled off a dark scarf, turned her head and looked slowly from side to side like a wary cat. He could see her eyes glint. Gone was the hijab that framed her face and he realised he had only seen such a small part of her before. Maybe he wouldn't have even recognised her in the street but her beauty would have attracted his eyes. She toyed with the strap on her shoulder bag, a nervous action. The meagre light from flickering candles outlined her slim figure. Her long, dark hair fell almost to the top of her jeans and was highlighted by a spectrum of colours from the leadlight windows.

She shot another quick glance from side to side and then her face broke into a shy smile, maybe a smile of confidence that she was safe for the moment. 'Yes. I ...'

Theo couldn't speak.

324

She glided towards him and stopped again, looking up into his eyes. He realised how petite she was. Theo stood still, looking at her, unable to do or say anything. He could hear the sound of the street, almost like a distant ocean.

She took the last step, looking him in the eye, and then threw her arms around him, an urgent gesture. Theo responded as if instinctively, there was nothing else he could do. He put his arms around her and for the first time in a long time he felt that everything in the world was alright, nothing could change in that moment. He slowly manoeuvred her around and gently pushed her against the wall and kissed her. Theo could feel the electricity; the same almost fever-pitch intensity as when she brushed his mouth with hers three weeks ago. She now responded with a honey-warm kiss, as if it was the most natural thing to do. Their mouths searched for a second and then remained locked, like two lost souls not wanting to break the spell.

He felt the weight of her warm body and her small, hard breasts pushed against his torso. He didn't know if it was her heart or his hammering. After a time their mouths moved to light kisses and he buried his face in the fragrance of her jasmine hair.

She gently pushed him away. 'We cannot do this thing ... I mean ...'

Theo knew exactly what she meant. They both were aware of it escalating out of hand. He couldn't stop himself and reached out. She fell into his embrace again for a long minute and then they separated.

She took both his hands. 'I have only been thinking of you. I hoped you would want to see me too but I always ask why you want to be involved with my problems? Then I see you with western girl, I ... I ... not know what to think.'

Theo didn't know how to respond for a moment; he was entranced with her unique, soft, beautiful voice and her interesting way of expressing herself.

Then he said, 'She is a friend, that's all. She has a husband; he was only just around the corner. I ... I have been thinking of you, too. You were all I thought about when I was in jail, you kept me going.' He smiled, finally almost in control.

She took his hand and led him to a pew and they sat down. She looked up at him with dark penetrating eyes.

'Theo, I have been planning this thing for many months ... getting

325

my passport and visa so I could leave Malaysia to get away from my family, and when they promise me to Mahmoud I try to hurry up process. Then you come along and Mahmoud frame you for drugs. Mahmoud very violent to me, bash me hard, so I have to go away. Razak help and other good friends, too. I so thankful to God you have friends to get out of jail as I not be able to help.' She appeared slightly embarrassed about rambling on but she could not stop. A tear glinted in her eye.

'Don't worry,' he said. 'We will sort something out.' Theo had to stop there, not wanting to make promises he may not be able to deliver. He stroked her hair and pulled her closer.

A door opened. They both tensed at the same time. Theo said, 'Quick, kneel.'

A man in a cassock genuflected as he walked across the aisle and then disappeared through the vestry door, leaving it ajar.

Theo could feel Biru trembling slightly. 'It's okay,' he said to her and held her hand tighter. She kissed him on the ear.

The man returned a couple of minutes later with what looked like a handful of candles and he replaced the short stubs of candles burnt out.

Suddenly two people, a young man and woman, walked in through the front doors, well away from where Theo and Biru were kneeling. The doors shut with a padded thud, absorbed by the vastness of quiet sanctuary. They went down the aisle and shook hands with the man in the cassock. Theo could hear them talking quietly but not make out what they were saying. In that moment Theo understood what they were doing.

He leaned so his head was buried in Biru's hair. He didn't want these few, precious moments to go away. He whispered, 'They are rehearsing getting married.' She smiled and laid her head against his shoulder.

Theo further realised no-one could hear, nor would they really care about him and Biru because it was a church and open to everyone. They would be seen as simply a couple praying.

He was jolted out of his nirvana. She whispered, warm fragrant breath into his ear, 'I do not know what to do. I still am having problem getting Malaysian passport which means I cannot get visa for Australia. I need permission of my family and of course they not know where I am. If they find out where I am, I get punished by them and local imam.' She told Theo she had doubts about her faith and the unreasonable power men had over women. Someone coughed and she looked around as if someone from her family was watching. 'Brian say he may be in position to help?' It was framed more as a question than a statement.

'Yes, we will speak to him.'

Another door opened and a small group of people wandered in, whispering and chattering excitedly. A short plump man came through the vestry door and sat down at the organ and started tuning up, obviously for the wedding rehearsal.

'Time to see Brian, I think,' said Theo. You wait here and I'll speak to him. He said he would wait around in case you needed to talk.' He kissed the top of her head and eased out of the pew and towards the side door, well away from the wedding party.

He slunk through darkness to the administration building and to his relief, Brian was still there, cup of tea almost to his lips. 'Aha, my boy, so good of you to call in on me.'

Theo explained their need to talk about visas and passports and Brian said, 'We have a spare office off the kitchen and card room. Bring her there, stick to the shadows and come round the back, not through the front, alright old chap?'

Theo returned to the church and crept in another door.

Biru was not where he had left her.

Chapter Seventy-Three

Theo glanced in all directions and apart from the wedding group; Biru was nowhere to be seen. Sweat clouded his eyes as he wandered the circuit, looking frantically in every possible place. He arrived at the alcove on the opposite side and glanced in.

'Theo, I am here.' She was kneeling in front of the small altar.

He didn't recognise her for a second in the semi-darkness because she had the scarf over her head. 'Why did ..?'

'Sorry, I felt nervous where I was, a man came in, he looked at me but I think it was okay, he went down the front to the wedding people. I thought it better I go here.' She stood, looked around like a wary ground-cover bird and quickly went to Theo and hugged him. He could feel her trembling.

'It's alright.' He held her for a moment. 'Let's see Brian.'

As casually as possible they headed for the nearest door and stepped out into the humid darkness.

Brian stood up from the seat behind the desk. 'Aha, I finally have the pleasure of meeting this young lady. May I say you are more attractive than I had imagined.' He nodded an old-fashioned, very British, gentlemanly half bow.

Theo couldn't help but smile.

Theo had to release her as Brian grasped Biru's hands in his, a very fatherly gesture. 'Please, please have a seat, we will not be disturbed in here,' he added clicking, the lock on the door.

They sat and Brian went back behind the desk. 'Now, how can I help?'

Biru quickly lost her nervousness and explained the difficulties encountered trying to obtain the passport. The Australian visa was not really a problem but she had to have the passport before she could finalise that.

'I see,' said Brian, leaning back and steepling his fingers on his chest. 'Mmmmm.'

Theo grabbed Biru's hand again.

'Right, we will see Jack. He has contacts that may be helpful.'

Theo's forehead crimped. 'What contacts?'

Brian smiled, eyes almost disappearing as he held up a wise index finger. 'That's what we will ask him.' He could see the others looking urgently at him. 'Don't worry, I took the liberty of ringing him a few minutes ago and he should be here any minute. Tea?'

Theo looked at Biru. They both nodded.

She pulled out a sheaf of papers from her shoulder bag. 'I have application here, filled out for passport but staff there say because I am Muslim woman I have to have this form also. She handed the sheet to Brian. 'See, I have to have signature of both parents, or in my case guardians, and also local Imam. My local imam is good man but I think he have no choice but to inform family.'

'Yes, I see the difficulty. Jack has contacts, he may have an idea.'

There was a quiet rap on the door. 'Open up, you sinners.'

'Ah, Jack the joker,' smiled Brian, who unlatched the door.

Theo awkwardly rose to his feet and was about to stumble through introductions.

Jack walked straight over and grabbed her hand. 'Biru, I presume?' Her nervousness disappeared, she was clearly charmed. Then he looked at Theo with a wink. 'G'day mate,' he said and gently slapped him on the shoulder. He reached for Biru's other hand and said, 'Theo and I are going outside to talk for a minute. It is important but you can relax, it has nothing to do with you, it's about home, family stuff alright? Brian will entertain you with some of his corny jokes for a few minutes.' He patted her hand and gave a thumb for Theo to follow.

They walked out into the card room. Theo said nervously, 'Is Mum ..?'

'Naaaah, no worries, it's nothing to do with home, just bullshit. I need a few words in private. Look cobber, what I wanted to ask you was, are you rock solid with this sheila? I mean ... fuck, you know what I mean.'

Theo felt hot. His nerves prickled but he felt a level of contentment about himself and Biru. He looked Jack in the eyes. 'Yep, from what I know everything she has said is true, oh, well maybe there are a few things can't be verified but aside from what she says, there's Razak, Yuman …'

'Yeah, yeah, but what about you and her? And … you know? I mean what she might do when she gets to Australia, her money situation, her obedience to Islam, what her parents might do to her – and you for that matter. Mate, all of that.'

Come on Theo, show some guts. 'Jack, I really like her, who knows about love but, I mean …' He rolled both hands outwards in a helpless gesture.

'Are you committed?' Jack chewed on his bottom lip.

'Yes.'

The pensive look left Jack's face; he nodded and faked a soft punch to Theo's upper arm. 'Let's go.'

Back inside, Biru looked at him with wide brown eyes.

Theo said, 'No worries,' and took her hand again.

Jack took up position on the side of the desk. 'Right, kids, how can we, or more specifically I, help?'

She began the story and did her best to explain her situation. Brian gently took over and Theo at first thought it a bit rude but he quickly realised Biru had trouble explaining it clearly in English. He also noticed Brian expanded and added extra pointers whilst Jack nodded and said yep and nope intermittently.

Brian looked at Biru. 'I apologise if I seem domineering, Biru, but Jack and I have much knowledge of these matters. *The Wayward Travellers' Haven* next door regularly has to help tourists and the like, people who either lose or sell their passports, some souls also who have entered illegally or been tangled up with a religious cult or, perish the thought, have recently been released from jail either here or elsewhere in Asia; and there are some who simply turn up here without documentation, sick in mind or body or both. Of course we do our best to reunite some with their families to obtain money or assistance to get them back home. You would be surprised at the number of people who for one reason or other fall through the cracks.' He looked at Jack.

Jack asked Biru questions regarding her family, the local Islamic community and some pointed questions about Mahmoud. Theo looked on, eyes wide. He could feel her tension down the length of his side.

'Right, there is a chance we may be able to get your passport sorted out. Our mission next door has links with a women's group called World Women, WW, and they help women in domestic violence situations. They may be in a position to help with the passport as I know of a couple of cases where they have spirited women out of the country.' Jack rubbed the stubble on his chin in a pensive, pincer movement. 'They generally rely on trying to resolve the family situation, sometimes bringing in the police, but obviously in some cases the women end up in further danger.'

Theo felt her relax marginally but she was still tense. She squeezed his hand.

Jack added, 'You, Biru, will have to come to Kuala Lumpur with me and it will be essential you stay in their refuge – a safe house. You won't be coming back here, at least for the time being, but let's focus on the fact that they can help you.' He half pointed at Theo. 'You will have to remain here.'

Theo opened his mouth. 'But ...'

Jack held up his hand. 'We have to wait and see what they can do, if anything. No point in you being there because you can't stay there and won't be able to see her anyway, it's a secure compound. We have to accept the fact that she is in danger. Anyway, we will still have Brian as the contact here and you and Theo will be able to talk over the phone, once you,' he looked at Biru, 'are safe in Kuala Lumpur. I'll explain it all tomorrow after I've made enquiries. We have done this on a few occasions for people who are being followed or in fear of their lives. You have to try to relax and don't build your hopes up too high, anything could happen, but at least you will be safe. It will be up to you when we arrive there tomorrow ... I'll be there, you ... we have to convince them of the seriousness of your situation.'

Biru tried a smile. 'Yes, thank you, I ... I don't know what to say ...' her eyes filled and she sniffed, wiping her nose and eyes with a tissue, clearly overcome with emotion and embarrassment. Theo gently put his arm around her.

Jack added, 'Now, do you want to go ahead with all of this? Are you sure? If you decide to leave Malaysia, you *may* never be able to return and you may never see your friends again. It is a big decision. However, times change and in years to come, who knows?'

Theo held his breath. A wet cloud of silence hung for a second.

'Yes, I am certain.'

'Righto,' said Jack, 'Where are you staying at the moment?'

Biru explained she was staying with a school friend and her husband but said they were becoming increasingly concerned about being discovered harbouring her.

'Can they be trusted?'

'Yes, of course. I stay with her sister's friend in Miri when I run away from Kuala Lumpur. They are most sympathetic to my situation as they also help his sister who was in a violent marriage before. They are brave because if I get caught, they get punishment, too.'

Jack looked at Biru. 'Do they know anything about Theo, or us for that matter?'

'Yes, they knew I was meeting him but they not know about you.'

'Okay, I think it best we don't involve them any further but you should tell them that you are leaving soon and you will be safe. Do not mention anything about us or what arrangements we are making. Yeah?'

She nodded.

Brian stood. 'Yes, that is for the best but you will be able to contact them at a later time.'

Jack grabbed Biru's other hand and looked her in the eyes. 'Please, it is most important you don't tell your friends or anyone about this. Most important, okay?'

She nodded, 'Of course, I get this far by devious means,' and she smiled weakly.

'Sure, I didn't mean to, you know ...'

'I understand,' she said firmly and looked at both Jack and Brian.

Theo felt as if he was watching a tennis match, looking from one person to the other. 'Maybe I could come too, be of use somehow?'

Jack shook his head. 'No, Theo, bad idea. The less you are involved in any of this – and be seen to not be involved – the better. If the authorities got wind of you having anything to do with her, particularly as she is a missing person, or fugitive in their eyes, they would arrest you at the drop of a hat. Sorry mate.' Jack moved to the door, his limp just noticeable. 'I have a car with my own driver out the back and I think it best if I take you home tonight. Tomorrow morning I will pick you up early, at say six am, and maybe Theo can be here then to see you, right?' He looked at Brian. You can be here in the ..?'

'Yes, I will be here doing my service in the administration of the Lord's requirements. No one will be about much before eight.'

'Brian and I will leave you two for a few minutes while we sort out a few arrangements and then Biru, I will drop you off and you can pack all your stuff ready for tomorrow, okay?'

The two older men went outside, closing the door.

Theo and Biru stood looking at each other. His heart raced, 'This is all happening fast. We finally get together and then you have to go away.'

'Yes, I know. How you do feel about me going away and I may not even get to Australia for some time, that is if I am to get out of Malaysia at all, I mean I would have to apply for asylum wherever I go.' Her eyes glistened with tears. 'I have no choice at the moment and can only trust your friends. I need help to do this thing, I have no other direction.'

He had to calm her down as well as himself. 'No problem, I will be here and we will talk on the phone when you know what is going on. Jack and Brian have said they will be there for you, don't worry.' Something occurred to him. 'Do you have enough money?'

She looked away embarrassed. 'I ... er ...'

Theo felt guilty for not thinking of offering her some money earlier. He dug in his pockets and handed her all the ringgits he had. She hesitated. 'Take it, go on.'

She closed her hand around the money and tears filled her eyes. 'I feel so helpless; have to rely on others ...'

He unzipped the back of his wallet and pulled out a wad of 100 ringgit notes. 'There. I also have travellers' cheques and I will get some more money to you somehow.'

She looked at the money. 'I can't take this ... I have money saved but difficult to get at moment ...'

He closed her hand around it and drew her to him. 'Don't worry, no more talk, you will need money for things.'

They hugged for several minutes. She said, 'I am sad I leave you so soon. It makes me very happy to be with you again, Theo. Let us hope we see each other again soon after I go.'

They kissed; Theo felt the warmth of her hard, slim body against his. He knew he had to push her away this time. The tap on the door separated them.

Marking Time

Chapter Seventy-Four

'Yes, she left this morning,' said Theo, lighting a cigarette. Even though he was with friends he felt distant, picking at his food.

They were having breakfast at the Planter Station just off Lebuh Cintra.

'Eric and I wanted to meet her,' said Franka. 'But I understand the problem. So long as she iss safe, dat is what counts.'

'Yah,' added Eric, 'We meet her when we come to Australia and stay at your place.'

Theo came to. 'Stay at my ..? I don't have a place but I'm sure my mother could find a spot for you. When are you coming?'

'I only just kidding around, ve not able to travel for a while or two. It seems I haff to work in my father's business for a time but I'm sure ve will come to Australia one day, yay Franka?'

'Okay, for sure.'

Theo filled in the spaces as to what had transpired over the last few days but he downplayed the complexity of it all.

'So you now a lonely person for a while?' said Franka, giving him an all knowing smile.

'Yeah, seems like it but hopefully not too long. I'm holding off on confirming my flights because I hope to link up with Biru somewhere, that's if she can get out of the country. I hope it all works out, I mean she left in disguise this morning as Jack's floozy. Even if you knew her you would be hard put to recognise her.' Theo smiled, despite the tight queasy feeling in his stomach.

Eric inclined his head. 'Floozy, vot is diss floozy?'

'Oh, girlfriend, young companion, maybe even ... er mistress, something like that.' It made Theo smile.

∞

He recalled Jack walking into the administration building, arm in arm with a young Indian woman in a sari with a scarf partly hiding her face. The picture was completed by a red dot in the middle of the woman's forehead. Theo had to look more than once. Biru looked convincingly Indian. They all laughed, Brian most of all because it was his idea. Jack gave Theo a quick run-down of the plan and he and Brian left the room. They only had a few minutes together.

Theo felt strange when he grabbed Biru for a final hug but the firmness of her tight body pushing into him and then her warm, sweet lips released the familiar electric charge between them. They both separated at the same time, knowing the moment had to end.

She looked back as she walked out the door, stopped, glanced quickly into the next room, spun around and covered the distance between them in Nano time. She planted a hot wet kiss on his lips and scooted out, not looking back.

Theo leaned against the desk, breathing hard as if he had sprinted around the oval. His hands had trouble lighting a cigarette when Brian came in with a tea tray.

'Brian, I forgot that she will need money, I don't think she has much, I gave her ...'

Brian waved him down. 'Don't worry, Jack will give her some.'

'Right, right it's ...'

Brian waved him down. 'Tea?'

One thing Theo felt sure about, more confident than anything in his life, was that he really did want to see her again. He also knew the next few days were going to be agony not being able to hold her. Imprinted in his mind was the departing view out the window; almost a serene scene, an older man with a slight limp, arm in arm with a young Indian woman walking away under the frangipani trees towards the back gate.

∞

Eric jolted him out of dreamland, telling him about their time in the Cameron Highlands. Eric arrived at the present. 'Ve go to top of Penang Hill today as final tourist thing, back to hotel and then to pack and pay up too. Den ve go to airport and fly away into yonder. I regret not being able to spend time with you here. Hopefully ve come back one day, you must keep in touch and make sure to get together before ve get a lot older, yah?'

Theo saw them again before they left and even though the future looked bright, he still felt a darkness descend on him when they climbed into the taxi at the end of the lane after a prolonged group hug. The emptiness inside him with the absence of Biru was compounded more than he wanted to admit by the departure of Franka and Eric.

Theo figured a change of scenery would jog him out of his malaise. He commissioned Tung to pedal him around for a sightseeing tour and he made the young Chinese boy stop and sit with him at a café where they drank a cold lassi. Thunder threatened the coming storm so they headed back to the Hotel Happiness where Theo went to straight to his room. He pulled out his notebook, *Theo's Adventures* but he couldn't concentrate. He lay back on his bed scrolling events of the last 24 hours. He was pleased Jack and Brian were able to spirit Biru away to safety but there was still the underlying possibility things could go wrong. He kept telling himself that everything would turn out alright in the end because he trusted in Jack. Before they left in the morning, Jack had told him not to worry, which was easier said than done.

Thoughts surfaced in relation to the bigger picture – if Biru and he linked up, where would they go? There may be no choice. If or when they arrived in Australia, if it *was* Australia, what then? What about the job he was supposed to start soon? He could put that off for a week or two but no more. Sorting out citizenship for Biru was the easy part. Would they live together? Marriage? Maybe, but what about her religious beliefs? She was a Muslim and Theo realised they had never discussed serious things such as religious beliefs. He knew he would never convert; religion was something he rejected. Theo wondered how she really felt about her religion, how seriously she viewed it. Would her religion allow her to not be a Muslim? Would it be a problem for their future relationship? He had never observed her at prayer. Theo was aware that although there was a deep attraction between them, there was an extraordinary amount to learn about each other.

'Bugger!' he said aloud, startling himself, as the rain began.

He remembered one thing she said when they were in church, kneeling. 'Theo, in the last few months I have been questioning my religion.'

He knew from playing football, you had to let the ball bounce; no-one could ever have total control over an oblong football. The more he practised the better he was at anticipating which direction it would go but there was always the time when it bounced the wrong way. So what chance did he have of trying to anticipate any outcome now? All these balls in the air.

Looking at his watch did not make the time go any faster.

He pulled out *Beyond Pardon* and tried to continue from where he left off. Hayley was explaining the punishment dished out to inmates for offences which took his mind off Biru for a while. For some reason, he felt he could identify with Hayley. Of course he couldn't condone the man's actions, being apprehended with heroin, but Theo somehow could understand his plight. After all, Theo and his mates had smoked dope on plenty of occasions, and although marijuana wasn't in the same league as heroin, it was still illegal, even in a broad-minded society like Australia. He recalled something that Spud Morgan had said and he eventually found the reference. '*A crime is only a crime if the law deems it so.*'

Theo lay there, watching the well-balanced ceiling fan cutting through the tropical heat as the rain fizzed down outside. He remembered his early intention to score some marijuana or hash here in Malaysia despite *all* the warnings at the airport and the printed handout with the immigration document that *he had signed* – he was *still* prepared to score some drugs. Just as well he did not actually do it. The stint in jail taught him a great deal. He licked his lips; his throat was dry suddenly so he reached for the water bottle.

The rain ceased so he decided to go out into the tropical garden, grab a beer and have a go at reading some more of *Slowly Down The Ganges*. He settled into a cane chair, lit up a smoke and started reading.

'You want beer?' said Mama.

A couple of minutes later she returned with a Tiger. 'Smoking bad for you. You give me one?' She laughed the laugh of the jolly as Theo offered her one. He didn't think she would accept but she slumped her weight down into a creaking cane chair and he lit her up.

Theo didn't really want company but very quickly he warmed to her vivacious personality and they spent a comfortable ten minutes. She had the bearing of an auntie/sister figure rather than a mother. He spoke of home; she spoke of her hotel and family.

'I go back to work, someone have to keep show on the road.' She looked him directly in the eyes and touched his hand. 'You be careful with Muslim girl, okay?' She stood with some difficulty.

He bristled. 'How do you know I am even seeing ..?'

'Chinee very observant, you in love, written all over face. I have work to do, no standing around here talking to guest otherwise place go to rack and ruin. Thank you for cigarette but that not make any discount for your bill, yaaaaaaaah!'

Theo lightened and nodded. She left him thinking about his mother and what she was doing today, and again he wondered what he was going to tell her about all the events on his holiday. How could he tell her about Biru or his stay in jail?

The call to prayer stereoed from mosques afar and some bells jingled at a temple nearby. He looked at his watch again, still hours to go before he could ring Biru. He went and rang his mother instead, planning to tell her a few truths.

Chapter Seventy-Five

Theo was surprised to not see Tung out the front but he didn't really care too much either. He didn't want to have to engage with anyone for a while so he followed the sound of a lingering call to prayer which he guessed to be coming from the Acheen Street Mosque. He knew Dr Sun Yat Sen's place was in that direction so he made his way through the busy streets.

The phone call to his mother didn't go the way he'd planned as she was on her way out and someone was out the front waiting in the car. There was no way he could weave into the short conversation any of the things he had wanted to. When it came down to it, there was no way he could even mention Biru's name. The voice in his head told him to tell her about Biru but not mention the Muslim part. He was able to say he was coming home soon as planned and was going to sort out the flights soon. He filled in the spaces and talked about Jack and how well they were getting on. She asked questions about him, obviously interested in what he was doing. There was a silence on the line when Theo told her Jack had married again and had a son. He had asked, 'Why?' After a moment she said she was slightly shocked because Jack had been married before and she never thought he would settle down and do it again. She had to go and Theo promised to talk again when he knew his travel arrangements. Although he was unable to confide in his mother about the things in progress, he felt buoyed hearing her voice.

Out in the street he felt more confident among the people and even though he had the day pack slung over his shoulder he didn't feel quite the tourist. Only a few rickshaw drivers offered him a lift and with a smile and a polite 'No,' they left him alone as did most of the other street hawkers. It caused him to think that either he gave the impression he was almost one of them or they had seen him around often enough to know he had been subjected to every scam on earth since arriving.

'You want lift?'

'I'll be. Tung, how did you know where I was?'

'Aha, special extra senses only Chinee have.'

Theo laughed and jumped in. Tung added, 'Only this time I cheat and Mama tell me, ha! You look like you need time on your own. I only speak when you ass me to, okay?'

Tung was a mind reader, too. Theo was happy for the company of a friend who it seemed understood. He was able to muse. He had made many friends in Malaysia and felt sure he would return one day. Then it occurred to him that Biru would probably never be able to and it made him think about the boundaries people put around themselves and others as well. It seemed here in Malaysia with so many different cultures, religions, languages and so many people, there needed to be a certain rule of personal restraint and order. Malaysia was so incredibly different to the life he had been leading in Australia and in some small way he felt he had grown up, if only by a few degrees.

'Dr Sun Yat Sen place, leader of Chinee revolution, him Penang base. You look?'

Theo jumped. 'What? Yeah, righto.' He fought his way through the touts, paid the small admission and wandered in. Fortunately he found a reasonably quiet section where he read newspaper clippings and items of interest stuck to the walls. As he walked out the day was surrendering to the night and a cool breeze had sprung up.

'Mosque?'

'Yep, do you know if I can go in?'

'Sure, sure, no problem but you lee shoe out front, make sure you get receipt and be sure to pay when you lee because otherwise rogue not let you take them, okay?'

Theo looked down at his thongs and they laughed together. 'Righto,' he said.

The minaret loomed up and the crowds thickened. Tung dropped him off at the front and surprisingly to Theo no-one seemed to pay him any attention. He walked up the steps and over to the shoe rack. A busy little man in a whiter than white full-length shirt tore receipts out of a book and handed them to devotees as he yelled and directed a young boy as to where to place shoes handed in. Theo took his thongs off and the man managed a smile as he barked at the boy. Clearly no-one other than westerners wore thongs. A sign with some writing he couldn't read showed the number 5 with *sen* following.

The crowd out the front must have already prayed because as Theo neared the entrance it thinned out and he could see the bulk of the interior with men kneeling.

A smiling man beckoned him towards the back, realising he was just an observer. 'You most welcome Tuan; please you maybe sit comfortable against wall – backrest okay?'

The praying process was almost hypnotic and Theo was reminded of Biru's faith. He couldn't get his head around it and wondered if he ever would. He supposed understanding the language would go a long way. After about ten minutes he felt he'd had enough and unobtrusively sidled out. He paid the officious man in white with one ringgit because he didn't have anything smaller. The man frowned and looked around with great concern, thinking he had to find change, but when Theo waved and walked away he seemed to relax and yelled, 'Terima kasih.'

Tung took him to three Chinese temples with smoky incense leaking out the archways. They were very noisy with drums and bells and people chattering, some yelling. Theo was not really in the mood so he directed Tung to take him to the quietest place in Penang.

The Indian eating house wasn't exactly quiet but Theo was able to sit in a corner under a fan, drink beer and make notes in his exercise book. He ordered some dahl and samosas recommended by a young smiling boy in white pyjamas. He was glad he did because he discovered how hungry he was.

At nine thirty he returned to the hotel. Mama said there were no calls but he didn't expect any anyway. He took his usual seat and dialled Brian's number. His heart thumped and the plastic handpiece felt sticky.

Chapter Seventy-Six

'Biru is staying there as expected but they couldn't promise anything,' said Brian.

Brian explained it all went fairly well but the shelter was busy. He gave Theo a number to ring and her code number 221, no names allowed. It was a general phone and the residents had restricted access only. He said they asked that you not ring tonight but tomorrow morning would be okay.

'Could they help with the passport?'

'Well, they evidently said they would do their best, that's all at this stage.' Brian could sense Theo's anxiety. 'Theo, it could take a while. I know how you feel but you will just have to wait.'

'Yeah, I understand.' Theo's stomach twisted.

'Jack is on his way back and he will see you in the morning. He may be able to tell you more. Rest assured, the ladies at WW are experienced in these matters and I'm sure things will work out, alright?'

They went on with general talk and then hung up.

Theo realised he was supposed to be going out with Harvey the next day.

Before leaving for Kuala Lumpur, Jack said Harvey was keen to show him around and a car had been organised for the day. Despite the anxiety of waiting for this present matter to resolve itself, Theo figured a day out with Jack's son would do him good.

∞

Next morning, Theo was up early and had already tried to ring Biru three times at the refuge. Unfortunately the phone had been engaged and he had the sinking feeling it might be like that all day. The tropical night had him battling with tangled, damp sheets imagining every possible life scenario, looking forward from this day. It wasn't only the complexities involved with getting her out of the country but what he was going to do when they reached Australia, if they ever did. The same question kept gnawing away, how was he going to explain this to his mother? He tried to convince himself the best policy was to do nothing; simply because there *was* absolutely nothing constructive he could do right at that moment, anyway.

The scolding from Mama for picking away at his breakfast jolted him into the real world. 'You definitely in love.'

He'd just finished another coffee when Jack turned up.

'G'day mate, looks like you've got a hangover.'

'Do I look that bad?'

'No, not really, but it looks like you didn't sleep too well.'

'That's observant. Anyway, how did it all go?'

Jack told him much the same as Brian. The supervisor at WW, a woman named Gloria, an expat Englishwoman, had told him it would be difficult to get the passport because fast tracking was only ever done when women had been bashed and raped but there was not a paper trail to back that up in Biru's case. Gloria had promised to give it top priority but Jack could see they were flat out. Jack knew the woman personally because he'd had dealings with her before and she had assured him they would do whatever they could.

Jack relaxed back. 'Biru played her part well. Er … did you know she was abused by her stepfather?'

'No, she never said.'

'Well, Gloria the supervisor told me. I know that is in confidence but it explains a lot. I wasn't present for the whole interview but she felt I should know. Gloria said most women are embarrassed and ashamed of that sort of thing and she's sure Biru was telling the truth.'

Theo looked into his coffee cup. 'Yeah, of course. Oh, by the way, money. Brian said you were probably …'

'Don't worry about it, it's the least I can do. Yeah, I slung her some bucks, it's alright, don't worry. Right mate, we have a car out the front and little Harve is just about widdling his strides to get going. I didn't bring him in here because I wanted to speak to you in private, first. He doesn't really know much only other than a girlfriend of yours has gone to Kuala Lumpur and you will be meeting her in a few days.'

'Right. Er … how is Biru, I mean ..?'

'She'll be alright; there are many women like her, most of them running from mongrel blokes. The staff might be a bit evasive on the phone too because there are blokes out there who will stop at nothing to locate the women who, they believe, have jaded them. The men who do this sort of thing should be whipped in public but sad to say, it's the women who seem to get blamed for somehow being the cause of it all … and they get publicly stoned, beaten or worse in some places. I don't get it, never will.'

'Could I ring Biru? I've tried a few times this morning but the phone is engaged.'

'Yeah, sure, make sure to use her code number, my driver has taken Harve to get a banana lassi and then they were going to stop at the end of the lane. I'll see you out there, okay?'

Theo tried again. This time someone answered in Malaysian but quickly switched to English and he asked to speak to 221. She said there was no-one allocated that number. The woman sounded quite abrupt.

Theo's heart raced. 'What? She was taken in by you yesterday. My name is Theo Perry.'

Silence hung for a moment. 'Sorry sir, even if there was a 221 she would be unable to take private calls.' The woman had a North American lilt to her accent.

Theo shook his head in frustration and fear surfaced. He mentioned Gloria's name.

'Ah, I see. One moment please.' A conversation took place nearby and the woman came back on line. Her voice softened. 'Okay, I understand. I'm sorry if I was rude but we get many men contacting us trying to locate women. All of the women here are in danger. Please, 221 is unavailable but Gloria has meetings with officials and says you should ring this evening because nothing has happened with the case so far.'

'Right, yes, I'm with you, thanks.' He sighed and hung up.

Mama wagged her finger at him on the way out.

Chapter Seventy-Seven

'Theo, over here,' yelled Harvey from the window of the car.

Theo jumped in the back alongside a wide-eyed Harvey who shook his hand. 'We will drop Dad off and then we will go for a drive,' and he spread his hands, 'everywhere.'

Jack turned around from the front seat. 'This is Chee,' he said tapping the driver on the shoulder. 'He knows the place inside out. How did you go with the call?'

'She couldn't take calls, they said to ring tonight.'

'Yeah, there's not much we can do until Gloria speaks to her contacts and all that. Try to enjoy the day.'

They dropped Jack off at home and continued on to Penang Hill where they caught the funicular railway to the top. Harvey tried very much to be the grown up by playing tourist guide, pointing out landmarks way below. They visited the mosque and Hindu temple. Theo was surprised at the depth of Harvey's knowledge of not only the religious places but of the history of Penang and Malaysia. They visited the Buddhist Kek Lok Si temple which was said to be Burmese at the top, Thai in the middle and Chinese at the bottom.

Theo wondered where Harvey fitted into the religious circle, knowing Jack was not religious in any way, but he had noticed a small Chinese altar or shrine, or something, with burning incense at their house.

Harvey beat him to it. 'We are not very religious at our place but Mum is Chinese, a Buddhist. Buddhism is not a religion, she says it is a way of life and I think Mum and Dad both agree, trying to be the best person you can be is the best religion to have.'

From an 11-year-old boy, Theo was impressed with the young person's view of things. The boy was also very curious.

'Are you religious, Theo?'

'No, not at all.' His reply made him instantly think of Biru and the bounds of her religion.

The boy looked at him, willing him to continue. 'Oh sorry. Mum made me go to a Catholic Sunday School but I guess because she is not religious and nor was Dad for that matter, when I turned about ten or so she could see I wasn't interested so she let me make up my own mind. I didn't go after that because I'm not a believer, I guess.'

They drove to Batu Ferringhi and Theo was amazed at the number of tourists, backpackers and package-deal older types. They had a swim and sat around at a tourist restaurant café on the sand.

'Dad says this is the place to come to get a good Captain Cook at the sheilas,' said Harvey, laughing.

Theo smiled at the use of language. Jack was right. It was clear that Theo's generation didn't follow the suggestions given in the guidebooks in relation to dress codes so as to not offend locals. Tourists, and interestingly not all of them young, wore close to nothing, possibly more daring even than in Australia. Some females removed their tops in the water and when sunbaking. Theo remembered going to Maslin's nude beach, near Adelaide, with his mates a few times. This was nearly as good because the northern Europeans were not afraid to show it all when at the beach.

'Mum forbids him coming here but he reminds her he goes to Thailand often and there are plenty of beaches like this there. He says it doesn't hurt to look anyway. She just laughs and says men are all the same. Do you think men are?'

Theo looked at the boy. 'Yep.'

Harvey asked. 'Do you think I will grow up to be like that?'

'For sure.' Both of them laughed, almost hysterically.

They toured along the northern beaches and had more swims. Harvey was enjoying himself and Theo found it infectious. Several times during the day he realised he had forgotten about his other issues. They sat at another café on the sand listening to the thunder and watching the spectacular lightning show zapping out to sea. Then the rains came and drowned out the conversation, and Theo realised they had both been talking non-stop all day.

On the way back, lights were coming on and they visited the colourful Thai Wat Chayamangkalaram where a huge reclining Buddha holds the stage. By the time they arrived at the Koo Kongsi temple it was dark and they wandered around listening to bells and gongs as well as lighting incense, burning play money and making wishes. When they arrived in front of the lane near the Hotel Happiness it was after seven and both of them were yawning.

Harvey stepped out of the car to say goodbye. 'I'm going off to school in Singapore for the first term tomorrow. I guess I won't see you again, for a while anyway.'

'I suppose not,' replied Theo.

The boy stood staring at him for a second and held out his hand.

'Here, a handshake isn't good enough, mate,' and Theo grabbed the boy in a bear hug. The boy had the smell of youth as well as sand and salt from the beach. When they released each other, Harvey had wet eyes.

'I have really enjoyed today and … I don't want you to go away and I don't want to go away myself but …'

'I know, but mate, we will get together again one day …' Theo realised how hard it was to reassure such an intelligent and open-hearted 11-year-old.

'Will you come back to Malaysia and see me again?'

Theo knew he would break up if he did not end the conversation. 'Yes, of course … I promise, one day.'

Harvey smiled and said, 'Yippee,' and clapped his hands. 'Great.'

'I had a really great day too, Harve, you're a good kid and you will love being at your new school. Don't forget to keep your eyes on the sheilas.'

Harvey waved through the back window as the car disappeared. Theo felt a tug in his chest; he knew he would miss the boy.

He wandered to the hotel and Big Buddha Mama said, 'You have big day, you get sunburn. No phone call for you. You want to use phone? Telephone company go broke without your calls, ha!'

'Yes, I need to make a call and could I have a beer, please?'

'You want beer delivered to your private table, too?'

Theo could afford to be as cheeky as she was. 'Yes, please and on the double.'

She frowned at him and wandered off to the kitchen throwing her hands up, exclaiming something in Chinese, as Theo took the phone to his private table. He rang Jack who had not heard from Biru or Gloria. Jack thanked him for taking the time to go out with Harvey and said the boy had enjoyed the day. Jack suggested they meet the next afternoon at the Saigon, confident they would have more information. Jack also wanted to give him his father's possessions from the safe. He rang off.

A beer arrived and Theo took a big breath and dialled. 'Could I speak to 221 please?'

'Sorry sir, no one has been allocated that number.'

Shoebox

Chapter Seventy-Eight

It was a different person this time. Theo gave his name and, despite his beating heart and the lead feeling in his stomach, he managed to relay to the woman that he had been through the same thing earlier in the day. At the mention of Gloria's and Jack's names, the woman put him on hold and went to locate Biru.

'Hello, Theo?'

'Yes ... it is me,' he managed to say.

'I have been waiting for this moment.'

'Have you ... sorry ... how are you?'

'I am fine. They good people here, no problem, many women much worse off than me. Gloria has put in my application for fast track but there is no way of knowing anything more until the government person gets back to her.'

Theo saw no reason to dwell on something he couldn't influence. 'Do you ... have enough money for things?'

'Yes no problems, Jack make me take money. We are not allowed out of this refuge unless we sign something to say we don't come back. The compound has armed guards so no-one can get in or out. This morning a Chinese man came to get his wife. Somehow he found out she was here and it took three security men to hold him down. He in jail now. His wife badly beaten two days ago and she come here for protection. She in infirmary now, broken arm and bruises.'

Theo murmured, 'That's ...'

She changed the subject and continued, obviously excited and somewhat agitated. 'People here do wonderful job but very busy. I have to share room with four others; two have children but I help. Theo I miss you, I hope I get out of here soon, don't know if I can stand it for a very long time. Gloria say to relax but it is hard for me to because if I not get passport, where I do go then?'

'Biru, I … miss you too. Look, everything will be alright; it should only be a few days. There is nothing anyone can do until you find out from the government. Jack says the visa part of it is no problem because when you get out of the country you can apply for one when in transit, if you really have to.'

'Yes, I know this but I nervous about it, too.' She seemed to brighten. 'I only wish I could see you, it would make me stronger.'

Theo could hear voices in the background and she said something to someone. His heart sank for a moment. *Come on, mate, remember, nothing either of you can do, trust the future, alright?*

She continued, 'I have to go now, I miss you so much …'

He knew he had to be strong. 'I miss you too but no matter what happens we will see each other again soon, I promise.' It was a silly thing to say because he had no control over that.

'Time to go, I can't make phone calls from here at least at the moment but please ring again tomorrow night,' she spoke to someone, 'about ten they say when I hope there will be some news. Bye bye, I love you, Theo.'

He didn't get a chance to reply, the line went dead.

∞

Next morning Theo tried to be in a positive mood so he asked Tung to take him to a quiet place to give him a chance to catch up on reading, as well as updating his exercise book. The café overlooked the sea and apart from some 60s western music on the stereo sung by Filipinos or Thais, he was able to sit in a cane chair, drink kopi and have a smoke in relative comfort.

He started with his *Theo's Adventures* exercise book and scribbled together a basic business plan for the articles or columns he was going to write. He flipped open *Beyond Pardon* and sped read the pages of information on Hayley's visitors – Amnesty International, two civil rights groups, Australian Embassy and government officials as well as others. Spud Morgan asked Hayley about his family.

M: Tell me more about your family. How are they coping?

H: Yeah, I know I let them down badly, particularly my mother who is too upset to visit anymore. The old man comes as often as he can but it costs money you know; flights, accommodation, all that. I'd rather not talk about them if it's all the same to … (he broke off and bowed his head, clearly distressed.)

M: Sure mate, I didn't mean to … I know it's hard for you. What about the lawyer, can we talk about him; you said he was a good guy?

H: Yeah, Shan, Shan Manesh. He always brings me what he can and my father has actually stayed at his place. Without him I think I would already be dead for sure.

M: You mentioned before that someone you worked for has helped out a bit with money for legal fees?

H: Did I? Oh yeah, I don't know who it is, the lawyer won't tell me but I can't complain. All Shan said was that it was someone I worked for. Could be anyone I guess …

It was early in the day and the meeting with Jack was not until three so he decided to have a beer. He considered *Beyond Pardon* to be a great reference book for the articles he was going to write for the Adelaide Advertiser.

He read some more *Slowly Down The Ganges*, ate rendang curry and watched the boats out in the sea. By the time he arrived at the Saigon the slightest of breezes stirred the listless trees lining the roadways.

'G'day, Theo,' said Jack from behind the bar. 'Beer?'

'Why not, thanks.'

Jack grabbed a couple from the glass-faced fridge and pointed to a table near a big fan. He also had a cardboard shoebox under his arm. 'Here, this is for you, sorry to say, your Dad's worldly possessions.'

They clinked bottles. 'Cheers yet again,' nodded Theo, opening the box, eager to inspect. He quickly flicked through the items.

Jack gave him a couple of minutes and then broke the silence. 'Nothing like a cold beer on a hot day, eh? How did you go with Biru? I haven't heard anything yet by the way.'

Theo put his bottle on the table. 'Well, it's like this,' and he rolled his hands in an open gesture. 'No news, at least last night. She said there was no point ringing again until tonight.'

'Yeah, Gloria said it could take a few days, I mean she has to speak to her friends in the government and convince them of Biru's dangerous situation. But if she can do that, the passport thing is fast tracked. There is a special department that handles fast processing of documents, mainly visas and passports for business people, legal types, people who have to go somewhere else for urgent medical treatment, and of course, bloody politicians.'

They sat in silence for a minute, listening to John Lee Hooker singing about the freight train being his only friend. Theo couldn't ignore the box. He gently picked through the items. 'Not much here for a life, Jack,' he said looking up, 'is there?'

'I'm afraid that's true, mate, just be proud of your old man, eh.' Jack's face was devoid of the usual humour.

'Hey, his medals are here! And a diary.'

'Yeah, unfortunately not much else though, he lived a sparse existence. That's his ashes,' said Jack, pointing at a smaller plain cardboard box. 'Er they are in a small plastic urn, for travel, you know ...'

Silence hung between them for a moment. Jack continued, 'Only thing he did apart from work was read. He read a bit of everything, I think. The diary might have some interesting stuff in it. Even though I was a mate, I chose not to look through it. I thought it is, sort of private, should belong to you ... er ... and your mother, you know?'

Theo looked up and nodded a smile.

Jack said, 'He drank a bit and ...'

Theo inclined his head. 'And ... and what?'

'Oh, nothin,' I didn't mean to ...'

'Does it matter anymore, what he did or didn't do? He was my father; I'm not surprised by any ...'

Jack's brow tightened. 'Well, he was using quite a bit of heroin.'

'How much is a bit?'

Jack signalled in the direction of the bar. It seemed to Theo as if he was weighing up what his answer would be. He lit a smoke. 'I guess it doesn't matter. He was using mobs and I was surprised when he handed me that money, you know the money I sent you. As far as I knew for probably about a year before ... before he died he was using heavily and had some difficulty holding things together and I didn't think he had much dough. When he went on to tell me, I wasn't surprised.'

'Told you, what?'

Two beers arrived. Someone put on Neil Young's *Loner*, loud. A connection was loose and the track jumped. Jack looked over. A man wiping tables yelled, 'Hey Foo, fix that thing, will you?'

Jack looked back and took a deep breath. 'He was dying, Theo, he had stomach cancer and I think he knew for some time before because he really went downhill rapidly, not that he wasn't almost rock bottom anyway.'

Theo leaned forward suddenly. 'No-one told us he was ill.'

'I really don't think it made any difference, Theo, he'd had enough of this life.'

Theo nodded slowly.

Jack looked away; Theo thought he could see tears in Jack's eyes. There was no need to speak.

Theo busied himself sifting through the items in the box during the long, heavy moment. He changed the subject. 'Jack, did you ever use heroin?'

'Yep, used a bit in 'Nam but not again until I went to Bangkok, when I left Australia after I arrived back. When your father went there we both did for a while. It was readily available but after a time both of us sort of gave it away, went cold turkey and then a few months later we started again, but you know casual use, and you can do that if you only use say once a fortnight or so and only one session and you don't get withdrawals. But for most punters, they never really give it away, heroin is not like that because they keep using regularly and if you do that it's real hard to stop because of the withdrawals. And of course we both continued to dabble but it was under control because we had plenty of hash and booze to pad it out. When we came here to Malaysia, it was also available through the places we worked but when my boy was born not long after, I swore off it. Vince, your old man, never did completely, kept it under control for years but he only started using heavily towards the end … end of his life and I guess it was for the pain as much as anything.'

Two more beers arrived. Theo decided to change the subject. 'Harvey and I had a really good day yesterday. He seems pretty grown up for his age. He had opinions on almost everything, including religion, politics …'

'Yeah, he's a bright boy. I want him to have a good education but I don't want him to have anything to do with the life I led. I get clothes, mainly shirts, made in Thailand and send them to America and Australia, also sell plenty in Thailand and I am looking at the potential in Bali. I can get things made there too. Van is becoming more involved and I'm hoping that when Harve finishes school he'll probably do law or medicine – but if he doesn't we want him to become involved in the clothing business and even backpacker accommodation and adventure tours. It's all legit. I can sell the backpacker interests in Thailand and keep this place as a hobby. There may come a time when I might need to leave Malaysia, that's why I have Australian passports for Van and Harve. Who knows if the wind may change but overall, I like it here.'

Theo didn't know if Jack was proud of his family, proud of his business or both. Maybe he was content he had found a spot for himself and his family in a place where he fitted in and was accepted for who he was?

They drank on for a while and then Jack bailed Theo into a car and they headed for Batu Ferringhi. An elegantly dressed Van met them at an exclusive bar, on the penthouse floor of the highest building, with 360 degree views. They sipped cocktails and looked out at the ugly clouds building on the skyline. Not long after the sky slowly darkened and thunder rumbled. Lightning zapped over the sea as the storm headed their way.

'You don't get a show like this in Adelaide, Theo,' said Jack. It was the old Jack Theo remembered as a child, with his impish, disarming smile. Jack and his old man, smoking and joking.

Theo was almost overcome with emotion. He said, 'That's for sure,' and looked away to hide his demeanour. He knew he was among friends, Van and Jack. The only one missing was his father. And Harvey.

The rain blanked out all surrounds for about five minutes and they could have been at street level or in a closed room. The rain eased to mist and the vista returned.

They went into the restaurant which was up-market Chinese and were able to select their fish from a huge water tank on the way in. The view was spectacular and Theo was reminded constantly of the might of Malaysia. Even though Australia was big, it was sparse and so very different to this. Lights blinked as far as he could see in all directions. Out at sea, the intermittent lights of large cruise ships, tankers, fishing boats and junks punctuated the darkness in front the backdrop of mainland Malaysia. The occasional strobe of light from the air force base in Butterworth cut a path to the heavens and across the horizon. Stars mingled with the flashing lights of air traffic across the night sky.

Theo was once again astonished at the wide variety of food choices and he left it to the others to order. It once again made him think of home and how different it was. They had individual fillets of fish, cooked in an Asian style and enhanced by a crowded table of complementary dishes.

'We don't get food like this in Australia,' Theo said, looking at Van. 'The best we can do is the local Chinese, and there are a few Thai and Indian restaurants too which aren't bad, mind you, but this is ...' He opened his arms to indicate the spread. 'Mum and I have never been to places like this, closest was a wedding but it was typical Aussie food like soup, a few prawns for entree and a whopping big steak, tough as, with peas and spuds.'

They all laughed. Theo added, 'Yeah, I'm sure there are places that serve high-end eating but I bet it wouldn't be as good as this.'

Van said she would miss Harvey but she said she would be going to Singapore with him for a few days and then planned to visit him every couple of weeks. 'Singapore is not so far,' she said, 'even by bus, only one day.'

She asked him questions about his mother and then Biru. Theo felt comfortable talking to her. Jack looked on and added a comment every so often. Full and happy, they went back down to the foyer and Jack said, 'We'll drop you off.'

They dropped him at the corner of the lane which had become familiar territory for Theo. Van pulled his face to hers and pecked his cheek as he opened the door.

'Thanks again for a really great time; I er … might have trouble leaving here.'

Jack said with a wide grin, 'Yeah, I know exactly what you mean, that's probably why I'm still here.'

Theo was about to say he was going to ring Biru when Jack said, 'See how you go with ringing Biru tonight or tomorrow morning and get a message to Brian. He will be there and I will be next door speaking to wayward travellers.' He emphasised '*wayward*' with his fingers.

Theo thanked them again and stood for a moment in the street, watching the car drive off. He thought what a beautiful person Van was, what a lucky bloke Jack was and what a lucky couple they were to have a son like Harvey.

Theo tucked the cardboard shoebox under his arm. He looked forward to rifling through the contents again as he walked down the lane to the Hotel Happiness. 'Aha, it's ten o'clock,' he said aloud, glancing at his watch. A few people mingled out the front but no-one paid him any attention. It was time to make a call. His heart beat harder.

Chapter Seventy-Nine

There were no difficulties this time; Biru was waiting by the phone. She spoke quickly, obviously excited. 'Theo, Theo, good news I think, I have been waiting all day for information and also to hear your voice.'

He smiled into the phone. 'Have you got your passport?'

'No, no, not exactly but almost, Gloria say I have passport tomorrow. I get photos of me from office staff with camera for passport and visa. I look different to how I look in Muslim uniform. Fast track process good for passport but to get Australian visa I have to have family sponsor.'

'Family sponsor?' Theo rubbed his jaw.

'Yes, I have to have Australian family to guarantee my um ... resident ...'

'Residency, yes I have heard of it, Vietnamese boat people have had to do the same. How long will that take, did she say?' Theo instantly thought of his mother but discounted it quickly.

'No, but shouldn't be a problem; there are people on list who help in this circumstances.'

'When can I see you?'

'Soon I think. Gloria say I can maybe fly to Bangkok if not Australia from here, be safe there and then when paperwork finish I can go to Australia. All up in air at the moment.'

Theo's heart jumped. All he could get out was, 'Bangkok. Yeah, sure whatever ...' Theo reminded himself to be patient; just because Gloria said the passport would be ready tomorrow, didn't mean anything.

'Yes, Theo I am so excited, to see you soon and give me hope...'

'I can't wait to see you again Biru and I just realised, do you have enough money for fares and ..?'

'Yes no problem, I save for years and have to hide cash but money with friends now in Penang. I let them know and they pay credit card. When I get to my destination they transfer money to account in my name. Problem for Muslim woman, not allowed to have bank account unless approval by man, that why it so hard for me to do anything. I pay back money to you and Jack also.'

Theo was amazed by her ingenuity and her strong will to survive. 'No, no, there is no need, it's okay. Right, we'll talk again soon; I'll ring you ... when?'

'Tomorrow afternoon, I think Gloria say three, maybe?'

'Right, I'll ring you at four in case.'

'Okay, I have to go, woman waiting for phone. I miss you Theo and I so excited I not be able to sleep before I speak to you again.'

'Yes, I miss you, too ...'

'I love you, Theo, bye bye.'

'I ...' The phone disconnected before he could finish.

∞

Theo tipped the contents of the shoebox on to the bed; the small urn, diary, medals and other things. There were a few barely readable receipts stapled together, two American fishing magazines five years old and two old paperbacks, *The History of Indonesia*, and *The Kill-Off* by Jim Thompson. Both books were well worn but Theo knew he would read them at a later time. He wondered if the diary would tell him more about his father. It had 1968 embossed on the front, was dog-eared, grubby and worn and appeared to be a sketchy account of things his father had jotted down during the war. Theo skipped through it, reading odd snippets of mundane activities, and from what he saw he figured he would need time to go through it one day. The entries were short and varied, things like, '*off on patrol today to ... looking forward to R and R ..., must remember to ..., Richo and Stan wounded today ...,*' and he also saw his and his mother's names, here and there. His eyes prickled with salty tears and he had to look away from the small book.

He knew there was plenty of reading for some time in the future when he was settled. Theo knew he was not ready at this point.

He peeked into the urn box, thinking of the sum of his father's life and then he placed it with the other things. He pulled out the photographs, the black and white shot of Vince in uniform, ready for a world of excitement, a young man off to a war that would change his life forever, and the other photo in colour of the same man. Theo could see the damage, not only the age gap but the face that portrayed a look of hopelessness. The likeness to a swashbuckling Errol Flynn was nowhere to be seen. He whispered, 'Dad, I hope you will forgive me.'

For a while he sat motionless, staring through heavy eyes at the meagre pile of possessions, wondering many things. Why Vince had kept the old diary, curious if his father had read the books and if he liked the genre, why he kept faded old receipts? Was anything there significant in any way and if it was, to whom or what? He lit a cigarette to break the spell. After this time of reflection he yawned. There would be plenty of time to wonder about things later.

He had a long shower and then lay down for a while. A short time later he fell into a restless sleep, waking regularly until he forced himself to think of Biru and then he dreamed of good things to come.

Chapter Eighty

Theo rang Brian the next morning and explained what Biru had said. As he talked, the fingers of his free hand fiddled with his father's medals. Brian hadn't seen Jack but suggested Theo come over when he felt like it. He couldn't stop himself and looked through the things in the box again and then flicked casually through the diary again as well, in quiet reflection.

A short ride later, he walked into the Wayward Travellers' Haven. Jack had just finished talking to a young couple so Theo came in and sat down.

Jack offered a cigarette. 'Seems as if she is almost there. I spoke to Gloria earlier and the passport should be ready today.'

'She mentioned something about being sponsored,' said Theo.

'Yeah, that's pretty straightforward. They have a list of do-gooder families who offer to sponsor asylum seekers, even though Biru, strictly speaking, is not. Well not politically anyway. WW have links in many countries.'

'Wouldn't she have to be sponsored by a Muslim family?'

'No, not necessarily, they're usually Christians, in Australia anyway, other countries I guess it varies. It's a league of generally good people who believe in helping those in need, I suppose. The family is responsible for her until she attains citizenship – in Australia they usually have a ceremony once a year. They usually try to organise a job, find somewhere for them to live, help them learn English, maybe put them in touch with their own community etcetera. We have asked for a family in Adelaide.'

'Great. How long will it take for her papers to be ready?'

'A day or two. They will book her on a flight when she is ready, should be able to get you both on the same plane. Who are you flying with, Aeroflot?'

Theo took a moment to get it then they both laughed. 'Qantas, mate,' he said.

Jack said, 'You won't be able to see her in Kuala Lumpur because the refuge is crawling with security. You will have to meet in the airport. They will take her, under guard and probably in disguise, to the airport, and then through customs and immigration and all that. You will meet her at duty free or the boarding gate. If all goes well …'

Theo looked at him, eyebrows raised.

He continued, 'What I mean is, it will all go well. You should give me the details of your ticket so if we can, or Gloria can, we can get you both on the same flight. Once again, nothing is guaranteed, you may not even be sitting together but could possibly be on the same flight.'

Brian came in with a tray of tea and biscuits and they sat around, three friends talking easily. Theo told them he wanted to go back to Kuala Lumpur to say goodbye to Yuman and Razak. He would wait there until Biru had her papers approved and organised with the authorities. Jack offered to drive Theo to Kuala Lumpur because he had some business to attend to.

∞

Theo spent his last day soaking up the sights of Penang in the discomfort of Tung's rickshaw. He revisited some of the eating places and had kopi or beer, and also managed to scribble some more details in his exercise book. Some of the time he spent looking out onto the blue-green sea, or out into the street at the people and their lives.

He called into St John's and had a cup of tea with Brian. Theo expected some words of wisdom from him and was not disappointed.

'Theo, you have made up your mind so stick to your guns and see it out; you will be a better person for the experience. The journey may be rocky for a bit but life is like that. Things will turn out well for you, I'm sure. Please do call and see me again one day or I may have to come to Australia.'

They hugged and Theo was amazed he had made such strong friendships and emotional ties in the short time he had been in Malaysia. He felt he had known Brian his whole life.

Big Buddha Mama made some wisecracks about his personal phone line and his personal office table nearby. Also she said she looked forward to him leaving so it would stop her from going broke from paying the phone charges.

He rang Biru mid-afternoon and she was obviously hovering by the phone. Everything was in order, passport in hand, but she still had to wait for the sponsorship papers. When she indicated someone was waiting for the phone, Theo quickly said, 'I love you.' He beat her to it and felt like an idiot but he was very happy at the same time.

He spent the evening with Van and Jack at their place. Once again Theo was surprised by the beautiful food presented, seemingly as a normal occurrence. He told them he didn't know how he would be able to exist on Australian food when he returned. At the end of the night, Theo said goodbye to Van with promises of seeing her and Harvey again one way or the other and he hoped it wouldn't be long.

'Maybe for visit to Australia,' she said. 'Harvey would love to go.'

Jack said there was always a chance and if not, Theo was always welcome to come and stay because they would be moving to a bigger house. On the way back to the Hotel Happiness Theo felt happy and content but a sudden thought surfaced. Biru could never come back here if Mahmoud was alive or her family knew she was here. He wondered if it would make any difference if they were married. She would be an Australian citizen even if she didn't marry him. Would her family still want to come after her? He was worldly enough to understand there was always a slight undercurrent of negativity to balance every perfect situation and only time would clarify things.

In the morning Theo had breakfast and settled the bill with Mama. She hadn't charged for phone usage at all, just the cost of calls detailed on a printout.

She hugged him tightly and kissed both cheeks. 'You still be careful with girl, okay?' She ruffled his hair and added, 'Maybe you tell all your frens to come to Penang and come to stay at Hotel Happiness, best place, yaah!'

He said his goodbyes to other members of the staff and it was an emotional parting. He walked away from the hotel feeling sad but happy at the same time. Tung wasn't around; he had dealt with that the previous night. The young Chinese was philosophical about the fact Theo would return. They both laughed, Theo thinking it was a good bet he was right. The young man was grateful for a large wad of ringgits; a bag of medications not needed any more that Theo knew Tung could sell, a Swiss Army knife and two packets of cigarettes.

It was before eight and Jack wasn't there. Theo had time to reflect on the good people he had met and the relationships he had formed, whether he would see them again or not. He thought about how he had made friends and how others seemed to genuinely care for him.

Some of the people in the street who had seen him before, noting he had his backpack, smiled and nodded at him. A car horn jolted him out of dreamland.

Back to Kuala Lumpur

Chapter Eighty-One

The trip through the oil palm groves speckled with rice paddies, small villages and large towns to Kuala Lumpur took less time in a car than the bus. Jack and Theo sat in the back and Jack explained that he had spoken to Gloria and things looked good, hoping for the paperwork to be clear by the following afternoon. Patches of silence were punctuated by Jack's stories of his time in the army whilst training at Puckapunyal as well as some warm, funny moments about the pranks he and Vince got up to.

Jack was staying with a business friend so he dropped Theo off around the corner from the Hot Spot. He gave Theo his warehouse phone number and they promised to keep in touch in relation to Biru's situation. On parting, Jack said he would try to catch up with Theo for a meal later that evening and if not, the next morning for breakfast. Theo recommended the Splendid Coffee House.

Theo stood there with his backpack and watched the car drive off. Immediately he was surrounded by touts trying to sell him accommodation and other things. He smiled, remembering Dempster's advice, and said, 'I know where I'm going, I've been here before, okay friends?'

They scattered and headed towards a bus just arriving. He smiled and walked up the steps of the Hot Spot Hotel.

'Do you have any rooms?' enquired Theo in an exaggerated fashion.

Yuman looked up from writing in a register. 'Aha, Mr Theo, you surprised me. 'What ..?' The young man with the chipped front tooth skirted around the counter and shook Theo's hand warmly. 'I'm so happy to see you … you want room?'

'Yes, just the one.'

Yuman was very excited to have Theo back and they talked together like old friends over a cup of kopi. Theo explained that he had to go back to Australia to start his new job and he was sorry he couldn't spend more time in Malaysia. Yuman told him Biru was in a women's shelter, in Penang he thought. Theo felt guilty he wasn't as honest as he could have been with his friend but he said that he had met her and she was alright, awaiting her passport.

Yuman said, 'Are you going to meet her again?'

That put him right on the spot. 'Umm, yes, I hope to.' He didn't elaborate.

Yuman smiled and nodded, this time not tapping his nose in that understanding gesture. Theo was certain Yuman knew more than he was letting on. Theo also had the feeling Yuman felt the same about him.

The afternoon was hot but Theo wandered through the streets to the Hotel New Islamic. Even though he didn't know Razak very well, he wanted to thank him and say goodbye. He walked up the familiar steps and at the desk Razak was hanging up the phone.

'Aha, Mr Perry, you back in town?'

They talked for a while and Theo thanked him for storing his possessions and also helping organise the lawyer to get him out of jail. Razak apologised about the drugs episode and said he was sure Mahmoud planted them. Theo was about to expand on the topic of Mahmoud but quickly decided to leave the matter alone.

He simply said, 'It was not your fault, mate, don't give it another thought. Everything turned out okay in the end.'

Razak nodded and then explained he hadn't heard from Biru for a while but he knew she was safe. Theo was certain that Razak, like Yuman, knew more about Biru than he was letting on but there was no point in saying too much about it.

Theo said, 'Thank you for looking out for Biru, too. I have seen her and she *is* safe.'

The other man's eyebrows went up. He slowly said, 'I see,' and smiled with Theo. He added, 'You must come again, Mr Perry, maybe next time your stay be much better.'

He told Razak his stay turned out very well and he had a good time in Penang. They shook hands and parted.

Theo walked to the restaurant street and had a beer whilst watching the parade of life in the mall. The touts, drug peddlers and opportunists mingled amongst the backpackers and tourists, and he was once again reminded of Roland Michael Hayley. He made some more entries in his *Theo's Adventures* exercise book, happy he had a direction with the articles he was going to write for the newspaper. Thunder in the distance hastened his decision to return to the hotel and have a shower. Not long after, he stood in the shower as the rain came down. After dressing in the cleanest shorts he could find he pulled out *Beyond Pardon* and went straight to the last interview.

Last interview - 17ᵗʰ December, 1987.

The day before Roland Michael Hayley was hanged in Pudu Prison, Kuala Lumpur, Malaysia.

Hayley was led in by two guards on this occasion - our final meeting. I asked one of them, why two? All I received was a shrug. Hayley was un-cuffed. He looked pale and drawn and I'm sure he hadn't slept in days. His stoop was more pronounced and he had the look of a man devoid of hope. His skin reflected a yellow pallor.

Hayley: They think I'm going to make a run for it. (He laughed which brought on his characteristic smoker's cough.)

(The guards helped themselves to the cigarettes I had placed on the table. I told them to take the packet because I knew they would leave the room and smoke with their colleagues. After they departed I handed Hayley his plastic bag of Milo, biscuits and cigarettes.)

H: Go on, Spud, it's okay, you can say it. How am I feeling today? (He smiled and lit up.)

Morgan: Yeah, sure. Alright, how are you feeling today?

H: How would anyone feel the day before they were to die?

(Note: The interview progressed from here more like a chat between friends, except it felt like there was unseen pressure pulling the ceiling down on our heads. I decided not to document most of this part of the interview because we covered mundane matters and things we had talked about before. He mentioned he'd had the last meeting with his father only hours earlier and his family was holding up as well as could be expected. He seemed very upset at this point and openly sobbed which indicated that his family and he were not coping. When I asked if he wanted me to leave he declined, saying he really wanted a friend with him at that moment, which made me feel honoured but sad. Then his speech became slightly jumbled and his thoughts erratic. He rambled on and seemed confused for the next five minutes or so; I tried to bring him back by directly questioning him.

Morgan: How is your current health? You look really unwell today.

H: Man, I have bad hepatitis, but it probably doesn't matter. Hanging me tomorrow will only allow me to cheat God because for the last few weeks I have been a bit crook. I was allowed to see the doctor, hoping I might get a more comfortable place to stay in the infirmary but the doctor said I wasn't sick enough to warrant that. They don't bother blood testing you for these diseases. Hey, it costs money, right? I reckon I'm going to die soon anyway. Could get anything in here, eh, sharing needles, all that, you know. I wish I could score enough to end it all, eh. No way would that be allowed to happen - the guards would get hung alongside me because the warden and the government want me to be alive and kicking when I die, as a statement, you know, to the world.

(His hands shook slightly during this conversation and there was an ever-present movement of his head from side to side which I put down to his increasing anxiety.)

Theo read on and noted a couple of other points of interest:

H: Yeah, mate I'm not sure if it's because I'm going to be hung tomorrow or if I am going to die of one of the blood diseases that I most certainly have but I am really, fair dinkum scared about dying. I feel like I'm in a vacuum, you know. My head buzzes, my guts are churning … I am not ready to die. I'm in isolation here which makes it …

(At this point he became incoherent and some things he said did not make sense. After a cup of water he seemed to stabilise and I was able to bring him back to the interview.)

M: Roland, what do you feel now about religion? Have you found any comfort in any religious path?

H: Yeah, beat this. The Catholic priest, he's the guy who talks to westerners who need counselling or just want to chat – a lot of blokes get the religion in here, can't help it – anyway Father Milton they call him, he came to me years ago when I first got here and I told him to fuck off, wasn't going to have anything to do with God, was I? But just last week he comes to see me again and I actually don't mind talking to him. We got talking and I knelt down and we prayed. It has helped me, not sure about whether I'm going to be let into the Kingdom of Heaven but he seems to think I will if I receive God into my heart or some such bullshit. So, beat that mate, me finding

God, well, not really, but maybe finding a little solace in a bit of God.

M: Will you be having any more visits before … tomorrow? (I was hoping he would say something more about his parents or family.)

H: Yeah, my lawyer, Shan Manesh is coming later on today, that's all, not up to seeing any more people, know they mean well …

At this point Roland Hayley said a few unconnected sentences and then hung his head and didn't say any more for a minute or two. Then he looked at me and said:

H: That's about it, mate. Thanks for coming to see me.

(He rapped the table a couple of times and the two guards came in. One of them told me Hayley was now to be taken away to his new isolation cell where he had to be examined by a doctor. We both stood. It was one of the few times in my life where I was completely lost for words. I think back to that moment and I just couldn't find anything to say. He made eye contact with me and gently pushed the guard's arm away so he could extend his right hand. They understood and Roland Michael Hayley and I shook hands for the last time. He tried a weak smile.)

Hayley: Well Spud, until next time, eh?

(I smiled back and it took until he was almost out of the room before I could speak.)

M: Farewell, my friend.

(The rear guard closed the door behind them and there was a loud clunk of the outer metal barred door. The clunk jolted me into realising the finality of my relationship with another human being.)

I had to sit down again and I remained staring

at the closed door for some time. It was one of the saddest days of my life …

During the time I knew him, I came to respect Michael Hayley as a human being. It may sound strange as he was indeed a drug trafficker and he did break the law, AND he openly admitted that. The question, 'Why break the law?' troubled me. I keep asking myself and the reply is a recurring, 'Don't we all'? From slipping a pen from work into our pocket, to speeding, to stretching the truth to the taxman, and more. We all do it. He just got caught, that is all. And it is up to us to decipher whether the law is just or not. I salute him for having the courage to face this terrible end to his life with such dignity. The humbling thought that became obvious to me throughout was that a crime is only a crime if a law deems it so.

S. Morgan.

∞

The evening call to prayer woke Theo from a contented sleep. He had dozed off with *Beyond Pardon* lying across his chest. He went to the window and looked out into the rapidly decreasing tropical light. He was amazed how quickly day became night, lacking the extended twilight of Adelaide.

Theo realised that if he used the phone in the Hot Spot Yuman would know details of the number by call back so he wandered out into the street in the direction of the restaurants and stopped at a bank of payphones. He rang Biru's number. She was not available, nor was Gloria. There was no new information and he was told to ring back later.

Chapter Eighty-Two

'Hey, Tuan, Mr White Boss, selamat tengah hari, apa khabar? I have something for you!'

Theo had hoped to see her before he left but at that moment his head was elsewhere. 'Aaaah! Old Woman from Borneo.'

'You have cigarette for me?'

'Maybe, do you have a book for me?' He opened his packet, she took three. He showed mock surprise. 'Smoking will stunt your growth, Old Woman.' He could feel the motherly warmth and the smell of jasmine and cloves.

She placed two cigarettes in her small wooden box and pointed to the other cigarette, already red from betel nut, in her mouth. He lit her up and she exhaled a cloud up in the air. 'I have book for you to read on plane. You ready to leave Malaysia; I think I see very soon.'

He loosely wondered how she knew. Then he smiled; of course, she did not need to be a clairvoyant to know he had to leave soon, all tourists do. He laughed, 'Yes.'

'Here is book ready-made to give greater knowledge.' She wound her scarf around her neck covering the turkey wrinkles. He could see the tribal tattoo on the back of her hand.

Theo had heard of it. *One Crowded Hour* about journalist Neil Davis, written by Tim Bowden. How did she know Sean Spud Morgan had teamed up with Neil Davis as a young foreign correspondent years ago? Easy, she sold him *Beyond Pardon* didn't she? 'How much?'

Theo squatted down alongside her. She unwound her scarf slightly which revealed her very dark wrinkled neck. Again, Theo could again see clearly the tattoo on the back of her sun-hardened hand. Two silver rings glinted.

'Special going away price, for you only once in lifetime chance. Eighty?'

'Hey, that's too much. Twenty.'

She wagged a finger at him. 'You make fun of old woman, take advantage, see back page still in situation. Fifty.'

'Fifty is too much. Here let me look.' He looked at the back page and it was there. The book appeared new also. He turned it over. The RRP had been scratched off. 'How much is the retail price?'

'One hundred. Okay, going away present, forty.' She looked defiantly at him.

His legs were aching from squatting. 'Thirty.'

'Oh mah Gard, robbing old woman. Thirty five, last price okay, done.' She started to wrap it up.

'No. Thirty.' He made her wait. 'Oh, all right, Thirty five.' They both laughed. He knew he was getting done.

'You very shrewd, I learn plenty plenty from you. I may even survive in jungle now,' she laughed in her half cackle.

She wrapped it up in newspaper. He gave her a fifty ringgit note. 'Gift for you, Old Woman,' he added, 'from Borneo. No change.'

She smiled, displaying the betel-nut red teeth. 'You good, young Tuan, I now give you free future telling. You have woman who care for you.'

Theo thought it was a soft prediction. There were many women in his life who cared for him. Biru, his mother, Big Buddha Mama, Franka, Van or ... even her, the Old Woman from Borneo.

She continued, 'Most important to read detail in first book, you have missed something.'

Another ambiguous statement. 'What detail?'

'Information in book to link up with what someone say.'

He stood. 'I must go to ...'

'You meet friend ...'

Theo figured she could not lose with a prediction like that.

She continued, 'Also you must ask him important question, okay?'

'Thank you, Old Woman from Borneo, I,' Theo hesitated, he wanted to say something more. 'I ... I'll miss you.'

She looked at him for a long second and then her face lit up with a smile. 'I will miss you too but I know you will come again and we will talk. You will be wiser then.' She held her hand up like a stop sign and looked up into the night sky. Her demeanour changed, a dark look took over her face. 'One more thing, beware, someone is keeping eye on you. I think they up to no good, can't quite get full picture. Be observant.' She brightened and looked at him again. 'Cigarette for old woman?'

Theo smiled and nodded politely. He pulled out his cigarettes, handed her the packet and she held his hand. He could feel the rings. She hung on longer than was necessary or maybe he did. 'Go on your way, young wise Tuan, never look back.'

He stood and walked away. When he arrived at the corner he turned and looked around. She was gone. He said softly, 'She told you not to look back, Theo.'

Action

Chapter Eighty-Three

Theo walked on towards the Splendid Coffee House. About half a block away he felt the presence of someone alongside. By the time he reacted, each arm had been gripped, vice-like, wrist and elbow, and he was marched stiff-armed around the corner into a dingy lane behind the shopfronts.

His instant reaction was to struggle but the grips were tight. He was slammed against the wall.

'Aha, whitey boy Tuan, eh? We meet again.' Mahmoud gave an oily smile.

'What the ..?' barked Theo, trying to gain some dignity.

'You will be quiet.' Mahmoud grabbed Theo by the throat with a strong hand. 'Now whitey boy, young white boss, young Tuan, you tell me where Biru is, eh?'

Theo could hardly breathe let alone talk. His adrenalin kicked in and all he could think about was getting the first one in. The added fear gave him the primal strength to twist his body in one mighty effort which enabled him to knee Mahmoud, who was quick, in the upper thigh. Mahmoud gasped in pain. Theo knew how much a corked thigh hurt.

The two henchmen slackened their grip for that second and it allowed Theo to lash out with his boot because Mahmoud had stepped back a fraction.

'Whitey boy,' he hissed, 'you pay for that.'

The slightest of nods gave the henchmen approval to punch Theo below the ribs, a solid punch each side at the same second. Stereo. Theo gulped and struggled to breathe and his body slowly sank a fraction. He was jerked up tightly against the wall again.

'Now whitey boy, you think you are smart ass, big shot Tuan, eh? Where is Biru?'

'How the hell should I bloody well know?' Theo did his best to glare but fear of the unknown gripped him as hard as the intruders. He wanted to say, 'I owe you for planting dope in my room, you arsehole,' but he was in no position to do that.

Mahmoud swung his boot out. Theo managed to move slightly to the side and the kick grazed his calf. Theo registered the pain but tried to draw an analogy with being hit in the pack, on the football field.

'You better tell me young Tuan, where is she?' Mahmoud pulled out a flick knife. *Click!*

Different rules now! Theo moved his head a fraction to see people walking past at the end of the lane only metres away. 'Listen, mate I don't know where she is,' he blurted, 'alright? How should I, eh? I've been in Penang for the last few weeks. Mate, there's no need to be doing this.' Sweat poured into his eyes. Theo knew his situation was serious, pinned to the wall, no room to move, trapped.

Mahmoud continued to stare. The sound of a video clip from one of the nearby backpacker places emitting gunfire and explosions, drifted across the laneway. Sounded like Rambo.

Theo tried to focus on stabilising his heart rate and slowing down his breathing but he was shaking inside. He was astute enough to ease back on the aggression; there was no point in getting stabbed. 'Mate, let's talk about this, I … I don't know where she is; I mean last time I saw her was before I went to jail.' He kept his stare on Mahmoud but tried not to make it too intense. He attempted to shrug, which was difficult, to back up his denial but his eyebrows indicated his feelings.

Mahmoud still stared at him and Theo sensed some doubt creeping in. It seemed as if the man was wondering what to do next. Theo moved slightly forward and to the side to protect himself from a kick. The knife held vigil against his throat, dangerous and imposing but as light as a feather.

Mahmoud gave his oily smile again. 'Why should I believe big-shot whitey boy like you? Eh?' He moved the knife off Theo's throat for a few seconds, glanced at each of his henchmen momentarily, and then focused on Theo again. He glared and put the point of the blade back on Theo's neck; just enough to prick but not draw blood. It caused Theo to turn his head, a natural reaction for someone in his predicament.

Then Theo saw him.

Chapter Eighty-Four

An innocent tourist with a map, asking directions. 'Hey, 'scuse me fellers, any of you guys know where the …' Jack covered the few feet in a second and punched Mahmoud in the side of the head. The knife clattered to the ground from a karate chop at the same time and then Jack turned and grabbed the closest henchman.

Theo's trembling body was like a spring and he elbowed the man on his right as hard as he could in the stomach. The man crumpled to the ground, too busy gasping to make any other sounds.

In such a fractured second, Jack had smashed the other man's head into the wall. The sound made Theo jump as he turned to see the man hit the ground with a thud. Blood poured out of his ears. For a second Theo thought he was dead but a groan emanated from him. Theo stood in shock.

Then Jack's voice, directed at Mahmoud, centred him. 'Right smart arse, think you're fucking brave with a knife, eh? And three onto one. You're a fucking coward, mate.' Jack had Mahmoud by the collar, pinned against the wall.

Mahmoud was still groggy as Jack looked towards the man Theo had winded, who was starting to get up. Jack kicked him in the head and he fell back unconscious. 'There dickhead, tell that to your mates, eh?'

Mahmoud shook his head and glanced at his offsiders lying unconscious on the ground, one in a widening pool of blood around his head, the other motionless. His eyes widened, at last realising the predicament he was in.

Theo stood gawking, shocked at the level of violence perpetrated in the last five seconds.

Jack slapped Mahmoud across the face. 'Now mister big brave man, you want to go one on one with me, eh?' Jack slapped him again, almost a punch, harder. Even though Jack was about Mahmoud's height, he was thicker in the upper body.

Mahmoud moved his head and his eyes boggled as he tried to focus and then there was fright. He was together enough to see what would happen next.

Theo could see Jack's right fist bunch up, he could feel the tension. He knew too what Jack was going to do. He tried to yell but couldn't. He reached out and was able to grab Jack's arm. It felt like a piece of railway line.

Theo forced a deep breath and it took every ounce of control to find words. 'Leave him be, Jack … please.'

Jack turned and looked at Theo, mild surprise on his face but madness in his eyes. He froze for a moment, then let go of Mahmoud's collar and took a step back but he continued to stare at the man, breathing heavily.

Theo moved and stood in front of Mahmoud. He was shaking as much as Mahmoud because he knew Jack would have probably killed him. 'You are an arsehole for planting that dope in my room. I went to jail for that, you prick. That's bad enough but slapping Biru around is unforgivable.'

Theo looked him in the eyes for what seemed like a full minute. Mahmoud may have thought he had been spared. Theo punched him as hard as he could in the stomach. The blow had all the force of pent-up fear, anger and frustration that had been eating away at him ever since he had been confronted by Mahmoud. Mahmoud slumped to the ground.

The action had Theo breathing hard. When he regained a level of control again he said, 'Listen here, you bastard, Biru is none of your business any more. Get it? If I hear even the mention of your name or your family's ever again I will come after you, alright?'

Jack picked up the knife, looked around, stabbed it into a crack in the wall and snapped it. He wiped the handle on Mahmoud's shirt and whispered as he dropped it, 'Cheap knife. Let's piss off, this way.' He pointed in the direction of the far end of the lane. 'No need to advertise this little scuffle, eh mate … just in case.' He tapped Theo on the shoulder and they walked briskly away.

It was only when they alighted from the lane that Theo registered what Jack had said. *Just in case. In case what – that one of them was dead? Christ Almighty!* He also became aware of Jack's slight limp. He recalled he had not noticed Jack's disability throughout the whole episode. The speed at which his father's friend had moved, and the professional execution of the job in hand, left Theo free-falling inside.

'Er … thanks, Jack … mate … I don't know what to say,' he panted, 'you saved my arse good and proper. Never had a knife thrust in my face before.'

'I guess there is a first time for everything, eh mate. Let's have a beer but away from here, we'll get a taxi.' He said it is if they had been to the football and it was time to celebrate.

Theo's insides were eggshell fragile, his heart rate was still nowhere near normal. The previous few minutes had shaken him. He couldn't possibly eat but some alcohol was exactly what he needed.

As they jumped into a taxi, Theo recalled the look on Jack's face back there. It was almost as if he enjoyed the violence. He felt a shiver down his backbone, goose bumps joining up. The weather was far from cold. It weighed on Theo's mind, Jack being calm enough to wipe the handle of the knife. *Fuck.*

Chapter Eighty-Five

Twenty minutes later when they arrived at a restoran kedai that Jack knew of, Jack ordered the beer and Theo went to the toilets. He threw up and then splashed water over his face. He just remembered in time not to drink the water. The image looking back at him from the mirror showed no damage to his face other than a tiny red dot on his throat. The damage was inside, he knew that. He had just played with the big boys, for higher stakes, bigger than grand final stuff. Theo kept telling himself he was alive and well and there was no need to worry about Mahmoud anymore. He smiled weakly about telling Mahmoud he would come after him if he ever heard of him again. Theo thought about the pub fights but the difference on this night was that the others were playing for keeps and perhaps more so, Jack. Theo would never know if Mahmoud would have killed him. He was jolted out of his reverie by the click and whoosh of the door opening and two men walking in.

Back inside, Jack and Theo had a few beers and after a while, Theo decided he was hungry. Jack was perceptive enough to see Theo was still lost in thought so he brought on a number of combat stories, somewhat toned down, Theo thought. Jack pointed out that in situations like this you had to act instinctively, quickly and decisively, otherwise you could easily be dead. 'I know it's easy to say but you have to kick tonight loose, put it down to experience.'

They drank on for another few hours.

When he arrived back at the Hot Spot he tried Biru again. His words were slurred and his head was full of things he wasn't sure he understood. *How could things escalate to what happened tonight?* When he was told nothing had transpired in relation to Biru's situation he felt instant alarm but the woman told him Biru was fine and he should ring in the morning because there was a line-up for the phone for other more important matters. Somehow he was pleased he didn't have to talk to someone he cared about because he was not on top of things.

Theo slept very well because he was drunk and emotionally exhausted. The call to prayer in the early hours roused him and it took only a few minutes for the events of the previous night to cram his head. The first thing that came to mind was the question: was someone dead? Jack had advised him last night to deny anything in the event of police enquiries. If there were any enquiries. Jack had carefully reviewed the events. The only person who could actually confirm Theo was there would be the Old Woman from Borneo. No problem there. Jack said he couldn't recall speaking to anyone and was confident no-one could place him there. So it would be his and Jack's word against anyone else's. No-one could place them in that laneway. Theo convinced himself there was no case to answer.

Jack had made the point that it was usually locals beating up tourists, not the other way round and police would almost definitely put last night's confrontation down as some local criminals feuding. And after all it was Mahmoud who the authorities were after anyway. 'Relax, Theo, relax.' Theo realised Jack didn't say anything about the possibility of someone being killed.

Theo went out to reception and asked Yuman a pointless question about paying his bill and the use of the phone in an hour's time. He figured Yuman would say something if there had been police around the area. It made him feel easier; at least more confident no-one had died.

Chapter Eighty-Six

Theo wondered what he was going to say to Biru about Mahmoud as he nervously dialled the number. His head hurt from alcohol and too much information. After a moment she came on the line.

'Hello Theo, I have so missed you, I am excited we can go away together today ...'

Her sweet voice seemed to dissolve all the negative things in his head. 'Hang on, hang on,' he laughed, instantly feeling better. 'I have missed you too. You say we can go away together today?'

'Yes Theo, it is so exciting, Gloria say sponsor papers all in order, I have new family in Adelaide ...'

'That's great, Biru, but you are saying we can go today, doesn't that seem a bit ... I mean I have to confirm my flight ...'

'No, that is all arranged, Gloria fix it all but big disappointment.'

Theo's heart jumped. 'What?'

'We not sit together, different seat numbers, but if I know you there on same plane we hold hands in gallery, okay.'

Theo took down the details of the flight and after romantic banter he reluctantly put down the phone. He willed himself not to think about what could go wrong. Also he did not get around to mentioning Mahmoud, not that he knew what he would have said anyway.

He rang Jack and was not surprised to find he had already spoken to Gloria and was probably instrumental in organising everything anyway. He asked if there had been any activity in the area that morning but it was suggested Theo lay low in case Mahmoud was around looking for revenge. Jack seemed to think that unlikely.

Jack said in closing, 'I'll pick you up at about five and drive you to the airport, save you going by bus, alright?'

Theo took Jack's advice and only went two doors down to the Indian restoran. The samosas didn't hit the spot as a breakfast staple but maybe it was because he was excited and his stomach was flittering and eating was furthest from his mind. At least the coffee was okay. He realised he had become used to Kopi and wondered how the coffee would taste at home.

He killed most of the morning looking out at the street scene, tourists of all kinds, young people, middle-aged people and the local Malaysians, all buzzing around like an afternoon at the football, trying to make a day of it or make a living. He constantly thought of Biru and how wonderful it would be to touch her face, her hair … His gaze was often attracted to the beautiful young women wandering in the street but he realised he did not have any interest in them.

He returned to his room and began the task of organising himself for the trip. He slowly went through his father's belongings again, almost playing with them, looking for some order of things. The old receipts stapled together? He couldn't decipher much, a room he rented in Butterworth, some clothes and car hire? The other scraps of paper didn't seem to say anything or mean much. Some pieces of paper flittered out of Jim Thompson's book, *The Kill-Off*, when he fanned it. A scribbled note caught his eye. He looked up suddenly finally feeling some attachment to his father and the whole tragic story of his life.

Theo sat in that pose for a couple of minutes and then snapped up the book *Beyond Pardon*. At the same time the Old Woman's words buzzed around his head, '*Most important to read detail in first book, you have missed something.*' He quickly turned pages, back to front and front to back. *Where did you see it?* Jack had said something when he was drunk. *What was it?* He shook his head in frustration; it had to be there somewhere. *Aha!*

After about half an hour of reading and re-reading certain passages he was sure. He wiped his forehead with the towel. 'I'll be stuffed,' he said and looked up at the wobbling fan.

He tipped everything out of his rucksack and repacked as neatly as he could, wrapping the plastic urn with his father's ashes in clothing. The dirty washing was rammed in the separate bottom section. He wondered whether he would still wash his clothes in the shower when he arrived home. Then he realised he might not be even living at home and it made him once again wonder what he was going to do.

Packing done, he laid out what he was going to need on the plane: *Beyond Pardon, One Crowded Hour, Theo's Adventures* and one of his father's books, *History of Indonesia*. He had finished *Slowly Down The Ganges* so he found a spot for it in his rucksack.

He realised what a stroke of luck it was that Biru had a sponsor family, and was able to find someone in Adelaide. Jack had told him there was a sizeable Lebanese population there and they were offering sponsorships. Surprisingly, they were mostly Christians not Muslims, but as Jack had pointed out, they were willing to help anyone in strife. Also Adelaide was popular because many Vietnamese boat people had arrived, most looking for asylum after the war.

Biru having somewhere to stay probably let Theo off the hook with telling his mother when he arrived at the airport, which made him realise she would not be at the airport as it had been too late to contact her. He had not really made an effort to contact her because of complexities of having to deal with Biru and what he was going to say to his mother. He felt guilty so he went out to reception and tried her number but she did not answer. He paid his bill to be sure there were no last minute things to be done when Jack arrived.

Back in his room, the sound of thunder rumbled in the distance; it felt almost as if it was indented in his life now. He knew he would miss it and the call to prayer as well. Lightning flashed intermittently, not necessarily coordinating with the thunder, but when it did the thwat and flash often took him unawares and startled him. He stood at the window, lit a cigarette and glanced out. He wondered if he would have trouble giving up tobacco but he quickly concluded it should be easy because they were only clove cigarettes. He wondered for a moment if they were available in Australia.

The rain started, big blobs at first and then steadier; in minutes it was heavy, drowning out the thunder and flooding the drains and roads. The grey blanket of hammering rain continued for half an hour and then it eased and became progressively lighter to allow the sun to peak through. Then it stopped. Theo breathed in the freshness of the air. Even with the pollution of the huge city of Kuala Lumpur, the rain somehow made the air fresh and sweet if only for a short time. The bark of a motorbike, the ding of a bell, the beep of a horn, the yell of a vendor seemed to drift through the vacuum. Theo realised he would miss this place. He looked at his watch and smiled, nearly five o'clock. Again the storm had arrived on time.

He looked around the room for the last time and walked out. At the desk he asked to use the phone. His mother answered this time. His heart kept jumping the whole time, willing him to tell her everything. He told her his flight details.

'It's been really good with Jack, we get on well, he's taking me to the airport. You know, Mum, I'm going to miss him, he's a really great bloke … and … anyway, I have to go.'

Theo was glad that was over. He walked out to reception.

'This should cover the call,' he said, handing Yuman a fistful of ringgits.

'But Mr Theo, there is too much.'

'Well mate, you will have to stick the rest in your pocket then, won't you? Yuman, thanks for all you have done for me.'

Yuman put out his hand. Theo ignored it and gave him a man-hug. 'Handshake not good enough for friends,' he said, shouldered his pack and went down the stairs for the last time.

He walked to the corner. His heart felt warm with excitement, balanced with apprehension. It was two minutes to five.

A skinny dog looked up at him wagging its tail. 'I might even miss you and your mates, too,' said Theo but was not game enough to pat him.

Chapter Eighty-Seven

Jack was full of stories but Theo didn't hear much. He constantly looked out the window, observing landmarks that had become so familiar to him over the last month. They went through Chinatown, chockers with small laneways and people, onto the bigger roads, and then onto the mighty main thoroughfare of Kuala Lumpur, Jalan Pudu. They stopped at lights almost in front of the bustling Puduraya Bus Station and Theo instantly thought of his visits there and also the times Roland Michael Hayley had spent hustling backpackers. As they passed Pudu Prison, in his mind, he imagined he saw Hayley standing at the edge of one of the guard towers, arms outstretched and flanked by a contingent of wise monkeys, looking out over the city.

Jack said, 'Pretty grim place, eh?'

Theo knew he said something. 'Sorry, what?'

Jack repeated what he had said and went on to say that many westerners had spent time in there. Theo didn't really pay attention to the rest of Jack's information as to where the prisoners had been transferred to when the jail was closed. He nodded and looked out again.

Jack continued to chat about Harvey, Van, the Saigon bar and other things. Theo politely smiled or gave acknowledgement to the one-way conversation. His mind was on the friends he was leaving, the country he felt some attraction to, Biru and his mother. There was another matter too.

They slowly made their way towards the airport, through the crowded roadways and endless traffic lights. Theo was thankful the car had airconditioning as the day was still hot and humid and the fumes from vehicles and bitumen choked the city. They passed tall, listless palm trees, jacarandas and other tropical varieties.

Theo glanced over at Jack, who was looking out his window and talking to the driver. His thoughts went back to earlier in the morning and the things scrolling through his head as he had rifled through his father's belongings again. Eventually he had found what he was looking for.

Theo's heart beat harder as they drove in the direction of the airport. *How are you going to handle this, Theo? You are going to have to bring up the subject soon.*

Confession

Chapter Eighty-Eight

He was saved, to a degree anyway. Even though he was keen to see Biru at the airport, he needed a few minutes with Jack.

'We have plenty of time before take-off, maybe we should have a coffee and a few minutes together before you go, mate. I'm going to miss not having you around.'

Jack tapped the driver on the shoulder and rattled some Mandarin. They pulled into a Kedai and picked out a quiet table in the shade.

'There's something …' Theo fidgeted.

'Sure, mate, fire away,' replied Jack, Jack-the-lad, prankster, smiling.

'Um … I'm going to miss this place and … the people and friends …'

It was clear Jack could tell Theo was slightly unhinged and uncomfortable.

'Come on, mate, what's up?'

He took a deep breath. 'Roland Hayley was Dad's drug mule, wasn't he?' A statement as much as a question.

'What?'

'Hayley was his drug courier, wasn't he?'

It seemed as if Jack wasn't going to respond for a moment. His eyes shifted slightly so he wasn't directly looking into Theo's. Then he looked back.

Theo was not sure what to say next. He had known it was not going to be easy. He awkwardly lit a cigarette and kept eye contact.

Jack refocused. The boyish, rascally looks hardened. 'How did you find out?'

Theo knew he had to be firm. '… Er, does it matter?'

Jack seemed to relax. He breathed out. 'No, I guess not.' There was a heavy silence for a moment and then he continued. 'Yes, Hayley was our mule, mine too. It was a bastard he got nabbed but …'

'What happened?'

'I guess you have a right to know. Hayley worked for us for a time bringing in heroin from other places; we fronted the money but he didn't know it was us. We knew him but he didn't know us if you get my meaning. We only dealt with an agent, a middle man or two so that if anyone was caught they wouldn't be able to blab. I mean the cops would beat it out of a suspect, but if the bloke genuinely didn't know then he couldn't blab …'

'You said you didn't use heroin after, you know …'

'Yep and that's true, I didn't but, well your old man did and we had to make a living.' His demeanour hardened. 'Mate, in Nam we killed people, burnt villages, destroyed families, property, farmland, all of that stuff, all under the name of something. I feel deep guilt about all that shit, deep guilt, but it was the way it was, a point in time …'

'Jack …' Theo could feel the piano-string tension emanating from his friend, the same as the previous night when Jack had almost killed someone.

'But when I, we, came to Asia after returning to the shitty welcome we received in Australia, we were still young and bitter and all that. I don't have any guilt about selling smack, or dope or illegal alcohol for that matter, but put simply, yes, I have used it and that was a choice I made. I also made the choice to stop using it too. People make their own decisions about it. If they want to use, well they do.' Jack had a do-not-judge-me look on his face. 'Hayley became greedy and was caught, pure and simple, crappy as it is but that's the truth.'

Theo sat there and drank his coffee with difficulty. Even though he had thought about this and he was sure it was true, he was still shocked at the admission; his father and Jack were involved with a man who was hanged in Pudu Prison only months earlier.

Jack looked away and almost mused, 'Even though it was Hayley's fault we felt rotten about it, more so your old man. Vince had a dogged loyalty towards anyone who he worked with. I guess being in the army kind of instils that sort of thing in you; you sort of have to because you may very well not survive if you don't. Both of us shelled out money to the lawyers to pay the legal fees. Some of our hard-earned was wasted on bribing officials and got pilfered away. Hayley was to be made an example of, no correspondence entered into. But, mate,' he turned and looked at Theo, a hard stare. 'It's the way of the world. We all make our choices, sometimes we have no alternatives, sometimes we do. Sometimes we make a decision to do something harmless, maybe slightly illegal, and then shit hits the fan and you are confronted with a range of bad options but you have to decide on one of those and you make another decision, and that might be only a slightly bad decision, then another and it compounds and you get deeper in the shit, and it gets worse as you go but you just have to cop it sweet. Hayley was busted a fair while back, in about '82 or '83 and he was hanged at the end of last year. A lot of water has gone under the bridge in that time.'

'Jack … I … I'm not judging you, I remember what you said about my Dad, not to judge him too harshly, I mean, hey,' he said with a small smile, 'I've grown up a bit in the last month or so. Jail, a couple of brawls …'

The tension lightened in the gap between them. Jack almost smiled. 'How did you know?'

'Well, I have this book called *Beyond Pardon*, written by an Australian journalist, Spud Morgan, who ran a few lectures for us, you know at uni, and he interviewed Hayley right up to the last day.'

Jack sat up straight. 'Fuck! What …'

'I wouldn't worry too much; it's just that … Morgan mentioned Hayley and others were given Greek and Roman God's names when talking on the phone.'

Jack inclined his head and his brow tightened. 'So?'

You mentioned the name Bacchus when we were pissed that first night at the Saigon, remember?'

'Er … nup.' He shook his head slowly and rolled his hands outwards. 'Mmmm … yeah, maybe.'

'I looked up in the Record of Arrest in the book and Hayley had told the cops his codename was Bacchus and whilst under duress he told them all he knew about his employers was what his connection had told him; they worked for a couple of veterans. That in itself doesn't necessarily mean much, it could have meant, like professionals, you know? Anyway, and then a note fell out of the Jim Thompson's book of my father's, from the box of stuff you gave me. It was grubby and hard to read but it went something like ... *'Shan needs more money for Bacchus'* ... and then, I stumbled upon, in the appendix of *Beyond Pardon*, the fact that Shan, Shan Manesh, the lawyer, works for the same firm as Josef Ibrahim, my mate, your mate, the same bloke you hired to get me out of jail. I wouldn't worry. You said Dad's landlady hid the stuff from the cops but even then, if they did go through his things, who knows, would they have registered any of that? I very much doubt it. These coincidences made me curious ... that's all ...' He let it hang.

Jack said, 'What did you do with the note?'

'I screwed it up and threw it down the dunny.'

The troubled look slowly left Jack's face. 'Obviously, Harve doesn't know any of this, that's why I'm pretty straight up and legit these days.'

Theo quickly said, 'Jack, I wouldn't say anything to him, you know that.'

Jack brightened. 'Well, you pretty much know it all now, Theo, and I feel better that you do.' He looked directly into Theo's eyes and Theo held his gaze and nodded slowly. 'We'd better get cracking, international flights don't wait for anyone and I'll bet my balls you are itching to see Biro.'

'Biru, Jack, Biru.'

Jack slapped him on the back and laughed. 'Right, mate, let's go.'

After a battle with traffic they finally pulled up in the drop off-zone at the Kuala Lumpur International Airport.

'Well matey boy, this is it. I won't be coming in with you.' The old smiling Jack was back.

396

Chapter Eighty-Nine

The driver pulled Theo's backpack out of the boot and went to pay a parking fee to a short, harried, turbaned man with a moneybag over his shoulder.

Theo, recalling a thought, said, 'Jack, there's something you could do for me if possible.'

'Yeah, no worries, if I can.'

'You might remember Tung, a rickshaw driver, um he took you back home after our first meeting ...'

'Um, yeah, I do.'

'He looked after me, I mean, if you need a good worker you could always give him a job.'

'For sure mate, see what I can do, any mate of yours is a mate of mine. Right, you'll need these, it's some copies of things in relation to Biru. When you get through Immigration and all that, you should see her smiling kisser in duty free. If not, show immigration people this.' He pointed to an official-looking document.

'Jack ... er, I'm going to miss this place ... and ...'

'Well, mate ...' Jack opened his arms. 'No need to say anything. I'll make sure we catch up again soon. Harve won't settle for anything less.'

They hugged and broke. Theo said, 'Hang on, I have a present for you.' Theo fossicked in his day pack to give him enough time to hide his damp eyes. 'There!' He handed *Beyond Pardon* to Jack. 'I can easily get another copy. I might even get an autographed one because I'm going to see this bloke; he's given me some good ideas about some stuff I want to write. Relax, I won't say anything about, you know.'

They hugged again.

Jack said, 'I can't advise you not to make a fool of yourself with that young sheila because you already have.' He laughed. 'Don't worry, son, us blokes always seem to. Good luck, I think she is a real catch.'

'I hear you.' Theo nodded, looked Jack in the eye, spun around and walked through the crowd past the barrier. He turned. Jack was there. He saluted. Theo raised a hand.

The call to prayer drifted across the airwaves from several directions. He stopped for a moment to listen. He smiled to himself and the voice in his head said, *Yes Theo, you will miss this place alright.*

He walked through the automatic doors into the airconditioning of Kuala Lumpur International Airport.

United At Last

Chapter Ninety

The slow progression of the line in front of the check-in was frustrating but eventually it was Theo's turn. He mentioned Biru's name but not only wouldn't the hostess confirm she was on the flight, there was no way of organising seats together. Customs and Immigration were much faster and he walked almost straight through. His excitement level was cranked up by rapid breathing and a hammering heart. He walked into the duty free area and glanced quickly in all directions.

'Theo, over here.'

He hardly recognised the young woman in jeans with long black hair. 'I'll be,' he said and he covered the ground between them quickly but not fast enough to be too obvious. Theo's heart pumped as he took her in his arms. The fragrance of her was almost overpowering as he buried his head in her hair. Then they kissed for a long minute oblivious to people walking around them.

She took half a step back, still in the embrace, and ran the back of her hand down his cheek. 'I nearly go mad waiting for you, Theo. I am so happy we are together.'

All he could add was, 'Me too.' When he managed to get a good look at her he could not believe how beautiful she was.

They wandered around the duty free shops, totally absorbed in their world, seeing nothing but each other.

∞

Biru was clearly excited by her first trip up in the sky. He could see her eight rows up in the aisle seat and every so often she would turn and their gazes would lock. Theo had told the hostess part of his story and she informed him that it might be possible if she could persuade someone to move. After about an hour two seats were made available. Theo and Biru were at last united, side by side. Finally they could touch each other without feeling guilty.

The nine-hour flight was eventful and exciting for both of them because food and drink was always available. They had no need to watch videos or read. They chattered away for the whole trip, covering subjects about their lives, their families and their dreams. Theo told her all about his adventures with Jack but he left some things out. He thought it was the best time to tell her about his encounter with Mahmoud but once again he downplayed the confrontation. He summed up by telling her that Mahmoud would not bother her ever again. When it came around to talking about family in Australia he tried to skirt around the information about his mother.

Biru was wise to it. 'Is your mother coming to meet you at the airport?'

'Um … yes.'

She looked sideways at him. 'Have you told her about me?'

'Um … no,' and then he laughed. 'I don't know what to say to her but I will find out soon.'

'Do you think she will not like me?' She asked, eyes wide.

'No, of course not, I mean, yes, she will like you, it's … everything will be alright, we will have to see if your new family has arranged accommodation for you, and a job.'

'I am supposed to be meeting an official person from Immigration and then I will be taken to meet my new family. Theo?'

'Yes?'

'Will we be able to be together?'

'Yes, of course, but it might take a day or two. You will have plenty of paperwork to deal with. I'm not sure if I want to live with my mother but we will … sort something out soon. You are considered an adult in Australia and you can do whatever you want, within reason of course.'

She looked deadpan. 'I not have to get approval from man to do things, okay?' They both laughed but Theo knew it was actually a very serious matter for her. She became pensive for a while.

They settled into the only silence on the trip but it didn't last long and she was all smiles again and he reassured her everything would be alright. He showed her the information on her new family and gave her relevant paperwork with his mother's home details address. Gloria had told her she would probably be shunted through another door and into a section of the airport where she would have to undergo a medical and go through a series of procedures before meeting her new Australian family.

They touched down at Adelaide International Airport about nine hours after leaving Kuala Lumpur. Wide eyed Biru squeezed his hand tightly as the huge aircraft thumped the ground and the jet engines reversed with a screaming roar. Only when they began to taxi did she release her grip. They looked at each other, two travellers who hadn't slept, bone tired but full of enthusiasm for the future.

Theo had never been so happy but one thing still played on his mind. What was he going to tell his mother?

Home - Tell

Chapter Ninety-One

Two other international flights landed almost at the same time so the queues were long, noisy and full of irritable, tired, shuffling travellers. Only three immigration booths were open for Australian nationals and many people grizzled openly. Theo took Biru to the Foreign Passport and Visa Holders Special Booth, which was the one she was instructed to go to. Fortunately there was only one person in front and she was processed quickly. Theo explained Biru's situation to the official in the booth and he was told she would be going through another door and he had to line up with all the others.

Biru kissed Theo, that honey-sweet brush of lips, and she was led away. 'Theo, I will see you soon.'

He stood like a dejected dog for a second and then managed a smile. 'Yes, righto, ring me today or I will ring you … the number you gave me.'

She was gone.

The lines were still long so he stepped back into duty free and bought a bottle of Absolut Vodka, the one his mother liked. He glanced at the cartons of cigarettes and continued past with some difficulty. He returned to the Immigration area. Fortunately some more officers came on duty and the crowds started to move steadily. As he had his passport stamped he became acutely aware of being home. He could hear familiar jargon, *G'day mate, she'll be right, no worries, too right, bloody oath* and more. It made him smile and he was jolted out of his reverie by a Customs officer who said, 'You must be so happy you're home, mate.'

Theo wandered out through the barriers at Adelaide International Airport, looking in all directions for his mother but thinking he might get a glimpse of Biru.

His mother waved, she looked older than he remembered. Within moments she was in his arms. He realised how big he was or how small she was. He took in her motherly aroma. When she stepped back she had tears in her eyes and it took all his strength to not do the same. Her smile told him they were tears of joy.

'I missed you, Theo,' she said and gave him another hug. 'Let's go, I watered the lawn when you were away and now it's ready to mow.'

He felt like a smoke. He was home.

Chapter Ninety-Two

On the way home his mother related news of things that had happened since he left, things that probably were important but seemed mundane. As he glanced out at the dry Adelaide suburbs he realised he had changed. It was probably more like he had grown up in many ways and the magnitude of lobbing in a foreign country for six weeks, not really knowing anyone, had stamped a different perception on his world. He knew he had to tell his mother about the woman he cared about who was a foreigner. But he decided to wait until they arrived home.

The roads appeared almost deserted and apart from the occasional piece of rubbish, the roadsides were tidy. The light was harsh and bright; the sky was clear and brilliant blue and the air desert dry; it was vastly different from Malaysia.

Theo watched his mother driving; her concentration seemed more acute than he remembered. He had the feeling something was wrong.

When they pulled into the driveway it was as if he had not been away at all yet the family home where he had lived all his life seemed slightly strange. Hose rolled up at the tap, lawn with a slight tinge of green but heading towards brown and crispy, roses battling. All the familiar things.

'I'll get you some brekky and we'll have a cuppa and a chat, eh, like old times,' said his mother as he held the creaking flywire door open for her to unlock the back door.

Before stepping into the kitchen, he looked out at the Hills Hoist where a couple of tea towels fluttered. 'Yeah, no worries, I'll get rid of this.'

He dragged the pack into his bedroom, threw it on the bed and looked around. Yes, his old room. The bed seemed too small. He hadn't grown any more in a month, surely. Now was the time to tell her about Biru.

He walked down the passage. 'Mum, I ... I ... here I bought these for you.' He handed her the bottle of duty free vodka, and a headscarf bought at the night market.

'Thanks, you didn't really need to ...'

'Mum, I've ... I've got something to tell you.'

'Well, son, there's something I want to tell you and it's best I go first.'

Theo's heart dropped, thinking maybe she was ill.

*

Chapter Ninety-Three

They sat down and she placed mugs of tea in front of them. She cleared her throat, more a nervous gesture than a need. 'There have been many times over the years I have wanted to tell you what I am about to say but, you know, I chickened out, thinking maybe it was best you didn't know, but then I'd get the guilts and convince myself I'd tell you later. And this went on forever.' She twisted the tea towel.

He was about to say, 'What?' when she continued. 'I'm going to tell you straight and Theo this is very difficult for me to say. Now that Vince is dead I think you have a right to know. Jack Deere is your real father.' A solitary tear rolled down her face but she was brave enough to keep eye contact with him.

He was the one to break it. 'Fuck,' he said, and stood up.

She didn't reprimand him about his language like she usually did. 'I really wanted to tell you before you left, thinking you'd find out. But how could you? Anyway I backed out again, I just couldn't ...'

Things began to spin in Theo's head. 'Jack and Dad – Vince, were mates. Vince saved Jack's life. How could Jack do that to Vince?'

Gail anticipated the question. 'Jack didn't know, nor did Vince.'

He took a couple of steps back and leant on the chair. 'Christ.' He wanted a cigarette.

She still didn't reprimand him. 'I know it's a shock, Theo, but ... it's the way it is. I'm still your mother and I love you. That is why I have to tell you the truth at last. I am really sorry it ...'

Theo stared at her and then sat down again to give himself time. 'I really don't know what to say. All those years you let me believe Vince was my Dad …' He let the statement hang in the space between them. He took a sip and gently shook his head. 'Did you have an affair … when you were married?'

She looked him in the eye. 'It wasn't like that.'

Jack had fucked his best mate's wife, the mate who saved his life? 'What do you mean?' Suddenly, Theo realised it was really none of his business. He was about to apologise for his questioning tone when she answered.

'It was something that happened … Vince and I had a huge argument and had decided to not get married, we sort of broke up. A few weeks later, I happened to be at the same party as Jack … we were a crowd that hung around together, you know … anyway Vince snubbed me and went off somewhere else with another girl. We were all really drunk, Jack was there, he caught me crying … we, you know, one thing led to another …' Her eyes filled.

Theo recalled one thing he had learned in the last month. Not to judge too harshly. He felt like an adult. 'Mum, it's alright, you don't have to …'

She answered the question she must have thought he would ask sooner or later. 'A woman knows these things; I knew you were Jack's baby. Not long after the party, Vince and I got back together again, and a month or so after that we were married. I was only eighteen, a lot younger than you are now, I didn't know for sure I was pregnant either until after we were married but I knew … I knew you were Jack's kid.' She wiped her eyes with the tea towel.

He stood up, went behind her and put his arms around her. 'It's alright, Mum, it's alright.' He had tears in his eyes and he was thankful she couldn't see.

The two of them remained like that for a while. 'Mum, don't worry …'

She squeezed his hand. 'Those phone calls we had when you were away, the way you got on with Jack it seemed as if you *knew* he was your father. I sort of figured you would find out, some way, I don't really know how, maybe intuition … but Jack doesn't know. I still have to tell him, he had no idea, it's not his fault …'

Theo felt as if he was now the adult, there was need for him to be.

'Mum, it's not anyone's fault, it's … it's like you say, it's something that happened.' Suddenly he felt very tired; the weight of a night without sleep and the jet lag clouded him. 'I might go and lay down for a while, didn't sleep at all on the plane. Mum, please don't worry about it, it's all okay. We can talk about it later if you want, but only if you want.'

She nodded and reverted to her role, dutiful mother. 'What about some breakfast?'

He squeezed her again, 'Not really hungry, had plenty of food on the plane, thanks. It's alright, mum.'

Chapter Ninety-Four

Theo went to his room, lay down on the bed and looked up at the familiar ceiling. For some strange reason, although important, all the things his mother told him didn't seem to matter. His mother didn't owe him anything; he owed her for looking after him. Vince was dead; he wouldn't think any less of the man who he thought was his father for so many years. And the idea that Jack the larrikin, bodgie Jack was his real father? Theo realised he did not mind. It also meant Harvey was his brother. He laid back, hands behind head, churning over the words his mother said before he left for Malaysia, 'You might find out things you don't want to know about?' Within seconds he was asleep.

A few hours later he woke and it took him a couple of moments to orientate himself. Crows in the gum trees, Theo, that's all it is. There were no bells or gongs, no call to prayer, no-one yelling, no motorbikes. Only the dog down the road barking. The thought of what he was going to do with his father's ashes came to mind, then he remembered. Finding out Vince was not his Dad did not matter at all. Vince may not have been his father but he had done the best he could; he had loved Theo and his mother.

Theo lay there for a while in comfortable free fall. Suddenly he realised, with an uneasy feeling, he hadn't told his mother about Biru.

'Oh bugger,' he said, shaking his head.

He stumbled out into the kitchen. She was at the sink.

'Mum, I've er … I have something to tell you. There's this girl I met …'

His mother turned and smiled, 'Oh, you mean Biru? I just spoke to her on the phone a while ago; I didn't want to wake you.'

Epilogue

Jack limps, pivoting every step on one good leg, dodging boxes, baskets full of live chickens, oil drums and other types of freight. Vince stops intermittently and looks back. Moths and Christmas beetles crash-dive into the wharf lights high up. The recent tropical shower has left puddles everywhere and blobs of water drip from the rusty guttering of the Butterworth Shipping Office and Warehouse. The whiff in the humid night air has progressed from a delicate fragrance of frangipani and coconut, through the aroma of chilli, garlic and satay up in the main drag, to all things base and fishy. As they clamber up the gangplank the air changes again and envelops them with diesel fumes from the two stacks on the top deck. They make their way to the open stern of the Palau Barung. Jack looks up at a sign on the bulkhead. The words behind the cracked Perspex sign designate the craft as a mixed passenger, freight and vehicle ferry. The lights off Penang Island twinkle in the distance.

They both lean on the rail and look along the dock where Malay wharf labourers warble to each other, dragging freight around. Monkeys skitter on top of the pallets and bales and tease the dogs.

Vince pulls out a cigarette, cups his hands around the lighter, and takes a drag. His hands shake violently. He turns and looks at his friend. Smoke billows out of his nostrils. 'Of all the shitty things I've done in my life, the worst thing I ever did was walk away from my boy. The second worst thing I did in my fucking life was to treat Gail the way I did.'

Intermittently a sharp clank echoes from somewhere below, or above. A spanner, a metal crate, a piece of chain -- metal to metal. Diesel fumes hang in the humid air that has almost turned to fog. The big steel ferry sways with the gentle ebb and flow of tide and embraces the dock

412

in a sleepy rhythmic waltz. Jack turns and looks at him. 'Maybe you need to lay off the smack, mate.'

'Wouldn't make any difference, now.'

Jack raises his eyebrows.

Vince continues, 'Things have really gone to shit, not like the old days. I feel really lousy about Hayley.' He chuckles cynically, 'I mean Bacchus … whose idea was that anyway?' It didn't require an answer. 'Anyway, nothing we can do now.'

Two long, mournful hoots from the ship's horn seem to hang in the damp night.

Jack lifts his prosthetic leg onto the foot rail. 'He got greedy, mate. We passed the word down the line, advising him not to use when he was moving stuff across borders.'

'Yeah, but he is … he's going to hang in a few days.'

The conversation is drowned out, and their attention is drawn to a group of Chinese, probably a family, yelling and remonstrating as they drag their bags on board. The long mournful departure horn punctures the air again. The diesels change pitch which instantly excites the crew and other passengers. The big steel ferry reverses, jerks and clanks gears, and then slowly moves forward, trying desperately to find a magic pitch to outsmart the dancing, loose steel rivets. The Malay crew pulls the gangway on board with a thud and the ship rumbles and bubbles its way to the main channel. The last, almost empty midnight ferry heads across the Selatan Strait towards the island of Penang, twenty minutes away. The vibrating deck calms down as the engines reach running speed.

Jack gazes at the speckle glow of lights slowly fading on mainland Malaysia as he flicks his lighter and takes a drag. 'He tried to screw us, overstated the cost of the last load of smack. Took us for how many grand? Glad we never dealt directly with him. He won't talk; he doesn't even know who we are. And, remember we got some bucks to him to help with the fucking lawyers, and the bribes — lost all of that.'

Three Malay crew members come out the back and squat in the other corner. They light up fragrant cigarettes and chatter away in their native language. The ferry has relaxed into its corkscrewing motion. The breeze negates the crippling humidity, out in the sea, between the land masses.

Vince chucks his cigarette into the wake that is folding a sprinkle of *fluorescent bubbles as it splays out. 'Yeah.' The ferry moves on. 'I'm going to die, I'm sick, Jack. Cancer. I don't want to go on.'*

'Yeah, I know, or suspected something. But, mate, you can beat it. We could scheme-up some bucks from somewhere, and get some decent medical care ... just like old times, eh?' The boat sways slightly and Jack grabs the rail to stabilise himself.

'We've been mates forever; we've been through a lot. I've made up my mind. Would you ... would you give this to Gail and me boy, Theo?' He grabs Jack's hand and closes his fingers around the envelope.

Jack's brow furrows. 'You saved my life over there in Nam, mate. I'd do anything for you, you know that, but why don't you give it to them?'

The lights ahead grow in number and become brighter and Georgetown seems to get bigger.

'Why don't I do it?' Vince shakes his head. 'Why don't I do it? Because, old mate, I'm just too fucking ashamed, that's why.' Tears in his eyes pick up the glint of the weak upper deck lights. 'I just can't face anything anymore.'

Vince turns, walks quickly to the rail and steps over into the boiling churn of the props. It happens quickly, almost one action.

'Vince!' bellows Jack, reaching out and stumbling forward on the slippery deck.

A Malay crewman jumps up and starts yelling.

– The End –

Acknowledgements

I acknowledge and thank my many colleagues and friends from the Coolum Wave Writers (CWW), the Sunshine Coast Literary Association (SCLA), my secret writing groups, Virties, Livistonia Institute, Swig and Old Scholars. Also, thanks for the support, help and encouragement in many ways from: Beryl Corris, Peter Nolan, Morgana McCloud, Steve Reilly, Robin Storey, Alison Quigley, Bob Goodwin and Rob Armstrong.

I acknowledge and thank Jan Bentley and friends at the Noosa Arts and Crafts Association (NACA), Queensland Writers Centre (QWC) and Australian Society of Authors (ASA).

Without serious critique, editing, guidance and assistance from the following friends, it would have taken longer to reach 'the end' of "Crucial Step":- Bronwyn Cozens for mentoring and always making time to help me no matter how trivial the question, Pam Hardgrave for rescuing me when I was struggling with the pen, Andrea Rankin for proofreading my draft and believing in me over the years, Rosemary Laver for taking the time to bring out the red pen, Michael Doneman for those long sessions honing the finer skills of writing, Jan Forbes for a multitude of tasks and Jeff Scrivener for keeping my computer alive over the years.

A big thanks to my partner, Denise Miller for supporting and encouraging me, especially brainstorming and for suffering through my many questions.

I wish to acknowledge my parents, Ina and Bob Laver who were always there for me and believed in me over the years, my siblings Rosemary and Peter, and sister-in-law Alice, as well as my extended family and friends who have supported me through my writing journey.

Critiquing editors - Bronwyn Cozens, Denise Miller
Proofreading, editing - Andrea Rankin
Cover photo and map images – Ian Laver
Cover design, map design, graphics, website and Facebook - Jan Forbes

About the Author

Ian Laver is a fiction writer living in south east Queensland. A short working life in the government gave him a solid grounding in writing fiction. Also, many years in the building industry and travelling the world has added to his story-telling experiences. He was editor of a small country association magazine and had a regular column in an on-line magazine.

Ian has been associated with many writing groups and was President of the Sunshine Coast Literary Association. He has two novels and three collections of short stories to his credit as well as numerous writing awards, including two Henry Lawson Emerging Writer. At present he is involved in a Haiku poetry group, writing short stories and finalising his next novel.